JON HURLEY was born in Rathfarnham, Co. Dublin. He eventually made his way to England and served the usual Irish apprenticeship: working in coffee bars in Soho, freelance writing on boxing and jazz, doing evening classes on Euripides, firing steam engines, making British Rail sandwiches, packing Cadbury mints, winding field coils for Lucas, and conducting buses on the Isle of Wight. Finally, he entered the English wine trade and for the past thirty years he and his wife Heather have been running their own company: WineWeekends, www.wineweekends.com. He writes and lectures on wine, walking and local history and his published works include books on those subjects as well as on pubs and pugilism, and a book of poetry. He has also co-authored a play.

It's Late Very Early is Jon Hurley's first novel. It is based on his own impoverished childhood from which he emerged lacking direction and with a tendency to emulate the last person he'd met. Fortunately, he met a lad whose father was a newspaper editor. *'He was a lovely man with a soft Cork accent, a truly great man. I often wished he was my father. We ate burnt pancakes together, and talked well into the early hours. I wanted to sit in courtrooms wearing a slouched hat, with a fag in my lips, like Bogie. That's what got me writing.'*

Also by Jon Hurley

BIOGRAPHY
Tom Spring, Bare-knuckle Champion of All England

'Hurley has meticulously researched the history of Spring's life, as well as his exploits in the ring, enabling him to colour his account with vivid pictures of life and society, adding a real flavour of what was essentially a brutal era in English history.' *The Independent*

'Read Hurley's vivid fight analysis. His descriptions . . . often border on the poetic.' *The Times*

DRAMA
Labels, co-authored with Peter Terson

LOCAL HISTORY, AND WALKING
A Ross Anthology
Paths and Pubs of the Wye Valley
The Wye Valley Walk

POETRY
The Wicked Wind

WINE
Wine for Game and Fish
The Wine Label Book

FORTHCOMING
Wine, A Matter of Taste

Jon Hurley

IT'S LATE VERY EARLY

GROWING UP IN 1950s DUBLIN

og ma

First published in Great Britain in 2004
by Ogma Publications
25 Nover Wood Drive, Fownhope,
Herefordshire, HR1 4PN
E-mail: margotmiller1@compuserve.com

British Library Cataloguing in Publication data available.

ISBN 0-9541161-3-5

Design www.dowling.biz
Printed and bound in Great Britain by
Antony Rowe Ltd, Eastbourne.

FOR MY PARENTS JOHN AND ALICE HURLEY
AND ALL MY BROTHERS AND SISTERS.

ACKNOWLEDGEMENTS

I would like to thank:

Beryl Bainbridge for sitting up late in the Goose Shed reading the manuscript and offering warm-hearted advice.

Fay Weldon for her enthusiasm.

Peter Terson for practical advice and encouragement.

My editor Helen Wire for painstakingly wading through acres of blasted Irishisms.

My publisher Margot Miller for lots of wine-fuelled discussion and long (very!) friendship.

Rosemary Jones for her typing and unfailing cheerfulness.

My wife Heather who has endured a gestation lasting thirty years.

My family both sides of the Irish Sea and across the pond.

GLOSSARY

acushla darling, an endearment

bockedy unsteady

bonniv small pig

bowsie low-class, mean or obstreperous person

chainies pieces of broken crockery

crubeen pig's foot

culchie rough country labourer

gansey pullover

garda, *pl.* **gardai** member of the **Garda Síochána** police force in the Republic of Ireland

gossoon servant boy

gouger low-class city lout

gurrier Dublin dialect for a low-class, tough, ill-mannered person

porter dark sweet ale

poteen illicit alcohol

Seannachie storyteller

slàinte mhath or **slàinte** Good health, a Gaelic drinking toast

1

THE BOSS WAS young, serious and intense. His feet were small, his hands large and callused. He had a hole in his coat, and in his heart. With small blue eyes he surveyed the scene. In spite of the beating sun he kept his hat on. He gazed over the nuns' vast yellow fields, the manicured hedgerows, and the stout stone barns. The view filled him with a hatred.

Inside Cullen's, men sat smoking, spitting and retelling old stories. Spotting the trilby-hatted stranger they carried their slopping pints to dusty windows and watched. The Boss saw them out of the corner of his eye. Idle, nosy bastards. Over the ensuing months the men in the pub observed the stranger arrive and depart without a word. He seemed transfixed by that flat slab of useless ground. His clothes were cement- and paint-stained. The men assumed, correctly, he was in the building trade.

Without bothering to remove his bicycle clips the Boss walked around the bit of land, examining it from every angle - sometimes even getting down on his knees. In Cullen's the men's heads ached with curiosity. With sunken cheeks they pulled hard on their Woodbines. Surely the stranger wasn't thinking of buying that half acre of dirt? Any shitehawk would know it disappeared under water every winter.

They offered the stranger pints and free advice but were rebuffed. It seemed the man didn't want friends. With teeth clamped on soggy butts they talked side-faced. One man moved his head and the ash from his Woodbine powdered the dandelions at his feet. 'Leave him alone,' he said, 'he'll want our help one day.'

The Boss stood with his hands on his hips like a matador facing a pawing bull. He would tame that feckin' river. The curly black hair that grew out of the sides of his head was troubled by the breeze.

'Miserable fecker,' one man observed as he heeled a fag-end into the lino. 'Looks a tough little gouger,' another said. They swigged their pints. The Boss glanced at them, revealing the white of an eye. Moronic sods.

Wild flowers bobbed in the long grass, rusty dock stalks waved. A butterfly alighted on a nettle. He couldn't afford the land but he would have it. 'An' ta Hell wit' the begrudgers,' the Boss growled to himself.

The barman mauled the counter with a germ-laden rag. 'First flood an' he'll be washed away,' he said. The men gulped their Smithwick's.

Like a fox sizing up a chicken-run the Boss returned. He stalked the plot, ready to pounce, claws spread, curved fangs glistening. The land would be his.

'Jesus Christ,' a drinker gasped and his smoke curled on the breeze. 'Look at the state a the man. Yeh'd t'ink he'd won the feckin' Sweep.'

The Boss mounted his bike and rode away furiously.

2

THE BOSS RETURNED next day with a sketch of the house he intended to build. As he stabbed sticks into the rough ground, he became aware of another pair of eyes. They hovered for a while before settling on him like dungflies.

The Boss turned his head slightly. A shadowy figure stood in the porch of a tin shack on a small island in the river. A collapsing gate led down a clinker path to a shabby door. From a rusty corrugated roof a crooked chimney protruded. The old man stood gaunt and silent, his tobacco-stained whiskers drooping. Jack Perkins was spent and bitter.

Perkins had killed two Black and Tans when he was seventeen. A tattered double-breasted suit hung slackly from his bony frame. His dirty shirt was open at the neck. He had lived in peace for twenty years - now this bloody stranger had to arrive to fuck things up. His nerves twanged. At last, Perkins shouted. 'Hey! Mack, wha'd'yeh t'ink yeh're doin' there?' It was the bark of a flea-bitten collie weighing up a belligerent pitbull.

The Boss looked up. 'What's it t'yeh, yeh bollix?' he snarled.

'Frig off then,' Perkins said and he shuffled indoors.

The Boss's fists curled. He expected trouble and relished the prospect.

For the next few weeks the Boss visited everyone he knew to beg for a loan. His guts were empty and his shirt clung to his back. Leaning on their sticks, the gentry were pleased to see him. He was a good hard-working young man, not like the IRA thugs or the shysters who lived off the State. The Boss removed his hat. The bushy hair sprouting out at the sides gave a false impression. He was in fact as bald as a crow's egg. Hatless he felt emasculated.

The toffs politely listened to the man's story and with shaking, liver-spotted hands, offered tea in china cups. The Boss forced sycophantic smiles and told them of his plans for the plot of land. Suds gathered on his lips. He wanted to get married and raise a family. He must act quickly.

The old folk nodded like dogs in the back of Cortinas and glanced at Ormolu clocks on marble mantelpieces. They shuffled on slippered feet when the Boss mentioned money and politely showed him the door.

The Boss cycled off damning all the English shaggers to Hell.

At night in his rooming house, he scribbled more names on scraps of paper and each day cycled to fresh humiliations. Hallway lights shone on him as he stood in the street like some villainous actor in a depressing play. His jaw locked, he cycled on oblivious to the birds singing on the wires.

At last, he visited a woman with fine black hair. Her sympathy was a lifebelt. Once inside her door the Boss smiled frantically, his small blue eyes dancing like forget-me-nots. Women were wonderful. He could always rely on them to give him a fair cut of the whip.

He sat on a hard chair and decanted the contents of his soul on to her carpet. She rushed to a polished bureau and wrote him a cheque. Jesus, Mary and Holy St Joseph! The Boss's voice became small. Tears blinded him. He folded the cheque with thick fingers and placed it in the pocket of his dungarees closest to his heart. He wanted to grab the woman and hug her.

The Deeds to the land secured, he worked furiously, levelling heaps of dry-filling with his flashing shovel, planting trees by the water's edge. All the while, he argued with himself, his voice carrying in the dark. The owls were hooting in Neary's field by the time his tail-light twinkled back over the hill.

Every day he worked, the veins on his neck standing out like caterpillars. Every pickaxe blow was through the skulls of priests, every slash with his sickle was cutting through the throats of women who had deceived him. Every grunting, gasping, rock-lifting, muck-shifting shovelful was a remembered evening of little Johnny Dunne working in the vast, twilit gardens of Orlagh College.

He had been ten at the time, turning over soil in the walled garden, raking and manuring, tilling the land for the spring sowing. With pudding-basin haircut, elbows poking through holes in his jumper, the boy had worked under the gaze of the young priests who came to watch.

Johnny Dunne saluted the priests as he'd been trained to do from birth, and waited head-down for the blessing to come. With after-shave-scented chins, they studied the bockedy-kneed boy with his hand to his fringe and laughed. They walked down the brick path leaving him saluting. They would live to regret hurting Johnny Dunne.

That night he filled a sack with stolen parsnips, beetroot, swedes, eggs from the Jesuit's hen-houses, threw it over the handlebars of his bike and headed down the drive. As he approached the iron gate, a bug-eyed curate from a Victor Hugo novel emerged out of the darkness. The old priest snatched the sack and emptied its filthy contents on to the path. Beetroot ran like rats. The smack that followed shocked and stung. 'Yeh won't be takin' anytin' from this place again! Get out a here quick, an' don't come back, yeh little bastard.' With a flutter of his stained habit, the old priest melted into the shadows.

'God forgive me, but *yeh're a cunt*!' Johnny shouted as he rode away.

His ear still tingling, he returned to Ballycullen. His father was sprawled in the glow of the turf fire. A pool of puke lay like spilt soup beside him. Johnny said he'd lost his job. Liam his sickly brother put down the racing pages to sneer. Gripping the stone sink with her bony hands his mother shrieked, 'Why didn't yeh tell th'ol' fecker a pack a lies? Yeh bloody gobdaw.'

Johnny sat at the table in silence as his father unravelled himself from the floor. Snot decorating his jacket like Russian medals, the man swayed and cursed, drawing himself up to his full five-two. 'Yeh bloody little shite,' he roared. 'Yer feckin' mother's disthroyin' yeh. Yeh're a feckin' softie. D'yeh hear me!' Like a gob-festooned Charlie Chaplin, the old man gazed blearily at himself in the wardrobe mirror. 'Yeh're not a man at all,' he slurred, and sucked his teeth while surveying his image. Then, grunting, he picked up one of his hobnailed boots and studied the hard metal tip for a few seconds before smashing it down on his son's hands. Liam went back to his racing pages. Dry-eyed, Johnny stared at his father. That night when the brothers went to the same bed, Johnny turned his back to Liam like a woman with a sudden headache.

Johnny left school and found work. He was strong and willing, with an appetite for pain. He now had a few pence to throw at his father, like a keeper would fling rotten meat to an old lion.

Robbed of his childhood, Johnny Dunne walked miles talking to himself. If his father disappeared, it was Johnny who was sent to bring him home. He would search the pubs until he found his father asleep on his own arms, his nose running. Releasing the pony from the lamppost to which it had been tied all day without food or water, Johnny lashed it homeward, his father lolling in the back like a Plague corpse on its way to the communal pyre.

One night, goaded beyond endurance, Johnny hit his father and laid him out. His reason gone, he dragged the old man across the stone flags, the grey head bouncing like a ball. His father wriggled and cursed. Seeing his father's bootless dirty feet, Johnny Dunne could easily have finished him off with a few well-placed kicks.

When Liam said, 'Leave the poor old fecker alone, yeh good-fer-nuttin' bastard,' Johnny's eyes grew as large as a bull's.

'I'll feckin' good-fer-nuttin' bastard yeh when I get me hands on that bloody pitchfork,' Johnny screamed and ran to the garden shed. Liam bolted into the street slamming the door behind him, and was last seen that night heading for Firhouse.

Johnny sought work, anything considered. Desperate and bare-necked, he had cycled across the Dublin mountains, peddling madly against the accursed wind with only the odd lolloping hare for company. He got a job on a building site, and eventually swore and sweated his way to being foreman. Soon, they were calling him *the Boss.*

3

BURSTING WITH PRIDE, the Boss shovelled and levelled his bit of land. In his delirium, his thoughts turned to happier times - to dances, sitting on the stage playing his accordion, watching the girls kicking up their legs. Stretching the squeeze-box, his tanned face serious, he tapped a foot. How he revered those new shoes. How snugly they slotted over his tiny feet. Scrubbed and keen he cultivated an expression of stylish solemnity. It worked with the women and later in his grubby sadness, he would open an album and review those good, sepia times. He'd had a full head of hair and a mouth full of his own teeth then. When the girls put on their headscarves, the Boss put his accordion in its decorated box and walked them home. One night he walked into Bridie Mansfield.

Bridie was red-bloused and red-mouthed. She danced like an African, her haunches sawing, the cheeks of her arse hanging from her like panniers. She plucked men from the walls and whisked them around the floor like mops. By day she packed Kimberley Creams in Jacob's factory. When he saw Bridie the Boss tugged on his accordion with gusto, his shiny shoe tapping like a heartbeat.

They danced together and she allowed a callused hand inside her blouse. They wrestled in cow-pats and kissed under streetlamps haloed with mayfly. When he proposed, Bridie laughed. The Boss's fists bunched, but he still bought her presents and watched her smile as she opened them.

Supervising his work gang on building sites all over south Dublin, he thought of Bridie. She was beautiful and malleable; most of the other girls wore Legion of Mary crosses like padlocks on their breasts. When he teased her about other men, she tickled his dimpled chin. He twisted her wrist until she cried out. He wanted to kill her. Lucky for Bridie she escaped, flying away one day like an exotic bird on technicoloured wings. The Boss put away his accordion for the last time and began searching for a virgin.

He found her bent over a big silver-wheeled pram, tucking in a baby. Mary Hogan, shy and gauche smiled at the handsome foreman watching her from some scaffolding. Mary had left Galway with only her bus fare. Country girls made great skivvies. Dublin ladies fed them on pigswill, paid them nothing and kept them in unheated attics. Dark-haired with a big mouth, Mary blushed when the Boss asked her out. In her narrow bed in her tiny room above glistening suburban streets, she hugged herself. She could hardly believe a good-looking Dublin man would choose a poor ignorant country girl. Dublin Jackeens usually had the pick of the crop.

Mary wrote to her friend Eileen back home in Galway. Eileen scrawled back on blue lined paper: 'Watch them dirthy Dubs. They're only after the one thing.' In her box room, Mary sat at a scratched table. What did Eileen know? Poor thing'd never had a boyfriend. Alone in bed, Mary smiled at the cobwebbed ceiling.

Reeking of *Brilliantine*, the Boss took her to the Stella cinema in Rathmines. Mary sat on the crossbar of his bike, her cheek next to his. He told her of his contempt for every human he knew, especially the men in Cullen's pub. He told her about Perkins, the cadaver who watched him from across the river. 'If them bastards t'ink they're goin'ta run me out they're mistaken,' the Boss whispered with menacing finality.

Sitting in her velveteen-covered, tip-up seat, Mary looked lovely with her freshly washed hair fuzzed out and her big lips painted like Dorothy Lamour's. The Boss pretended to be watching the film but his mind was on his land. 'I'll push that oul' fecker right inta the bloody river,' he said. A woman behind them told him to, 'Shush!' And he turned and gave her a look.

In the shade of a cedar that spread its branches over a lawn, Mary parried his advances with her big country girl's hands and chastely kissed him. He waited for the door to close behind her before snapping on his bicycle clips and cycling up the Rathgar road to Terenure, then through Templelogue to his rented room.

Next morning, as she made beds, dusted, and shovelled ash on catshit, Mary worried. Johnny had so many battles on his hands.

In the backroom he shared with three Longford labourers, the Boss's brain whirred as he lay in his stale bed that night. Some scutter in a suit was bound to take advantage of her. She was weak and stupid, like all Galway women. The Boss grabbed the blanket and flung it off. He got up, walked to the window, and looked out. It was yellow outside, road lights, houses, stray dogs. He needed to finish building his house. He wanted to get out of this place and get married.

4

MARY WAS ALONE but very contented. She smelt the smoke of cigars rising through the floorboards. Below there was the clinking of port glasses, ribald laughter. When she heard them leave, the men calling out fruitily, their women hushing them, Mary crept downstairs to clear the table and wash up.

The Boss's sister was expecting a bastard. The family had gathered in a backroom in Ballycullen, sitting around the table like a card school. The Boss moved like a jockey on his chair as Molly tearfully unveiled her sin. She sobbed as the family lobbed grenades.

'Yeh're a bloody slag,' Liam said with thin-lipped pleasure. Molly wrung her handkerchief.

'Yeh're a dirthy slut,' her mother hissed.

The Boss stared at the walls in wild disbelief. 'Wha'cha goin'ta call it? Bastard?'

Molly wept. What can you call an eyeless lump that lies blind and unwanted inside you?

The door's violent slam made everybody jump and shook the cups on their hooks in the dresser. Their father was home, bleary-eyed and spoiling a fight. Stupefied, the old man stood swaying, short-arsed and lethal. His moustache stained with dried porter, his clothes exuded the fug of second-hand tobacco. He looked down on the assembled family, one tiny knuckle on the table for support. Hazily, he gazed from one to the other, panning slowly from the Boss to Liam. His eyes rested sleepily on his wife, who glared back at him sourly.

'What she done?' he slurred. Molly was his favourite.

'She's fallen be the wayside,' the old woman snarled, as if her tongue was coated with paprika.

The old man closed his eyes. 'She wha'?'

'The bitch's melt's gone an' got shafted,' Liam said.

'That's enough a that,' the old woman rasped.

'Hey, Mol, d'yeh hear what they're sayin' aboutcha?' The old man swayed closer to his daughter who sniffed his beery breath. His daughter had dropped her knickers to facilitate some filthy stranger. The thought of it was shocking - done in a mad few seconds of disgusting lust. It was a crime against God. His own daughter harbouring her rotten secret right there in the house - the filthy thing growing inside her. The old man should do something - hit someone - but he collapsed on to the sofa and snored, his moustach rising and falling.

When the Boss cycled to meet Mary under the big yew that evening he felt cold and sad, as if a fever had grabbed hold of him. His hands bare on the bike, he weaved to and fro like a horse with the staggers. He was shaking as he took Mary's gloved hand and gripped it hard. Neglecting to give her the usual kiss, he parked his bike in the garden of the big house, chained it to a tree. His boxer's walk, balanced and light, was replaced by a short and leaden stride.

'Well?' Mary was smiling from under a throw-me-down headscarf the lady of the house had given her. The dress she wore was a thing with big red roses like gunshot wounds all over it. It was a tart's dress, the Boss decided. She was asking for it - just like his sister. He would take her down the Dodder path and ram his fist between her legs. That was all they wanted, the hoors.

They walked in silence past Mount Carmel Hospital, through the trees and over the footbridge with the Dodder flowing smoothly below.

'What way diyeh wan'ta go?' Mary teetered on second-hand high heels. She was so delighted to see him after a humdrum three days.

'I don't care,' the Boss said quietly.

'We haven't been this way at all,' Mary said. She had been thinking about their walk all day. It would be great to get out of the old house with its smell of damp and the kids running all over her scrubbed tiles. The family never talked to her, except to give orders. Mary played with the children. She loved children. Children were not critical.

Mary and Johnny - she was a head taller than the little south-Dubliner - followed the Dodder to the bridge. They passed the tiny tributary Dargle and heard it falling from the castle grounds, tipping like broken glass into the river. They sat on a bench under an umbrella of alders, the tree that gave Rathfarnham its name. The trees huddled like eavesdropping old men while Mary babbled on about her weekly bus ride to Rathmines with some of the other maids to window-gaze. From her handbag she produced a letter from Eileen. She read it out loud in her mellifluent brogue. The Boss couldn't care less about Mary's primitive relatives but he would want to know in future who was writing to her. Letting the Boss into all her little secrets was something Mary would later regret.

They walked a little further along the misty valley. Mary left gaps in the conversation which Johnny seemed reluctant to fill. They covered another half mile before he spoke. 'Sit down,' he ordered. He took a white handkerchief from his pocket and wiped his eyes. 'Me sister Molly's expectin' a bast– a baby. She won't tell us who the fella is.'

'Ah well, that's good anyway,' Mary said. 'Yeh can tell her congrats from me.'

The Boss let go of Mary's hand. His face was twisted into an ugly scribbled thing. 'Me on'y sister's ruined,' he said, 'and yeh're not takin' it seriously.'

'Oh no,' Mary said. 'I was, honest. I was just tryin' t'be, yeh know . . .' Mary was frightened.

'Listen, in future, before openin' yer feckin' big culchie gob,' the Boss snarled.

Now Mary had seen the other side of him - she should have walked away.

Instead, she sat, her legs blue with cold, her big feet squeezed into shoes a size too small, holding her handbag in front of her like a sporran. She was stunned by the nastiness of his rebuke. She hadn't meant anything. 'I'm terrible sorry,' she said. She massaged his thick neck and looked into his pained face. 'I didn't mean anytin'.' She tried to kiss him but he turned his face away.

'If I on'y knew who the fella was,' the Boss said quietly, 'I'd take a gun an' blow his fuckin' brains out.' Mary shuddered.

It was a long time before he took her hand. He remained silent for a few minutes then he said. 'I wan'ta marry yeh, Mary, but I hav'ta be sure.'

Mary was smiling with relief and happiness. 'Sure of what, darlin'?'

The Boss tried to find the words. Sex was such a hateful subject.

'Well?' Mary asked.

'I want . . .' The Boss stopped. He couldn't look her in the eye. 'I want . . . tibee certain yeh have . . . I mean . . . no experience of other men.'

Mary smiled. 'Is that all? Well, I can tell yeh that I have never–'

'No,' the Boss said and his tone was sharp, 'I can't accept yer word.' He pushed her away. 'I need ta have it certified.'

Mary's mouth opened and closed like a fish in a bowl. The Boss smiled thinly. 'It won't cost yeh anytin'. A doctor of my choosin' will hav'a look. It's betther ta be on the safe side.'

Mary wept quietly.

'C'mon, wad'yeh say?' the Boss said as if he were haggling over the price of a pig. 'It'll on'y take a few minutes. Come on now, stop that cryin'.' He put a hand on her. 'An' after that yeh can go ahead an' organise th' weddin'.'

Mary looked up at him. Her big eyes were pools of tears. Instead of clouting him with her handbag and racing down the riverbank and catching the next bus back to Rathgar, she said through the tears, 'All right, Johnny, if that's what yeh want.'

Mary was intact. Overjoyed, the Boss gave the doctor his Judas money. Later, when blows and tears fell, Mary in her tattered cardigan would scream, 'Yeh never trusted me. I should never a married yeh.' In the ensuing years, Mary would cry and cry, her shoulders pumping, a square of torn sheet in her hand to stem the endless tears.

But in her cold attic, all she could think about was poor Molly. In the Fifties, Irish girls expecting illegitimate babies had to suffer the priest's lash and wear the crown of thorns. But for the Grace of God . . . Mary thought.

Molly's confinement was more like the expulsion of a cancerous growth. She had a fair-haired boy without celebration. He was taken from her, and Molly cried. She was three weeks short of her eighteenth birthday but her life was over. She was allowed neither a visit nor a letter. No one was allowed to renege on a deal brokered by the clergy.

5

THE MEN IN Cullen's pub watched how the site altered, how manically the stranger worked. The Boss was recharged by the news of Mary's purity. On Sundays, after catching seven o'clock Mass in Terenure, he rushed to the site and worked while other men went to football. In the setting sun, he was still chopping and sawing. He reclaimed more land, forcing the river back, piling up muck and stones to built a barrier against it. He burnt flotsam and jetsam, his bonfires spluttering and sparking into the night. Gilded by the flames, the Boss piled on uprooted trees with his bare hands.

The pub men waited until the tail-light of his bicycle had disappeared over the hill like a bloodied eye. Then they leapt off walls and ventured on to the Boss's sacred land. Like dogs inspecting an aborted foetus, they sprayed everything with their piss.

'Jasus, he's takin' more'n he's entitled ta,' one man said, making a feeble watery arc.

'Sure, that bit belongs t'oul Neary beyant,' another agreed as he buttoned up his flies.

Jack Perkins, too, watched the site alter.

Soon the men in Cullen's had something new to talk about. The Boss drove a big Albion truck on to the site. It was filled with broken bricks, plaster, dust, nails, old torn wallpaper and broken tiles. The men spat and adjusted their caps. The stranger had got one up on them. The Boss milked a steering wheel as big as a dustbin lid as the truck rocked and wobbled across the swamp with black smoke issuing upwards as the Albion sank roaring into the marshy ground. The men prayed it would turn over and trap the little shite underneath. But, leaping out of the cab, the Boss grabbed his big shovel and flung the dry filling over his shoulder like a starving cur searching for a bone. His face powdered by dust, his trilby white, he scattered the load, then with his sides heaving, he paused for breath. When the Boss removed his hat to wipe the brim, the men saw the Boss was bald.

'No wondher he keeps his feckin' hat on,' one said.

'Ah come on lads,' a man known as the Dowager said, 'Fair play ta the fella. He's turnin' that oul' swamp round.'

All summer the Boss worked, the Albion's headlights sweeping the Corporation houses, bathing the faces of children sleeping three to a bed. Crunching the gears, the engine revving, the Boss yanked the levers in his broken hands, and rumbled off for another load. Tons were delivered and pulverised. The river was defeated. The ballast soaked up the water.

'He's feckin' done it,' one man said.

'An' more power to his elbow,' the Dowager said.

When winter came the men huddled around Cullen's fire. Gloveless, with steam billowing from his mouth, the Boss began to build a house from buckled corrugated iron, old telegraph posts with the earth still clinging to them, straightened nails, used washers, knobs and hinges. He threw up an A-frame, hung doors and fixed windows. The building rose quickly. It was a tiny dwelling lapped by water but to the Boss it was his Wagnerian castle perched above the thundering Rhine.

Half a mile up the road the lacquered gates of St Gatien's opened to a sweeping drive and an elegant house. A pot-pourri of perfume billowed from the flowers and herbs in the neat gardens. Along the high stone walls pears drooped like breasts, strawberries glowed in their beds, lilies shone like lamps on dragonfly-haunted ponds. The old maids who owned the house quietly wandered its boundaries, whispering as they snipped roses with gloved hands while speculators cruised by like sharks waiting for them to die.

At the back of the Boss's land sprawled Neary's farm. How the Boss envied the Protestants their big red barn crammed with sweet hay, bales of yellow straw and a Massey Ferguson. 'Rotten swine have everythin' in this bloody counthry,' the Boss railed. If he could only charge across the field and take it from them at gunpoint he would. Irish laws were framed by foreigners.

6

THE STREAM TOOK to its new course without complaint, tumbling over the weir, creeping around the grounds of Rathfarnham Castle where the Jesuits, the seventh sons of watery-eyed fundamentalists, strolled about in their new boots. Choking on bile, the Boss worked without song or a soothing voice to ease his troubled mind. On a paint-spattered ladder, his eye followed the curve of the paintbrush as it filled every crack and fissure with army grey. A few shrubs were planted in old manure and a handful of bulbs were thumbed in. Big rocks torn from the riverbed were strewn around the yard like a miniature dolmen. A seat he'd made from planks polished by the flood was placed by the door. A toilet stood like a sentry box.

At last, the house was ready.

The men from the pub came at night with torches to peer in through the newly glazed windows at the few items of furniture. A small dresser with chipped plates and jugs, a Singer sewing machine, a ewer and a bowl. A galvanised bath hung from the door.

'We might ketch a look at yer wan's diddies,' one of the men said.

Unbuttoning his flies another attempted to thumb his fat cock through the Boss's letterbox. He was sent flying with a kick. 'No yeh feckin' won't,' the Dowager said, 'the man deserves a bit a privacy. Even if he's a bollix.'

The men in Cullen's sipped their pints, tipped back their caps and opened their shirt buttons to give their necks an airing. They had never seen a man expend such energy.

'Jasus Christ, sure that fella makes me tired just watchin' him,' the Dowager said as he watched the dungareed figure with the hobnailed boots stand proud in front of his house.

Young Johnny Dunne had proved his drunken father wrong - he was not so weak as when he'd planted his little body between his roaring, punching, gouging father and his screaming mother; been hurled against the wall, punched in the guts and told he was a good-for-nothing. As he listened to the stream chatter and saw the sun dancing on its uneven surface, the Boss had a right to feel vindicated. He would live on his estate. He would take care of Mary. Enjoy seeing her bent over, as she dug white parsnips and red carrots from under the dark loam, scraping off the good dirt and rinsing them under the tap he had fixed by the back door. There was more work to be done. Soon he would start building the pigsties. He would die here - be Mary's guardian. There were so many people out there who wanted to hurt her.

The Boss planted thick willows, bound them with barbed wire.

The men in Cullen's rolled cigarettes and rooted in their pockets for matches. The barman topped up their pints one by one. Shadowy and capped silhouettes, they watched the Boss.

'Poor bugger, sh'be in here wit' us havin' an oul' pint a da black stuff,' the Dowager said. 'I couldn't work like that wit'out sust'nance.'

'Yeh couldn't work, full stop,' another said and the men laughed.

7

MARY LISTENED TO the rain on the ivy. She was happy. Surrounded by billowing white material, she was making her wedding dress. Outside, trams sparked and clattered, a drunk rattled the iron railings with a beer bottle. Together with Eileen, Mary was filling her trousseau. Before slipping under the blanket, she knelt on the gritty floor and prayed.

Eileen was there at the crack of dawn to help her best friend prepare. Mary's employer allowed them to dress in the master bathroom. The country girl could not get over the size of the bath - and the towels were like bedspreads.

The Boss married Mary in Bohernabreena church. A warm sun shafted through the coloured windows and fell on Mary's relatives. Shy countrymen nursing their hats, they sat in angular silence. Mary, her dark hair brushed to a lustrous sheen, waited nervously for her man to mouth the words of affirmation. Smelling of carbolic soap and hair oil, his hired suit tight against his powerful body, the Boss pressed the thin gold band on to Mary's finger.

Mary's brothers, as shy and suspicious as Amazonian Indians in stovepipe hats and feathers, gathered to shake her hand. They could hardly wait to get back on the road and head west. Dublin was a neon-lit hell where their poor sister Mary had been forced to go to avoid starvation. Now she was marrying a Jackeen, God help her.

Both families went to a dusty pub and mixed warily - the sharp-suited Dubliners and the circumspect men in creased suits from Galway. While the country people waited for instructions, the Boss's family noisily dived in and cornered the grub. Mary's father, a long man smelling of pipe tobacco, sat in a chair looking misplaced while the Boss's father confidently spouted words with his elbow on the mantel-piece. The countrymen hated the look of him. Please God, the little shite would soon be throwing up his ring in the graveyard next door.

While Mary mingled easily among both families, the Boss stood like a statue. He had little in common with his own lot so what was there to say to those from the reeking arse of Ireland?

Mary cried when it was time to say goodbye to her family. She lingered as they clambered into battered cars and spluttered away, trailing smoke. She waved until they disappeared. For a moment, she felt adrift without them but the Boss was smiling. He was ready to take her home.

The men in Cullen's saw smoke rising from the chimney. It was a victory signal. With his hands in his pockets, his tie loosely knotted around his bull's neck, the Boss walked his domain. He heard a trout jump, and the weir roaring. Removing his trilby he ran thick fingers over his naked cranium. He had shown those useless feckers.

Perkins was watching him through the trees.

The Boss went indoors and lunged at his prize. Mary dodged his hands and ladled a rich stew. In an old bed with squeaking springs the Boss did what was required of him, enjoying Mary's innocence and her lamblike softness beside him. Lying on her back and transfixed with terror, she let nature take over. As he fondled his new wife, the Boss fretted in case the blood-soaked mystery that had unfolded between them had been tainted by another's spore. In spite of the doctor's certificate, Mary's purity would always be questioned.

8

THE BOSS PLANTED his first crop of potatoes. He talked to himself as he worked, bunched his knuckles and swore. As Mary hung out her washing, her black hair long and gypsylike, the men could see she was already pregnant. Mary turned away when they called to her.

'Yer man's a fast worker all right.'

As she went indoors she heard them laugh.

'Yer woman's up the feckin' pole already,' one said, and the others guffawed.

Soon the small garden was full of savoys as big as footballs, purple onions and yellow marrows. Mary made thick soup, sometimes flavoured with a bone. Most days, the Boss was away working but his mind was always on his empire by the river. It worried him to leave Mary on her own. He raced home as soon as he could. Sometimes he would sneak into the yard and search the sties and sheds like a bear looking for honey. He was hoping to catch some miscreant so that he could give him a good kicking. He would stand listening as the wild geese honked across to Neary's lake.

Once, when Mary suggested he took a break from working all the time and maybe go to Cullen's, his face twisted. Why did she want him out of the house? Did she have some chancer with a full head of slicked-back hair lined up?

Next morning, he began to build a wall around his property. He stood up to his thighs in the red bog water, with a crowbar he levered great stones into place, cemented joints and backfilled. It was ferocious work and he was drowning in his own stinking sweat. Mary brought him mugs of tea and thick slices of buttered bread. She sat with him for a while. Brown trout came to look and with a mud-turning flick were gone. Mary wanted to talk, but the Boss's mind was on other things, his brain working like the flywheel on a manic pump.

'Yeh've done a grand job there, Johnny,' she ventured but the Boss, hearing distant voices, chewed slowly and stared into the river.

'That feckin' wall,' he said, 'it'll still be there when we're rottin' in the ground.' The thought made Mary shiver and she went indoors. The Boss carried on until dark, determined to finish the job. Hollow-eyed he was too fatigued to eat his supper and went to bed early. Mary joined him.

The Boss heard the first splash, and shook Mary.

'What the f–?' he jumped out of bed and went to the window. A ginger-headed youth was illuminated by the lamppost. He was cursing and laughing as he pushed the wall into the water, watching it fall a yard at a time like concrete dominoes. Without bothering to pull on his trousers, the Boss tore out of the door.

'Hey! Stop! Yeh feckin' sleeveen,' he yelled. The youth froze, then bolted, stumbling sideways over piles of rock and plunging through sand. The Boss flew after him, his pyjama coat open, not feeling the cuts inflicted on his bare feet by the sharp black slates he had chopped up to make a dry footing. With a wild snarl the Boss caught up with the youth before he was swallowed by the night. He slammed him to the ground.

'Gotcha, yeh bastard!'

At eleven stone and only five-six the Boss was giving away eight inches and several stones, but he held on to the youth, sinking blows into every inch of the fat body.

'Wait, gi'me a chance, I'll tell on yeh . . .' the boy said, getting to his feet.

'Yeh'll tell, will yeh?' the Boss hissed, sinking a savage left to the boy's guts. 'Yeh'll tell me.'

Bang! Another massive dig, this time a right-hander to the pudgy face. The Boss was insane with anger. Enough punches landed to bring the boy to his knees, where he knelt in supplication at the Boss's muddy feet - his mouth split, his nose burst. The Boss continued to fire punches that would have downed a heavyweight.

Screaming, the boy rolled over in the dark. The Boss lugged him upright by the lapels. 'Now, tell me yer name so's I can summons yeh, yeh connivin' little bastard.'

'Corbally. Eamonn Corbally.'

'Where d'yeh live?'

'Saint Bernard's Cottages.'

'Well, get back there and t'ank yer lucky stars I'm not wearin' me hobnail boots or I'd kick the shite out a yeh.'

'T'anks very much,' the lad said, scrambling to his feet. He slouched off, looking back fearfully, his mouth running blood.

The Boss listened to the sound of his own breath. Both hands hurt where he had punched the boy in the teeth. Mary bathed his wounds.

'I hope yeh didn't hurt the poor lad,' she said, as she applied neat Jeyes Fluid to the cuts.

'I sh'da killt him,' the Boss gasped. 'Afther me workin' all day fer nuttin'. In the name a God, what did yeh expect me ta do. Kiss his arse and give him a tenner? Whose side are yeh on anyway?'

'Yours a course,' Mary said, kissing her husband's cheek.

In bed she comforted him.

With bandaged hands, the Boss was in the river lifting the heavy stones out and placing them in order on the bank. A man appeared and stood by the riverside for a while, watching. Eventually, he came over.

'Hello there,' he said.

The Boss looked up. 'Howyah. Some cannat's afther destroyin' me day's work,' the Boss said.

'It was me son that done it,' the man said.

'Oh, was it now?' the Boss replied, expecting not just an apology but compensation.

'I think yeh wor a bit hard on the lad.'

'Hard? Huh,' the Boss's eyes glinted. He climbed out of the river to gain the higher ground.

'Yeh should a seen the state a the poor lad when he kem home. His mother t'ought he was run over be a car. He was covered in blood.'

The Boss looked the man in the eye. 'Next time, it'll be murder,' he said. The man shook his head and walked away.

The Boss had no more trouble.

9

MARY HAD COMPLICATIONS with her first pregnancy. She ached and bled, prayed and staggered to church in the evenings. She met Eileen in a teashop in Harold's Cross and needed to talk about it.

'Ah sure, it's yer man's big cock that's done it,' Eileen said with a wall-eyed chuckle. Mary was shocked. 'Yeh know what they say about small jockeys,' Eileen continued in the same vein. 'Don't they always have the biggest w'ips.' She laughed coarsely, lit a Craven A and blew smoke over her shoulder.

'Cut out that filt'y talk,' Mary said looking round her.

'Shag off,' Eileen said, waving joyously to the waitress for more cake. With the gait of a bruiser looking for action, the vocabulary of a striking miner, and the complexion of a jockey's arse, Eileen was not afraid of the Boss. In fact, no boxing promoter could have dreamed up a more attractive match. Like a great she-ape, Eileen would protect and defend a crippled mate, to the spilling of blood and the tearing out of hearts if necessary.

'First time yeh done it an' yeh're in the puddin' club,' Eileen said. 'Now, is that good plannin' or what?'

'Our religion doesn't allow fer plannin',' Mary said solemnly.

'Oh, feck the same religion,' Eileen snorted. 'Yeh haven't got a penny ta yer name an' yeh're havin' kids already. It's madness, Mary. What chance are they goin' ta have, the poor little feckers? I'll tell yeh - none.'

'They'll have all the love that's goin',' Mary said.

'Love is it?' Eileen said drawing the smoke deeply into her lungs, 'yeh'll soon find out love won't fill their bellies. Why didn't yeh use one a them gadgets?'

'What gadgets are yeh talkin' about?' Mary asked.

'Them oul' rubber t'ings the fellas do be bringin' back from England. They come all shapes an' sizes,' Eileen said with a husky giggle. 'They slip 'em over their oul' langers and that's it. No more babies. It's as aisy 's that.'

'That's disgustin',' Mary said.

'Oh, is it now?' Eileen said. 'Well, ask yer brother Damian, he's the one that told me.'

'Sounds like Damian's goin ta Hell,' Mary said.

'Oh, he is,' Eileen said happily, 'on horseback, in the nude, wit' a rose up his hole!'

'I've heard enough of this,' Mary said, 'it's time I went home.'

'Yeh can even suck 'em like lollipops,' Eileen said. 'They come in all sorts a flavours.'

She burst out laughing at the sour look on Mary's face.

'I don't like dirty conversation, an' yeh know that,' Mary snapped.

'Anyway,' Eileen said, 'go an' see oul' Nurse Smit'son above in the village. That oul' hoor knows her stuff.'

Mary kissed her friend goodbye, caught the number 17 bus to the Castle and hurried through Rathfarnham village. Passing the Church of the Annunciation she went in, knelt and whispered a few prayers. Mary loved the smell of churches, the incense, the paraffin from the heaters.

When she arrived home the Boss was standing at the gate. 'Where the hell did yeh get to?' he asked angrily.

'I wen'ta see Eileen fer a chat.'

'Yeh don't want to be seein' that bloody tick,' he said. 'An' I saw Perkins lookin' atcha as yeh kem in. Yeh don't wan'ta be encouragin' them oul' shysters who have nuttin' better t'do than spy on fine women like yerself.'

Mary removed her headscarf, shook free her beautiful hair and looked at her shoes, then at her husband. She was tired and pregnant. Tears came to her eyes. 'I don't encourage anyone,' she said.

After a while, the Boss took her gently by the arm. 'I was on'y jokin',' he said softly. 'C'mon now, can't yeh take a joke?'

Mary stood like a chastised child in her second-hand coat. She blew her nose.

'There yeh go,' the Boss said, 'pregnant women have their tears close ta their eyes. C'mon now, snap out of it. I'll put th'oul kettle on.'

10

WHEN THE TIME came for Mary to have her baby, the Boss accompanied her to the Mater Hospital on the number 17 bus. On the return journey his mind raced, there was so much to do now, so much to haul, dump and deliver. Then there was all that scrap iron and the old car batteries he was seeing on building sites and in the backyards of garages. Like a toothy old beaver building his dam, the Boss gathered more sticks, planted more hedges and erected more barbed wire.

While Mary was away, he began looking for a pony and cart. He cycled up to Tibradden where a man bought and sold ponies. The fields were as close-grazed as the baize on a snooker table. There were horses with doleful eyes and feathery hocks, some with scars in their hides, others that were jumpy and unbroken, old mares with dipped backs that were fit only for O'Keefe's the knackers. They stood around with their backs to the keening wind, waiting for their daily wisp of hay.

'They're not much good, any a them,' the Boss said. 'I want somethin' strong an' energetic ta pull a cart.'

The horse dealer stood with smoke rising from the Sweet Afton cupped in his right hand. 'There's one over there - Kitty - she'd suit yeh, Johnny,' he said.

'Which one would that be?' the Boss asked doubtfully. 'They all look like dogmeat.'

'Over there be the wall, the little nag wit' the star on her face. She's a game little pony. Strong as an ox. I took her off a tinker on'y this mornin'. Kick the shite out a yeh, quick as lookit yeh.'

The pony was a decent sort, fourteen-two, four good feet and well muscled around the withers. She flattened her ears and exposed her teeth. The Boss moved nearer, unafraid. 'Mind her now,' the dealer said, 'I won't be held responsible if yeh tease th'animals.'

'C'mon now,' the Boss said. Kitty turned and flung out both heels, missing him by inches.

'Why, yeh bitch's bastard,' the Boss said quietly. The dealer retreated as fast as his mucus-filled lungs permitted. 'C'mon now Kitty,' the Boss cajoled. The pony looked at him peevishly, then squealed and walked off. The Boss followed, stalking her gently, all the time talking to her in a low voice.

He saw in the pony the qualities he was looking for: spirit, and a wiriness that meant she could live on fresh air. 'Get me an oul' halter,' he said. And the dealer brought up a broken old thing which the Boss, still talking, fitted around Kitty's ears, then he led her to the gate.

'She'll need breakin'',' the dealer said.

'I don't want her broken,' the Boss said, 'I want her as she is.'

'T'irty quid,' the dealer said.

'Yeh're pullin' me leg,' the Boss said. 'I'll give yeh a tenner.'

'Twenty-five,' the dealer said.

The Boss gave him eight crumpled pound notes up front and with regard to the remainder, he said, 'I won't ferget yeh, oul' son.'

He led Kitty home; the horse trotting meekly beside him as he pedalled his bike. It seemed she had found the owner she was looking for. The Boss searched the small ads in the *Evening Mail* and kept his ears open. Within hours he had a cart in need of repair, and a set of harness in very poor condition.

He worked hard all afternoon and evening - by the time he returned to the empty house, he was pushing a cart that was brightly varnished with new bolts and the holes repaired. The harness was stitched and oiled.

The Boss felt quite pleased with himself as he cycled in to the Mater to see his wife and new baby daughter, Babs. The tiny black-haired creature looked up at her father. He touched her smooth skin as she lay swaddled and pink as a newborn mouse.

Kitty responded to regular feeding and watering. As the Boss curry-combed her dusty hide and teased the burrs out of her mane, talking softly to her all the while, she stood quietly, the resistance gone out of her.

He tacked her up for the trip to the hospital to collect Mary and Babs. The pony flashed the whites of her eyes as the heavy hames was hooked around her neck. After a brief trial around the Hermitage and across Taylor's Lane and back, the Boss had her mastered. Kitty, he soon discovered, would not yield to heavy-handedness. She required a gentle approach. Her hooves rang on the tarmac as the Boss held the reins lightly in his fingers. He drove her through turbulent traffic, past the hiss and clang of factories. At the maternity hospital he leapt from the cart, tethered Kitty to a street sign, and galloped up the steps to collect his precious daughter.

Mary looked remarkably fit and well as she stood on the hospital steps with her baby in her arms. She was impressed at the elegance of the pony and cart, and wisely said so. She sat by her husband, holding her baby tightly to her. The Boss produced from his pocket a cellophaned packet of Ritchies peppermints, and peeling off two he gave one to his wife. Smiling and chatting they sucked mints all the way home, back to the little house now hidden behind tall trees.

Mary, her large full breasts filling her blouse, carried the baby as if she were a primed grenade and laid her gently in a pram the Boss had liberated from some garden. Bab's small pink head lay like a rose on the pillow, her little hands curled, the tiny blue-veined legs as bandy and restless as a jockey's. Her tiny body tired from its messy and mysterious journey, she slept, her little bird's breast rising and falling, black hair sleeked like a Chinese doll, her pale cheeks dimpled.

The Boss went out into the yard and commenced hammering and banging. He had a reason now to finish things. Life was short, he needed to get on. He felt the weight of more responsibility as he worked and talked to himself, his lips moving furiously, his strong hands clutching like claws, the sweat making a vee on his back.

When he returned to the kitchen several hours later Mary had a simple meal on the table. Two boiled eggs sat in wooden cups like teed-up golf balls, a plate was piled with buttered bread and a brown teapot was full of strong tea. The Boss washed his hands and ate, smashing the head off the egg and downing the contents in a couple of spoonfuls. 'A fella needs t'get on,' he said, 'if he duzzen wan'ta be left behind by them lazy hoors that do be hangin' round the pub.' Mary let the words come. It would not do to block them. The Boss's mind was a banked-up stream; it needed to drain to relieve the pressure.

As he slugged his second cup the Boss was absorbed. Mary reached into the pram and scooped up Babs who appeared to have been staring at a fly looping the loop above her. Mary modestly peeled back her blouse and taking the heavy breast in her hand she discretely directed the thick dark nipple towards the baby's questing mouth. Babs suckled noisily, her small white-nailed fingers touching her mother's full udder. The Boss averted his eyes and wished he had a newspaper to read, but his eyes were soon drawn back across the table. He was used to animals and wasn't disgusted but to see a breast as something other than a sex object was new. Mary already knew when Babs had had enough; so much of it was instinctive. She covered herself and, putting the baby against her left arm, she patted the tiny back with her right hand. Babs flashed her father what looked like a twisted smile. As he reached over to touch her she burped and gummily grimaced at the strange noise she'd made. Sour milk covered her fat little chins.

When Mary began to unpin the thick nappy the Boss returned to the yard. He offered Kitty a rotten apple which she ate out of his hand. 'Bedad, that little Babs is a fine little t'ing,' he told the pony, who nudged him, wanting more. As he shovelled and dug, stitched and tugged, the Boss's mind was occupied by something other than his own doings and dealings, his jealousies and ambitions.

Babs was a godsend. A lovely present. Every morning and evening after work they admired their suckling infant, and enjoyed a tea of boiled eggs and buttered bread. On one of these wonderfully happy evenings the Boss unveiled another surprise - a radio he had been given. It was a small Bakelite set with all the main stations. He turned it on and filled the little house with music.

Over the ensuing months the Boss watched Babs grow and change. Although she had still not reached the weight of a decent capon she took over the house with her cries and needs. As Babs grew, the Boss patted her dark hair and tweaked her snub nose. He splayed her tiny hands with his stubby working man's fingers and marvelled at their soft perfection. Babs smiled up at him. In a life of poverty that had been filled with hate and doubt, he had never known a love such as he felt for this small creature.

For a short, sweet time, Mary, Babs, his house and his land were all that mattered to the Boss. But as Babs crawled, then toddled and walked with him hand in hand, there would soon be no room in his heart for anyone else. Babs ate the good food the Boss grew, and developed into a shiny-haired, blue-eyed little beacon that lit up his life. Other babies would follow, a miniature procession of boys and girls, but none would ever be so cherished by their father. Mary was fecund and willing. Father Orlston visited and told her to keep making little soldiers for His army. Willingly, she complied.

11

FOR A WHILE husband, wife and baby prospered. There were eggs in the hen-house, greens in the garden and rabbits in Neary's fields. The Boss made brass-wire snares; fat rabbits lost their lives and their skins. Their blue-veined carcasses went into the stewpot, garnishing the swedes and parsnips. The young couple occasionally rewarded themselves with a day in the mountains.

Kitty zigzagged along overgrown lanes where cow parsley met in the middle. They sallied under dark, unkempt trees, trotting past old stone walls scabbed with lichen. Sitting on a blanket, with Babs protected from the mountainous wind, they ate scallions from the garden and soda bread which Mary had baked that morning. They drank cold tea out of bottles. Mary, her country face blushed with good health, her black hair wild and blowing, had never felt happier. The Boss in slacks and Sunday trilby, tickled Babs' toes.

But when he looked across to Orlagh College his face darkened. 'I hoed them paths from dawn ta dusk,' he said sadly, 'me poor guts empty, an' them feckin' priests wouldn' give me as much as a slice a bread. The black-coated bastards.'

''Tis a sin t'blame the priests,' Mary said, 'they wor on'y doin' what God instructed 'em t'do.'

The Boss shook his head like a tormented bull, and gritted what was left of his rotten teeth. 'They didn't have ta be such ignorant bollixes,' he snarled.

'I won't have yeh runnin' down them priests,' Mary said, 'it'll bring us bad luck.'

'Luck is it?' the Boss asked. 'Yeh make yer own luck in this bloody world.' He was on his feet as if a great wind had blown him upright and wiped the smile off his face. The precious day was at an end.

The Boss whipped Kitty into a fast gallop all the way back to the house, and locked the gates behind them.

12

THE BOSS PUT down his shovel. The Dowager was standing on his property. 'What is it yeh want?' the Boss asked. 'I'm a busy man.'

The Dowager cleared his throat. He looked into the trench. 'Jaze, yeh got yer work cut out here,' he said. 'Worra yeh doin'?'

The Boss looked hard at the unwelcome visitor. 'I'm diggin' a feckin' trench.'

'Oh, yeah,' the Dowager replied.

'Well?' the Boss prompted.

'Meself an' the lads beyant,' the Dowager nodded in the direction of Cullen's pub, 'wor goin' ta ask yeh over fer a pint. We wor t'inkin' maybe yeh'd be needin' a little . . . yeh know, refreshment.'

The Boss stood up. He seemed to be twice the Dowager's bulk. 'I wouldn't be at all interested in that sort a caper,' he said. 'I've got plenty t'do here.'

The Dowager waited for a moment but the Boss returned to the trench. Like a police dog looking for a child's corpse, he was furiously flinging black riverbed earth over his head. The Dowager spat a green gob of phlegm on to the ground and returned to the pub.

The Boss didn't need friends. Why couldn't they accept that and leave him alone? He had more trees to plant - he wouldn't be happy until every bit of the pub and the labourers' cottages beyond were hidden from view. Then, with his little Babs by his side, he would build more pigsties. He kicked off his wellingtons and went indoors. He rolled up his sleeves, exposed his neck and washed at the sink. Mary said Grace, her hands joined in front of her.

The Boss attacked his food, his elbows out like a youth on a motorbike. He ate noisily, sucking the juicy fat and marrow through stumpy teeth. After he'd wiped his plate with a slice of bread, he read yesterday's *Evening Mail*.

As she put Babs to bed Mary whispered prayers until the infant collapsed into untroubled sleep. Leaving her baby, pale in the moonlight, Mary returned to the tiny kitchen to drink tea and read *The Messenger.*

In bed they lay together, wrapped around each other like eels under a rock. Mary was soon pregnant again.

'It seems yer man on'y has ta wave his feckin' trousers at yer woman, for her t'be up the bloody pole,' Mrs Dowland said in Rice's shop. The harpies from the Corporation houses queueing behind her laughed.

'She's fertile all right,' one said. 'And t'ink iv'all the lovely Children's Allowance yer man is pocketin' - he's no feckin' fool that bugger!'

Pam, a sweet and vulnerable ball of fluff, was next to fall from Mary's womb. Her little hands gripped the Boss's finger. Life was going to be more difficult with another mouth to feed. If only Mary could be stitched up with thorns like some primitive tribes did to their women.

The Boss planted apple trees and rhubarb, raspberries, a cherry tree, and a wisteria. More sheds were erected from materials begged, borrowed and stolen. More sties were added and the Boss went out again looking for work to pay for them. Anything considered, legal or otherwise.

Babs loved her little sister and gurgled with pleasure as she touched the baby as it suckled Mary. When darkness dropped like an iron door the Boss, washed himself all over in a tin bath. He ate his supper and when Babs came over to put her fat little hands on his thigh, he picked her up and finished his meal one-handed, avoiding spearing the little hand that wallowed in his bowl.

Now the trees had grown, Mary was unable to see passers-by going down the Whitechurch Road to the Church of the Annunciation, but she saw her husband cross the bridge lugging something heavy.

'God won't be too hard on me,' said the Boss from behind the pigsties as he stashed away the two brand new sheets of corrugated iron he'd stolen from the convent.

When Mary said stealing was a sin, the Boss had to stop himself from hitting her. He made lean-tos and clinker paths. Mary asked the priests for advice: they topped up her blessings and told her how much God appreciated her efforts.

Babs was now a bright and sparky three-year-old who followed her father around like a faithful sheepdog. For Babs, he would lay down his shovel and share his jam sandwich and bottle of milk, thumbing morsels of food into her tiny mouth, allowing her to suck from his bottle. To feel her tiny body through his shirt made it all worthwhile.

The trees were now so tall, they were erasing the convent bell which now boomed the Angelus unseen. The tall chimney of the Bloomfield Laundry - on whose stone wall lolled the ghost of James Joyce - ejaculated filth into the clear sky.

Seven more sties were built out of tea-chests and biscuit tins. The Boss cemented broken bottles into the floors to keep the pigs from ripping them up. 'A cut snout'll soon cure them feckers adat habit,' he told Babs as she helped him mix cement with her little wooden spade. Only eight of the completed sties actually held pigs and they were runty things the Boss had picked up at the market for a few shillings each. He earned a little extra exercising horses for toffs and mucking out stables.

The two little girls slept belly to belly in an old double bed with sagging springs. Mary was expecting again.

13

BRIDGID WAS THE next child to burst from Mary's womb like a chestnut from its spiky shell. She suckled noisily, and constantly howled for more. She was a big-boned baby, round, fat and heavy, with mischievous eyes. She ate her mashed potato and her bacon rinds before normal children did. Bridgid wobbled around with her bockedy walk, her nappy hanging off her. She raided cupboards, scattering cups and saucers and pulling down a clattering avalanche of utensils.

She copied her mother cooking, pouring sugar on the tiles, adding water and a broken egg. Mary pulled Bridgid away and hugged her protectively before the Boss got to her.

Mary was kept busy, as well as knitting and making dresses out of old clothes. Her glasses on, she worked nimbly with pins and thimble, her love for her children driving her. She took Babs to church on Sundays, dropped her last few pence into the collection box and listened to a sermon on chastity.

Mary was soon expecting for the fourth time, and prayed, 'Please God let it be a boy.'

Each baby was another boulder for the Boss to carry. The house was not big enough. Like the grizzled captain of a sinking tramp steamer, he could hear the waves crashing, the ropes uncoiling from the slippery decks. With paint and putty - he plugged holes.

Mary sat by the fire feeling the new baby already astir in her belly. It felt like this one was taking penalty kicks. It was going to be a boy, thank God.

The Boss trimmed hedges for farmers up the mountains and dug gardens for old ladies in Rathmines. He cleared rubbish from the shops and brought it home on the cart to burn. Like a madman on an out-of-kilter escalator, he was running with a scowl on his face, comically falling down and bouncing up again, only to trip over his outsize braces and land on his arse. One day, Mary, her belly stuck out in front of her, walked all the way to St Columcille's Holy Well with its big weeping trees flapping with rags and holy medals, and collected water from the well to make tea.

The Boss laughed when she told him. 'Superstitious shite, the lot of it,' he said. He could just imagine her big arse bending over the well, with the Tallaght gobshites looking at her veins. Mary was going back to her roots, all that feckin' fairy stuff she was brought up on. What more could you expect from that bloody bunch of culchie savages?

'The holy tay'll bring us luck,' Mary said. The children gathered round and gazed at her with big questioning eyes. They watched as their father slugged his holy tea, expecting to see him suddenly clothed in golden robes and wearing a crown.

'Feck off ta bed,' he growled, and the children trooped off, looking back just in case they missed a miracle.

Eileen brought fruit and high spirits to the maternity ward, which resembled a byre filled with intensively farmed babies and lugubrious pregnant women.

'I've a belly a slop,' Mary complained as she lay swollen and red-faced on the bed.

'Niver mind,' Eileen said, 'yeh'll get over it. But don't do it again. Yer man's cock seems to hypnotise yeh like some kinda big oul' snake.'

'Ah, stop, fer God's sake,' Mary sighed. 'It wearies me ta hear yeh talk like that.' She shifted in bed for the hundredth time. She knew the baby was lying crossways inside her.

'Here, have th'ol' grapes at least,' Eileen said, plucking grapes off the stems and swallowing them in handfuls like purple marbles. 'Yeh'd betther hurry up or I'll ate them all meself,' she said, laughing as she fed her face, the juice lying in the valleys of her chins.

'They don't even give yeh an oul' shot of an'tin' ta kill the pain in here,' Mary whined.

'The bloody priest tol' them not ta,' Eileen said, wiping her hands. 'They warned the bloody doctors they'd rot in Hell if they were caught helpin' a poor woman. Bloody perverts.'

'Will yeh stop that blasphemin',' Mary groaned. 'I can't stand any more of it.'

'Sorry, darlin',' Eileen said. 'Here - have a grape, there's two left. I know how yeh're suff'rin' bu'rit's yer own fault. Stand up ta that Jackeen. Cross yer legs an tell'im ta piss off. Yeh won't find me in here lyin' like an oul' baste with me bare arse in a strange bed.'

'I hate babies, too,' Mary sniffed.

'Now yeh're talkin',' Eileen said. 'They're all smelly little feckers wit' yella arses.'

'This is the last one,' Mary said. 'I'm fed up. I wan' ta go home.'

Mary had lost interest in her friend and was dozing. Her stomach was bubbling and acidic, her legs filled with water.

She slept fitfully and began to dream. Father Orlston was astride her, his fat face was sweating, his complexion unhealthy and his teeth were black. He was humping like a dog on heat. 'There. Now yeh have number five in the bag,' he said, doing up his surplice. Mary was laughing in her sleep. Now she wouldn't have to go to Hell. She woke up smiling when Eileen kissed her.

'Hey, that was a wet wan by the look a yeh,' Eileen said.

'What?'

'The dream! Oh niver mind. Look I'm off. Keep drinkin' the gripe water.'

'Bye darlin'.' Mary kissed her friend goodbye and slipped back into her delicious dream.

Eileen mounted her bike and felt the breeze on her face as she rode away, glad to be single.

14

WHEN THE NURSES came to deliver Mary she swore and gripped the blankets. The pain was ferocious. The nurses loosened her fingers and raised her shift. Mary tried to beat them away. She closed her eyes as the rubber-gloved hands entered her. Her legs spread wide like the trophy carcass of a white hunter, Mary prayed. Bog Latin, Irish hymns and Sanskrit tumbled deliriously from her. When she heard her baby's first cry, she forgot the pain and humiliation. When the midwife put the clawing, squirming, messy thing on her bare breast, Mary cried with joy. It was a boy. Thanks be to God.

Mary was washed and relaxed when the Boss arrived in his best trilby. He was clutching a bouquet that drew comments from the women in the other beds. 'They're from Lady Moore's garden,' the Boss said. He had cycled up to tell the old lady his wife was having another baby. She might have dropped him a ten bob note but all he got was: 'You poor man. I'm sure you will cope. Take your wife some flowers.' Lady Moore directed the Boss towards a spectacular flowerbed.

The Boss watched the old woman go down a lavender-scented path before helping himself to several armfuls, some of which he sold to Brady the florist in Terenure.

'They're nice,' Mary said but she was more interested in what the Boss thought of his first son. 'I t'ink we should call him John in honour of yerself,' Mary said with a smile. 'Jack fer short.'

When Mary opened the embroidered white shawl as if she were delicately unwrapping a precious gift, the Boss glanced disinterestedly at the plum-coloured nestling, and was filled with contempt. He recognised in his first son a rival, a mother's boy. The thing that lay rheumy-eyed in the shawl would never be a man like him: a steely-eyed, iron-willed, blue-chinned Pluto.

Jack had rickets and bad ears from the start, which made it easier for his father to dislike him. He looked a potentially ungainly child, the sort that toddled drunkenly between chair-legs, banging its oversized head and slipping on its own droppings.

While Mary would no doubt love the scrawny wretch the way mothers do, the Boss, like a tiger after jettisoning his sperm, wanted nothing to do with the result. The smell of Jack made him gag. Pig crap smelled bad but they made money. Children brought nothing with them except pain, dirt and expense. If Mary hadn't been such a bloody fool with her stupid Catholic superstitions, the Boss would have been happy with one child, his lovely dark-haired Babs. She was a miniature version of himself with her fine delicate looks and bright intelligence. Mary got no thanks for bearing Jack. Why should she? Any recipient of a man's seed on any Saturday night in any back alley or behind any ivy covered wall could have done just as well.

The Boss glanced at the tiny screwed-up face. 'It's all right fer him lyin' there while I'm out there workin' me guts out t'feed them pigs.'

Mary said nothing. She felt so let down.

Revolted by the smell of breast milk and constipated oul' ones from the Libertys slum, the Boss impatiently fiddled with his hat. He so obviously wanted to be outside in the fresh air.

'That bastard Perkins is annoyin' me again,' he grumbled. 'D'yeh know what he's doin' now?'

'Sticking rocks up his arse,' Mary wanted to say. The Boss blathered on. Mary couldn't give a tinker's curse about Perkins. But a life of enmity with her neighbour was a horrible prospect.

The Boss's sat on the bed looking pained. His mind was so full there was no room in it for Mary or her son. She wondered what she could say or do to please her husband. They were like strangers.

Mary felt squashed and broken. Soon she would be back in the dreary, friendless shack behind the trees. She wasn't looking forward to it one bit. Please God, Eileen would call to see her, because she badly needed a friend to talk to. 'C'mon,' the Boss rasped and departed in a hurry, his boots squeaking on the tiles.

Mary blessed herself as she clambered into the cart with little Jack and held him to her milk-ripe bosoms. 'There goes another one,' the Dowager said as he watched Kitty trot by Cullen's. 'Don't know why they want so many. Yeh never see the poor little shaggers out playin' on the road like the other kids.'

'Jasus, will ya look a' her, she's gettin' as big as a house,' another drinker observed.

'More fer yer man ta get a hoult of,' the Dowager cracked. The men laughed and returned to their pints.

Stepping warily, Mary entered the gates and walked under the trees that darkened the windows and hushed the stream. Little Babs made tea and fussed. Pam and Bridgid rushed to hug their mother, and inspect the infant. After tea they sat by the fire. The children with their hands on their knees, listening to Mary's hospital tales while the Boss read his paper with silent indifference. At bedtime Mary sent him to the single bed like a disobedient hound.

15

MARY WAS TOO sick and depressed to do much more than feed her new baby. 'It's that blasted baby takin' it out a her,' the Boss told the pigs who grunted in agreement. When he eventually visited his wife, Mary lay as if weighted down by her two huge, milk-filled udders.

'What's wrong wit'cha?' the Boss said sharply. He put an icy hand on her brow.

'Ach, I don't know,' Mary said, 'I jus–' Her voice went. She was too exhausted to finish the sentence.

A week passed, and there was no improvement. Babs prepared a childish meal and carried it on a tray which she placed by the bedside with a single wallflower in a jam jar. The Calvita sandwiches remained uneaten. Babs mopped her mother's brow with a damp cloth.

'Can yeh get me the statcha of Blessed Martin de Porres?' Mary whispered. Babs took her mother's request to the yard where the Boss was digging a hole to take the oily pools of muck that leaked from the sties into the river.

'She says she wants the statcha of Blessed Martin de Pour Rayse,' Babs said.

'What's gorrinta her now?' the Boss asked, his face crinkled with irritation. 'Who's this fecker anyway? Izzy a doctor or what?'

'I don't know,' Babs said. 'It's a statcha. Mammy wrote it down fer yeh. Yeh have ta get it from the convent. He's a good black man, Mammy says.'

'There's no such t'ing,' the Boss said.

'Well, this fella is,' Babs said, 'the nuns wouldn' hav'im if he wasn't. He's standin' in an alcove in the school reception area, be the door, on the left as yeh go in, Mammy says. Ask the Mother Superior if yeh can have a lenda him ta make the Novena.'

'I'll go an' get it now,' the Boss said crossly.

Leaving Babs with her mother, he walked briskly to the Loretto Convent and rapped on the door. Sister Anthony opened it.

'All a them bloody nuns is ugly bitches,' the Boss said later, 'but Jasus that young one is as sweet as a nut.'

'Yeh shouldn' talk about nuns like that,' Mary cried. 'Anyway, didja say it was fer me?'

'Course I didn't,' the Boss laughed. 'I was too busy lookin' at yer woman and wondherin' why she wanted to be a nun.'

'Me nerves is playin' up,' Mary said. 'This should do the trick.'

The Boss unwrapped the eight-inch plaster statue.

'Oh God,' Mary said, reaching out, 'give him t'me.' She snatched the statue and kissed it all over while the Boss and Babs looked on. 'God forgive me,' Mary said, her rosary binding her hands. 'Please God, absolve all me sins.' Tears flooded her instantly. The Boss glanced at Babs and nudged his daughter. Hunching his shoulders and secretly laughing, he left the room.

Mary slept with the statue by the bed. Every time she woke up, she kissed it and prayed. It worked. She got better. 'There now, I told yeh,' she said when the Boss brought her tea.

'Ah, sure he isn't yer man, the great black fella!' the Boss joked. And when Mary scooped out a large breast to feed her son, the Boss left the room to go to the pigs. Babs stayed, fascinated by her little brother. The colour had returned to Mary's cheeks and the smile to her face.

She put Jack down beside her and was making herself comfortable when her right elbow caught the statue and sent it crashing headlong on to the uncarpeted floor where it lay shattered, the black head rolling under the bed.

'Oh Mammy, yeh've broken it,' Babs said and she bent down to pick up the body in one hand, the head in the other.

'Mothera God,' Mary said, crossing herself, 'Jesus forgive me. Oh Babs, hurry an' tell yer Daddy. He'll get it mended.'

'I know jus' the fella,' the Boss said as he collected the broken statue. 'I'll take it inta him tamorra.' Instead, he took the broken statue down the yard and sent both parts spinning through the air, the black head following the white-robed body, until they plopped into the deep pool below the weir. 'That's where that oul' black man belongs,' the

Boss said to himself and returned to his work.

Unable to motivate herself, Mary went back to bed and stayed there for several days. 'She shou'be up be now,' the Boss growled to himself as he worked in the yard. 'It's all in the 'magination'.

Eventually, Mary was washing clothes, darning and ironing. In spite of her discomfort, she didn't complain. She had put on weight, her legs were heavier, her arms thicker but she never blamed her babies. They were a godsend who collectively tapped into a great reservoir of love - something her husband would never understand.

16

THE BOSS WAS happier now that his wife was on her feet, back at the sink where she belonged. A fortnight's contact with his first son had not cemented any sort of bond with the scrawny, yellow-tinged baby. Mary adored the jaundiced brat as if he were made of gold. Suckling her creamy milk, Jack thrived but days and nights spent in an unheated room with condensation weeping from the walls gave him catarrh, making him cough and splutter like a sick kitten.

'Little fecker's lookin' fer notice,' the Boss grumbled, 'when I was his age I was walkin'.'

That night over supper Mary asked about the statue. 'Ah, didn't I tell yeh,' the Boss said, 'yer man did a grand job on it. I gev it back ta the nuns.'

'Oh, that's good,' Mary said, 'broken statchas bring bad luck.'

The Boss mopped his gravy with a heel of bread and made no further comment .His pixie ears twitched. 'Who the hell's that?' Someone was rapping on the windowpane.

When Mary saw the moon face, the nostrils pressed out of shape against the glass, she cried, 'Eileen!'

'What does that culchie bitch want at this hour a the day?' the Boss asked angrily. Mary shuffled to the door. Eileen brushed past the Boss's chair as if she was a prison warden and he a broken-down old lifer.

'Where's the little yella fecker?' Eileen asked. 'I'm dyin' t'see him.'

She fingered back the blanket. 'Ah, sure, he's a little dote,' she said. 'Jasus but he's the spittin' image a yerself, even down ta the feckin' big snout. Poor little shagger.' Dropping her voice, she added, 'Make this the last one fer Jasus' sake, Mary, or yehz'll all starve.'

'Maybe yeh'll be havin' one yerself one day if yeh can get a fella,' the Boss stirred it up from behind the *Mail*. Mary elbowed her friend into silence. Eileen gave the newspaper a vigorous two-fingered salute.

'Wouldja like a cuppa tay?' Mary asked.

'Bejasus, I t'ought yeh'd niver ask,' Eileen said. 'Sure, me oul' belly t'inks me feckin' t'roat's cut.'

'It would be if I had me way,' the Boss was thinking.

Like two tinkers round a campfire, the dark-haired Galwegians drank strong tea and munched Lincoln Creams. Mary claimed her raven hair and aristocratic nose were due to some high-born young Spanish officer who'd been swept on to a Galway beach after the break-up of the Armada.

'Some oul' wandhrin' gypo more like,' Eileen said, 'which reminds me: Damian, that sexy brother a yers, has bought a business in Cabra.'

'God help him - he deserves it,' Mary said.

The Boss's brown forehead visibly contracted. He disliked all Mary's relatives but he had a black hatred for Damian, Mary's favourite - although she would never condone her brother's womanising. Damian was so handsome and so charming, no woman was safe from his glittering blue eyes and fluttering hands.

'It'd be grand t'see him again,' Mary said.

The Boss cracked the paper like a bullwhip.

Babs cut up the cream cake Eileen had brought and after the Boss refused the first slice, the two women ate most of it with some help from the children, who wedged great slices into their talking mouths and licked their fingers. They laughed and talked of old friends and old times, of Galway far away in the west. Mary's complexion improved and by the end of their meeting, she looked healthy and optimistic. Before she left, Eileen shoved a five pound note into Mary's hand. 'Buy sompthin' for yella Jack,' she said kissing her old friend goodbye.

'I'll take care a that,' the Boss said after had Eileen left.

To keep the peace, Mary meekly handed over the fiver.

'Stupit hoor,' the Boss said. 'Time she got a man. Pity there's no one that desp'rate.'

'Poor Eileen,' Mary said to the children who were fighting over the empty cake carton, 'she'd give yeh her last penny. That's what I call a friend,' she added defiantly. The Boss pretended to read but his thoughts were on Damian, Mary's filthy brother. Any girl who gave herself to that animal deserved horsewhipping in public.

17

BABS WALKED ALONGSIDE the pigsties, gently shaking the big second-hand pram. From its depths, young Jack gazed like some desiccated Chinese dwarf. 'Ah, look Daddy,' Babs cried, 'he's suckin' his t'umb.'

The Boss went from barrel to barrel, forking the putrid contents into the pigs' greedy pink eyes. Babs was determined not to be ignored. She tilted the pram and showed it to the Boss, who stopped, sighed, and back-handed the sweat from his forehead. 'There, Daddy, look - isn't he lovely!'

'Jasus Christ, can'tcha see a fella's busy,' the Boss said, 'fer Christ's sake - take that infant up fer yer woman ta look afther. That's her job.'

'I will Daddy, but on'y when yeh've said hello ta him first. He's so beautiful,' Babs sang.

The Boss, with his shovel shouldered, peeped into the pram as if it contained a nest of poisonous snakes. He did not want more children. They brought with them poverty and ignorance. Thanks to Mary - his ambition was gone, his world shattered.

'Hello!' he bellowed, making the baby jump.

The Boss mused as he gave the pigs' water. If only he were like the men in Cullen's - the wasters, the layabouts, who never paid their bills or accepted any responsibility for anything. She, being from Galway, worried about nothing. Sitting up there in the nice house he built her single-handed. There she was, thriving on doing feckall. Now she has this bloody baby. Boy - me arse! The Boss resented a male child gulping down his wife's milk, his bloody little fists cupping her tits with pleasure. Little fecker. It was disgusting. The whole bloody thing was revolting - the blood and the placenta and the headaches and the jam rags. Filthy bitches - women.

He lowered his shovel. 'Ge'rim up ta yer woman before he has an accident,' he growled. Babs turned the big pram with difficulty. As she pushed it slowly towards the house she cooed, 'Who's a good babby then!' and her ringlets danced.

When Babs reached the kitchen door, she yelled, 'Mammy I t'ink Jack's afther doin' his doody.'

'An', God help him, how can he control his little bowels,' Mary said, nuzzling her baby with her big nose. As Babs watched, she laid him on the table and unpinned his soggy nappy.

'Will yeh wash the droppin's out a that?' Babs took the stinking bundle to the sink and without complaint ran cold water over it and watched shit and water swirl down the plughole. Warm and dry, Jack, with eyes closed in pleasure, sucked the thick red nipple and kneaded the fat soft breast with tiny hands. When the Boss came in for his sandwich, his eyes darted towards his wife then were quickly averted. He ate his grub silently and returned to the pigs.

It wasn't long before Mary fell pregnant again. No one knew whose fault it was this time. Perhaps the Boss's feeling of despair made him reckless. Perhaps God intervened, shooting his celestial sperm from outerspace. Mary didn't mind and her latest confinement brought a big satisfied smile to Father Orlston's plump face.

Jack survived the rickets and an ear that wept pus, to grow into an undernourished and nervous child with straight black hair and his mother's long nose, which was always running. He conquered potty training hopelessly late, and wiped his nose on his sleeve so much it was soon stiff with dried mucus. Babs looked after him, fussing around, grabbing his nose and wringing the snot out of it until he cried. The children played in the solitude of the cramped yard with only the tops of the trees and the sky to look at.

From the moment of first awareness, Jack had feared the Boss and tried to please him. Shouts and curses were his daily diet as he staggered round giving his daddy presents of stones and handfuls of sand. He would be the Boss's slave. Babs was the one born to shine.

The big double bed sagged in the middle with the weight of the four children. Babs slept at one end with Jack in her arms, Pam and Bridgid at the other, an arrangement that lasted several years.

'Yeh can't have them childher sleepin' in the same bed now that Jack's growin',' Mary said.

'An' why not?' the Boss asked. 'Sure, he'd be no good at that either.'

18

AFTER MONTHS OF lively discussions with himself - in the pigsties and on the cart with Kitty trotting out in front - the Boss decided he would build a real house out of cement blocks and girders, with fireplaces and chimneys. It would make the dross, who pissed their dole money up the wall in Cullen's, puke with envy.

Barely literate, the Boss made room for himself on the kitchen table, ordered Mary to keep the children quiet, and got to work. Over several weeks he sketched plans and priced the job. After many abandoned schemes, he came up with a squat bungalow containing two bedrooms, a parlour and a kitchen.

Feeling like some grey-bearded archaeologist digging up an ancient civilisation, he picked and shovelled out the foundations. With Herculean strength and single-minded commitment, he built his house. He worked with Kitty, her mane dusty, her thin flanks lathered, her eyes bulging. No whip was needed, the pony seemed to accept this was important to her master. The pair hauled bricks, wood, slates and bags of cement. The Boss nailed rafters, hung doors, tiled floors and put in fireplaces. The original house was cannibalised and recycled. Like children in a country devastated by a natural disaster, the children gawped as their room was eaten away.

The work made the Boss tired and angry. 'I'm doin' it all single-handed, fer yehz,' he said as he ate a sandwich and slugged tea. 'Them shaggers in Cullen's watched me lift that big joist on me own an' not one a them lazy melts lifted a finger t'help a poor fella.' Although fourteen children would spring from his loins, the Boss would always consider building that bungalow his greatest achievement. It was his *Iliad*, his *King Lear*, his Golden Gate Bridge, his discovery of penicillin. Babs offered to help but the Boss grimly told her to go indoors. 'Bye, Daddy,' she said, waving and smiling, her thin little legs taking her up to the shack. When the Boss came in, hungry and slack-eyed, Babs sat on his lap. She shoved the bread towards him and watched him wrench at it with his few remaining teeth. He went to bed and slept like a fallen tree.

He pebbledashed and whitewashed the walls. The bungalow looked exactly the way the Boss wanted it to look, powerful, squat - built to last. At the bridge he built massive gateposts like tank traps. Surely now, those who lived in State housing would have to accept he'd finally arrived.

As a man of property the Boss worried all the more. What would happen if the kids upturned an oil lamp and burned the new house to the ground? What a laughing stock he'd be. This and worse calamities occupied much of his waking hours.

Led by Babs, the children crawled all over the new bungalow and made their own little houses in the corners out of sacks and sticks. Mary stood in an unpapered room and felt very proud. If only her doubting relatives could see her now. On his knees and in his trilby, the Boss painted skirting boards, doors, picture rails and walls. There were the Dublin mountains through a south-facing window. St Gatien's was behind a giant walnut tree, and Rooney's house sat on the fronds of a Douglas fir. With the children romping behind, Mary paraded round the bungalow like a queen.

Their footsteps echoed on uncarpeted floors and they oohed and aahed. They visited both bedrooms, the parlour - reserved for social occasions - the big kitchen with the cooker in a corner and the scullery for hanging up onions.

'It's a bit dark in the corner where yeh're puttin' the cooker,' was Mary's only criticism. The Boss bridled like a lashed mule. Was there no pleasing her?

'But it's grand - so it is,' Mary said.

The Boss accepted her apology with good grace. He went to his secret cache and returned with two bottles of stout. Ceremoniously he drew the corks and handed one with the foam oozing out of it, to Mary. They clinked bottles and drank each other's health.

'Here's t'Paradise!' Mary said. It was her idea to name the new house after a little conversation she'd had with Father Orlston. Please God - life would be good from now on.

When the day came to move in, Jack was first across the threshold, crawling over the step and falling flat on his face on the concrete floor inside. His face twisted with pain, he lay there as helpless and pathetic as an upturned woodlouse. The girls followed, dragging boxes of stuff from their room and claiming the best beds. It was an exciting day. That evening Mary cooked her first meal on the new stove. The Boss ate his fill and after he'd checked on the pigs, he urinated in the stream and hoped Perkins was watching.

19

FOR BAB'S SEVENTH birthday the Boss ordered a cake from Landy's with her name written on it in icing. She sat on her father's lap and hacked it into segments: a nice big one for Mammy, a bigger one for Daddy, one each for Bridgid and Pam, and a tiny wedge for Jack whose jaws bulged as he crammed it into his mouth and immediately began to splutter, scattering it on the floor.

'He's chokin', the greedy little shite,' the Boss said.

Mary cleared the blockage and ate it.

Mary, of course, remembered all her children's birthdays, not just Bab's. She made tarts and stabbed them with candles, and she cheered when the children blew out the candles. One year she made a doll's pram for Pam out of plywood. She cut slices of log for wheels, and made the holes for the axles with a red hot poker. When the children were in bed she hammered, screwed and painted the crude contraption canary yellow and the wheels strawberry red. Pam shrieked hysterically when she saw it. Mary wished she had a camera.

As the years had passed, Mary - although still young - had slowed down and was always jaded. It was hard work trying to feed the children with what scraps the Boss gave her, and to clothe them as best she could from cut-up leftovers. She became awkward and cantankerous as her relationship with her husband withered. The Boss turned to Kitty for comfort, the best buy of his life. With the pony's help he collected scrap, bones, bottles, wire, and old horseshoes from the blacksmith in Templeogue - anything he could sell on for a few pence. He stashed most of his money in a coffin-like box he locked and shoved under the bed. Who knew when a volcanic eruption in Sicily might have a catastrophic effect on Rathfarnham?

The Boss, too, had lost his sheen and whatever was left of his optimism. He was never going to make a fortune and it hurt. He kept himself to himself and looked down on the scutters in their State-owned houses. The Boss would rather be an individual not a sheep. He often bayed at the moon, 'I owe nuttin' to no man!'

Perkins remained a source of anxiety and suspicion. While the Boss was away, the old man might just pay a visit. For all he knew, Mary was giving the filthy old reprobate more than her Galway smile and cups of sugary tea. Dirty deeds were probably happening in the Boss's bed. The thought of it drove him mad. Down in the yard, as he worked with his greasy trilby pulled low over his eyes, in his tattered jacket and wellingtons, he looked over at the light in Perkins hut and cursed the old man.

Alone in the dark he ranted, his voice carrying up to the sparrows and mice sleeping in the eves. He abused Mary loudly for her unfaithfulness, and wished Perkins a slow and incredibly painful death, preferably from a brain tumour but only after he'd survived an horrific traffic accident in which a foot of railing had gone up his arse.

20

THE CHILDREN PLAYED in the sand the Boss had dumped under the pussy willow tree when he'd finished building the house. Babs, Pam and Bridgid threw sand in each other's eyes and cried under Mary's abstracted gaze. When she dragged a chair into a pool of sun in the yard, the children clambered out of the sand and crowded around her like ants around something jammy. Babs crawled up first and made base camp, while Jack, his mucused ear bandaged, mewled at his mother's buniony feet. Mary sat patiently in her squeaking chair, trying to drink tea while six arms and legs threshed about on her lap. Jack, his snotty face triumphant, was scaling her varicose-veined legs to get on board when he fell back and hit his head. Howling, he gained top spot.

Smiling gummily, Mary cuddled them all like an armful of squeaking weasels. Her children were her only reason for existing. Without them - life was nothing. And it was nice to know God approved.

Down in the yard the Boss, unloved and troubled, railed against the world - even though the sun was shining and finches sang in the newly-blossomed apple trees.

A scrape against the pebbledashed wall made Mary look up.

It was Eileen. 'God, doncha yeh look grand. Here, I brought yeh an oul' currenty cake.'

'Ah, yeh shouldn't have.' Mary said reaching up to hug her friend. The children examined their surrogate aunt, watching her pockets for the bag of sweets she regularly brought them. Mary noticed Eileen's crooked eyes had a spark flashing brighter than usual. And her make-up was more accurately applied than usual. Then there was the shortish skirt, revealing her thick, unlovely Galway legs.

'Guess what?' she said. 'I'm gettin' hitched.'

'Yeh're not!'

'Oh yes I am!'

'Yeh're not, are yeh? Who's the lucky fella? Jasus, I don't believe it!' Mary squealed into her friend's massive bosom.

'Yeh wouldna know 'im, he's an accounts clerk.'

'An accounts clerk? My God, how did yeh manage ta snare a smart fella like that? An *accounts clerk*, if yeh don't mind,' Mary said, unable to hide her envy.

'He's a quiet old shite, burr he'll do me.' Eileen laughed. 'D'yeh get it? . . . Do me. Oh Mary, I wan'ta be done from all angles. I'm dyin' fer a taste ath oul' mickey. I'm gaspin' fer it. Sure, I've been near on starvation since I left Galway. All me dir'y talk, wouldn' yeh know it. He's fifty-two, half dead, but beggars can't be choosers. Anyway, I'll pizen his bloody cocoa if he's any throuble!' she laughed loudly. Mary shooed the children away and picked Jack up.

'Get yer Anty Eileen a cup a tay,' she shouted after Babs. Then to her friend she said, 'Reveal all,' and because she was laughing so much, she could hardly get out, '*immeedjetly*!'

Eileen's harsh culchie brogue and her coalminer's bellow brought the Boss up to the wire fence to peer through the holes like a performing artist wearing multiple spectacles. The fat legs crossed and the skirt hitched way above the knees, caught his eyes like a fisherman's hook. He opened the gate, bulkily entered the small concrete space by the kitchen.

'Yeh're lookin' smashin',' he said, eyeing a triangle of knickers.

Eileen, who'd never had such a compliment paid to her by anyone in her life, smiled, her wall-eye filled with pleasure. She noticed for the first time that Boss possessed a certain animal attraction: him in his shirt sleeves with his bulging muscles and his sun-browned skin. Jasus he was sex in wellingtons.

Eileen brazenly teased him by crossing and recrossing her massive thighs. Mary was annoyed at her husband's intrusion. She wanted to hear everything from Eileen firsthand, in the minutest and the most intimate detail. The Boss's charismatic presence put a stop to that.

'Eileen's gettin' married to a clerk in Clery's,' Mary said.

'Soooo, there's now!' the Boss said archly. 'Gettin' marrowed are we?' He couldn't take his eyes off that sweet triangle. He took a step closer and peered down Eileen's bovine cleavage. Jasus - but the hoor was well-served in that department too. 'Did yeh offer the woman a cup a tay at all?' the Boss asked. His smile, Mary noted, was the fullest it had been for six months, and there was a telling drop of froth on his chops. While Eileen was talking, the Boss sat himself on the warm concrete with his knees up. It was a ringside seat. When Babs brought the teapot, he ordered her to get him his personal mug. Mary was disgusted but intrigued. She hadn't seen him in such good form for ages. For him to take time away from his darling pigs for a cup of tea was very unusual, especially with Eileen. Maybe he was changing back to the charming man Mary had fallen in love with that day in Rathmines. It seemed such a long time ago.

The three chatted but Mary was hived off to the edges of the conversation while the Boss talked as light-heartedly as he'd done when he and Mary were first courting. There was no doubt about it - the charm was still intact. Mary had often wondered why she had married such a miserable bollix, and now she could see why. The Boss in this sort of form was engaging, even genial. If only he could stop worrying his poor head about everything and put his trust in the Almighty.

'Listen Eileen,' he said, placing a hand on her knee, 'le'me show yeh the t'ree lovely pigs I bought from the market last week. C'mon.' He pressed his black nails into the plump arm and almost dragged her towards the pigsties. Eileen looked in mock helplessness over her shoulder at Mary as he disappeared through the gate and down among the pigs. The Boss's domain was usually sacrosanct. Entrance was forbidden to all females, except for Babs. Everywhere was her playground. Now, Eileen - plain, old gunner-eyed Eileen from Galway - was melting under the Boss's charm.

'In here,' he said. Flies buzzed up from the darkness of the sty. The smell was strong but Eileen, like Mary, was born on a farm with the smell of animals in her nostrils. The Boss opened the sty door. 'C'mon,' he urged. Eileen tiptoed around the piles of dark excrement. 'Now,' the Boss said softly, 'get down on yer haunches. That way yeh'll see them betther. Aren't they the nicest t'ree pigs yeh've ever seen?' Eileen got down as she was bidden. 'Yes, lovely,' the Boss repeated. His face was close to Eileen's bust. 'Lovely!'

He could smell her perfume over the pigshite. Jasus - inside that flimsy dress there were illicit delights the like of which he hadn't tasted for a very long time. Not since the days of his wavy hair and his accordion. The Boss was hungry for excitement. He had recently been missing sex to avoid babies. Before he knew it his hands were between Eileen's legs.

With a scream and a curse, she kicked out and sent him sprawling on his back in the shit, looking up at her like an injured beetle. 'Don't yeh ever try that oul' trick on me again,' Eileen hissed, her lip curled, her wall-eye wild and aflame.

The Boss regained his feet and like an embarrassed boxer, claimed, 'Jasus,'that oul' shite's slippy.'

Eileen hurried from the sty, hobbling on her high heels over the cobbles, back to her friend who sat quietly feeding her son.

'Ah, there yeh are,' Mary said, making room for Eileen to sit down. 'What was that commotion all about?' she asked, shoving away her tit.

'I saw a feckin' big rat in there,' Eileen said, 'frightened the crap out a me. Yeh know how I am with them rats. I'd kill the feckin' lot a them.'

'Didja see the pigs?' Mary asked.

'Let's jus' say I saw more than I bargained fer,' Eileen said ambiguously. 'I'll tell yeh another time.'

'Wait,' Mary said. 'What did happen in there? Yeh kem out lookin' flustered an' yer man looks sheepish. I know that look.'

'Nuttin', nuttin' at all,' Eileen said. 'He fell over that's all. I have ta go now.' She kissed Mary and with a wall-eyed wink she was gone.

'Yer woman left in a bit of a hurry,' the Boss said.

'Yeah,' Mary said. 'She seemed a bit disturbed.'

'Disturbed, me ring. Yeh know I never liked that culchie hoor,' the Boss said. 'Babs!' he roared, 'will yeh get these oul' cups and wash them up - then we'll go out on th'ol' bikes.'

The Boss's bike was propped against the white railing round the Holy Well. Father and daughter knelt in front of the caged Christ. Babs, in her pink coat and maroon beret, the Boss's trilby on the ground, the chevrons on the soles of his old wellingtons all but erased. Black fist clenched, he beat his craw, his lips quivering in prayer, while Babs - slyly observing - copied him. It was unlikely he was begging forgiveness for attempting to molest Eileen - culchie women were fair game for dashing Dubs. They were all gagging for it - from anything breathing.

After a few moments of meditation, the Boss suddenly stood up, crossed himself violently a number of times and donned his hat, first sweeping the cold sweat from the brim with his palm. His breath warm on her ear, he told Babs how badly life treated him. 'A fella hasta work hard enough just ta stay alive,' he said.

Babs, her head full of her own happy thoughts, sang to herself.

21

FOR A WHILE Mary worked happily in her new house. There was room to wash clothes, somewhere to hang them when it rained. One morning while on his rounds, the Boss rescued a three-piece suite destined for the dustman. It was balding in places, probably had the mange too. The Boss brought it home - shoved, pulled and cursed until it was ensconced in the kitchen. That evening under ferocious interrogation, the suite yielded two pencils, a bob in copper and fifteen hairclips. When it was washed down with soap and water, disinfected with Jeyes Fluid, it fitted in nicely beside the handmade form and the pine table with the wood-wormed legs. The children loved the suite and piled on top of it pretending to be on a ship wobbling on choppy water. Their laughter blessed the new house, making Mary smile and feel glad for them. The Boss's brow wrinkled once or twice but he did not object to the outbreak of gaiety.

Mary reread a pile of old *Ireland's Own* magazines. The new house was bright and spacious. It seemed there would be peace at last. After a long day grubbing for pennies, the Boss needed comforting and his feet shifted and stamped until it was time for bed. The lights went out quickly, doors were hurriedly bolted; Mary and her husband were alone in their bedroom. Soon the thin bar of light under their door was extinguished and the Boss wrestled Mary by the light of the roadside lamp. There was another infant in the making.

Babs had prepared Jack for his newly-painted cot in the corner. The children lay quietly. They would soon be asleep - their little hearts beating as they lay with their faces to the bolster, enjoying the smell of fresh paint. The water rushing under the bridge and crashing over the weir by Perkins's shack, muffled any sounds from their parent's room. When at last satiated and content, Mary rolled over like a big filled-up bear and snored. The Boss lay awake, the roadlight casting a yellow glow over the bungalow, making the luminous hands on the green alarm clock dance.

'Feckit, it's on'y ten,' he muttered. Why couldn't he sleep? He got stealthily out of bed, dressed, armed himself with the handle of a pick and walked out on to the road. Maybe he could catch some gurrier from the Corporation houses breaking in. On tiptoes he walked by the houses and peered in at lighted windows. All was quiet, but the bastards were probably planning an attack.

In the morning, bronzed by the sun, the Rhode Island cock stretched his long neck, arched his back and let rip from his perch on top of the manure heap. It triggered crowing from backyard henhouses all over Rathfarnham. The Boss was quickly up and dressed, his shadow pulling on drawers and thick socks. He wanted to be out in the yard before the sun burnt off the mist. He opened the window a notch, to allow any overnight body gasses to escape. Unlike Mary, who, when she could, preferred the sedentary life, the blood was always pumping in the Boss's veins. He had to get out in the open. He swallowed a good mouthful of fresh air and glimpsed a sliver of water flow under the bridge.

Buckling his belt, he went out to the yard. Kitty's big head stuck out from her stall. She greeted her master with a soft whinny. 'Y'ol' hoor,' the Boss said and affectionately stroked her long nose. He checked the sties, and let out the hens who fluttered their wings and headed for the corn that glinted like grains of gold in the dawning sun. He harnessed Kitty, and placed a basin of food under her nose, then left her waiting in her blinkers while he breakfasted on a slice of Mary's home-baked bread and a new-laid egg. He sat alone and ate in silence. He was happiest in his own company.

With the sun still thinking about breaking through, he set off with two big wooden tubs side by side in the cart. When he undid the big lock and drew the heavy chain through the wrought iron bars, Kitty charged, wheeling left for Rathfarnham, with her master madly trying to climb on board. The air was a little raw so the Boss drew a sack across his knees. His estate flew by as he opened a packet of Ritchies mints and dropped one on his tongue like communion.

Nelly Crimmins's shop was shuttered, the big plate-glass window opaque with condensation. 'Ol' maid from the counthry, got the first penny she ever earned,' the Boss muttered as the cart flew past.

The black gate to the Mill House next door was locked. A row of low-sized cottages welded together ran along the right hand side, their symmetry broken only by Rice's sweet shop with its larger window in the middle. Here, children gathered to salivate and gaze on aniseed balls, liquorice pipes, fizzbags and Crunchies. Babs was too young to go there but she thought about Rice's a lot. Whenever she passed the little palace of exquisite sweetmeats, she looked longingly at the knot of lucky kids who jangled their pocket money while noisily planning their purchases. Babs' prayer was that one day her father would prove his love for her by letting her go in there and come out with a cone of pink ice-cream or a bag of sweets from any of the glass jars sitting so mouth-wateringly in the window.

As the Boss's trilby slowly slid by the houses, a few people lay in their beds and knew it was him. No one else in the whole of Rathfarnham was ever on the road as early. The Boss swung past Cullen's, Kitty's ears twitching as she trotted. Cullen's pub was quiet, just the odd carrot-garnished pool of vomit on the pavement outside. Two empty Smithwick's bottles stood forlornly by the wall, piles of squashed cigarette butts lay where the barman had emptied the ashtrays. The drinkers were all in bed. Working men still had a few minutes beneath the sheets before their wives elbowed them out, leaving the retired and unemployed to snore on in their dirty shirts. They could get up whenever they wanted. The Boss didn't envy the lazy sods.

Pony and cart sped past the Bloomfield Laundry and a few hundred yards later, the Rathfarnham Boys National School. The Church of the Annunciation was next. The Boss blessed himself, 'In case there's sumpt'in' innit afther all.' Past The Yellow House, Kitty girding herself for the incline. Shops, their fascias garish in the morning light, were stone dead. Litter gathered in the gutters. Outside the newsagents papers lay in bundles. The Boss stopped, slit a bundle with his penknife and helped himself to an *Irish Press*.

Her blood now warmed, Kitty tore along at about twelve miles an hour. The Boss would call on every household who had agreed to keep their kitchen waste for the friendly man who always had a smile for the ladies. Sleepily, they opened their windows for him, showing their unharnessed bosoms as they leaned out the windows to wish him a good morning. 'An good mornin' t'yeh Missus, isn't it a gran' day!' The Boss looked up and smiled like a boy hoping a ripe apple might fall from the tree.

First stop, Crannagh Road where almost every house had a full bin outside. The Boss leapt from the cart and poured potato skins, stale bread, fish heads and eggshells into the big tubs. It was not yet eight o'clock but the sun was up. It was tiring work and the Boss was wondering if Mary was being faithful to him.

Back at the bungalow Mary was out of bed. She woke the children with kisses and went to the kitchen to fry them bread and to crack dirt-streaked eggs. The children ravenously tucked into yellow yolk and frilly white, juicy fried bread and mugs of strong tea. Babs dressed for school. She had just started at the Loretto Convent, half a mile or so away. With her black hair tied with a bow, she was nervous but ready for the challenge. She had made her bed and the other children's as well and swept the room. The postman called - a rare treat. He was carrying a letter. Mary could hardly wait to open it. No one in Ireland wrote to her. But it was from Damian, her wayward brother. He was calling in to see her.

'Jesus,' Mary whispered, how could she break it to the Boss?

Feeling insecure and tense, Mary washed the breakfast things, swept the kitchen and took the shaped plywood case off her ancient Singer sewing machine. She stitched and sewed, a measuring tape around her neck, her brass thimble flashing. Then she waited like a child with her neatly folded creations, to show the Boss on his return. Mary sang softly as she worked. A favourite tune was Stephen Foster's Jeannie with the Light Brown Hair. Through the open window her pure voice poured into the small garden, as with intense concentration she sewed on buttons, lowered hems or fitted zips.

With both barrels full to overflowing with decomposing kitchen scraps, the Boss was on his way back, whipping Kitty, the two of them tearing down the hill to Rathfarnham.

When Mary heard Kitty's hooves on the bridge, she hurried to put the kettle on and placed two cups and saucers and a fancy plate piled with Marrietta biscuits on the table. As the Boss worked for a while in the yard, the tension rose within Mary.

In the sties, the Boss argued with himself. What was he going to do now that the house was built? Maybe he should leave her, disappear off somewhere to begin a new life? With the experience he had, he could make a better job of it. But he knew if he left Mary, he would go insane with jealousy. He could never leave his Galway virgin. What would happen to her without him? The thought of her with another man would drive him to commit murder.

Mary heard his boots on the concrete as they approached the kitchen door. She licked her lips like a terrified cat. 'I gotta letther this mornin',' she blurted before he'd kicked off his wellingtons. The Boss stopped as if she had said, 'I've had a lover this morning'.

'Who from?' he demanded.

'Em . . . em . . . Damian. He wan'sta come an' see us, em . . . maybe stay the night.'

The Boss's eyes almost closed. 'Feckit in the fire!' he said, 'that dirthy bowsie's not comin here!'

'But he's on'y droppin' in for a . . .'

'I wouldn't let that blaggard sleep wit' the sows!' the Boss shouted. 'I'm not havin' the melt under me roof. And that's final.'

Mary returned to her sewing with tears in her eyes.

22

THE CHILDREN LEAPT from their perches like chimps gesticulating, laughing and pointing. 'What is it?' Mary asked as she lifted a curtain. 'Mother a God!'

A smart Wolsey was revving its engine as it edged forward, its sleek coachwork reflecting tired geraniums in a flowerbed the cats used as a lavatory. The driver got out and lit a cigarette. It was Damian. He was a culchie Scott Fitzgerald in a smart jacket, cravat, slacks and piebald shoes. His companion was a cuddly blonde. Mary opened the door six inches as if the pair were Jehovah Witnesses.

'Damian!' Mary said. 'How are yeh now?'

Damian hugged his fat sister to his thin, smoker's body. Removing the cigarette from his mouth he kissed her, his pencil-thin moustache tickling her nose. 'Melody,' he gestured towards the blonde. The woman smiled broadly as if she were about to sell something. 'We wor jus' passin' an' I said ta Melody I t'ink 'tis time I saw me poor old sister Mary an' sort a caught up.'

Mary charged round like a stunned hog in a slaughterhouse. She didn't know whether to make tea, beds or confess that it was a lousy time for them to come and that the Boss would extract enormous pleasure from killing the lot of them when he returned. She got out the lace doilies she was given as a wedding present by the old lady in Rathmines. 'I'll get a room ready fer yez.'

'Oh, Jasus no,' Damian said. 'I heard all about yer man an' him a right bloody tyrant. I don' wan'ta make it bad fer yeh, Mary.'

'Yeh must stay,' Mary pleaded. 'I want yehz to. I wan'ta know all about Gownagh and me mother and father an' all at the farm. Look, I'll jus' put out some towels and do a bit a sweepin'. It won't take a minnit, honest ta God. Babs won't mind a bit if I move her.'

'No, no, no, Mary that won't be necessary,' Damian said. 'We'll be out a here before yer man comes back, no problem.' But Mary was already stuffing Bab's clothes into drawers, sniffing the chamber pot and Ewebanking the strip of threadbare carpet. She returned to open all the windows. 'Johnny hates smokin',' she said.

'He hates everyt'in' from what I understand,' Damian said lighting another cigarette. 'An' yeh'd bether move that car, udderwise when he comes back he'll put a big dent in it. It'd be a shame because it's a grand motor. Yeh're doin' well Damian. How d'yeh manage it at all?'

'Yeh can't bate buyin' property,' Damian said. 'I gor'in at the right time. Yer man coulda done, but he t'inks small, that's his problem.'

The sound of the steel cart wheels grinding over the bridge caused Mary to panic. 'Here he comes,' she said.

Seeing the Wolsey, the Boss left Kitty harnessed to the cart and ran into the house. He stopped when the cool figure in the neat sports clothes approached, cigarette in hand. 'Johnny, how are yeh?' Damian's smile was viperish. Like a heavy roller in a Vegas casino tipping a lackey, he fondled a roll of notes into his brother-in-law's pocket. The Boss wanted to spit in his eye and ram the money down his fecking culchie throat, but he took the money and shook Damian's hand.

'Melody, my current girlfriend,' Damian said.

Resisting the urge to count the money, the Boss looked at her. She looked what she was, a tart with no brains and no morals. All her bits were on show like a display in butcher's windows. The Boss instantly felt like giving her a good fuckin'. It was clearly what she wanted. 'Will yez be stayin' a night or two?' the Boss enquired, his eyes flitting from tit, to arse, to leg and back again.

Mary was smiling too, she could hardly credit what she was hearing.

'That's very kind,' Damian said. 'What d'yeh t'ink Melody?' Unaccustomed to making decisions that excluded taking off her clothes, Melody shrugged her shoulders. 'We'll stay a night,' Damian decided. 'We have a long oul' thrip tamorra. But don't worry about food Mary, there's a new Indian in Rat'mines. We'll thry that.' Seeing the Boss in his trilby was mystified, he added. 'We're partial ta'da oriental cuisine, yeh know.'

'Jasus, yehz wouldn' wan'ta be puttin' that shite in yer guts,' the Boss said. 'The story has it them fellas do be atin' dog's giblets an' every bloody t'ing.' He laughed. He was such a comedian when the girls were around.

That night, the Boss watched the luminous hands on the green clock move slowly. The front door was unlatched, a terrible thing with the whole world outside just waiting to walk in and help themselves. When would those culchie mocks be back so that he could rush out and bolt that feckin' door. Then, the walls of the room were lit up by the Wolsey's powerful twelve-volt headlights. The Boss feigned sleep and waited for the push on the door. He heard the pair stumble laughing to their room. He heard them undress as he lay under the blankets.

After a painful wait for something to happen the Boss fell asleep. He was awoken almost immediately by the twanging of elastic, the rustle of petticoats and the sound of lips glued in frenzied passion. The Boss shifted up on to his elbow. The rotten bastards were up to it in his child's room. Please God, Babs was asleep. The Boss slipped out of bed, threw on his trousers and a jumper and crept into the yard.

Next morning the deadpan face of Damian was playing footsie under the table with his pungently scented companion while Mary was frying the bacon and eggs they'd brought. Mary drank tea and chin-wagged.

Eventually, Damian rose, saying, 'I t'ink we'll have a bit of a drive round. It's a while since I seen Rathfarnham. See yeh lather sis.'

As the Wolsey drove away the Boss came galloping up the hill. Damian tooted the horn and waved.

'Fancy invitin' that rotten cunt to stay under my roof an' me with a houseful of young girls,' the Boss hissed.

Mary stoically hung the hand-washed sheets in front of the fire, trying her best to make light of a potentially dangerous situation.

'Arrah, isn't he a young man with no roots or ties,' she said. 'He jus' hasn't found the right girl yet.'

'Well, the fecker's tried enough a them,' the Boss snarled.

Young willing flesh. Oh! how the Boss had enjoyed it when he was the melodian player with the tong-curled head of hair, the sky-blue eyes and the spotted dicky bow. And how sweet were the honeyed words that flowed out of his mouth to seduce those little girls. In those far off, careless days, the Boss was as lustful as the next man. Behind the ricks after the dance he did his share of fishy pawing, heard the giggles as the little blondes and the redheads let his thick fingers probe, and felt his tongue like cold liver on their necks. 'I'll give yeh ten minutes ta take yer hand away Johnny.' What fun it was then. Now, all he had was poor old, careworn Mary, his only source of fleshly pleasure.

The Boss went back to work, cursing Damian's looks, youth, and his hair. His country boy's attraction to pliant women with milky breasts and raspberry red nipples. Women like Melody with a hairy arse that wiggled and wobbled when she groped for a light as she staggered naked to the cold toilet to wash Damian's Galway juice off her matted loins. Did she know a pale blue eye was watching from outside in the yard?

'That rotten fecker will leave this house or I'll split him in half with th'axe,' the Boss raged.

Mary, in defending her wayward brother, assumed guilt for which she would later pay. She would always have to pay while in cowshed and barn, toilet and garden, what had occurred in the night would be enjoyably raked over and amplified in the Boss's head.

The visitors returned from their expedition laden with parcels. Melody looked cool and fresh in a flowery frock, her breasts heaving impressively. The Boss nosed near, and like a boy faced with a bowl of sweets, he couldn't resist putting a paw on her well-upholstered backside. Melody smacked the Boss's hand away as if it had leprosy. The Boss was stunned. He was so convinced any woman who lay all night waiting to be taken by a low-down Galway cur, must be easy meat. Damian saw the incident and his hackles rose but he remained charming. Murder, he heard, wasn't beyond the baldy Jackeen.

The Boss ate without pleasure, his small eyes zipping around the table like black bees. He had been put down by a hoor, he wanted revenge. In silence, Damian nibbled; he wanted to be away from this awful place as soon as possible. He wouldn't have bothered except it would have been a pity to drive all the way back to Galway without seeing his poor sister. Stupid, gullible, soft-centred woman that she was.

Damian could think what he liked. The Boss didn't care. The sooner they left the better. Galwegians were an ignorant and primitive tribe. They left half their fields unploughed for fear of fairies for Christ's sake. How could anyone benefit from knowing such scum? Except, and the Boss tapped his pocket. Ten lovely notes. The culchie bastard.

Damian flushed the toilet and pulled his natty waistcoat around his slim body. He walked stiffly past the Boss's chair like a conquering, but wary, tomcat. Mary trailed after them to the door, a worried smile etched into her blue cheeks. The children lined up like Royal servants in the hallway to see Uncle Damian off. He kissed each virtuous cheek and tousled Jack's hair. He counted five new notes from his wallet and left them on the table in the hall. 'For the kids,' he said.

The Boss stood on the doorstep, his head tilted, as Melody swung her legs into the car. Damian reversed the Wolseley out over the bridge. 'Bye now and t'anks,' he said and drove away.

Mary watched until the car was out of sight, then with a sigh she returned to the kitchen.

As if electro-charged the Boss leapt from his seat, showering her with filth from his bottomless septic tank of a mind. Upset at her brother's departure, Mary looked into her husband's insane, hate-filled face. Her lips moved but she said nothing. She stood, her feet over-flowing in the glossy shoes she had slipped on over her ugly corns and bunions. Her clean apron hung limply and her shiny eyes behind her glasses gave her the glazed look of a corpse.

'Answer me!' the Boss screamed and, grabbing his wife's shoulders, he shook her. His eyes were cold and pitiless. In his mind's eye he saw Babs backing against the bedstead, Damian cutting off her retreat. He saw him rip off her clothes as she pathetically tried to defend her virginity. He saw Mary, corrupted and beyond salvation, smile and encourage him. 'Jasus,' the Boss's roar was that of a wounded animal. 'I'll fuckin' kill yeh!' Seizing Mary by the throat he pressed on her windpipe with both thumbs. One by one the children appeared and watched in horror. They saw their mother, so pure in thought and deed, with her legs apart , struggling to get a grip on her assailant.

Jack's screaming set off the others. Babs tried weakly to separate them. 'Mammy! Daddy! Stop!' she cried. The architects of their own visionless and wretched existence were killing each other. Mary fighting for her life picked the knife up off the table and rammed it towards her husband. The Boss caught the blade on his arm. As he watched his blood spurt from a deep wound he let out a banshee howl and retreated backwards out of the door.

Babs picked her steps over the dung to him. 'Are yeh all right, Dad?' she cried. The Boss was trying to bandage his arm with a piece of his shirt. 'The hoor, what did she wan'ta go an' do a t'ing like that fer?' he said, grimacing as if his entrails were falling out. Babs helped him tie the knot. He stayed there for an hour, sitting glumly, the blood seeping through the bandage. Babs sat by him chattering away. Pam arrived to announce tea was ready.

The Boss walked to the house trying to look like a wounded soldier. Mary's dress hung from her in shreds, showing her big, fat, blue-veined thighs. The Boss had a knife hole in his jacket. Both appeared relaxed and almost happy. Some sort of pressure valve had been opened by Mary's use of the knife. The children watched in awed silence, waiting for more explosions, but there were none. The drama was concluded, the actors were washing off the greasepaint and changing into their workaday clothes.

23

JACK STOOD OBEDIENTLY behind the Boss as his father tugged at the mouldy door bell. 'Now, yeh listen t'me,' the Boss whispered urgently. 'When this fine lady speaks ta yeh, for Jasus's sake speak up. D'yeh hear me now.'

Jack nodded. His father exhaled a white vapour as he whistled nonchalantly, his eyes slyly raking the dirt- and rain-streaked windows of the old house for a sign of life.

'What d'yehz want comin' here?'

Startled, the Boss whipped round and saw Geraghty, a crooked old retainer, hobbling out of a rustic shed which a thick-stemmed wisteria was attempting to wrestle to the ground.

'Good-day ta yeh,' the Boss said smartly. 'I have an appointment wit' her Ladyship fer t'ree a clock.'

Geraghty looked suspicious. He was troubled by the appearance of these two strangers standing on the doorstep he would wash with his tongue if ordered to. His eyes peered out of red sockets, and each one had a substantial bag under it.

Geraghty stared as if deciding what to do. The Boss made up his mind for him by seizing one of his withered arms. 'Now listen, me oul' son,' the Boss said. 'I don't know who yeh're, an' I don't care, but I have an official appointment with the lady of the house. Now, be a good man an' go an' tell her.'

'Come on then,' Geraghty said as he shrugged himself free and testily stumbled round a laurel hedge to the side entrance of the massive grey-stone house.

The Boss made rude gestures behind the retainer's back as he disappeared through the door. 'Bloody oul' fool,' he said. 'Collectin' good wages fer doin' shag all. Will yeh look a' the cut'v'im: like sometin' out'a bloody Frankenstein.' The Boss laughed quietly.

Father and son waited. Eventually, there was movement within as

Geraghty struggled to open the heavy door. Lady Moore stood, her grey hair neat, her face stern.

'God save yeh, Ma'am,' the Boss said, rushing to take her hand. 'It's very nice of yeh ta agree to see me.'

As frail as old lace she stepped forward and took the Boss's hand. Looking very superior at Jack, she told him, 'Your father is a fine hard-working man, always remember that.' Then she instructed the retainer to, 'Show this gentleman to the library please, Geraghty.'

The servant stalked forward, down a musty corridor to a splendid drawing room. 'Sit here,' he said.

'Be dad, we will,' the Boss said. He had taken an icy dislike to the old fellow who stared dumbly at the visitors, his lower lip hanging.

The Boss looked round the room, taking in the giant marble fireplace, the Grinling Gibbons carvings, the huge portraits of gentlemen in tricorn hats on terrified horses, trampling on guns, dogs, rods, dead pheasants and antlered deer. Under small glass domes dead songbirds stood on twigs and moss. By the door a sawn-off elephant's foot acted as a receptacle for shooting sticks. How the Boss wished he worked for a fine woman like Lady Moore. He might have married her daughter. Jasus, wouldn't that have put him on the pig's back.

Lady Moore sat in an ornate chair. 'Well,' she said. 'And what can I do for you this time?' The Boss started into his rigmarole, his history, his dedication to his family, his attempts to keep them fed and clothed in spite of everything. The old lady nodded and smiled as the words cascaded over her. Then she tilted her fine head. 'Please tell me what can I do to help,' she said.

'Oh right, yes, well yeh've always been a great friend.' The Boss glanced at Geraghty who stood quietly, hardly distinguishable from the stuffed bear in one corner of the room. 'It's a sensitive matther I'm goin' ta bring up.'

'Just a moment, Mister Dunne. Excuse me, Geraghty. Would you mind leaving us for a moment?'

The old man shuffled off, and the Boss smiled with satisfaction.

'Carry on please, Mr Dunne. Sorry to interrupt you.'

'Ah sure that's all right, yer Ladyship. Anyway, it's me teet'. Actually, it's me an' me wife's teet'. I'm afraid we never had the benefit of the

Colgates an' our poor oul' teet've rotted in our heads causin' us bot' pain and distress.'

'Yes, poor things, they must do.'

'Well, as I was sayin' yer Ladyship, yeh can get false teet', yeh know, but they cost an arm an' a leg.'

'Yes, I do understand these false teeth are very expensive. But at the same time they are quite effective if properly fitted. So you were, erm, wanting some financial assistance to enable you to buy two sets of false teeth? Am I assuming correctly that is the purpose of your visit this afternoon?'

'No, no, no,' the Boss said. 'I was jus' t'inking maybe a little letther from a lovely Lady like yerself ta the Healt' Department might open a door or two fer us. It worked wit' the glasses. Money is short.'

'Of course I will. If you can give me a few days I can compose something and send it to you.'

'Ah, that's grand,' the Boss said. 'Well, many t'anks again,' the Boss said. 'An' may the Little Flower and all her angels look down on yeh wit' all her favours.'

'Thank you,' Lady Moore said. She smiled and got to her feet, signalling the end of the interview. Finally, she asked about Mary.

'Ah sure, isn't she in the pink a condition, atin' up everyt'in' put in front a her,' the Boss said.

'I am glad to hear that. She is a wonderful wife and companion for you.'

The Boss's smile said, 'Yeh don't know the half of it.'

Lady Moore pulled on the bell. Geraghty instantly materialised, eager to show the Boss the door.

Waiting until they had left the drive the Boss turned to his son. 'Them's the hoors wit' the clout in this godforsaken countrhy. Yeh have ta bow and scrape ta'da likes a that oul' dame to get an'tin' from this rotten government.' He rubbed his gloved hands together. 'Me an' yer woman'll be laughin' when we get th'ol' one's letther,' he said.

As they trudged along the twisting, Whitechurch Road the Boss opened a new packet of Ritchies mints.

24

THE BOSS SAT in Cullen's like a man waiting for the lever on the electric chair to be pulled. Like a bloody fool he had been bamboozled by that old cannat the Dowager to come to the pub for just one drink. The Dowager had elected himself peacemaker. He was determined to integrate the Boss into his warm pub family.

The Boss was intrigued. It was against his nature to do anything unpredictable. He hated and despised these men. His instinct told him it was a mistake. Then why did he allow the weak-minded Dowager to lead him by he nose? The fact that the Dowager was essentially a good man who saw only good in others did not come into the equation. Good meant weak and vacillating in the Boss's kiltered world.

'Jasus, Mary,' the Boss murmured as the smell of men, piss and vinegar invaded his nostrils. The pub atmosphere was unfamiliar and alien. It was Hades, he thought, where all the lost and useless men went, men who had no control over their own destinies. He wriggled as if in bondage. What a bloody shitehawk I am. That bloody woman always encouragin' me ta 'Go an' have a dhrink wit' the men. It'll do yeh good.' Worra gobshite I am ta listen ta that stupit bloody pile. Did she have another reason?

The men crowded round the Boss like they were anthropologists examining the Wild Man from Borneo. Pints were ordered and lined up. Full packets of Craven A were pushed in his face. The Dowager took charge and sat beside the Boss, the savant eager to touch the magician's wand. The Boss saw his own hand reach out and take the slippery pint glass. He saw it raise itself to his lips, and he felt his throat convulse as the bitter liquid went down and into his stomach. The men talked and gestured. For a man famous for his lyricism when in the presence of young women, the Boss was oddly silent. There was nothing he wanted to say to these men who so shamelessly prostrated themselves in front of him. Even in drink they were tactful enough not to mention Mary. That would require a level of stupidity even beyond the men who frequented Cullen's pub.

The Boss was pumped about his background, but the interrogators were naive and drew little of substance from a man as wary and as potentially vulnerable as the Boss. Like a nuclear spy under KGB arclights, and the threat of nailpullers, the Boss resisted all blandishments to talk. His past was none of their business. Why should he share his secrets with such men? It would be very foolish to arm the enemy and he had no intention of doing so. To reveal anything would be a sign of weakness. The whole truth about the Boss's past had never, and would never, be addressed. Not even to Mary. The Boss gingerly took the second pint and, like a spotty schoolboy with a pint of scrumpy in a bus shelter, he messily gulped it down. The taste was still bloody awful. The drink was sour and cold. How did anyone like it? The Boss belched. Another pint stood blackly on the wet counter, then another.

When his bungalow was hailed as 'nuttin' short of a miracle consitherin' the shite that was there', the Boss smiled with the superior air of a brigadier praised by his men. Smoke coiled from pipe, cigarette butt and cheroot, gathering like soiled cotton wool under the pub's amber ceiling. Pints slopped, slipped and skidded along the bar. The noise grew to a banshee's bellow. The Boss, his face glistening with sweat, sat in the same spot, his expression stern and lifeless, his bladder filling, his stomach distending. Jasus, this was some kind of torture. He felt hemmed in, the way he felt when the old priest in Orlagh locked the big wooden gates and he was trapped behind the high walls with no chance of making a run for it. He was up to his neck in holy shite. The Boss remembered every line and vein in the face of the twisted old perve who hit him.

The Boss was dying for a gulp of fresh air. The bastards had him where they wanted him, paralysed and helpless. Why couldn't that feckin' priest let him escape, his tattered shirt blowing as he flew like a madman down the mountainside, the priests after him like black crows.

The men in Cullen's leaned closer, their eyes smiling. The Boss saw their rotten teeth and he knew they were making fun of him. The truth was out. He couldn't hold his drink and they knew it. At the dances he'd always drunk lemonade. He hated the stench of beer. He had to be focused to play his instrument. And a clear head always got the best of the girls. The Boss took another pint and drank it. That would show the hoors. They handed him another. At least he wasn't paying. He must have another for the sake of revenge, and another.

Drink was a fool's game. Drunken men were incapable. They vomited, swore, pissed themselves and fought. What bloody fools. Sober men ran the world. What drove men to drink? Weakness. Most men felt uncomfortable in the presence of teetotallers. Non-drinkers were pariahs. The Boss guzzled another. His bladder felt like a Morris man's balloon. He couldn't tell where the lavatory was. It was outside somewhere. From on top of the cart he could see the shit drying on the riverbank, the torn, shit-streaked newspapers. It slithered into the brook like chocolate and floated and bobbed all the way to the Jesuits at the Castle. Nice present for the gay bachelors. The thought pleased him. But he must get out of here. He was bursting.

Staggering through the mob of jawing men the Boss pissed against a car outside. His head resting on a hot roof. He looked down at his penis, and the yellow water spouting from it and he felt ashamed. What was he doing? These men were not his kind. They were low types, bent on dragging him down to their abysmal level. They were barking like dogs now, he heard it coming out of the windows. He could not go back in there. The drink had not just taken away his brain, but his pride and his strength.

He must escape. The sun shone in the windows of the pub. The Boss's trained ear picked out the sound of wagtails on the rocks in the middle of the stream. He heard a woodpecker hammering on a hollow bough. He heard the muffled lowing of Neary's cows as they plodded home, nose to rump. It was funny how in his blocked way he still heard nature speak to him. He was an animal like them, and like them he liked his freedom.

He staggered on to the road, buttoning his flies. His legs were rubbery and they disobeyed him. A little girl like Babs was watching him. Even she could see a man who had lost his self-respect. The Boss grinned at her and swayed. ''S'all right,' he slurred, 'com'ere.' The little girl ran away. The Boss's shadow staggered alongside him bent and leaning. Holding on to a whitewashed wall he climbed the hill. His breath was coming in sharp lung bursts. His oxters and the crack in his arse were clammy with sweat. He could smell himself and he hated it.

The Boss rested on a round coped wall and looked over the stream, and across the sun-glistened fields to Neary's barn and talked to himself. 'Lovely fields them. What a poor fella coulda done if he on'y had the few bob t'buy a field like that. Yeh would'n see feckers like the Nearys in Cullen's in the middle a'da day. Not them, crafty oul' Prods. They didn't mix with poor ignorant Catholics. The Neary brothers were too feckin' respectable, wit' their fine farm and their fat cows, t'mix with the Pope-lovin' peasantry. Oh yeah, I seen the pair a them drivin' their shiny Humber Hawk to the church at Kilmashogue. Sittin' under the stained-glass windas that commemorated th'English soldiers who'd died fightin' fer the King.'

An old woman on the way to Crimmins's shop walked around the Boss as he railed. 'No, it couldn't be,' she said to herself. Then, looking back, 'Be God, it is. It's yer man Dunne above in the bungalow wit' all them poor kids hidin' behine the trees. The poor man looks distracted. God help him.'

How the Boss wished he had a practical God. Instead, he had one that was out to trap him, to plant his feet in glue, to humiliate him. What sort of God was that? Why couldn't his God bring richness. 'There's not a pauper among th'Raffarm Prot'stants. Them shites is the chosen few. The Rev'ren' Handy, he's a Proddydog, an' him ridin' his oul' pushbike roun' the parish. Smart lookin' fella he was too. A handy job that, jus' countin' money and takin' tea with respectable oul' ones. Will yeh come in, Maurice. Mind th'ol' bulldog there. I'll call Mary, the maid. What wouldja like? I have sev'ral kinds a cake. Mary's not a bad cuke fer a Galway girl.' . . . The Boss felt a tremor in his guts. He opened his throat and watched the beer sail over the wall. He wiped his mouth on his sleeve. The smell was awful. 'Sure, Handy wasn't one a them grazy little boyos from the bogs yeh saw in the chapel. The same kinda rotten hoors that ballyragged and bullied poor Mary inta havin' more childher when one was plenty enough. Yeh'll have a little priest next, they told her. I know their bloody game. Black-coated spies. Soljers a God, me ring. That little Handy is a gentleman.' The Boss's rambling was interrupted by more retching but less came up this time. 'Battherin' poor gobdaws like Mary wit' their bloody missals while they, the connivin' melts, go off ta the Curragh to watch the bloody Derby from the stan', their pockets full a money they stole from the poor.'

'Way, hey! Y'all right Johnny?' The Boss's dribbling, glaring, reverie was curtailed by the arrival of the Dowager who gently took his arm. 'I'm sorry oul' son,' he said, 'I didn't see yeh go. T'oughtcha wor jus' havin' a piss.' The Boss tried to wrestle free but the Dowager held firm and guided the drunken, lurching, dead-weight man up the Whitechurch Road like an embarrassed miscreant. 'It's not sacrilege gettin' fluthered once in a while,' the Dowager said. 'Udderwise God would've disthroyed us all long ago.'

Perkins was waiting at his door with a consumptive sneer. 'So the big fella can't hold his porther,' he said.

'Feckin' Jasus tanight,' the Boss roared and the Dowager held him for all he was worth. 'I'll kill that dir'y oul' git.'

'C'mon then, yeh little scutther,' Perkins said, adopting a ludicrously old-fashioned boxing stance.

'G'wan, lay off or go inside,' the Dowager said, 'this man's in no condition.'

Perkins looked amused as he stood in his porch watching the little maneen brought to heel by drink. Who'd have put money on that? Mary, watching from behind the lace curtains, withdrew as the Dowager arrived with her husband leaning on him and looking as green as a man pulled out after a week or two in the Liffey.

'There yeh're now,' the Dowager said, 'aisy does it.' The Boss turned to walk out again. 'Now, now, Johnny,' the Dowager said, 'Perkins the great white hunter is afther watchin' yeh. He shot a couple a' Tans yeh know, a pair a kids makin' a po'ra tay be the roadside. Yer man kem up on a bike, shot them in the back and rode away. Some feckin' hero. I mane ta say, he's no Audie Murphy is he?'

The Boss frantically pushed the old man away.

'Don't worry, I'm not comin' in,' the Dowager said after the Boss blundered back through the gate and left it swinging open. Like a man drawing together the petticoat of a drunken prostitute to protect her dignity, the Dowager pulled the gate to.

Mary had moved to the kitchen and stood observing them both. She heard the Dowager say, 'Take care now,' and saw him soberly march back across the bridge and return to the pub. In Cullen's the Dowager dodged and fielded questions and comments.'He didn't buy a round,' one man complained.'Here, take it out a this,' the Dowager said throwing a crumpled ten shillings on to the beer-soaked counter. 'Youse fellas,' he admonished and took off his hat and left it on the warm windowsill.

The Boss stood holding on to the chicken wire like a man caught in a hurricane. His jaw was gaping, his throat was dry and his head seemed to have been invaded by bees. He stumbled to the lowest shed and, with the help of a barrel left there, he managed, after a number of collapsed attempts, and a backward roll into a puddle of muddy water, to make it to the top of the shed.There, under the sally-willow boughs that hung, fan-like, over the cool tin roof, the Boss fell asleep.

'I see yeh, Daddy,' Babs said, squinting up at her father. She had returned from school and was sent by Mary to find him.The Boss lay as if dead until Babs climbed up and shook him.

'What the feck–?' He woke up, disorientated, his eyes red-rimmed and blazing.

'It's all right, Daddy, it's on'y me.'

The Boss felt for her and patted her.'I'm sorry, Babs, fer cursin' in front a yeh,' he said.

'Don't worry,' Babs said,'I'm used ta that, c'mon.' She tried to push him upright. 'Hurry up, Mammy's got the tea ready. She made a big cake wit' sultanas an' candy peel.' Babs skipped up the yard towards the bungalow.The Boss staggered after her, pausing to dip his face in the water butt. He entered the kitchen with all the mobility of the Tin Man in *The Wizard of Oz* and sat down heavily. His head was still spinning and felt as if it was cracking open with the agony. In a new apron that bulged over her latest pregnancy, Mary poured tea and offered her husband a slice of fruit cake.

The Boss said nothing but the pain of the experience would stay with him for a very long time. He had dropped his guard and allowed the bowsies to take advantage and have a good laugh at his expense. It was the last time that would happen. He would keep to himself in future as he had always done in the past. It was that fool of a woman who put him up to it: 'Why doncha mix with the men from the village?' All that shite. Men? That lot were mental and physical cripples. What could a fellow learn from the likes of them? Alcohol was a bastard. It was deadly. Those hoors were born to it. He wasn't used to it at all. He couldn't handle its sleep-inducing, mind-removing powers. The Boss had let himself down. He would never forget it. Quietly, he swore it was the last time a pint of Guinness or anything like it would be seen in his fist.

'Lovely cake, Mammy,' Babs said.

'Thanks darlin',' Mary said. 'Glad someone likes it.'

Back in the yard, the Boss went through his routine in slow motion. He cursed himself in the sties. Drink had made a fool of him. It would not happen again. It didn't - he never set foot inside Cullen's again. He would try to erase the experience and the village with it. Behind his stockade he worked repairing and extending the pig sties, buying tools as the money came in and erecting a workshop at the back of the bungalow. Work was good.

Mary meanwhile put Jack on the floor to begin his first wanderings while she waited patiently for her fifth child in as many years. Jack was reluctant to vacate his mother's warm lap. He was a slow child, still messing his pants and not over keen on having his ears washed. Babs took charge and he responded to her soft commands.

The Boss had forgotten his experience, or at least cemented it under some patio in the back of his mind. He had not seen anyone from Cullen's for months. A neutron bomb could have fallen on the pub and liquidised the clientele for all he knew. They would be no loss to society. Such men were easily replaced.

25

THE BOSS LOOKED up. He couldn't believe what he was seeing. 'What d'yeh want? I'm a busy man,' the Boss growled through rusty teeth. He stood impatiently in his wellingtons, his old jacket flapping open, his collarless shirt lending him the appearance of a disturbed and unfrocked priest.

The Dowager, low in stature and self-esteem, was creeping over the bridge, towing a greyhound on a string. The dog was shivering, its eyes fearful, its tail clamped between its legs. 'I was wondrin'–' the Dowager started.

'Get off me land!' the Boss said. 'And don't come here again.'

'But Johnny . . .' The Dowager's courage failed him. The idea might have seemed a good one in Cullen's cosy bar, but it was a different matter, standing face to face with the Boss, especially after what had happened last time

'Wouldja like a dog?' The Dowager blurted and he offered the string to the Boss who refused to take it. Instead, he looked at the creature and then at the Dowager who stood bemused and tiny.

The Boss relented. 'What in the name a God would a hard-workin' poor divil be wantin' wit' a feckin' greyhound? I have plenty t'do here instead a standin' chewin' the fat wit' the likes a yerself. Now, clear off back ta them that sent yeh.'

The Dowager ignored the rebuttal. 'Ta make it up t'yeh the lads t'ought yeh might like the oul' dog. It'd be great company, an' it's a real softy wit' kids. An' if yeh're interested in the racin' side of it–'

'I'm not a bit int'rested in dogs or bloody dog racin'. I've seen enough gobshites ruin themselves on the same racin'.' The Boss was thinking of his father who stood at the track with his nose running and his pockets empty, bemused, drunk, and broke without as much as his fare home.

'I'd be obliged if yeh'd let me ge'ron wit' me work,' the Boss said.

'He's got a pedigree.' The Dowager played his ace. 'If he wins anytin' yeh just pay me half.'

The Boss laughed. 'Look, I don't want a feckin' dog. They're all shite an' barkin'. Now, get of a my property an' tell them foolie ollies I am not goin' ta . . .'

'Daddy!' A small face appeared from behind the bungalow. 'Janey it's a dog!' Babs exclaimed as she ran to her father's side.

With a child's lack of fear she knelt down and put her arms around the greyhound's pointed head. It licked its lips nervously but when Babs began to pat its brindled back it seemed to lose its fear.

'Lookit the back on 'im,' the Dowager said. 'He's a fine animal from a good home.'

'Oh, yeah, an' how did yeh getcher hands on 'im?'

'Ah, that's a long story, but yeh can have 'im fer nuttin'. There yeh go. How's that?'

'Take the cursed t'ing away. D'yeh hear me!' The Boss's voice rose. The Dowager took hold of the string.

'But Daddy I want him,' Babs said. She embraced the dog again and kissed its muzzle.

'Jasus, don't do that,' the Boss said. 'That t'ing's alive wit' maggots and fleas.' Babs threw herself on the dog.

'Ah, please, Daddy, let's keep him. What's his name Mister?'

'I can't remember. Here, hold that,' he said, offering Babs the string. The Dowager rooted for his Rizlas, sprinkled a pinch of tobacco on one, rolled it, and ran a pink curling tongue along the gummed edges of the fag paper to make a thin cigarette. He lit it, drew the delicious smoke into his tattered lungs and exhaled with a gummy smile. He bent low at the waist to get closer to Babs' level. 'Ah there, isn't he a grand fella?'

Babs led the dog towards the bungalow. It bristled and showed its fangs as she walked it past a cage where the Boss had a sickly rooster. The terrified bird croaked and flapped its wings. The greyhound pulled free and tore at the cage. Pam and Bridgid came out of the house to see the Boss clump up in his wellingtons and bury a toe in the dog's ribs. It yelped and cowered. 'C'mon quick,' Babs said and she ran with the dog and her sisters to the kitchen door where it thirstily lapped the cat's milk and ravenously despatched the crusts Mary had left out for the birds.

The Dowager waited.

The Boss' face softened. 'G'wan get goin',' he said. The Dowager smiled, a cagey old man's smile. He took out his tobacco and his fag papers and offered them to the Boss.

'No,' the Boss said. 'Smokers are gobshites.' The Dowager rooted in his pocket again and produced a slip packet containing three Woodbines. 'Maybe yeh'd like the real McCoy,' he said. He shook the packet until the cigarettes were protruding at one end. The Boss shook his head. 'Good luck wit' the dog,' the Dowager said, as the Boss escorted him to the gate as if he were a trespasser.

Spring-heeled, the Dowager walked down the road towards Cullen's. He had crossed the Boss's bridge again, like the first soldier into a conquered country. He proceeded past the Corporation houses and Jack Perkins's shack. Perkins was waiting at the door. As the Dowager approached the old man dredged a gob of green phlegm from his lungs and flung it over the wall.

'How yeh?' the Dowager asked.

'I seen yeh fraternisin' wit' the enemy again,' Perkins growled.

'Ah, I wouldn' say that,' the Dowager said. 'Every man's got sumptin' good inside him.'

'Wit' a few notable exceptions,' Perkins said. 'If yeh seen what that bastard's doin' ta my land. He's pushin' me inta the river. An' have yeh seen the wather? It's full a pig shite. He's dumpin' the shite in the river. Jasus, the smell. It's a killer. I'll have the law on him.'

'Give the man a break,' the Dowager said. 'He's a hard workin' poor hoor, an' he's got a nice little house up there.'

'He robbed most of it,' Perkins said. 'I've heard him stashin' it away in the early hours.' He shuffled back inside his shack, and the Dowager went on to Cullen's.

'So, yeh're still alive then, an' he didn't tell yeh ta stick the greyhound up yer arse?' one drinker asked.

'A pint a the finest there, Curate,' Dowager said. Tranter, the new barman, a country boy with weak eyes, a slow gait and jug-handle ears, carefully pulled the pint. The Dowager took a long gulp before coming up for air. 'I suggested he raced it at Harold's Cross, bur he's not a gamblin' man.'

'Can't handle the dhrink, doesn't smoke or gamble. What else is there?'

'Shaggin', he does a lot a that,' the Dowager said and the men laughed. 'I'm dyin' fer anudder jar,' the Dowager said. 'Jus' talkin' ta yer man makes me t'irsty. Slàinte.' The Dowager came up from his second pint with a café au lait moustache which he flicked away with his thumb and forefinger.

Jack and Bridgid had toddled over, shrieking, to stroke the dog. The animal licked their grubby hands clean. The children's eyes opened wide with tremendous and unusual pleasure. Pam found an old curry comb the Boss used on Kitty and began to groom the dog like a hair-dresser, holding and combing fringes of hair. The dog looked with soulful eyes and flinched every time a clumsy child's hand came down on him. That night before tea, Babs put the dog in a tea-chest in the yard with a small rectangle of netting wire stuck in front of it, and the children all trooped out, laughing, to see it again.

The greyhound wagged its tail, its eyes glowing like cigar butts.

'Keep the hoor outside,' the Boss yelled.

But Babs couldn't stop herself opening the door to the little cage. Scenting warmth and company the dog galloped into the house and raced around the kitchen sniffing at the quickly withdrawn bare feet and food-smeared hands. Grinning in unison the children reached out to touch the rushing pet.

'Ge'rout a dat!' the Boss roared, snapping his paper like pistol shots. The dog scuttled out of the door and sat pining on the mat. Babs took him to his crude kennel and kissed him. When the shaft of light from the kitchen was finally extinguished the dog curled up like a snake and slept.

Next morning, the children queued at the kitchen door, ready to rush into the yard to see how their new pet had survived the night. Babs tied the string to the dog's collar and led him round the garden.

'Look, he's doin' his doody,' Jack said and he sat on his haunches giggling with excitement as the dog wearing a beatific smile dropped three dry turds on the concrete. Babs replaced his water and filled a bowl with what she'd scraped off the plates and saucepans. 'You'll mind him when I'm at school, won'tcha?' she said to Jack.

He clapped his hands and did an ungainly little hop. 'Yes, yes,' he cried, 'please let me. I'll look afther him fer yeh. I will, I will.' He danced around like he had one foot nailed to the ground.

'No, I'll mind him,' Bridgid snarled as she pushed her brother over. Jack wailed and stared at his sister from the ground with tear-filled eyes. 'Jesus, what's that smell?' Bridgid said. 'It's yeh, yeh little fecker,' she said pointing to Jack. 'Yeh've shit yerself haven't yeh? Dirty pig. Can'tcha smell it? Have yeh no nose at all?'

'I have a nose,' said Jack, poking a finger up his nostril.

'Yeh are a dirty little shite,' Bridgid yelled, lengthening her neck to scold like a bad-tempered goose.

'Don't curse him. Please,' Babs said. 'By the way, I'm goin' ta call the new dog Biffo.'

Jack squinted in the sun, mouthing the dog's name. 'Biffo. That's a nice name.'

After school, Babs rushed into the yard, pulled back the wire and took the dog out for a trot. After being cooped up all day in a space half his size, Biffo galloped, sniffed and urinated. Then with his tongue hanging out like red bunting he opened his bowels. Nose to the earth he patrolled the garden perimeters, sniffing at the wire traps the Boss had placed to catch the big water rats which he imagined Perkins was breeding and sending across the river.

The Boss was washing his face in a bowl of hot water. 'I'll do that rotten oul' fecker Perkins one a these days,' he snarled, furiously ducking his red face and blowing bubbles into the water in temper. 'I've every right ta kill them rats any way I like, an' put me wheels in that river if I wan'ta. He doesn't own the river. Jasus, I can't believe yer man's gall. Tryin' t'stop a poor fella earnin' an honest livin'. God blast him an' all that knows him.' He dried his face, his skin twisting like rubber. 'Turn down that bit a gas fer Chris'sake,' he said out of a crooked mouth.

'Mammy, don'tcha t'ink Misther Perkins might shoot Daddy?' Jack asked, his big eyes both worried and questioning.

'No, he won't, worse luck,' Mary said, only half in earnest.

The greyhound scratched at the holes the rats had made and let out delighted little barks which eventually drew the Boss out from the kitchen.

'Keep an eye on that feckin' hound!' he thundered from the chair he sat on to pull on his wellingtons. 'We might try a race or two at

Harold's Cross. How wouldja like that?'

'That'd be grand,' Babs said. 'When he wins we'll buy a big roasted chicken fer all of us to share. Mammy won't have ta do any cukin' so we can all sit down an' enjoy ourselves.'

The Boss was almost whisked off on his daughter's magic carpet. 'This fella'll have to have a bit a runnin' in the field t'see if he's any good first. It's no use spendin' our hard-earned few bob on enthrance fees an' all if the dog's useless.'

Babs looked disappointed. 'I'll give him some more food,' she said, 'there's lots a bones in O'Rourke's shop. I'll ask Mickey ta keep them fer us.'

'An' the lovely marra that's in them 'll be good fer him,' the Boss said.

'If Biffo's goin' ta race, Daddy, we'll have ta feed him up.' Babs said, throwing her arms around the dog's neck. 'Havin' ta race on an empty stummick would be awful. Wouldn't it Biffo?'

Later that evening the Boss came into the kitchen holding something behind his back. 'Yeh wan'ta get yer man fit for the races,' he said, 'well, thry this.' He flourished a cage trap. In it, a big black water rat crouched, its tiny black eyes shining. 'This lad's yer sweet dish.'

'Jesus!' Mary cried. 'Get it out a the house. It's bad luck.'

The Boss looked at his firstborn, who was brushing her hair into twangy wavelets. 'What d'yeh t'ink, Babs?'

'Le'rim out, Daddy. Please,' Babs said.

'Yeh can't l'ave the poor rat in that awful cage. He's frightened. G'wan, Le'rim out, Daddy.'

'No I won't,' the Boss said. 'I've gor enough of them hoors riddlin' the banks wit' holes. I'm takin' him ta the Pit. We'll le'rim out there. See if that hound can ketch'im.'

'But that's cruel,' Babs said.

Pam looked into the trap with her big eyes, her face smeared with jam and dirt. Jack crabbed over to see what was going on and stuck his finger into the cage . 'No!' Babs snatched his finger away, and Jack's lip curled. But he didn't cry, he just gazed at the rat, his full nappy sagging. Mary picked her son up and rubbed him with her lips. 'Don't let him touch that filt'y animal,' she said.

'He wouldn't do it twice if that oul' rat took a bite out a him,' the

Boss said, laughing. The rat's brown incisors began to investigate the Boss's fingers as he carried the trap to the dog's cage.

'Come on darlin',' Babs said, looping the string over the dog's head and yanking it tight. 'We're goin' ta catch a nice big fat rat fer dinner.' And father and daughter walked out to the Pit in the direction of an old cement cowshed.

'Mornin' gentlemen,' said the Boss to two businessmen from the new houses who were walking to the bus stop, but his smile was false. 'In their Sunda' suits,' he sneered under his breath to Babs.

He stopped in the middle of the field. 'When I release the rat, coun'ta ten before lettin' the dog go,' he said.

'But what happens to the poor rat when he catches it?' Babs asked.

'He bloody well ates it a course,' the Boss said.

'Poor rat,' Babs repeated.

'Never mind the poor rat,' the Boss said impatiently, 'there's millions more where this one kem from.'

The Boss undid the catch. The rat sniffed the air before dropping awkwardly on to the grass. Barely visible above the green blades it ran, the grass bending before it like a small green tide. The dog plunged after it, dragging the string behind him. With a growl he plunged through the air. It took only a few seconds.

'Good man!' the Boss cried. Babs watched the dog sit on his tail with the rat in his mouth as though he was wearing a distinguished moustache. The rat wriggled and curled in silent agony. 'He's bloody quick all right,' the Boss said.

'But, Daddy!' Babs cried as she watched the rodent spinning in agony, its fur damp with blood.

'Drop it!' the Boss commanded. When the dog opened his mouth the rat was impaled on his canines. He pawed it off and it lay dead in the grass. The Boss put an arm around his daughter. 'Yeh know I t'ink this fella'll surprise a few people when he runs at Harold's Cross.' The Boss smelt money, and it smelt good.

26

NEXT MORNING, BABS left Biffo in his cage and was in her class at the Loretto Convent before the men from Cullen's were groping blearily for their tainted drawers. The Boss came into the house for breakfast. It was a meal he usually took in silence as there was nothing of interest he wished to discuss with his wife. This morning was different.

'Y'know sumpthin',' he said to Mary, who was peeling potatoes for the evening meal in between spooning food into Jack. 'I have a feelin' this oul' dog was sen'ta us be the good Lord. This oul' hound could be our saviour.'

'A bit a dough'd come in handy,' she said.

'This fella could be the best,' the Boss said. 'Yeh shoulda seen the way he caught that feckin' rat. Jasus he was lightnin'.'

'Ah well let's hope so,' Mary said, delighted to see her husband optimistic for a change.

As he swept the pigs the Boss dreamed of making a fortune. Here was a golden opportunity. Wouldn't he just love to gob in the faces of those who hated him. What better way to do it than by winning a few races at Harold's Cross then go on to triumph in the Greyhound Derby? A win like that would make Biffo worth a lot of money. Maybe a fella could buy an oul' car or somet'in', add another room on to the bungalow. That'd show them spineless feckers that a good man was impossible to keep down.

That evening, after the day's chores were concluded, Babs climbed on to the Boss's handlebars and settled snugly between his arms. With Biffo trailing behind on a string, the Boss's powerful lower body took the strain and, with his cheeks puffed out, they wobbled up the Grange Road. They passed Gooley Kennedy's dairy and the stumps of the Priory, where John Philpot Curran had lived nearly two centuries earlier, and who for entertainment organised events for a hedonistic group of young blades called the Monks of the Screw.[1]

A light breeze wafted over the fields from the Dargle Brook, carrying with it echoes of the men who rode to the Priory dressed as devils to drink champagne and cavort outrageously. With monstrous red phalluses they poked the naughty girls who leapt naked from giant cakes and ran among the diners. On the Priory's smooth lawns couples copulated by the light of the moon. One night in 1792 Curran's daughter Gertrude, a special child with beautiful dresses and a room of her own, climbed up on to the windowsill and pitched head first down to lie crumpled among the revellers. Curran buried her on the lawn and he grew old grieving for her.

'Isn't that where the ghost of the little girl is?' Babs asked.

'Like mine,' the Boss said, 'his poor heart was broken.'

'Whatja say, Daddy?'

'Nuttin'.'

Babs was sure he'd said his heart was broken. That was funny, he'd never said anything like that before. What Babs heard was the sound of snapping, the first stress fracture in the walls of the Boss's hitherto indestructible fortress. The steel hawsers that bound him were stretched to breaking point. Poverty, struggle, too many mouths to feed, a life that was doomed to end in a cul de sac filled with stench and litter. The Boss realised his optimism had been unfounded. His father was right, his life would never amount to much. The reinforced concrete that had protected him from his enemies was crumbling to dust. His physical powers were waning too, soon he would be as frail and as vulnerable as the men who spent their days drinking in Cullen's.

'C'mon, Biffo,' Babs called as the dog bobbed along on the end of the string, its nails scraping on the tarmac. 'Daddy, what did yeh say?' Babs asked.

But the Boss's mind had turned destructive and, as he glanced down at the dog trotting alongside the bike's turning wheels, its long ears flat

1 John Philpot Curran (1750–1817) Lawyer and orator, born in Newmarket, Co. Cork, Ireland. He entered the Irish Parliament in 1783, and opposed the Union. Master of the Rolls (1806–14).

against its skull, its intelligent eyes moist, its legs as thin and knotted as branches, he muttered, 'Nuttin'. Yeh jus' keep an eye on that feckin' dog.'

Babs went quiet. This was a strange man talking. This was not her father.

'Yer mother's nerves is gettin' worse,' the Boss said.

'What did yeh say 'bout Mammy's nerves?'

'Shu'rup an' watch that bloody dog.'

Babs felt the Boss's breath hot on her neck. His feet furiously gathered impetus, his knees pumped madly.

Having attained the Hermitage hill they sped down, the greyhound cantering like a miniature racehorse. Marley, standing white and massive entered the Boss's line of vision. Head down he rode past the grand house where La Touche the banker had lived until Tedcastle the coalman bought it off him, and he'd sold it to Ketton Love who still lived there.

'There's no love fer a poor hard-workin' man from that bloody lot a rotten English,' the Boss punned unintentionally. 'How did them hoors make their money?' he gasped. 'Buncha English bastards.'

'How should I know?' Babs pouted.

'Bey foolin' poor fellas like meself, that's how,' the Boss spluttered. 'Glenavy, that Campbell fella, the stutterin' oul' shite wit' the moryah speech impedementia that does be playin' golf at the Grange wit' them snots a businessmen. That ould imposter livin' in darlin' Rockbrook House.' The Boss got off the bike. 'Yeh'll hav'ta walk, Babs,' he said, 'I'm spent.'

Babs led the greyhound along the grass verge where it sniffed before dropping a curly stool.

Ticknock, Montpelier, the Pine Forest, Larch Hill, Taylor's Grange, the Lamb Doyles, the Three Rock Mountain, Stocking Lane, Billy's Bridge, Scholarstown, Cruagh and the Hell Fire Club. The Boss knew the area well. It was all foreign owned. He had walked every pennyworth of it, every grassy field and knoll. He had investigated every dump where old car parts might be found, every lane near every pub where empty bottles might be shining in the grass. They were worth a farthing each. The hills above Rathfarnham, which drew the wealthy with their views, was the Boss's thorn-filled Garden of Gethsemane.

Each day, as the pigs sized him up with their clever pink eyes, he beseeched his poor second-class Catholic God to let him win the Irish Sweep. Money would buy him a lift up in class. He was really a gentleman at heart. Wasn't his second cousin a doctor? And his other cousin a famous singer? He had the right connections, all he needed was the money.

'C'mon, Daddy, let's go home,' Babs said, 'I'm gettin' cold, and so is Biffo. Looka'im, he's tired too.'

The Boss put his burning cheek against his daughter's cold face and they freewheeled across Taylor's Grange, past Columba's College, where the golden sons of the English were studying in yellow light, their blonde heads in thick books, and back to the bungalow, the whitewashed flanks of which were lit up by the bright moon. The ferocious stench of the pigs hit the Boss in the face like a shovelful of shite as he put the bike away, padlocked the shed door and stuffed the dog into its cage.

The Boss tiptoed to a window and listened fer a while.

'What are yeh doin'?' Babs asked.

'Nuttin',' he said. In fact, he was listening to see if his faithful wife, the woman he had humiliated by having her virginity proven, was belittling him. He did not trust the one person in the world who would die fer him.

Mary was already in bed with Jack who lay like a small corpse, his mouth gaping, snoring softly in the moonlight when the Boss turned the key.

'Good-night now,' he said, handing Babs a bowl of warm milk. 'Gerrinta bed an' don't be wastin' that bit a light.'

'Night, Daddy,' Babs whispered.

27

THE FOLLOWING DAY Babs was playing with her new pet. 'Yeh can practise holdin' him,' she said, handing Jack the string. The dog pulled and the string flew out of his weak grasp. He waved his hands like helpless tentacles. The dog prowled around the garden. Its powerful sense of smell directed it to the cage where the rooster stood hunched and miserable in thick droppings. With a snarl the dog tore at the cage.

'Stop!' Babs screamed. Maddened by the smell of the bird the dog tore at the wire with his teeth. 'No, no, Biffo, that's not right. Don't do that,' Babs cried. The dog ripped a hole in the wire and sank his teeth into the bird. Babs screamed. Bridgid and Pam rushed from the house.

The clang of the gate announced the Boss's return from whatever wild goose he'd been chasing that morning. He jumped off the cart. 'What ar'yehz all doin huddlin' there? What's up?' He looked at the wrenched apart cage. 'Where's the bird? I hope that feckin' dog hasn't had it because I told yehz ta keep that hoor tied up.'

'He's down the garden with the cock'rel in his mout',' Bridgid told him excitedly. 'Babs is chasin' afther him.'

'Biffo ran away,' Jack said, smiling in wonder.

The Boss's eyes blazed. 'Jasus Christ lemme at that fecker.' He ran into the kitchen and returned with an old .22 rifle he'd bought for killing rabbits.

Babs cried out with a desperate anxiety in her voice, 'Biffo, Biffo, come here, please!' The dog, with bloodied fangs and reddened paws, wouldn't obey her. Babs sobbed. Only then did Biffo trot calmly over to his stricken mistress and kiss her hand with a curl of his bloody tongue.

The Boss thumbed in a slug and took aim. The bird lay on the ground, its yellow beak opening and closing in spasm. Kitty watched, her ears pricked. The dog panted, eager for another game. Babs' heart beat inside her chest like a trapped bird. 'Babs! Ge'rout a the way.' She screamed and flung herself on the dog who had now grabbed the dying cockerel and begun to crunch its bones. The Boss took aim from almost point-blank range. Babs screamed. Mary ran out of the house.

'What in God's name's happ'nin'?' she asked.

'Daddy's gointa to kill Biffo,' Babs cried.

'Why?' Mary asked, her eyes wide.

'Because the hoor's afther tearin' a hole in the cage and killin' the darlin' bird,' the Boss said. He could see the men from Cullen's laughing and could imagine the Dowager telling them how he had conned the upstart from Tallaght into taking on a dangerous animal that would destroy him. First the cockerel, then before long the rotten mongrel would be attacking the young pigs, then the children. 'I'm gointa kill the feckin' sonovabitch.' The Boss's finger pressed against the trigger as he said, 'Take them childher inside and shut the door.'

'Don't do an'tin', please Daddy!' Babs begged, her face scrunching up with remorse. 'It was my fault,' she squealed. 'I let him do it. He didn't mean it. He jus' needs trainin' that's all. He won't kill an'tin' anymore, Daddy.'

'I'll betcha he won't,' the Boss said. Babs sobbed, her hand on her Daddy's sleeve. 'Go to the house.' The Boss spoke remotely now, his expression as calm as if he were entering a place that precluded sympathy. He put the rifle to his shoulder, aimed at the dog's head–

Babs picked up a stone and cracked Biffo on the head. With a yelp the dog ran down the garden. The Boss followed him with the barrel of the rifle and fired at the swiftly moving hound's lean arse.

The rifle report made Babs gag. The bullet tore through the leaves of the drooping sallies, sped past Rice's shop and embedded itself in Dowling's wall. Babs ran to her father befere he could reload, and threw herself on his mercy.

The Boss's first impulse was to reload and fire again and again until the dog was stone dead and pumping blood. 'Will yeh ge'rout!' the Boss roared but his daughter was clinging to him like a snail to a flowerpot. The Boss stopped. He looked down at his daughter as if he were hearing and seeing her for the first time. 'What the–?' he started.

'Daddy, please!' Bab's eyes swam with tears.

The Boss put the gun down. After a moment, he took his daughter's upturned cheeks in his sandpapery hands. 'Right,' he said quietly, 'if that's the way yeh want it, but th'hoor's gotta go. He can't stay here.'

'Oh, t'anks Daddy,' Babs sobbed, and tried to grab her father's hand to squeeze it.

The Boss's small eyes looked into his daughter's. The deadly murderous look was gone. 'He'll hav'ta go,' he repeated and there would be no changing of his mind this time. 'I don't care where he goes but he can't stay here a minute longer. The rotten sod's gotta taste fer blood on his feckin' whiskers and from now on there'll be no satisfyin' it.'

Babs called Biffo, who returned to her side playful and bouncy, not knowing how near he'd been to death. He lurched forward and lay still at her feet, his tongue lolling , his breath coming in short bursts. The kitchen door flew back and Pam raced down the garden, her long hair flying. She cradled the dog who smothered her with licking kisses.

'That hoor would have had yeh next,' the Boss growled.

'No he wouldn't,' Babs said. 'I know he wouldn't. He loves me.' She wiped her eyes on her sleeve and asked, 'Daddy, what ar'yeh gointa do wit'im?'

'I'll thinka somethin', don't worry,' the Boss said, carrying the .22 back to the kitchen.

'He's jus' a dog,' Babs said to Pam, as she knelt down and stroked the dog's head, 'he doesn't know any betther.'

A shadow behind the thick leaves of the sallies had witnessed the drama. Carefully picking his way, Perkins slipped quietly back indoors.

Babs sat on her own, traumatised, clutching herself with her arms and murmuring, 'I've said goodbye t'him.'

The Boss had had enough of it. He felt guilty and wanted to read the *Mail*. 'He's on'y a rotten dog,' he snapped. 'Now, ge'rup there an' help yer mother.'

The incident opened floodgates of bile that had been building up between Mary and her husband. The noise of their fight went on until, eventually, everyone slept, except the Boss who wondered how he could buy back Bab's love.

Next morning after the children had set off for school, the Boss crated the dog and drove it to the mountains. On a windswept road, with neither tree nor house in sight, he released the dog. 'G'wan now,' he shouted. The dog sat on its tail and refused to budge. The Boss went to the cart and returned with Kitty's whip.

'Get the hell out a here!' he roared cracking the whip across the dog's back. The greyhound loped away, stopping every now and then to look back. Soon it was no more than an insect on the horizon.

The Boss drove back to Rathfarnham and told Babs that Biffo had gone to an old dame near Rockbrook. 'She'll trate yer man like a lord,' he lied. Babs was happy, and as Biffo was never seen again, so was the Boss.

28

THE SUN HUNG like a shiny badge pinned in a clear blue sky over Rathfarnham. It beat down on the straggly village with rare intensity, drying the grass in the hillocky fields and lapping the water from pools that had filled in winter. Variegated cows flicked their mucky tails and waddled in single file towards any shade they could find, accompanied by haloes of flies that settled all over them whenever they stopped to graze. A heat haze shimmered on the tarmacked road that unwound from the Dublin mountains, disdainfully skirting the village.

The Boss talked to himself as he worked, his angry voice rising above the ever-present sound of the river clattering past his half acre. After wolfing down the raw guts the pigs squealed for more. Without the pigs the Boss could be taking his accordion to dances, grinning, playing, and afterwards, in the dew-wet bushes, pawing the starry-eyed virgins who hung about the bandstand. The Boss often thought of those days of freedom and excitement; he should never have married. Why was his bloody life strewn with bad decisions?

Alone in the yard the Boss rambled on about the hand life had dealt him. And him a 'hard-workin' poor shagger'. Bitterness choking him, he looked up at the bungalow he had built 'single-handed, wit' not a bit a help from no one', and saw Mary at the sink by the window. He spat an oath. Mary was a poor choice for an ambitious fellow who had married her out of pity. Stalking around the yard like a rusting tin god, the Boss swore and prayed some awful fate would befall everyone he knew.

In the kitchen, Mary was making an apple tart for tea, moving slowly because she was pregnant. With a pastry-smeared finger she pulled back the dusty curtain and looked down the yard. Yes, the old bastard was staring at her, standing there as if he were posing for a photograph, expecting to see a lover fleeing around the corner of the house. Mary grinned, revealing gappy teeth.

Playing on the tiles at Mary's feet was Jack, the first boy after three girls. Round and round he spun, laughing at the way the funny Greek symbols on the tiles seemed to be spinning with him. As Mary transferred the tart from the table to the oven Jack got up from the floor to watch.

'Mind yerself darlin',' she said, turning up the gas.

Suddenly, the door flapped open, and the Boss stood on the threshold, his hat still on.

'Jesus, Mary an' Joseph! Mary said. 'Yeh frightened the life out a me. What d'yeh want?'

'I was won'drin',' the Boss said.

'What?'

'Yeh know.' He nodded his head towards the bedroom.

'Oh Jesus, haven't yeh had enough a dat lately? What about the lad?'

'Ge'rid a him!' the Boss snapped and he slipped off his boots, came indoors, and stood, loose-limbed and smelling of sweat, pressing down on the balls of his feet.

'Here,' Mary said, handing Jack a doorstep of bread and jam. 'Be a good man an' run off t'play.'

Jack, smiling with surprise, took the bread in both hands and waddled out into the sunny yard. He headed for the sandpit under the willow that every year rained silver bullets on to the concrete.

The Boss stared at his first-born son with no real feeling. He loved only one of his children: Babs, born when her parents' love was still warm. What set her apart from her anonymous brothers and sisters was the miracle of her eyes, shining deep, questioning and mischievious. When he had passed her cradle the Boss had looked down at the sleeping Babs and felt proud. She had opened her eyes; those big eyes that watched his every move. From the start, Babs was the star in the Boss's mucky firmament. Cossetted and loved from all sides, she grew strong in body and will. Angelically, she swam through the troubled waters of domestic battles, taking neither side, and consoling her mother when the battle ended.

'Yeh'd betther be quick about it,' Mary said as her husband slipped out of his dirty overalls. She lay on the bed, looking at the ceiling as the bed creaked and the Boss, his face florid, thrust into her. Within minutes he was back in the yard, putting a fire underneath the big black cauldron to boil the remainder of the guts for the younger pigs. The smell of burning rubber and cows' entrails in the big black boiler reached the bungalow and clawed at its windows. Mary was back at the sink peeling potatoes.

Jack played happily, a sand encrusted turd at his bare feet. He would soon have to be sent to school, so that one day he could work and bring in wages. His mind was on the neat little towers of sand he was making with a rusty bean can. Like a chick in a soiled nest he knew nothing beyond the tall trees that darkly surrounded the bungalow. There was a bridge over the river. He could cross it but go no further. Every school day he gripped the bars of the tall gates his father had made to keep out intruders. His sandy little hands reaching through the bars like a prisoner's, Jack waited for his big sister Babs to come home. When he saw her he beat his hands together, even though his father was standing behind him, because the Boss, too, loved Babs and wanted to hear what sort of day she'd had. As Jack reached up to his sister, softly calling, 'Up! Up!' the Boss whisked her away and left him clutching air. He would have to make do with Bridgid, who said things like, 'Aha, yeh little shite, that shook yeh, didn't it?' Pam too would drift past, her head in the clouds, clutching a ragged comic. Jack knew the piece of tarmac outside the gate, the people and cars that went by on it. He saw the Jesuits as they strode up the mountains with little khaki bags on their shoulders. Sometimes, he wished he was at school.

Babs, her white legs dangling, her feet in brown scuffed shoes and ankle socks, lolled uncomfortably on her father's knee as he quizzed her about her lessons. 'Yeh done well,' the Boss said, his face amused, his trilby on the chair, his bald head shining. 'G'wan now,' he would smack her soft little bottom, 'getcher bit a homework done.' Sliding off his lap, Babs flicked the hair from her eyes, and wrapping her fingers around a pencil, earnestly watched it scrawl across the page as she wrote a story with spidery illustrations about a treasure island. Mary knitted by the fire, the desultory flame painting her face as gold as an Indian's.

When she'd finished, Babs folded her jotter, put away her pencil and rubber then went to play with Jack. But not for long. 'Ge'rup ta bed,

Babs,' the Boss said brusquely, 'yeh've got school ta go ta in the mornin'.' Babs obediently left the room, taking Jack with her by the hand. The Boss watched her go. He didn't care much for children but Babs was his very own love. The rest were a bloody curse. He sat by a turf fire that smouldered throughout the year, and with audible glee read a lurid newspaper account of the slaughter of a local policeman. D.I. Sean McMahon. The *Evening Mail* was the Boss's only pleasure, he gleaned the ads: displays first, then the classified, sometimes with spiteful comments. 'Jaysus, that feckin' hoor O'Rourke's after gettin' plannin' permission for that lovely little field next ta the chapel.' When he'd left not a single word unread the Boss folded the paper, wound the green alarm clock and shouted, 'Willyehz lookit the time?' The room cleared with sighs and the scraping of chairs. Mary grunted as she shuffled off to the cold bedrooms that lay off a short corridor. 'Ah sure, it's late very early,' the Boss said. The children knew the phrase so well they silently mouthed it as they wandered off.

Most days, the Boss cycled around Rathfarnham looking for work, because there was 'feck-all in pigs'. He would build walls, fix leaking taps, mend holes in roofs, dig drains, shovel shit, anything for money. He would scale windy buildings, fearlessly swaying on makeshift scaffolding. He'd mend shoes, his mouth a cat's claw of tacks, his cobbler's last like the steel limb of a thalidomide victim. He dosed hens, scoured calves, mended gashes in the sides of cows, forcing his needle through the thick hide, pushing the slimy guts back inside with his hand, or stuffing the hole with straw until he got the animal to the abattoir. No one knew what went on in the Boss's mind as he worked, inhaling the smell of an animal's insides, muttering to himself. The Boss was a man of stone who nicked, plucked and grabbed what he needed to survive.

In the forlorn Kilmashogue hills which he trawled for work in the autumn dawns, when he was at one with the fox and the badger, the Boss collected velvety mushrooms. Looking down a valley, the wind tousling what remained of his hair, he watched with narrowing eyes the mess the bulldozers were making of a once fine old Georgian house. The speculators were moving in. Noting lead pipes and iron guttering hanging from the shell of the half-eaten mansion, the Boss promised himself he would return under darkness and spirit them away. As he pedalled his big Hercules bike back to the bungalow there was an aching space where his heart should have been. The Boss was a failure and he had to share that with his family. He collected bones and guts from the abattoir. Mary boiled the bones down for soup, a brothy concoction leavened with carrot, swede and onion. Sheep's heads made nourishing dinners, but the children gasped when they came upon a boiled eye staring at them from the bottom of a bowl. The Boss dumped the cows heads in a heap in the garden where they would be stripped by maggots and the black rats that swam across the river from the surrounding farms. The heads were piled high, their eyes melting in the sun, their worm-infested mouths grinning at death. Blood had dribbled from bullet holes in their skulls, horns stuck out like motorcycle handlebars. Their stench mingled with the aroma of the chicken coop, the pigs, the cabbage stalks decaying in the garden.

Sickly cats stalked the yard at night and slept in the ricks during the daytime. Jack called out to them, proffering a dab of jammy bread. Obsequious and weepy-eyed, they responded, licking the sweet stuff, purring to the rhythm of a small gentle hand stroking their emaciated backs.

'Don't be feedin' them melts,' the Boss would growl as he trundled by on some urgent mission.

The blackened boiler frothed and steamed in a corner of the garden and acrid smoke from the old car tyres kept the mosquitoes at bay. Swarms of insects buzzed up from the dark leafy pool of the river to sting and bite every warm-blooded creature in sight. A brace of bats flew out of Paddy Slavin's stone wall and criss-crossed the garden. As dusk descended, a percolating mist spread like cotton wool, blocking out the house. Soon, darkness veiled all but the nauseous, greasy smell of the boiler, the pigs, and the latest bones from Cosgrove's abattoir, heaped into a pile and crawling with rats.

29

THE TIME CAME for Jack to be introduced to the wider world of Rathfarnham. Lying snugly in his narrow little bed, his black hair stark against the pillow, he heard the commotion in the kitchen and knew something important was happening. He heard his father yell, his mother curse and Babs calmly intervene. Rows in the bungalow were as normal as birdsong but this one had an edge to it. As he lay there, worrying in case the flickering noises of dissent were fanned into punching and scratching, Bridgid barged into the room. She had none of Babs soft ways about her.

'Get yer feckin' arse into them trousers or I'll cut the bloody ground from under yeh,' she shouted.

Jack crawled out of bed like a blind mouse and wobbled around the room trying to hide his privates the way his mother had taught him to. Bridgid hit and pushed him in the direction of his new clothes and shiny boots with the gleaming brads. He had slept badly; he was sick to the guts with worry about the big school he could see from the garden. The black-robed nuns and the terrors of other children. He had never met a stranger before, except for occasional visitors to the bungalow but they were rare since the Boss seemed to hate everyone. Jack was forced into his clothes, his nose was pushed upwards because Bridgid's idea of washing was to dip a smelly rag in ice-cold water and thrust it into his face, making him jump with the shock. Like a stiff little doll, he was guided with prods and knees in the backside towards the kitchen where the Boss waited.

'Ate yer breakfast,' the Boss snarled, but Jack couldn't, even though Babs made a dripping soldier out of soft boiled egg.

'There,' she said as the yellow dripped on to the table. Jack's mouth seemed sealed and dry inside. He wanted to use the toilet.

Mary, at the sink wearing her caring face, turned and said, 'Don' be too hard on the poor little fella.'

'Ah, ta Hell wit' that, he hasta survive,' the Boss roared.

'But . . .' Mary turned her big back away and looked sad. She was stooped over the sink now, round-shouldered, the fat on her big arms shaking as she scrubbed an old black pot which had last night's stew ceramicked on the bottom. The Boss was less predictable in the mornings, so the least said the better.

His mouth wiped and his water passed, Jack was ready. Feeling stiff in his new clothes, his knee-length socks itching and his boots looking brazenly up at him, Jack clung to Babs' hand as they crossed the bridge with Bridgid and Pam, leaving behind Mary, her babies, her pain and the Boss.

Like an old wave-battered seal cow, Mary would cling to her icy rock and bellow defiance at anyone who swam close enough to threaten her pups, and that included the tuskery old bull, her husband - the Boss.

Jack followed his sisters rumps over the rusty gate that led into The Pit, a few acres of tussocky, bulrushed wilderness where Rathfarnham's children played, cried and were occasionally abused and hurt by men, rocks or thorns. The Pit was amphitheatre, Eton's playing fields, Croke Park and Dalymount to the multitude who used it. It had two holes for the caddies to pitch and putt while they idly smoked and waited to go to the Grange golf club to earn cash for fags and steamy visits to the Classic to see Victor Mature and Jane Russell. The Pit was sacred. It would never be built on because even the councillors, though stupid and crooked, could see it was the only amenity around. Stumbling over anthills and barging past islands of stinging nettles, Jack followed his sisters and their big stalking legs until they regained the tarmac of the road. With its reassuring firmness beneath his boots, Jack lifted them like a cartoon character, revelling in the delicious noise they made as he plonked them down on the road.

But as he neared the school's forbidden black gate, Jack now heard his boots echo like a death-knell. He saw Brennan's dray as it clattered past, his sisters' feet shuffling in unison like some huge insect. They passed St Patrick's cottages, the Corporation houses whose occupants the Boss called 'them lazy shites that don't wan'ta work'.

They came across a clump of roadmen standing idle. Babs skirted them, holding firmly on to her little brother's hand. The men leant on their spades, their broken hands pinching the shrunken butts of hand-rolled cigarettes. 'Mornin',' one yelled, and bent to catch a glimpse of the girls' knickers as they scurried past.

Jack suddenly felt as cold and shrivelled as a corpse. He heard the men's shovels grate metallically as they got back to work, exchanging oaths. Bab's dark head bobbed and her brother's boots pattered on the tarmac. In awe, Jack observed the Loretto Convent, a fairy castle glistening in the distance.

He jibbed like a stubborn pony when they reached the school door. 'I don't wan'ta,' he whimpered, his face ugly with fear.

'There's nuthin' ta worry about,' Babs said, hugging him. Jack peered squinty-eyed at the cavernous building. 'Come on now, yeh'll love it,' Babs cajoled.

Jack's knees unlocked and his feet stepped out again, but stiffly, like a mechanical doll. 'I wan'ta go home,' he wailed, but he knew his fate was sealed. From now on he would be a prisoner of the nuns. He would have to be a good boy, for ever.

The smell of chalk, sweat and warmth let loose when the classroom door was opened, terrified Jack. He clung to Babs until he was prised away like a whelk off a stone and led away, wet-eyed and sniffing. When he glanced back over his shoulder to see if Babs was still there the big door was closed. Jack was in the hands of those who would shape him according to God's will - or else.

30

FOR THE FIRST few weeks Jack hid and slunk about the classroom and corridors like a rat. He hated school. The days were hot and he felt trapped. The slates of the convent were glossy with sunshine. In the heat of the playground tattered sparrows danced. Jack envied them their freedom as he peered out of the window, his hands manacled behind his back with nerves. He was surrounded by bustling children, every one a stranger and according to his father a possible enemy.

Jack shrank with fear as, eager and shrill, his classmates anticipated the coming of Mrs Byrne, to test children's eyesight.

A magpie slipped from roof to pole to bench, not daring to touch down. It was a suspicious bird, always expected the worst, like the Boss. Jack hid behind the other kids, the boys with miniature fists clenched, the girls demurely holding hands.

He drew a crinkly sleeve across his nose, spreading a slimy cobweb all the way to his elbow. A small girl screwed up her face. Jack's heart thumped as each name was called. He went deaf with fear. When Mrs Byrne spiced her initial tone with impatience the lad behind punched Jack in the back. 'It's you, dopey,' he hissed. Trembling, his eyes moist, Jack edged towards the table where Mrs Byrne, fat, in glasses and polka-dotted frock sat, her magnified eyes bulging like blood-flecked marbles. Jack glued his gaze to her chest. Dots began to swim like tadpoles across his eyes. Desperately he struggled for control.

'Jus' stan' where yeh are,' Mrs Byrne said, rising like a balloon and drifting towards him. The card she was pointing at was miles away. Jack squinted, his hair was a mad lavatory brush, his jumper an unfinished moth meal. Mrs Byrne gave off a perfumed smell. 'Now,' she said, 'when I p'int me cane at the numbers an' letters all I wancha t'do is ta call them out in a clear v'ice. Got that?'

But the figures and letters perversely changed places as Jack tried to read them.

'G'wan,' Mrs Byrne prompted.

The beams of the roof pressed down.

Mrs Byrne began to melt like a big ice-cream, her voice somehow filtering away. Only echoey sniggers penetrated Jack's brain. He clawed at his side. The air was gone from the room, he was light-headed. Suddenly, a beautiful feeling engulfed him. Water dribbled through his trousers and streamed down the insides of his legs, deliciously soaking his socks and pooling yellowly around his feet. Silently, the children pressed near, some pointed at the dusty droplets disappearing like loosed ball-bearings between cracks in the floorboards. Others smiled at him, with the fixed smiles seen in school photographs.

Jack's ammonia-scented carcass was still there, but his spirit was out in the yard, the sparrows landing on his little sloping shoulders as if he were Saint Francis. Faintly, he could hear his own voice. It was still struggling over numbers like a tired soldier clambering over slippery rocks after a bloody battle.

'No, no, no,' Mrs Byrne was whimpering like a trapped kitten in the distance, 'dat's a six. Da next wan's a seven. Yeh're near'y dere.'

Jack stammered.

Mrs Byrne put down her cane. Like a prisoner he waited. 'Yeh can go now, g'wan,' Mrs Byrne said with a sigh. Jack trudged wetly back to his place.

The door opened and Miss O'Halloran, the headmistress, stood there fiercely framed. The children clattered to attention. They watched sensible shoes stride to where Jack, like a battered fighter, had slunk. Miss O'Halloran grabbed him by the collar, a knee in his spine helped him on his way. Grimly, he was dragged over to the pool he'd made. For one glorious moment the children thought he was going to have his nose pushed in it. That would have been a great gas.

'Look! Look! Will yeh look!' Miss O'Halloran barked. 'Is that a nice t'ing ta do in fronta little girls? Yeh hear me! Is it?' How she would love to batter this scruffy little bastard until he squealed for mercy. 'C'mon out a that,' she said roughly. Jack slithered out the door and all the way along to the sombre sterility of the headmistress's study.

The door slammed behind him. 'Stand up straight!' Miss

O'Halloran cried. 'Put yer hands on my desk. Now bend forward.' Her dentures fizzing, she glared with contempt at the grotesque object in front of her. 'Don't you have any pride?' she shrieked. Jack kept his head down like a tired donkey. 'What sort of holes do creatures like you crawl out of?' Miss O'Halloran bellowed.

As she waited for an answer Jack heard her anger ratchet up another notch. 'I am going to teach you that you can't do what you like in my school,' Miss O'Halloran said. Jack heard the desk drawer being tugged open. 'Didn't you see the whole school laughing at you?' she asked, her voice high as a girl's. Miss O'Halloran ran a thumb down the blade of her ebony ruler. 'What made you do it? You wretch!' Her face crimson, she lashed at the bony calves with the brass-edged ruler. Six, seven, eight. Children next door silently mouthed the blows.

When the beating stopped Miss O'Halloran was breathing loudly. Jack remained bent over. Although the pain scorched his very soul his expression was serene. The headmistress sat down and, with dead eyes, she looked at him. Jack, the little shit, was forcing back the tears. She knew it. Steadfastly, Jack wouldn't let them come. The calmness of the room drummed in his ears. Miss O'Halloran's voice started to caress him tenderly.

In the luscious silence, with only her breathing pulsing like a severed nerve, Jack was experiencing a new kind of tranquility. He turned his head and through a misty eye he saw her contemplating the ruler, saw his blood on the snow white blotting paper that lay on her desk. He turned to rest his wet nose on his arms which were folded under his face like a bony bolster, his teeth fastened on the soggy material. He knew he had bested her. He had made her suffer too.

'I've got something for you,' the headmistress said, breaking the silence. 'Look, come round here.' Her voice was stupid. She pulled Jack's head into the cleft of her skirt. 'I'm doing this for your own good,' she said. She opened the desk drawer again and he flinched. In her hand she held a large, red, boiled sweet. She found his mouth and he felt her soft fingers between his lips. 'I'm sorry, do you hear? You forgive me don'tcha? I'm lettin' you off early. You won't go tellin' the others now will you? Go out the back way, t'rough the garden.'

She shot back a stubborn bolt. Red saliva was filling Jack's mouth to choking. Outside he spat the sweet into a flowerbed. Sunshine washed over him. God's air was all he wanted. To hear birds singing, to see flowers and the big monkey-puzzle tree in the lane. Chaffinchs bobbed around fresh horsedung. Blue tits vanished into cracks in the stone wall that girdled the convent grounds. Pigeons arrowed high to their roost, where the big green bell hung. Jack burst out crying, tears poured from his eyes. He ran, casting a crooked shadow on the convent wall, his wet shoes pounding the road, his arms flailing, crying as he'd never cried before. Nature, lovely nature, was filling his ears with its pleasures and all he could do was cry.

As he wheeled away from the convent garden and out into the blazing sun he saw Billy Riley leaning on bronze arms, staring at him like a well-fed ox. The big convent labourer followed the fleeing boy with slowly swivelling brown eyes. Jack ran and ran but Riley's mindless guffaw tore after and overtook him. He looked back, his eyes wide. Riley was mad. The Boss said everyone who kept pigeons was mad.

Jack was out of breath but he kept running as fast as he could. Head down, he saw the quiet lane unravelling beneath his feet. On a hill, a man and horse ploughed. The air hummed, a sheepdog growled, the convent's bell boomed over the glass-topped walls. Nuns crossed the paths, quietly praying. The sound of a garden hoe clanged against cobbles. A necklace of pigeons flew round and round Billy Riley's loft.

31

JACK WALKED NOW, the tears dry on his face. Women in aprons, their hair spiky with curlers, hung out their washing and cackled over fences. Mongrels slept in hot yards, cats were draped over sheds. At last he could see the bungalow crouching under the pussy willow like an old woman under an umbrella. A smell of pigs was on the wind. Jack was home.

Squeezing through the half-open gate he tiptoed over the bridge and gazed around the yard. A scattering of hens scratched, the smell of pigs was strong and wonderfully familiar. A pall of black smoke from flaming tyres billowed and curled as if from the funnel of a steamership. The Boss, small and dogged had been chopping up old doors and window frames he'd removed from buildings in the city. Smoke teased the willows that ringed the garden. Jack watched the fire's orange tongue lick the tindery weeds that grew around the fat boiler. Animal guts trembled in a green sauce.

The smell of marrow, dung and decay seemed sweet to him. Flies swirled, defying the steam, unafraid, in spite of many of their sort being upturned and wriggling in the fetid froth. The liquid hissed and fizzed. The guts simmering in the moonlight would draw foxes from Fonthill Abbey. Rats would gather too, like wizened old men in threadbare fur coats. Like tiny parliamentarians they would stand around figuring out ways to get at the soft warm meat.

When Jack softly opened the kitchen door his mother dropped her three-day-old *Sunday Independent*, and stared wildly at him through her spectacles. 'Mother a God!' she exclaimed. 'What in His Holy Name ar'yeh doin' home at this hour?' She spun her son and felt his trousers. 'Ah, I t'ought so. Is that what's brought yeh trottin' home to yer poor ould mammy. C'mon, we'll get yeh out a them dirty ould wet rags in a jiffy.'

She ran her big kind fingers over the ugly weals on the back of her son's legs. 'Good God, is that what that oul' bitch done t'yeh?' She sighed wearily, but Jack was delirious with happiness and talked baby talk to himself. 'That oul' maid'll rot in Hell for this,' Mary growled as she towelled her son. 'God protect yeh but yeh can't help the way yeh are.' Jack hiccupped a tear and shivered as his mother briskly rubbed his pale body. He was secure again among familiar furniture; the two yellow Victorian dogs covered in dust on the mantelpiece, their mouths panting; the fly-stained picture of Jesus Christ spreading his bleeding hands; the wooden wireless with its green Cyclopsian eye.

Jack traced the flowery pattern of the wallpaper with a finger as his mother, glad of the company, pulled a fresh pair of woollen pants up his thin legs. 'Yer Daddy'll blow his top when he sees yeh here, so be off wit'cha now and make yerself scarce. God help yeh,' she whispered, with the sunlight reflecting chickens onto her lenses.

Jack, uncomprehending, looked up at his mother's eyes for a message. Mary patted his backside and steered him towards the door, and watched as he ran to the pile of sand under the pussy willow.

He was talking to himself and making castles with the rusty tin when he heard Kitty's iron shoes drumming on the bridge. When he saw the pony's fierce white-flecked eyes and rusty teeth appear round the gable of the house he dropped the tin and ran to the chicken-wire fence. His father brutally tugged on the reins and Kitty stopped as if shot. With an athletic leap the Boss was on the ground, dragging open the gate into the yard. Kitty tore after her master, almost crushing him against the gatepost. The Boss snarled and thumped the old pony in the ribs. Kitty snapped. She was over twenty, spent most of her life in the Boss's company and was as close to him as anyone would ever get. As he manoeuvred her nearer to a row of barrels with shouts of, 'Back there, c'mon now, back!' the Boss noticed his son. 'What are yeh doin' away from school?' he growled. Jack's head dropped. 'Yeh're not sayin'?' the Boss snarled. He despised those who couldn't speak up. Jack sneaked away back to the sand heap while Kitty, tired of waiting, dragged the cart away. As the Boss dashed over to haul her back he shouted, side-faced, 'I'll speak ta yeh later, yeh bloody sleeveen.' But Jack had mastered the animals' trick of setting off noisy alarms just before he was hit, and he didn't hate his father the way he hated Miss O'Halloran.

Flinging off his greasy jacket the Boss furiously shovelled pigswill from the cart into the barrels. It was a messy job, a pungent mixture of rotten tomatoes, stale loaves, yellowing cabbage leaves, milk-bottle tops, rusty razor blades, and even the odd knife or fork. The pigs kept up a raucous chorus, their trotters resting in benediction on the half-doors of the sties, their pink eyes darting from Kitty to the Boss.

Her head and shoulders framed in a window, Mary was suddenly busy. The Boss's presence worked on her like an electric prod. She was by the sink frantically peeling potatoes. Her arms and hands were red from the cold water, her hair hung in tangles around her worn countrywoman's face.

The Boss worked madly, demonically muttering to himself, sweat dripping from his chin. Occasionally, he shot a glance towards the kitchen window. 'Yeh hav'ta get up early in the mornin' to catch that bastard in bed,' the locals said about him. The Boss accepted it as a compliment. The villagers were beneath his contempt; anyone who sat gossiping in a pub all day was a 'bowsie' or 'fooly olly'.

A small sweet sound curled from the top of the pussy willow. It penetrated the pig noises, the sound of hammering from Perkins' yard, the swish of cars and the clip-clop of passing drays. Jack's big zany eyes crept around his cranium before looking up, blinking into the sun. The sound was coming from the beak of a thrush, a mottled ball of fluff on stalky legs. Jack forgot his fears as all his thoughts focused on the bird. A smile broke out on his tear-stained face. The bird threw out her little chest and blew a curlicue of beautiful notes that filled the yard.

So rapt was he, Jack only noticed Babs was coming in from school with Pam and Bridgid when she called out to her father. For no one else would the Boss leave his work and walk up to the wire fence. 'Howyeh?' he said, holding his shovel and smiling. 'Did them oul' nuns give yeh a hard time?'

'No, Daddy, we had a gran' day,' Babs said. 'Sister Anthony took us out fer a walk ta see some t'ings on the farm.'

At the mention of the nuns' great estate the Boss's smile faded. 'It's them barren bitches that's got this counthry ruined,' he said bitterly.

'What happened to Jack?' Babs asked. 'Why's he home early?'

'I'll see t'him later,' the Boss said, gloomily.

'Anyway, Daddy,' Babs said, recognising signs of trouble. 'I've gotta go. See yeh.'

'Don't ferget ta getcher bit a oul' homework done before yer tea,' the Boss shouted after her. How he respected education. If only he'd had any. He returned to the squealing pigs and had a mind to shoot the lot of them.

While Babs was engaging her father, Bridgid and Pam, knowing their presence was an intrusion into a private love affair, went through the gate to the kitchen, and slung their schoolbags on the table. Jack sidled nearer to them to share the warmth his sisters brought with them. Their animated, contradictory, accounts of the day sailed over his head.

Bridgid opened the dresser to see what she could gobble before tea. Pam, who had found a peculiar flower on the way home, put it behind her ear, and asked her mother how she looked.

'Dear, dear,' Mary laughed, 'who d'yeh t'ink yeh are? Mitzi Gaynor?'

Pam took the pink plastic mirror from the shelf above the sink, looked at her face from every angle and patted her hair.

'Jasus, will yeh looka'er,' Bridgid muttered through a mouth crammed with fig roll.

Mary had hidden the fig rolls behind a stack of baking tins for a sly treat when there was no one about. 'Can't I keep an'tin' from yeh, yeh greedy oul' sow?' she said good-naturedly.

'I'm sorry, Ma, but I'm bloody starvin',' Bridgid said, going for the last few biscuits and ripping the packet open like a wild animal.

'Oh no, yeh don't,' Mary said, 'they're mine.' She snatched at the biscuits, sending crumbs everywhere.

'Yer man didn't get 'em fer yeh, did he?' Bridgid asked.

'Christ, yer jokin',' Mary said as she scuttled from table to oven and back again.

'What d'yeh t'ink of me now?' Pam asked as she arrived from the bedroom wearing the mothballed fox fur Mary had been married in, and with a beret slanted across her head.

'For Jasus' sake!' Bridgid said, slapping her hands together to get rid of the crumbs.

Pam picked up the mirror again and looked at herself with a keen intensity.

32

JACK WENT BACK to the sand and played half-heartedly as he waited for his punishment. For a big woman, her belly swollen from breeding babies, Mary moved nimbly enough when her husband was around. She had no time for her son now. He would have to stew quietly, awaiting his fate. If the Boss was in a good mood Jack might escape with a smack in the face, but as the Boss was seldom in a good humour, a thrashing was a distinct probability. Jack would soon find out when his father's trilby bounced through the wire towards him.

Mary, the simple meal prepared, hung the embossed kettle over the fire and poked the flames until they licked its black bottom. The Boss liked his tea weak with fresh milk, and was finicky enough to create a scene if it wasn't exactly to his liking. The argumentative children threaded their way through any crossfire as best they could. While the children thrived on queasy fries he kept to the diet of a mannequin - a sprig of cress, a wafer of brown bread, a soft-boiled egg - and kept prodigiously strong on this little bird's food.

'Jack,' Mary called out in her soft Galway brogue. 'Would yeh like a slice a bread an' jam before yer Da comes in?' Jack crept back into the kitchen, his toes barnacled with sand. 'Yeh must try, darlin', ta control yerself, specially in front a the nuns.'

Jack returned warily to the yard, sporting a jammy moustache. He heard his father muttering, 'That bloody woman is no use ta me.'

Jack sidled away from those poisonous heretical words, pulled a wisp of hay from the sagging wet rick and took it to Kitty. The pony tugged at it ferociously, chewing with gums and teeth while waiting patiently to be released from her sweaty harness.

The Boss angrily shovelled food at the pigs' faces, and collected their droppings. Then he deftly removed Kitty's stitched and patched harness and hung it in the shed where he kept everything from old tools to every size of nail and screw. There were shelves for paint tins, bundles of rags, old newspapers, lengths of rope and wire, mole traps and snares. One day, there would be a use for everything.

When the last item of tack was removed from the pony's matted back the Boss levered the cart into a corner and left it with its shafts pointing like an aitch to the sky. 'Here,' he barked, 'take this an' give her a bit of a rub down.' Quick to ingratiate himself, Jack grabbed the wad of straw and gingerly approached the pony, who flattened her ears and made him take a step back. Everyone except the Boss was afraid of Kitty. The old pony was diverted just in time when the Boss kicked a basin of scraps under her nose. She raked the offering with leathery lips and raised her head and grinned. Jack pawed at the barrel-chested pony, feeling her tremble as the spiky straw touched the big veins on her belly.

'That's enough of that,' the Boss growled, 'get up there to the house.' Jack threw the wad away and raced to the kitchen. The pigs were squealing again, still hungry after gobbling up their scanty meal. The Boss, armed with a blackthorn stick, rushed along the line of half-doors and gave each protruding snout a wallop.

Indoors, Babs, Bridgid and Pam were busy helping Mary. The breakfast things had been washed and put away. Now the girls were wiping toddlers' faces, sweeping up and changing the baby. When Bridgid saw Jack, she rushed at him, clutching her wet rag. He whined and flailed ineffectually. Babs changed the baby, its podgy pink legs and arms waving about like an upturned piglet.

Jack watched the yellow-stained nappy, the baby's balls tight and wrinkled as a walnut. 'Do yeh like doin' that?' he asked, forgetting his father for a moment.

Babs picked up the soggy nappy as if it contained something precious. 'Someone has ta do it,' she said. 'Anyway, it's not that long since I was doin' it fer yeh.' Jack looked away. 'Babies like to be clean and full, don't they?' Babs said, nuzzling the infant's belly with her nose.

Jack gasped. His eyes swivelled to focus on the door. He could hear the Boss marching up the concrete path, his wellingtons slapping together ominously.

A bolt slammed, a sack was rammed under the door to keep out draughts. In stockinged feet, silent as a tiger, the Boss sprang. 'T'ought

I'd forgot yeh, eh, yeh litte hoor's melt.' He cuffed his son round the head. 'Feckin' little baby, pissin' yerself. That oul' mother a yer's sp'iles yeh.'

Jack reeled away, doing his screaming act.

The children, led by Babs, slipped past the confrontation to hastily occupy the crude wooden form the Boss had knocked together with six inch nails and old planks. Babs cared about what happened to Jack, and kept an eye on her hopeless, snotty-nosed little brother. Hers was the only face that winced when the flat of her father's hand made a final pistol shot noise that sent Jack sprawling across the floor.

Bridgid was unsympathetic. Herself, not a favourite of the Boss, took her slaps and insults like a man and had no time for weaklings. 'He deserves ev'ry bit he gets, peein' in his pants,' she whispered out of the corner of her mouth as Mary shuffled around helplessly in the background, like an incompetent referee attempting to stop a one-sided contest.

'Fer God's sake,' she screamed with a plate of food in each hand, 'hasn't the poor lad suffered enough. Haven't yeh seen what that oul' bitch done ta him?'

'If yeh'd done yer job right here,' the Boss said, 'there'd be no need fer it.'

'Don't be cursin' in fronta them childher,' Mary protested.

Jack lay on the lino sobbing, the weals on his legs visible, until it was prudent to take his place at the table. The children made room for him, and he quickly gulped down his food before stealing off to the haven of his bed. As he left, tarnished and disgraced, the skirmish he had initiated exploded into all-out war. Oaths filled the kitchen. He heard his mother's voice clattering like the cavalry to his defence, the crash of pots and pans, the discordant music of cutlery cascading against walls, insults raining from every quarter. The other children kept quiet as their parents stood face to face, snarling at each other like rabid dogs. 'Eat up,' Babs whispered to her younger brothers and sisters as she spooned food into the baby who, wide-eyed and open-mouthed, was drinking in the terrible scene.

Jack climbed into bed without praying, and curled up on the soap-scented sheet. Through the wall the battle between his parents rose and fell like the tide washing rocky cliffs, one minute crashing and spraying, the next becalmed and lapping. He heard his mother threatening, as she had so often before, to leave. Life without her would be unbearable for everyone. Jack heard his father's final curses, awful words that must have been his own property because he would let no one else use them.

'Right! That's it,' Mary said, 'yeh've hurt me enough. I'm seein' the priest tomorra about a separation. God, when I t'ink of how yeh begged me ta marry yeh, yeh in yer dandy little suit, yer hair all oiled and curled. Lookit yeh now, baldy and broke, nuttin' but hate in yeh.'

Jack heard his father reply, 'An' yeh, yeh feckin' pile, what did yeh ever do fer me? Yeh were glad of a roof over yer head, a good man ta feed yeh when them hoors from Galway t'rew yeh out ta skivvy fer them oul' ladies in Rat'down Park.'

Babs did the washing-up. Lights were switched off, the fire doused, the parents barged each other like little children as they fought to get to the one small and airless lavatory. Its door crashed against the wall: flesh on wood, bone on flesh.

Jack hid under the blanket listening to his sisters undressing. He heard Bridgid say, 'It's a row an' a half t'night sis. Will yeh listen ta 'em goin' at it. I'm sick of it. That feckin' brudder of ours needs his backside walloped fer bringin' this on our heads.'

'Ah, stop,' Babs said, 'it's not the poor kid's fault. There's somethin' wrong wit' him.'

Jack smiled.

'Me arse,' Bridgid retorted, 'he's just a lazy little fecker.'

Jack's expression under the blankets changed to sad.

Lullabied by the swarm of words, Jack drifted off to sleep. He was up in Heaven with birds and flowers when the door creaked open. 'Jack, Jack,' Babs whispered, 'are yeh awake?'

Jack dreamily turned his face to the presence in the dark room. 'Yeah,' he sighed, 'I am.'

'I jus' wan'ta say it's all right. Daddy's gone ta bed.' Jack felt her small warm hand caress his face as if reading its contours. He smiled and closed his eyes.

33

THE BOSS'S AFFAIR with Babs, his first-born, was gradual. At last, he had found someone worthy of his love. The new love was clandestine, pure and platonic. It manifested itself in shadowy ways. In a man cursed with the need to be cruel, Babs tapped into some unsuspected sensitivity. The Boss's voice softened when she pushed the gate open after school. 'There now,' he'd say, smiling, 'did yeh have a good oul' day?' And Babs would flash her sparkling, dimpled, fruit-eating, smile. Tender and innocent, she drew from the Boss a fierce, potentially dangerous affection.

Babs talked to her Da as if she were really interested in him, demolishing steel walls with her love. The Boss took her to Croke Park. The small girl, all bows and ringlets, stood in the shadow of the burly man who threw his head back and yelled obscenities at players, and at the crowd too if they wanted some. Most of the exchanges were good-natured because the Boss was a different person with Babs, and away from Mary, the squealing pigs, crumpled cats and the smell that hung over the yard. If only he could just go off somewhere and live with Babs, just the two of them, he would have been a happy man. As it was, the occasional match was the only precious time they shared. And if Galway, Mary's county, were the opposition, the tension within the Boss was fevered. His hands shook and his teeth ground. 'Get that country hoor an' smash his feckin' head in!' he'd scream, his voice carrying to the manicured turf. 'Ram yer feckin' hurley down the bastard's t'roat.' With his pale eyes blazing, the Boss leapt above the heads in front of him, roaring, while Babs took the amused glances of the other spectators with an innocent shrug.

On the way home the Boss cursed the beggars who haunted the canal banks. 'Get a feckin' job, yeh lazy melt,' or, to an old lady selling flowers, he'd yell, 'Yeh know what yeh can do with them bloody weeds missus.' If only he could make a sports star out of Babs but, perversely, she showed no interest.

'Worrabout camogie?' he asked as they walked quickly to escape 'the slum hoors', who would rob them of their few coppers.

'I don't wan'ta play camogie,' Babs said with a petulance the Boss admired. The Boss badly wanted a sporting child. If only Babs could play out there on the great pitch in her shorts and boots, her dark hair tied back, his life would have been adorned. As it was, there was nothing he could boast of, no brilliant children, except Babs, no young sports stars in the making, no one with his coordination of eye and foot. It was as if the children, Babs excepted, had inherited Mary's inbred weaknesses. They were all like her in Connaught, the barren land to which Cromwell consigned rebellious peasantry to live off furze and shavings of rock.

The Boss felt trapped inside a cave full of monkeys. The match brought out every ruffian in Dublin. They patrolled the streets around the stadium, hunger in their sly streetwise faces, waiting like packs of wild dogs to pounce on any weaklings who got separated from the milling herd.

The Boss hated people to get too close. He felt insecure in built-up areas. 'C'mon, let's get the hell out a this shagging kip,' he said. With him tugging Babs' arm almost from its socket, they ran to the bus stop, exhaling a breath of relief only when the bus was in Rathfarnham with Landy's Bakery, Cosgrave's the butchers, Jolly's Dairy, the Mascot Sweet Shop and The Yellow House pub.

The following day, when Babs returned home from school, the Boss grabbed her playfully and led her into the kitchen. In the corner stood a brand new camogie stick wrapped in brown paper. 'When yeh've had th'ol' cuppa tea givvit a bitova swing,' he said, his smile friendly and loving.

After tea and a slice of cake from the Boss's private hoard of appetising delicacies which he kept locked up in a stout cupboard, Babs joined her daddy in the yard.

'Hey, watch this,' the Boss laughed as he wrenched the stick from its wrapper. He threw an imaginary ball in the air and made a savage lunge.

'Bejapers that'd be sailin' over the convent beyant be now,' he said with a grin.

Babs, thin and wan, was laughing, too, at the burly figure, his thick arms coppered by years of weather, lustily cracking the invisible ball over the chicken wire. The Boss tenderly offered Babs the stick. She made a feeble, uncoordinated swing. The Boss laughed and tickled her.

He took Babs to a camogie practice but with her gentle disposition, she found it difficult to compete with the fat, manly girls from the farms around. The Boss leapt up and down, trying to curb his natural temptation to spew curses. 'Watch that fat bitch behin' yeh Babs, she'll cut th' ankle off yeh witta swipe.'

But Babs couldn't put her heart into camogie and gradually lost interest. The Boss took the stick, cleaned and oiled it, and put it away. But if he could read the future he would have smashed it to smithereens and thrown the accursed thing on the fire.

34

JACK WAS GROWING and filling out. He tore through brambles after blackberries, birds' nests and balls; skinned his legs on the Boss's crude barbed-wire fencing, and tumbled off hayricks. His body was stretching, yet he was riddled with agonising self-doubt, nerves and chronic shyness - easy meat for bullies like Terry Foley, who would make it to prison before he left his teens.

Jack, snotty, scared and taciturn, was an obvious target for sly pinches in class, kicks and punches in the school toilets and for holding the door shut when he was inside and sniggering at his frightened howls. Jack was 'a cowardy custard, a useless little fecker'. Foley's pinches became rabbit chops, handfuls of holly leaves were pushed down the back of Jack's trousers. Quietly whimpering, Jack endured the pain and humiliation.

Tortured, wet-legged weeks passed into months but Jack never spoke of his nemesis to anyone, least of all to his father. The Boss would side with Foley. And might easily inflict further punishment on a hateful, pathetic creature unable to defend himself in a man's world.

As he grew stronger and independent of his mother, Jack became interested in the wildlife that lived in the fields around the bungalow. He watched the jackdaws perch, beady-eyed, on the shattered oaks in Neary's field, their sequin eyes shining with greed as they contemplated the crusts Mary had thrown down in the garden for the hens. Jack especially loved the daws, their bravery, their cheek. But no matter how many crusts he laid for them, they wouldn't allow him to come nearer than fifty yards before disdainfully flying off, their legs extending, their claws bunching, as they landed lightly on the leafless branches of the oak.

The woodquest's coo also became familiar, as Jack snuggled in his bed listening to the girls murmuring audibly through the thin walls of his room. When up and about in the garden he saw nameless little invaders in flashy epaulettes landing in the apple trees, blending with the pink blossom, green leaves and lichen-fuzzed branches. He learned from Mary they were bullfinches, tits and linnets, a wondrous, colourful family with flashes of yellow, red, green, pink and blue, which for a while turned the dull mud, corrugated iron sties, manure and foul bone heap of garden into something exotic. Jack watched and smiled at their beauty and springy agility.

One day Jack went up to Terry Foley and produced from his bag an old, crumpled *Dandy*. Foley looked at it with amused contempt.

'Dis fer me?' he asked.

Jack nodded.

'Hey, com'ere the lot a yehz.'

Anticipating some fun at Jack's expense, Foley's friends ran towards him.

'Look what Snotty gev me. Isn't dat nice?' Foley held up the dirty comic that Jack had slept with for months. 'What the feck izzit, anyway?' Foley asked. He grabbed the comic, tearing it in half. 'Betcha he's wiped his feckin' arse wit' dis.' And he threw the torn fragments in Jack's face.

Picking up what was left of his present, Foley held it by the corner as if it were diseased, and smiled. 'Yeh poor cunt, yeh've no feckin' brains atall, givin' me dis is on'y goin' ta make it wurse fer yeh. I wouldn' shit on dis.' With that he sprinkled it like confetti over Jack's head.

Jack stared uncomprehendingly after his tormentors as they swaggered off.

When he arrived home Babs was already in the kitchen, her apron on, making little flat cakes decorated with blobs of jam. Jack ran his finger round the mixing bowl, licked it and smiled.

'C'mon out 'ere,' the Boss yelled from the sties, 'an' give me a hand.'

Babs bent down and kissed Jack. 'When yeh come back in I'll have them baked and yeh can have a nice hot wan fer yer tea.'

Jack exhaled, longing to stay and help his big sister kneading that soft dough, it had such a wonderful feel about it.

'Will yeh come out, or do I hav'ta come in there an' bate yeh out?' the Boss roared.

Jack rushed from the kitchen, pulled on his father's discarded boots and clumped down the yard to work.

The heron skimmed over the bungalow and landed softly in the pond in Neary's field. Stepping like a man in glue, beady-eyed, shining, bony beak poised, it waited. Jack loved to see the giant bird. No one knew where it nested, in what tree or bank. It visited when the air was heavy and grey.

One afternoon, Foley and his gang arrived. Like Red Indians they skulked around the cover provided by wildly overgrown bushes. As Jack watched, a hail of stones suddenly descended, hitting the water around the heron like torpedos. Surely the heron was too clever for Foley. Jack waited for it to lift off, squawking its victory. Instead, he saw it limp and floating. Jack rushed to the waterside. Foley was holding the broken heron like an old dowager's dusty fan.

'We go'rim, we go'rim,' Foley yelled, and he galloped back to the Corporation houses bawling out his victory.

35

BABS' EYES, BLUE and bright, highlighted a pretty if pale face. The Boss watched her progress with approving grunts, and all the affection he felt for her, she reciprocated. After school, Babs donned her wellingtons to help him in the sties. There, in the swampy heat of the dung-fermenting day, in the steam of guzzling, squealing pigs, she saw the red miracle of life as piglets spewed in slippery rows from the red crevice of the sow. Her face spotted with the prints of her dirty hands, Babs pawed a fuzz of hair from her eyes and talked to her father when he could spare a moment from tending the piglets as if he were opening presents wrapped in cellophane. There was an uneasy clamour about the yard, the discordant sounds that accompany drudgery. So much effort, so little return.

Jack, small and bandy, would soon have to replace Babs as the Boss's helper, when Babs went on to the big school. The Boss would feel the loss of his daughter and occasionally take out his frustration on his son.

Pam, almost two years younger than Babs, appeared with mugs of tea on a tray, dumped it down and returned briskly to the bungalow to reassure Mary all was well. For in her feverish mind's eye, Mary, was jealous of her husband and Babs. While Babs and her father innocently straddled a straw bale, their faces benign in the tea's mist, enjoying each other's warmth, Mary was at the stove cooking, thanking God her worst fears were not realised. Mary drew the dirty curtain and saw May Nolan passing by with her short skirt and pink cardigan.

'What's wrong wit' a bitch that hasta show her rotten legs offta any man. Tell me that?' she screamed.

Clear-eyed after her 'attack', with her natural kindness returned, Mary guiltily hugged Babs, who had come to the kitchen door, her hands filled with dirty eggs.

'Ah, sure, God an' me's got an understandin',' the Boss scoffed at dinner, picking Babs out from a line of children waiting for a loving sign, 'don't we?' Babs smiled uncomfortably. It was nice to be loved. She had the tips of her fingers on a crumb of it and wasn't going to let go.

'That wan is gettin' too big fer her boots,' Mary whispered. 'Now he's tellin' her t'ings she should'n' be hearin'.' After dinner she would pray in her dark room surrounded by fonts and with plastic saints staring down mutely from the bare walls.

Babs picked at her stew, she had begun to despise the flesh of animals. She wanted them to live out their lives, to see the blood flowing through them, their coats shining. She wanted to hear their friendly sounds, to smell their dung, and to watch them suckle their young. To murder such creatures and then devour their flesh was wrong. She pushed away her plate and reached for a potato, crowded like small, black-eyed beasts in the sooty pot that hung above the flames.

Mary waved her ladle as if to strike. What other mother could conjure up such tasty food out of pigswill? But Babs looked at the dog turds of old grey sheep meat setting in its fatty gravy, and her stomach convulsed.

'Her High an' Mightiness t'inks my cookin' is pizened,' Mary said, her words ending in a growl. 'Grrr.' She glared round at her brood, and they immediately gave her space, but the threat came to nothing more than the terrible scowl.

Finding a corner, Jack looked at his school book and tried to read. The room was packed with quiet strangers. On the mantelpiece, the alarm clock ticked hurriedly. Babs was perched like a frail bird on the Boss's lap. The whites of Mary's eyes darted their way repeatedly as she - bulky, broken and unloved - puffed and hissed with frustration as she tried to thread the Singer's needle. The whir of the sewing machine she pedalled in the corner voiced her unspoken lament. She was needed only for her cooking, her scrubbing, her expertise as the family clothier. Babs had siphoned off any love that had once been hers.

Her daughter's sounds of contentment drummed in Mary's ears as she treadled furiously, the Singer's needle stabbing the cloth, stitching together the cut and shaped pieces of an old blue shirt her sister, the children's Aunt Dolores, had sent from America.

36

'YER DADDY'S GONE ta McGrane's,' Mary said over her glasses as her heavy iron glided over Babs' blouse, flattening it.

'Can I go ta see 'im there?' Jack asked, his voice high-pitched with excitement.

Mary placed the iron on a small square of asbestos. 'Are yeh serious?' she asked, taking Jack's schoolbag and unbuckling its single strap. She removed the empty milk bottle with the sodden brown-paper stopper, and shook out the sandwich crumbs in the yard. From the door Jack watched the brown hen, that laid in a box beside the bungalow, tilt her head from side to side before warily approaching, clucking softly. Briskly, she pecked at the crumbs, her beak tapping like a blind man's cane on the concrete.

The thought reverberated like an explosion around Jack's silly cranium. He would walk to McGrane's. It was a thousand miles away at least and the route very dangerous. He only wished he had Black Bob from the *Dandy* with him, but he would do it just the same. It would please his father, show him his son was, after all, worthy.

Now that he had decided, spectres began to leap about in Jack's head. It terrified him to think about the disasters that could happen on that perilous and lonely journey. He had never gone anywhere before without Babs' guiding hand in his. Everything scared him. He even shivered when he crossed the road. Out there were noisy animals with frothy teeth and claws like fish-hooks. People were frightening too.

Mary was surprised but as pleased as she could be. The lad could do it. If only she had shown a bit of spunk in those early days when she'd had a bit of sway over her husband. She was now no more than a doormat for the Boss to wipe his dirty boots on. The courage had been thrashed out of her. She was worn down by constant verbal lashings; insults had made her feel stupid. Mary knew how it was to feel worthless.

She took her son's face in her hands. 'Yes, yes, darlin', a'course yeh can go.' But she was worried. The road was narrow and dangerous, there were cars out there without brakes or licences. But Jack could do it; he needed to. He was her favourite now that she'd lost Babs to the Boss.

It's two miles,' Mary reminded him.

Jack's expression changed. 'Two miles,' he said, moving closer. Could he find his way? It was an enormous challenge.

'Putcher runners on,' Mary said, 'the day's dry, yeh could trot there in no time.' She pressed a chunk of cake into her son's hand and washed the dried snot off his face.

Jack crossed the bridge, and soon the bungalow was lost behind the willows. When he looked back his heart beat faster. At Sheridan's garage he slowed to watch the men work on their baby Fiats. Cars without wheels, smashed up, cannibalised, forlorn, and abandoned, sat rusting among the nettles. Blackberries crawled over discarded axles and gearboxes, into the dead ends of Essolube bottles. Sheridan, in his grease-streaked overalls, a cigarette between his lips, a spanner in his hand, wheeled himself on a trolley under a little car jacked up at the front. Jack envied the mechanic, and his cigarette, delving into the oily mystery of cars. Ruffling the ivy that bound the coping of the wall, Jack saw a man sitting in a car, trailing blue smoke. It was Freddy, Sheridan's uncle, a clownish grease spot on his nose. He was revving a repaired engine. As he wiped his hands like a surgeon after a successful operation, Freddy spotted Jack.

'Howyeh?' the man said.

It was enough to send Jack scampering away, heading south. Soon, he was a mile from home, lost in the doings of every bird, animal or fish he inspected in hedge, tree or pool.

He reached a stretch of road darkly canopied by bare-knuckled branches. Old oaks, interlocking and interdependent, leant against and scratched each other like grotesque old men with fleas. Jack looked up through the branches at the filleted sky. The road was smeared with rotted leaves. Jack ran to the light like a grounded moth, past the gravelly ribbon that led up to Lady Moore's mansion. Panting, he paused by the gates, remembering treasures lay beyond the sweeping drive. Racehorses, thin-legged and coquettish, grazed behind white fencing. Jack gazed past the lodge at the gate, as it cowered under green laurel.

He could see the mountains, coiled and asleep in the distance. Up there somewhere his father was working. Jack must get there before the darkness apprehended him. The Grange Golf Club's wide gates accepted cars like the mouth of a famished giant. Jack paused to watch scented gentlemen and their powdered ladies in bright colours, take their clubs out of large boots. In awe, he spotted the putting green, smooth as a carpet outside the clubhouse. A lady walked on to the tee dressed in a symphony of yellow ochre and, with a palsied swing sent the ball scuttling like a mouse. A lad from the Corporation houses carried her bags.

Jack savoured the manicured course, was amused by the yellow flags fluttering on distant greens, and the players parading across the green canvas as if they were in a procession, silent and colourful.

'Oi! You! Fuck off!'

Bred to obey orders, Jack slid from the wall taking the skin off his knee. He ran. The quiet countryside seemed full of madness.

The tarmac shimmered as Jack headed for Kilmashogue. He dawdled to look down upon the mysterious chimneys of a house built below the road. He could see into its rooms, the gleaming furniture catching the sun, the beds, all white and made. In a tiled kitchen a woman in a spotless apron was washing up, her hands in yellow gloves.

A black dog bounced out of the door and gambolled on a lawn without daisies. The dog gnawed and tossed a ball, its coat shining. Jack heard the woman call to it. Accepting a bowl of food, the dog wagged its tail. Jack heard the woman murmur and saw her stroke its fat, vibrating back. A child's red swing stood neglected in a corner of the garden. There was neither a scrap heap nor a mountain of rotting bones.

The woman looked up. Jack saw her pale face before ducking behind a seedling growing from a crevice in the wall. 'I see you chum.' The brittle English voice rose up from the garden. The dog stopped slavering over his food and began to bark. 'I'll call the police,' the woman threatened. 'What a cheek, you naughty boy, spying on me like that.'

The dog, enraged with excitement now, was leaping up and down impatiently, waiting for a command. 'Go, get him boy,' the woman shrieked, her voice seeming to echo like thunder in the lane.

Anchored by fear, Jack didn't move until the dog was halfway up the drive, its head flattened by speed, its tail straight out behind like a rudder. When his brain finally gave a belated command, his legs, as if trapped in glue, slowly responded. He could hear the dog's claws grating on the gravel as it sped, open-jawed, towards him. Jack fled. The dog skidded to a halt at its boundary, thwarted in its mission to tear the intruder apart. Looking back, Jack saw the woman and her dog both mouthing their protest. The woman shook her fist.

Jack was tiring, the mountains seemed further away than ever. There were no houses. He passed a shack with peeling red paint behind a wild hedge on a patch of waste ground. Creeping by on tiptoe, he was almost past when he heard a chilling cry. 'Who the feck are yeh? An' worra yeh doin' here? Spake up!' Partly hidden behind blackberry bushes was an old man with a hat pulled low over his ears, and a red rag round his neck. He staggered on to the road, his face tortured, his eyes half closed. 'I astcha wha'cha doin' here?' the old man demanded. His eyes were rolling; only the whites were visible in their rheumy sockets. 'Who are yeh, yeh connivin' little bastard?'

Jack's mouth worked soundlessly. The old man went into a spasm and as Jack watched, he saw the old face break into a broad gin. The old man suddenly began to shake a trouser leg. As Jack watched a large turd rolled on to the road like a baked potato.

With an animal cry, Jack bolted past the old man and away, leaving him staring unsteadily after him.

He ran by Kilmashogue church, a gaunt place where Godless Protestants went to pray. Mary warned her children against going inside Protestant churches, there were devils there who would tear out their lights. Jack imagined long-tailed, half-men springing about like monkeys with English accents. He passed the cemetery full of Protestants rotting under their grand monuments. It served them right. A weasel on the wall, probably a Protestant devil in disguise, hissed at Jack.

He ran on until, behind a high wall, he heard the dull thumps of a hammer. Looking up he saw his father, strong and unafraid, hammering slates on to McGrane's farmhouse. As he stumbled down the overgrown drive Jack wanted to yell, 'Daddy! Daddy! I made it. I'm here, if yeh on'y knew what I've been t'rough.' Then a voice, so familiar Jack nearly cried with relief, growled, 'What kep' yeh?' From his vantage point the Boss had seen his son some way off. He teetered on the ladder, his neck a red, muscular twist, as he stared down with lifeless eyes.

'Wot in Christ's name are yeh doin' here, yeh bloody little gobshite. Who in the name a Jasus let yeh out.' Jack looked down at the boots that had transported him safely through his glorious adventure. 'Yeh shubby at home mindin' the place!' Jackdaws peeked from the chimney to see the reason for the commotion. 'Jasus Christ, that bloody woman putcha upta this. Wait 'n' I see her, the stupid pile.'

'She didn't,' Jack whispered.

'Wot!' The Boss wasn't used to interruptions.

'It was my own idea,' Jack wheezed, his hands curling.

'I've gorra good mind ta get down there an' give yeh a bloody pastin', yeh connivin' little washer.' The abuse was music. Jack watched his father stick the hammer into his leather belt like a gun and quickly climb down the long swaying ladder to the ground. He wanted to run up to him, throw his arms around that thick waist, but his father wouldn't like that.

'C'mere an' listen,' the Boss said, his voice dipping into the conspiratorial tone he used when something was up. 'Kitty's in the yard beyant.' Jack followed his father's nod and saw the pony's tail flicking at flies, her feet in piles of manure, a frothy pool of urine nearby.

'I lef' 'er there deliberately tibby nexta them mangolds. Listen,' the Boss said, his voice almost disappearing, 'put as manya them mangolds in the car' as yeh can, an' keep 'em covered. An' watch out for anyone comin', yeh hear me now? That oul' shitehawk O'Casey the milker, is roun' somewhere. If he catches yeh we're in throuble.'

Quietly and carefully, Jack filled the cart with fat, yellow mangolds from under the straw in McGrane's yard. It was wonderful to be under his father's protection again, stealing. He had made the journey. He'd proved himself.

37

THROUGH STORIES TOLD around the fire Mary shared nightmares from her past with her children when the Boss was at Confession or on one of his many forays into the surrounding villages looking for anything not nailed down.

Jack closed his jotter to move nearer the cluster of children hemming their mother in on all sides. Glad to be so favoured, Mary sat smiling wildly on her armchair and wrapped as many as she could of her brood in her fat arms. The children gazed up at her, the youngest on her soft lap.

'Now, what sorta story would yehz like?' Mary asked wickedly.

'A murdher,' Bridgid shouted.

'Yeah, a murdher,' echoed the other children.

'All right then,' Mary said, 'if yehz insist.' She was thrilled by the fear already alive in her children's eyes.

'Durin' the throubles,' Mary began, 'a woman in me own village in Galway was accused a concealin' an IRA man on da run. A lorry-load a Tans druv up an' surrounded the farmhouse.' The children pressed closer. 'But on the way there they'd stopped off at Allen's pub an' got fluthered. Wan a them gev the order ta get back inta the lorry. 'First, let's pay the bill,' the Captain said, an' he took out his pistol an' shot all the bottles off a the shelf. The udders drew their weapons an' fired holes in the walls. They go'rinta their lorry an' druv t'rough the night till they saw the light of the farmhouse. The soldiers crawled up ta the windas, and the Captain knocked on the door and shouted, 'We believe you're harbourin' IRA criminals in this house.'

A woman opened up. 'Is it criminals yehz're afther?' she asked. 'Well, the on'y criminals in this counthry is yerselves.'

The children laughed with Mary. 'Then a terrible t'ing happened.'

As one, the children's expressions changed to fear. 'The soldiers looked at the woman and looked at each other, an' they dragged her out ta the back a the lorry, an' bate her wit' pieces of wood an' straps an' t'ings. She didn't have an'tin' to tell so they took her back inta a field an' tortured her.' The children stared, wild-eyed. The baby started to cry.

'What did they do then?' Babs asked, a quiver in her voice.

'Well she was bleedin' and naked,' Mary said with relish. 'They t'rew her on the ground an' wanna them found a big owl steel door, an' he covered her wittit an' they jumped up and down till the weight burst her skin an' her poor ribs came out.'

Bridgid threw her hands to her mouth. 'Was she screamin'?' she asked incredulously.

'A course she was, an' covered in blood, God help her.'

'Jasus, Mary an' Joseph,' Bridgid said.

'Stop that,' Mary said. 'The worse t'ing was there was still life in the poor crature when they found her five days afther. The magpies was afther pickin' her poor eyes out.'

'Christ!' Bridgid exclaimed.

'There's no need fer that,' Mary said. 'But the funny t'ing is the man on the run was miles away. Got clean away,' she finished, her lips pressing together like a bullfrog. 'There now,' Mary said, 'wot didya t'inka that?'

'Horrible,' Babs said. Upset by such tales of horror, pain and suffering, Babs slipped unnoticed from the tangle of limbs that surrounded her mother and went to her room. There she whined, 'God, why does Mammy hav'ta tell such terrible stories? The poor woman. God help her.' She imagined the maggots crawling in the victim's flesh, and felt her supper slithering up her throat. Humans were so cruel. They were mad, mad, mad, mad!

Jack had crawled under the table and unwittingly looked up at his mother's bare thighs and the gap in between, through which he and his brothers and sisters had all slid into the peculiar mystery called life. He saw his mother's feet shift uneasily on the floor as if talking. Suddenly, there was pressure on the broken shoes, squeaking and bending at the lace holes as Mary stood up and they endured her weight.

'C'mon childer, 'tis time fer yer beds,' she said. Welded together with fear the younger children grabbed at her until she wrenched them off.

Dazed, the children went to their cold rooms, while Mary filled a galvanised basin with hot water. When she had the room to herself, for Mary was painfully modest, she washed by the fire, her big blue-veined breasts lolling and swinging to her waist.

Babs returned, giving her mother a fright.

Mary covered herself. 'What do yeh wan'ta be spyin' on me fer? Is it ta tell yer man?'

Suddenly, Mary whipped away the towel. 'Go on, look,' she said. Her hands reached out and she cried like a child suddenly grown old. She was terrifying, like a damaged refugee from some awful war. 'Tell him I love him, too,' she cried.

Quietly sobbing, Babs stumbled to her room.

38

BABS LATHERED HER body in the simple tub that filled one half of the tiny bathroom. She soaped the tangle of hair between her legs, the tufts under her arms and the round soft breasts. Her hands were scratched and strong like a man's, but her body bore the confirmation of an almost mature woman. She looked down at herself. Before she knew it, her skin would be creased and dry, her breasts lolling like her mother's, her belly filled out and sagging. Age would eat like rust across the face staring calmly at her from the hand mirror on the bath. She sluiced herself all over with clean cold water, dried herself and dressed.

Babs examined her face in the wardrobe mirror. There never was an uglier person, she thought. Her nose was long and pointed. She tweaked it, making it waggle in the middle. There was a mole on her cheek. She stretched her neck, reading her features, when the Boss appeared with tea and biscuits and closed the door.

They jumped when the door burst open.

Mary stood there. 'Well?' she demanded.

'Well wot?' the Boss snarled, kicking the door closed with his slippered foot. Mary pushed from the other side again and with a great fat shoulder succeeded in forcing the door open. 'What the feck's go'rinta yeh?' the Boss asked, a sick grin on his face. If he wanted he could smash the door, her and all with it, into a heap of broken wood, hinges, flesh and bone in the hallway.

'Why are yehz always lockin' me out?' Mary pleaded, her voice breaking. Babs took Mary's fat hand and led her into the room. Her mother was crying silently, attempting to wipe away the tears with the back of her hand. The children gathered round.

'It's nuttin, Mammy,' Babs said, 'nuttin' at all.'

'What's wrong wit' yer woman?' the Boss asked when they returned to the kitchen.

'Nuttin',' Babs said. 'Leave her alone.'

That night Mary made the Boss a nice big mug of cocoa and two slices of wholemeal toast. Maybe he would love her like he used to do, now that Babs had rejected him.

Babs had never known what it was like to have a boyfriend. The Boss would kill any male threatening his ragged little harem. By the light of the small paraffin lamp Babs wrote down her feelings to try to understand them. She hid the letter in the bottom of a drawer where not even the Boss would find it. Her head in shadow, her eyes open, she struggled with her thoughts. Next door, her father lay in bed. He too was awake, running the disappointments of the day through his mind. Fit to bursting, Babs tried to talk to Pam. Her sister swept her eyelashes with a tiny brush, pulled a face in the mirror and sighed. Bridgid trundled into the room and it went quiet.

'I know wha'cha talkin' about,' she said. 'Have yeh seen a lad's mickey yit?'

'What!' Babs laughed, 'Jasus, Mary an' Joseph, what d'yeh t'ink I am?'

'Bur it's natchral,' Bridgid said, running her long tongue slowly along her lips.

'Jasus, don't let Daddy hear yeh say that,' Babs said, 'or we'll all be killt.'

'I've had Jack's in me hand loadsa times,' Bridgid said. She looked at her sisters and they laughed. 'I did, really.'

But no one believed her.

39

THE GREEN CLOCK ticked on the mantelpiece, with the sound of bare feet on lino, Bridgid slipped out of the room. Swiftly muttering her prayers she stripped, letting her baby fat breasts fall as she pulled her nightshirt over her head and took off her knickers. Lying on the cold sheets she wondered if Jack would remember the arrangement.

Minutes ticked away on the big clock in the hall before he drifted silently to her bedside. Bridgid pulled back the bedcovers, took his cold hand and placed it on her breast. With her left hand she unbuttoned his trousers and kneaded his tiny penis. She then directed her brother's hand to the downy hair between her legs. Jack caressed it until it was damp. With a grunt Bridgid opened her legs and briskly guided his hand up and down, milking him furiously and in vain. Jack's mind was spinning.

'Ohoooh,' Jack groaned. 'No, no, no.'

Bridgid's fingers were like lightning, the bed groaning and banging against the wall.

Suddenly convulsing, she pushed him away and curled up, moaning. Jack waited, a quiet dark lump, for further instructions.

'Go away,' Bridgid said, 'but put yer mickey in first.' Jack obeyed and just avoided the first phalanx of toilet users bursting down the hall.

Hugging herself Babs walked down the dark garden. The apple trees stood in mute rows, their butchered limbs held aloft like beggars.

The Boss appeared, his torn cardigan smelling of pigs. 'What's on yer mind?' he asked.

'Nuttin',' Babs said. 'Why?'

The Boss's voice was soft. 'Them oul' nuns is not workin' yeh too hard? Otherwise I'll go over there an' see them.'

'It's all right, Daddy,' Babs said, 'ever't'in' is great.' Her teeth chattered.

'Will yeh c'mon in out a the cold fer Christ's sake,' the Boss said sharply, taking her by the arm and spinning her round.

Mary's shadow filled the kitchen window.

'C'mon,' the Boss said. 'A cup a cocoa, it's a sweet dish on these cold evenin's.'

They returned to the kitchen. The Boss filled a saucepan with milk and lit the gas. Feeling the distance between them, Babs just sat quietly as they sipped the hot drink. The Boss collected the used cups and took them to the sink. Babs slipped away with a murmured, 'G'night'.

Mary's lamp was a thin rod of light under her door as Babs passed. 'Good-night, Mammy,' she called but Mary did not respond. Babs prayed for her mother and father, and for her little brothers and sisters.

The Boss padded through the bungalow in stockinged feet checking every door and window, slamming bolts shut like rifle fire. Outside, an early autumn mist rose like smoke from the river.

With the Boss in a rare genial mood, Babs persuaded him to permit a family trip to the mountains to picnic or pick blackberries the next day. So seldom did happiness intrude into the family's misery that the feeling of joy was contagious and the children all galloped to bed almost whooping with expectation.

Next morning, the mountains, distantly basking in the sun, were visible from the bungalow's windows. Their heathered flanks gave them a hazy purple look in summer. In winter they were brooding and rain-swept, or glistening with snow.

Her self-esteem bolstered by the touching enthusiasm of her children, Mary was up early to make apple tarts as big as dustbin lids and frost them with caster sugar. Bridgid peeled and sliced the apples. Earwigs ran amok on the kitchen table and tumbled on to the floor, some dragging their half severed bodies behind them. Bridgid screamed.

'Put a foot on them hoors 'fore they 'scape under the dresser!'

Jack dragged Kitty's tack out of the shed for polishing. Pam fed the chickens, then groomed the pony. 'We mustn't be seen goin' t'rough Ballyboden wit' a dirty ould horse,' she said.

'Feck 'em,' the Boss grumbled, 'hungry hoors wit' their noses against the windas.' But he laid out a tin of motor oil and a brush for Kitty's hooves.

The mare looked splendid in the September sun, coat gleaming, horny feet rasped, mane plaited, brasses catching the morning light. Pam cut big earthy onions from the garden, their pungency bringing tears to her eyes. A choice piece of chicken breast was wrapped for the Boss.

'Will yehz hurry up,' he yelled. The children, raggedly happy, babbled about the journey. Blackberries were unique, a gift from God. The Boss pounded into the kitchen swishing his whip. 'If we're goin' atall will yehz hurry up!'

Most of the children sat waiting on the cart behind Kitty's swishing tail and the Boss, a row of reversed caps sticking out like platypus tails. Pushing, shoving and whispering oaths, Bridgid climbed in. Then Mary arrived, grunting as she tried to raise one heavy, varicosed leg on to the step. Hands reached down to give her a pull. 'Hope yeh 'membered ta hose down the cart?' she said breathlessly. After it had transported several loads of guts from the abattoir and manure to Lamb's raspberry fields, it stank.

'I didn't hear yeh offerin',' the Boss said.

Babs had leapt to claim the seat beside her father. Mary preferred the squash in the back, feeling the warmth of her children round her. Shaking with nerves she had her rosary within her fist, small silver crucifixions dangling and swishing with the rhythm of the cart.

The steel-rimmed wheels rattled over the bridge. Kitty swung left, heading for the city, but the Boss was ready for her and put such power into his tug on the opposite rein that the pony was forced, open-jawed, with eyes rolling, to turn for the mountains. Mary, wearing a hat for the occasion, tucked a sack about her legs. And the Boss had chosen the cleanest of his grease-streaked trilbies.

Kitty trotted willingly, although the load weighed heavily on her skinny quarters. The Boss flicked his whip angrily. They passed Rathfarnham. Green in parts, it was a friendly place where kids fished, climbed trees and robbed. New houses gathered on the horizon, waves of concrete gobbling up the timeless scenery. Once a familiar sight, the pony and cart raised second glances from parishioners going to Church or pub. One man, with slicked-back hair and a cigarette between his fingers, waved.

'Grand day,' the Boss said pleasantly and raised his hat, but after they'd passed by he muttered, 'Who's that gobshite?'

The children had the temerity to giggle at their father's drollery.

With plodding ease the miles unravelled. Soon the pony's hide was soapy with sweat. The Boss lowered his whip. Kitty snapped at overhanging branches and snatched at dandelions by the roadside. When stone walls gave way to tall hedges the Boss reined her to a halt. The cart emptied, folded knees were stretched, bottoms sore from bouncing on bolt heads were gently touched. Mary spread an old oilskin over the thistles, and Bridgid helped her unload. Babs took a party off to scout for blackberries. The Boss secretly urinated. Mary spread the food, insects homed in to investigate. 'Why do they wan'ta ate our food when God has provided for them?' Mary asked with a gummy smile. It was rare to see her so happy. Her children gathered round her. Bridgid helped her mother distribute the food. Pam wandered off to feast in silence on the panoramic hills. Jack gazed through his fringe at the powerful and silent scene and breathed audibly.

The Boss's fire took off with a fierce crackling. Soon smoky tea was handed round. Hands grabbed, laughter rippled. Trees stood by without a murmur, stone-chats perched on furze and embroidered the day with song. A disturbed hare stood gawking for a moment before shooting up the steep hill-face. The food vanished quickly, tea leaves were wrung dry and the sun slid upwards. Now to work, stealing berries from the bushes' protective thorns.

'Take a jam jar apiece,' the Boss yelled, 'spread out, strip them all, even the green wans.'

Mountain berries, small and sweet, were plucked; dresses were snagged and scratched legs leaked blood. As heads bobbed among bushes, hair was caught as arms stretched to capture elusive fruit.

Pam was dreaming of James Dean, her tongue blue from eating.

'That wan's afther atin' all hers,' Bridgid confirmed.

The Boss, loading furze for kindling on to the cart, growled. 'But she'll be the first ta grabba slice a' pie when yer woman makes it.'

Jack picked slowly, the thought of his mother's pie making his mouth water.

All containers filled, the pony trotted home, flicking her ears, eager to roll in the grass. The birds were shadows as they flew to roost. In the bouncing cart, blackberries glistened like a million malevolent black eyes. As the cart swayed into the village, boys leaning on bikes jeered. They were the new arrivals, children whose parents drove cars and bought the houses that had swallowed the fields. 'Heigh-ho, Silver!' one shouted. Another in falsetto gave a rebel yell.

The Boss reined in the cart and sprang to the ground. The kids brazened it out. Slick arrivals from the city, they were not going to run away from a tramp. As the Boss approached casually, one boy dashed for safety, another mounted his bike. The third stood his ground and was the surprised recipient of a bloody nose as the Boss caught him with a punch. The lad cried. It was an odd sound coming from such a well-built young man.

Jack smiled. If only he could be like his father. No one would dare stand up to him then.

'Yeh wouldn' do that ta someone yer own size,' one boy shouted from the safety of a hundred yards. 'I'll get me father fer yeh.'

'Get who yeh like yeh little shite,' the Boss roared as he strutted back to the cart and whipped Kitty into a gallop.

'Yeh're nuttin' but a dirthy bully,' Mary said, her ill-fitting false teeth clenched. Babs kept hearing the smack of bone on gristle and remembering the blood spurting from the boy's nose. The day had ended badly.

Babs suddenly felt sick. She sat with her hands on her lap. She was ready to go, anywhere, but where? Maybe Aunt Dolores would have her in America, but that was a long shot. The cart's wheels rumbled across the bridge. The Boss issued orders in his hard voice. The gates closed, to Babs it was as if a drawbridge had descended, separating her from the real life that went on outside the little bungalow. As she helped Mary unload, she watched Jack, a spectre in the yard, helping his father feed the squealing pigs.

What would become of him if she left?

40

JACK FELT THE throb of nature deeply, without books to guide him he taught himself by watching the tits in the stone wall flitting in and out of the tiny crevice like yellow-and-blue bumblebees. He saw the male, his mate safely incubating her eggs, chirping as if boasting on a blossomy branch of the apple tree. From behind the hayrick he twisted his greasy fringe and smiled. The dank half acre of garden was a wildlife haven. Crows swooped down like bombers to strafe the yard with beady eyes. If their luck was in, they might nab a filthy crust the hens had dropped. Starlings swaggered fearlessly among the bigger birds. Sparrows, quiet as mice, hopped about like little cripples, waiting for the bigger birds to miss a crumb.

The wall of trees the Boss had, over the years, planted for privacy couldn't keep out the birds. As they squabbled to survive, their presence brought hope to the grey yard. Birds were neither distrustful nor complaining. They didn't ridicule or hurt him. They brought something innocent and magical into his windowless existence. Every day the birds visited the dirty yard. Jack delighted in their antics. How he wished he could fly with them up to the highest bough of the old sally tree and see the river Glin as it streamed silvery below, peacefully curling through Neary's farm.

In Neary's field guinea fowl rasped. Jack knew all about the grey bird with the wagging red wattles. Like the Romans, he too had eaten the guinea fowl's coffee-coloured eggs and tasted her flesh. Their sound carried like a rusty hinge in the breeze. One hen laid her eggs in a hedge. The nest lay hidden for weeks while Jack searched. He observed the little helmeted hen bobbing through the long grass. At last, he tracked her down, having flattened a path through the wet cow parsley. The bird fled screaming into the trees. In a damp depression he found a dozen warm eggs. In her native land her eggs would have hatched on their own in scorching soil. In Rathfarnham it rained, and the sodden bird miserably deserted her damp nest.

Jack robbed the nest and took the eggs home to slip under a broody hen in a box in the bathroom. The hen, her feathers risen, squatted until yellow beaks began to batter weakly on the walls of the eggs. The imprisoning shells and soon the bathroom resounded to chirping and clucking. The hen, a fussing foster mother, with beak ready, threatened Jack's hand as he placed bread and milk beside her.

For a day or two the downy chicks' tiny hearts kept beating. Then, one by one, they succumbed to the sound of the rain beating against the window. Jack crouched on the cold floor, watching them die.

Soon, the torture was almost over. The last weak puff of life had wafted from every chick except one. Every morning before school, he scrutinised the red hen as she struggled to give her all to the doddery brown blob that lay curled and stiff in its bed of straw. Jack pretended he wasn't crying. The guinea hen grew and prospered. Sometimes, she perched on the pile of scrap iron, filling the serenity of the evening with her rough voice. Only darkness, clasping a dewy hand over the bird's misery, stifled its lament.

'The same feckin' guinea fowl is a wasta time,' the Boss said, as he collected the straw and droppings of the old nest to stuff into the boiler's crimson maw.

When the sun was going down, Jack sat by the weir watching the water polish the rocks. Below the weir a bronze surge was turning the deep pool into a fiery cauldron. Splashes leapt like fireflies. A young heron circled, drifting and wheeling, its granny-grey legs tucked up like old underwear. It flapped over the pensive boy below. Jack took his boots off and gasped at the cold of the water, his toes like slugs in the soft mud. He watched the heron swoop again. Speckled trout swarmed restlessly in the clear pool. With a harsh KRANK! the heron landed and immediately adopted the stiff walk of an old man, carefully placing one long leg in front of another as if feeling the cold.

It would remain until Jack went indoors, then it would hypnotise the fish to swim between its scaly legs to be gathered like flowers. Then it flapped upwards, carrying olive trout to some unknown nest. From behind the window Jack watched it rise like a small pterodactyl, filling the silence with the beating of its wings.

As darkness invaded the house the Boss allowed the light to be switched on as if he were the Mayor of Blackpool. Jack fiddled with his fringe and waited for the newspaper while his sisters made ready for bed.

41

ONE SATURDAY, THE Boss was at McGranes fixing something. At home nobody was crying, and Bridgid was taking Jack to visit Aunt Molly and Granny for tea. Molly was the Boss's sister. Like him, she was going bald. Like him, she was nasty. She had twisted hips and wasn't married. The Boss hated her and the feeling was emphatically mutual.

'That feckin' woman's got a filt'y tongue,' the Boss always said.

Aunt Molly swore like a trooper, but she made big cakes which Jack loved. She had learned her cooking while in service, working for 'an oul' lady with a bloody big garden'. Mrs Pollock got a kick out of helping the poor and the ignorant. She gave Aunt Molly big bones filled with marrow to take home and spread on bread.

'That lady mus'be a saint,' the Boss always said.

Aunt Molly lived in a cul de sac with her mother. None of the neighbours spoke to her, mainly because she was a troublesome loudmouth. And she wouldn't want to talk to them anyway, she said.

When Bridgid towed Jack around the corner and into the road, Aunt Molly's big arse stirred among the flowers in her tidy front garden. Looking over her shoulder for signs of vibrating lace curtains, Aunt Molly told the children, 'I've made a lovely big fruit cake fer yehz,' as she shooed them indoors.

The hallway was gloomy. While they waited for their aunt to change out of her wellingtons, Bridgid examined a framed photograph on a crescent-shaped table. It showed a nice young man sitting on a log. The lad's smile penetrated the fly dirt on the glass.

'Go on, ask me again who it is,' Aunt Molly said, her hand on the brass knob. 'Yehz always ask me,' she sighed, 'but I'm not sayin''. Ask yer ould fella. That git's never backward in comin' forward when it comes ta p'isonin' his poor sister's name.' Aunt Molly had a bastard son who drowned while swimming in a quarry. The boy's useless death had destroyed her.

Jack's Granny appeared at the sound of voices. She was ancient, like some lethal reptile with crinkly skin and a gummy, air-sucking mouth. Her husband, the Boss's father, had been a useless drunk who drove his gig to the pub and spent the family's money on filling his cronies with porter. Drinking till he was paralytic, he was invariably tossed into the gig and lay there splayed out in a dead faint, as the pony's rump was slapped so it set off and drag him home. The old man, like most feckless bastards, lived long. His legacy was poison and poverty. The seeds were sown.

But all that was far from Jack's mind as he contemplated the cakes on the table.

'Well, there y'ar,' Aunt Molly said grouchily as she noticed her mother shuffling in.

Her old eyes, bulging like a toad's, swivelled redly in their crimson sockets. 'Well?' the old woman enquired sourly. 'What have yehz brought me? Didn't that bloody divil ovva father a' yours give yeh a dhrop ta wet me whistle?'

Bridgid handed over the baby Power's. The old woman fumbled with the pink wrapping, screwed off the little gold top, then held the miniature bottle at arm's length, testing the colour against the bright shaft of sunlight pouring through her curtains. 'Yis, I t'ought so,' she snarled, pressing her shrivelled lips together. ''Tis the usual half water.'

Aunt Molly, nodding her agreement, told the children, 'Your father's a tight-fisted ould bollocks.' As she added a beautiful looking cake to the spread on the tablecloth, Aunt Molly sighed and shook her head. 'Even fer his poor ould mother that bastard hasta water the drop a Power's. If yehz on'y knew how this poor oul' hoor looks forward to the droppa malt. May Jasus an' his Blessed Mother fergive him.'

Molly ordered the old woman to divide the contents of the tiny bottle. 'Would yehz childer like a raspberryade while we ould ladies take our med'cin?' she asked with a screwed smile.

Bridgid nodded. Jack disappeared under the table after Aunt Molly's fluffy old tom. The cat mewed bad-temperedly before crawling off to settle under the dresser, leaving Jack to suck the bleeding scratches on his hands.

Bending her arthritic body and gasping with the effort, Aunt Molly poked the fire until it spat stars. The tea table looked gorgeous. Bridgid drooled and fidgeted. Several kinds of cake, tons of biscuits; a blackberry and apple tart, wobbling jellies. Jack reappeared and jumped up and down trying to see everything. Aunt Molly poured tea in steamy, amber spurts into small china cups while Granny chewed a feathery cup cake with her gums, her blood-flecked eyes staring. Bridgid reached for more.

Aunt Molly nagged through a spattering of crumbs. Wiping a scar of cream from her chin, she launched into another diatribe. This time against her other brother, Liam, the big racehorse trainer. 'That shagger hasn't set foot inside our door since he was up fer the Phoenix Park races,' she snapped. 'His poor ould mother is sittin' here, dyin', an' the divil bit do we get from that little scutther.' Uncle Liam, who made a comfortable living out of racing, owned the house his mother and sister lived in.

'Yer aunty's right,' the old woman growled, spinning her pink-veined eyes like a fruit machine. 'Not wort' a happort' a shit.'

Aunt Molly said, 'that's fine talk in fronta them childer.'

The children were too busy eating to listen as words flew round their heads like dandelion seeds in a summer breeze. The children ate and ate until they were packed with food.

'An' how's yer poor mother?' Aunt Molly asked. 'That mean little shite has her druv insane. Does she still be havin' the hallucinations?'

Local scandal flew around the table, as Aunt Molly chewed over and savoured each rancid titbit of it.

'An' you,' Aunt Molly's glazed eye settled on Jack. 'Has the cat gotcher tongue?'

Jack tried to think of something to say, but failed. He rubbed a foot along the curve of a chair leg.

'All right, don't talk ta yer aunty after yer loverly tea an' all. I don't know what's got into childer today. Malicious little bastards,' she concluded.

The clock pounded seven. The children were hurried into the hall. It was cold outside, and smelt of evening descending.

'Hurry up,' Aunt Molly said, 'it's bloody freezin' here an' me standin' wit' me t'in frock on.' As she shoved them into the street a sharp gust hissed from behind the pub, wiping the colour from their cheeks.

Bridgid held her brother's hand as they walked home.

'Jasus Christ,' Aunt Molly said, 'didya see the way the paira them demolished the lovely tay I made? That bowsie starves them poor t'ings.'

The old woman nodded miserably.

'God above, they left wan bit a the Dundee,' Aunt Molly said, gleefully, and her hand closed on the almond encrusted slice. Cramming it into her mouth she chewed with pleasure, her voice still for a moment.

42

MARY PUSHED BACK the faded curtain, swept the dead insects into her wrinkled palm and wiped the fly-dirt from the sill with a wet rag. The small window above her head was open. Through it the strong smell from the pigsties assaulted her senses. 'Bad cess to the same pigs,' she muttered, as she chased a spider into a crevice and dabbed it to death. On hot days, the stench from the yard was nauseating. It insinuated itself into her pores. Mary, her face drawn like the Turin shroud on the smeared pane, looked out at the yard and the dark, rusting sheds her husband had built.

She thought of her home in Galway. Fresians in the backyard. Gentle, grass-eating beasts, even their smell had been friendly. Standing up to their fetlocks in mud, their big horned heads used to gaze through the kitchen window as if waiting for something to happen. Mary's father had had a Hindu sense of a cow's immortality. When old and spent, their teats as milkless as sausages, they were left free to roam the rock-strewn fields, swatting flies with their tails as they grazed in hollows untilled since the days of Cromwell. On winter mornings they chewed their cud as winds sharpened by the Atlantic bent double the blackthorns leaning away from the shoreline. Mary flicked the squashed spider out of the window. How she missed home. She wondered if she would ever again lay her head on her own Galway bed.

'Me own fambly's round me here, an' I still feel lonely,' she mused. Treacherous thoughts. Unfair to the children. If the Boss knew he would kick her all the way to Portumna. Mary closed the window.

As Mary supplied babies the house grew rooms like goitres. Every plank and brick the Boss put in place, and paid for with an aching back and raw hands. Fiercely it stood. A defiant, two-fingered salute to the 'scum in them labourers' cottages, who live off the State'. Inside his isolated empire the Boss had imprisoned his family and locked out the village.

The garden was seasonally crammed with cabbages, leeks and cauliflowers. Apple trees drooped with fruit, the fallers welcomed by rooting pigs. The children tilled the ground and pulled the weeds. 'There's nuttin' fer nuttin' in this life,' the Boss told the children as they trekked out to toil in the garden.

Mary finished her dusting and opened the polish tin to buff the sheen on the ugly pieces of furniture cluttering every room. There were no books, other than prayer books. The Pope smiled down from the damp-stained walls.

The Boss had little time for Mary's fundamental Catholicism. 'Them priests is all shamshites,' he'd say, yet he never missed a Sunday at Mass. 'Yehz never know, there might be somet'in' innit after all,' he'd say with an oily grin.

With fecund regularity Mary dropped her babies. Anonymous, gurgling and trusting, they would grow up in ignorance. 'I'm after making a football team,' she joked. She loved all her children, and whenever she could her big arms protected them from the Boss's angry blows. She stopped going to Mass. She was afraid, but she insisted her children went. 'I wan'ta bring yehz up in the sight a' God Almighty. Folly His Divine path an' yehz can't go wrong.'

The children went to Mass for Mary. They read their prayer books, sniffed incense, daubed their faces with holy water and ash on Ash Wednesday. But they were glad to rush home afterwards. Safely indoors they were spared the cruel eyes of neighbours. Secure behind the Boss's willows the children played in the yard until they were old enough to work.

No pets were allowed, even though the yard swarmed with cats. Inbred and fearful, they lived incestuously in rick and barn. Deformed queens with bellies low-slung from kitten bearing sat around like images of death, mewing forlornly.

'Let them eat dem big rats,' the Boss said with a laugh. 'I'm not givin' them melts good food out a the pigs' mout's.'

When the pregnant cats edged closer to the bungalow in search of a comfortable place to drop their litters the Boss cursed and threw stones at them. The cats ran off to a safe distance and watched with their glittering eyes. By nightfall they'd be back, rows of them, their eyes glimmering behind the willows, their mangy fur quivering.

Babs' small window was always open for them. Driven by instinct, one swollen mangy-looking queen sniffed and stared at the tempting aperture. At last, she dared to jump and with easy agility slithered through the opening. Flattened, she slipped under a bed and immediately began to disgorge her slimy, squeaky cargo.

'What's that noise in the lassies' room?' the Boss demanded. Mary, in a hairnet, was reading a Roman Catholic approved novel. He lowered his newspaper, his forehead shrivelling. 'Jasus,' he roared, 'wanna them rotten cats is after shittin' under the bloody bed.'

Sheets of newspaper fluttering down behind him, the Boss tore into Babs' room, went down on his knees and dragged the cat out. With afterbirth streaming from her and whimpering responses to her blind kitten's weak cries, the cat unsheathed her dirty claws and fastened them on the Boss's arm. With a yelp he dashed the cat's brains out against the bedhead and threw the carcass out of the window. With breath held to choking, the children watched, astonished.

'That'll teach the rotten bastards,' the Boss said, clutching his bloodied arm. 'Ge'rout yehz filt'y scum,' he roared, firing handfuls of wet kittens out on to the concrete yard.

Jack came to Babs' bed and she consoled him. 'Daddy didn't mean it,' she said, 'he's just in a bad temper over the mess.'

A manic laugh came from the kitchen. 'Curiosity killed the cat,' they heard their mother sing.

The cat's blood splashed across her mind, Babs lay on her back in her nightdress, shivering with anger, and muttering to herself, 'How can I get out a here?' Surely, beyond this darkness other girls and boys are dancing. There must be music, money, freedom.

The Boss crept into Babs' room with a mug of cocoa. It was his way of saying sorry. Not for killing the cat. The thing deserved it. It annoyed him to have to be on the defensive. Feck the same cats, he thought as he sat on the yielding bed and saw his pale daughter, with her pile of black hair, rise like a corpse, covering herself with a blanket. 'Thanks Daddy, leave it there,' she said. 'I'll have it in a minute.'

'Yeh'll have it now,' the Boss growled, 'it'll be frozen slop in a minute.'

He sat for a while like a man waiting for someone to die, nothing to fill the silence.

'Are yeh all right now?' the Boss asked.

'I'm OK,' Babs murmured. Only when he had left the room did Babs reach out to take the steaming mug.

Downstairs, her father bellowed. He was blaming Mary for letting the cats in.

43

THE ROW OF RUSTY sheds where dung-caked pigs snoozed had become Jack's world. After school he worked with the Boss till dusk, daydreams unshared, industry unrewarded. Afterwards, manure-splashed and tired, he did his homework before going to bed on a bowl of bread and milk.

From the Boss, Jack learned to castrate a pig with a razor blade, grow fruit and vegetables, mend a chicken's broken wing, or cut its throat. The family album showed the Boss snapped against a background of happily rooting pigs. With shovel poised, his arms bulging, trilby shading his eyes, he was every inch the peasant - proud, tough, independent.

The children gave the pigs pet names: Netsy, Pigsy, Gulcher . . . The Boss's favourite was Barney, a Landrace boar he'd hand-reared. 'They're related,' Mary joked.

As each new baby began to toddle it came out into the yard. But one day, crawling and inquisitive Paddy, the latest baby, got into the yard, learning, touching things, frightening the hens. He played with the cats, murmuring happily to himself. When he saw Barney's ringed nose twitching and snorting under the sty door he crawled over to investigate, and reached out to touch the boar's nose. Barney grabbed. Human flesh tasted good.

Jack heard the scream as he was piling green droppings into the wheelbarrow. In giant boots he lolloped over to the sties to find Barney eating little Paddy's hand. The baby was screaming, gazing at his bloodied hand. Jack ran to his father, blurting and pointing until the Boss wanted to smash him with the shovel. 'Fer Jasus sake, what're yeh on about?' he yelled.

Jack led the way in his lumbering boots.

'Yeh feckin' gobshite!' the Boss roared. 'How did yeh let that babby get down here in the first place?' Jack hardly stammered before the

Boss was yelling in exasperation, 'Ah, yeh bloody dope, can't yeh see yeh left the gate open. I've a good mind ta–' He swung his fist, but stopped himself at the last second. Unbuckling his belt, instead, the Boss charged into Barney's sty and beat the pig mercilessly about the head. The boar lost an eye.

'It'll teach yeh to keep yer bloody hands to yerself,' he roared at the baby as he carried the hysterical bloodstained infant to the house.

That night the Boss brooded, not over his son's mauled hand, but his boar's pulped eye. 'Jasus, that grand pig'll never be the same,' he sighed.

There was no need to buy in young pigs when the boar matured and for several summers two or three pregnant sows flicked their big white eyelashes like beauty queens and grunted happily in the mud. Barney was much appreciated by the smallholders of Rathfarnham. At ten bob a head he was kept busy servicing sows driven into the yard by silent men in wellingtons and dubiously-stained clothing.

The sows arrived like pet dogs, led by Billy Riley. Grubby and smiling, like the owner of a tawdry Moroccan brothel, the Boss held open the gate. He had a willow switch in his hand in case any pig tried to escape.

'Good-day t'yeh, Billy,' the Boss said genially. 'Will yeh put yer animal in the empty sty nex'ta the wan at the end.' He pointed with the switch.

'How's she cuttin'?' Riley thundered but the Boss told him to move along quickly to allow the other sows room. Riley stung his sow's backside with his stick and she squealed and broke into a bouncy gallop, her big scabby ears walloping against her skin.

'Ah, the man himself,' Riley said when he caught sight of Jack peering at him through the lower branches of the pussy willow. 'I'm tellin' on yeh fer runnin' away from class t'udder day.' The man's persistence with this old joke made Jack anxious all over again. When he saw the frown darken the boy's face the fat fat labourer winked broadly, the side of his face hinging like a pub sign. Jack watched the big man in terror.

Riley enjoyed visiting the Boss, always desperate to please, he brought things he had stolen from the convent yard.

'I won't be bought, fergit that oul' son,' the Boss said, as he stashed the stuff away. How many times did those empty words sail over the half doors to Jack as he worked out of sight in the sties? In silence, except for the snoring of the pigs, he often heard his father's grunts as he stowed stolen planks or tools in the spaces over the sties. The pig men laughed and swapped obscenities as they waited for the pigs to perform. Standing in the open sty, urging Barney on with prods and pokes from a stick, the Boss stage-managed the performance. With parched throats his audience dreamt of wives and girlfriends. It was better than the cinema, and Barney even kept customers away from church on Sunday mornings.

When the first sow trotted out to cheers the men leaned forward, their dungarees pressing against the sty wall. Barney circled like a matador, grunting with excitement. 'Lookerim,' one man muttered. 'Jasus, he's sizin' yer woman up.' Another man loudly rattled the change in his pocket. 'Feckin' hell,' a third said, 'wouldn' mind a langer like dat.' Another touched his cap back and smiled a gap-toothed smile.

Jack, his eyes wide, watched Barney mount the sow, his every quiver and jerk closely observed by grinning, sun-swarthy, outdoor faces. The boar's penis wriggled like a blind pink snake, curling, driven as if by radar towards the opening. A man cried, 'Oops, narely dare, whoa, fuck me, the cunt's goin' ta come all over us.' With a fixed smile the Boss lifted Barney's penis with his stick and laid it on the sow's genitalia. Jack watched fascinated as it penetrated and the sow's ecstasy became obvious. 'Jasus,' a man shouted, 'I can't feckin' stand this any longer, must hav'a slash.' He disappeared behind the back of the shed. One after another, the men followed him.

Jack carefully negotiated Riley's great arse. The giant labourer was laughing, swivelling his jowly neck to look up at the house to see if any of the girls were about. He had once made remarks to Babs which, luckily for him, the Boss knew nothing of. After Riley's visit behind the sheds Jack noticed the gaiety seemed to evaporate, the voice went down an octave and quit altogether the babble of inanities. Without Riley's violent shrieks of encouragement, Barney too seemed drained. Quietly, Riley paid the Boss and drove his pig across the yard and out on to the road. Without waiting for the others he took his animal across the Pit to its tin sty behind the Corporation terraces.

Mary hated the dirty crew whose vacant guffaws and lewd remarks sailed through the open kitchen window to threaten her and her three pure daughters. The girls, chaste but inquisitive, had to be dragged from the window. Mary swore that anyone who took a delight in such activity would repent in Hell. Jack sneaked away from the pungent circle of men, hoping not to be noticed, but the Boss exposed him with a yell and he had to flee to the house pursued by a wild barrage of laughter and the Boss yelling, 'Ge'rup out a that or I'll set the bogey man after yeh.'

When the exhausted Barney withdrew, to curl up in the shade, the remaining dark men steered their animals out of the gate, some trying to hide bulges in their trousers. Mary grimaced behind net curtains, muttering, 'filt'y bastards, may yehz rot in Hell. God'll never forgive them, watching that dirty pig perform his foul antics on a Holy and Blessed Sunda' mornin'.'

Jeers hung in the air like kites as the men trotted their curly-tailed sows across the Pit. Good, healthy, white porkers would soon carpet every outhouse in the village.

Although fond of his pigs, the Boss was relieved when they were plump enough for the butcher's slab. Prior to this last brutal act the twenty or so animals selected for execution were fed unusually well, cossetted and kept clean for weeks beforehand. The pigs swelled, their backs broadening, their cheeks rounding into tasty hams for smoking. But it was food for the well-off. The Boss could never afford his own home-grown meat. When his family ate flesh it was grizzly off-cuts and maggotty sheep's heads which Mary would turn into stews and thick-crusted pies camouflaged with gravy.

44

'THEM LINNETS IS fine little birds,' the Boss said to Jack one morning as they watched their antics. 'Grand little singin' birds. There's oul' wans that'd pay good money ta have wanna them in their lounge singin' away for visitors.' The Boss put a price on everything, including all of nature's fine, free gifts. Jack turned his face to look at his father, weighing him up.

'Jasus,' the Boss said after watching the tumbling birds for another minute, 'I t'ink I'll ketch a fewa them little hoors before the mornin's out.' He rushed to the shed, returning with a sand riddle, a stick and a ball of twine.

As Jack watched, his belly stuck out like an old codger's above his baggy trousers and his dirty face screwed up with interest, his father busied himself preparing a trap for the birds. He tied the twine to the stick and propped up the riddle, then laid out the twine like a dynamite charge, across the garden, and behind the pigswill barrels. After sprinkling a pinch of seed under the riddle, the Boss hid, his trilby sticking up above the barrel like a cowboy in a shoot-out.

'Hey, square brains,' the Boss hissed at his son, 'ge'rin 'ere or yeh'll give the bloody game away. Them birds is a lot cliverer 'an yeh.'

Father and son waited silently. Soon a flock of birds landed near the trap like small green peppers on a dish. When greed overcame suspicion, several birds began to peck at the seed under the riddle and were trapped when the Boss yanked the string. Father and son rushed forward and Jack watched his father bend low, and his tough hand surround the birds with as much gentleness as if they'd been made from Christmas tree baubles.

Fluttering helplessly, the birds were picked off one by one. The Boss, triumphant, held aloft his handful of feathers and thorny-looking legs, then took them indoors with Jack trotting along, smiling, behind. The birds were crammed into an old cage and hung from a beam in the kitchen. After his evening meal Jack came to watch the birds, touched by their pointed faces peering and piping disconsolately through the rusty bars of their prison. He leaned back on the heel of his hand, watching them as the sun outside was slipping off the hedges, the flanks of Neary's oaks aglow with a pinkish light. But as he heard the trapped birds bidding farewell to the day he was overcome by a great swamp of sadness.

After homework he sat by the cage and heard the fluttering of wings as the dozing birds sensed his presence. When Mary lumbered into the dark kitchen (the Boss forbade electric light in more than one room at a time) to wash up, she grunted in surprise when she bumped into her son.

'Jasus, what are yeh doin' in here?' she asked.

'I'm watchin' the birds,' Jack said.

'Birds?' his mother queried. 'How can yeh be watchin' them birds and it as dark as pitch in here?'

'I don't like them t'be in there,' Jack said.

'An' neither do I,' Mary agreed. 'That bloody man'd do an'tin' fer a shillin'. Here, where are they?' She groped. 'Ah, there they are, poor little t'ings. What good'll it do 'im sellin' the little song birds.'

'Mammy,' Jack tugged at his mother's sleeve, 'we won't have any in our garden if they go.'

'Yeh're right son,' Mary said, then instinctively whispered. 'Quick, gi'me that bloody cage.'

Jack climbed up on to the table and took it down. Snatching it from him Mary took it outside, wrenching at the tiny wire door as she went, and shook the dozy birds out. They sat like stuffed toys on the window ledges and concrete where they had landed, their little dark shapes barely visible until Mary waved a sack at them and they flew off unsteadily to a bush.

'Now,' Mary said, 'if we leave the cage on the floor wit' the door open yer man'll t'ink the cats done it.'

Delighted to be part of such a conspiracy, Jack laughed and put his hand on his mother's blubbery arm.

As he lay in bed the next morning, dawn cracking under the strain of the birds' chorus, Jack heard his father curse the cats, and his footfalls marching to the shed to dump the empty cage. He snuggled down, thinking about the linnets in the bushes probably already greeting the new day with their lovely song.

'Yeh an' yer feckin' birds,' Bridgid came to the bedroom door. 'Daddy would a killt yeh if he'd found out, I've a good mine ta tell 'im.'

Jack squirmed under the quilt. 'Yeh wouldn', would yeh?' he pleaded.

'I would,' Bridgid said defiantly. Then she caught sight of Pam sitting akimbo on her bed picking hairs from the mole on her cheek, studying each one as if it were a cancerous growth. 'Yeh filt'y t'ing!' Bridgid cried. 'Yeh'll get warts fer doin' that.'

Pam, serene and ladylike, with a scrap of coloured silk around her neck, fluttered her mascaraed eyes and ran her tongue across her teeth tantalisingly. Pam was so in love with her own appearance she hadn't even heard her sister's rebuke.

Babs closed the shorthand pad she had been glancing through and joined the little band. 'Yeah, I heard about the linnets,' she said, laughing. 'Daddy'll be mad. He was hopin' ta make a fortune out a them. Said he had sev'ral oul' wans lined up ta take them.' Babs sat on the bed, put her arm around her young brother and pushed back his fringe. 'But it wasn't yer fault this time,' she smiled, 'wazzit? The oul' cats done it, didn't they?'

'Mammy done it,' Jack stammered.

'No,' Babs said, pretending to be shocked.

'Well, I hope she doesn't boast abou'rit too much,' Bridgid said, startling Jack with her gravity, 'or she'll be the sorry wan.'

'What's goin' on here?' the Boss slipped up on them without anyone noticing.

Babs stood up with a beaming smile, stretched herself, her breasts pressing against her blouse. 'Nuttin' Daddy,' she said, 'jus' talkin'.'

The Boss spotted the notepad on the dressing table. 'Get that ould Pitman's goin' again,' he said, tapping Babs' shoulder. 'Ya can't go wrong wit' the shorthand.'

The children dispersed, sliding like water round a big rock as they passed the stubborn bulk of their father that occupied most of the doorway.

45

JACK GREW TO love the pigs. The sows with their rows of little piglets nuzzling rows of crimson teats, the stout young boars raucous and ready to prove their virility by chewing through doors and uprooting the floors of their sties. The pigs got to know Jack and they fawned as he scratched the rough, lice-ridden skin behind their ears. With small intelligent pink eyes they looked upon their scruffy swineherd with fondness and trust. Mickey O'Rourke, the butcher, with his humane killer seemed a long way off.

But it was only a bare week away.

His work done for the day, his hands jammed in his pockets, Jack stood amid the whitewashed stones in the front garden, keenly watching O'Rourke, a loud man with multiple chins, splutter into the yard in his battered Ford. An air of gloom hovered above the place like a shabby condor. The lopsided-van door shrieked open and the roly-poly butcher emerged breathlessly, clutching the humane killer in his fat hand. Striding forward to gain the upper ground, the Boss greeted him. The two men enacted an annual comedy, enriching their exchange with archaic language seasoned with obscenities. Nothing could disguise the serious nature of O'Rourke's visit, but such spirited foreplay was an important part of their dealings.

The Boss took his squat companion on a tour of the sties, introducing each occupant with a trumpet of enthusiasm.

'Ah, come off it, Johnny. Them's not a spot on the fine pigs yeh sold me last year,' O'Rourke boomed, emphasising the negative with an elbow in the Boss's ribs. 'What price were yeh lookin' for?'

The Boss named an optimistic figure and watched with an irritated smile as O'Rourke went into his laughing routine. 'Ah, Jasus, yeh're coddin' me,' the fat butcher replied, wiping sweat from his brow with a grubby handkerchief.

'Now listen, Mick,' the Boss cajoled. 'Sure them pigs is as big as baby elephants, will yeh take a good look at the size a' them. Yeh'll make a fortune out a them.' The Boss was laughing, but his tiny blue eyes were dead. 'Them oul' wans from Terenure know what's good fer 'em, don't they?' he went on. 'Lookit the meat on them pigs.' He pressed a thumb down on the nearest pig's back, causing it to squeal. The men haggled, their trilby-hatted heads bobbing, until a price was struck. The Boss always claimed he got the best of it, but so did the cunning butcher.

When O'Rourke unboxed the humane killer and rattled a box of shells in a baggy pocket, Jack disappeared. Death would soon come to the pigs and he couldn't bear the zipping of the weapon as O'Rourke placed the cold muzzle to the centre of each unsuspecting skull. The gun went off, and neat holes spurted out blood and liquidised brain. The pigs kicked and struggled, unwilling to die. They huddled nervously, they feared death, smelt it, their dung running watery as they pressed closer to the door. Jack watched from a distance. His friends had seen their last rays of sunlight. Mary often said if her husband could watch with such detachment as lovely, intelligent, warm-blooded animals were slaughtered, he could do the same to her. And she was probably right.

O'Rourke loosened his dirty shirt and grunted with the effort of stooping to get his overweight body closer to each quarry. Phut, phut, the gun went and Jack could only stand in the cool, dark kitchen, a web of fear in his frightened eyes. He remembered Netsy and the others friskily chasing each other round the apple trees like tiny hippos, crunching the fallen apples, wallowing in the muck at the bottom of the garden. Now their lives were terminated, their blood making plum-coloured streams under the sty doors. Oozing slowly, it congealed in the fly-ridden heat. Outside, a tree creeper climbed a willow in search of insects, unaware of the drama.

The Boss opened a couple of halves of Guinness and, with dung-splashed hands, the two men put the bottles to their lips and drank. 'Sure, them's lovely animals,' the Boss burped. 'I told yeh they wor tops.' He wiped the froth from his mouth with a bronzed arm. 'Next year, they'll be even betther,' he added confidently.

'Jasus, yeah, as big as bloody elephants, I suppose?' O'Rourke joked, and both men laughed.

'They will be,' the Boss said, finishing his stout with a last convulsive swallow before standing up to accept the wad of used notes the red-haired butcher peeled off a grimy bundle.

With an expression that sent his forehead rippling, the Boss licked his dirty fingers and flicked through the bundle. He wouldn't put it past O'Rourke to slip in a few dud ones.

'Ah, it's all there, Johnny,' O'Rourke said.

What they really thought of each other was no secret. The butcher grinned. He scratched the top of his head, sweat seeping from his fat body, soaking his soiled shirt. The Boss, mouthing the last figure, stopped counting.

'On'y the bare few bob,' he cracked, then he wedged the money into his back pocket and did up the button.

'Sure, yeh're a hard feckin' man ta do business wit',' O'Rourke concluded as he fitted his paunch behind the steering wheel. 'Good luck now,' he shouted and the van, overladen with corpses, bumped towards the road. Passing the window the butcher raised his hat to Mary before clattering away in a cloud of black smoke. A trail of red spots followed him as his cargo of pigs lost their last drops of blood. When Jack came out of hiding the yard was still full of silent squealing and the deadly echo of the gun. Outside the sties where the killings had taken place the cats had gathered to quietly lap at the sticky pools.

The girls remained in the house. Pam cried quietly in a corner, her face covered in a scrap of black veil she had taken from one of Mary's old hats. She had made a particular pet of Netsy. Pam always made a pet of something.

The Boss cruelly abused his daughter for her silliness. 'Fer Jasus' sake, pigs don't have no souls,' he said. 'They're on'y pigs, fer Christ's sake.' To prove it he had often kicked Netsy back into her sty. The small sow, surprised at the sudden turn of events, ran as fast as she could to avoid further punishment.

'Daddy,' Pam whispered as she sidled towards the empty sties, trailing her delicate fingers along the wall, her eyes full of tears. 'D'yeh hav'ta do it, Daddy? Isn't there another way?'

'Heh,' the Boss gave a dismissive laugh. 'If yeh find wan, let me know.' And walked away, guffawing loudly.

'We could all be vegetarians,' Pam whispered.

'Ha, ha, ha,' the Boss said, 'that's a good wan. Vegetenarians, me arse.'

Bridgid didn't mind seeing animals killed. 'If yeh eat meat, or wear shoes,' she argued, 'yeh haven't got a leg t'stand on.'

Pam, like a torpid Madonna her chin in her hands, was exquisitely drowning in her sadness. Babs, like her mother, could not inflict pain on any living thing, but she understood her father's need to make his few pounds any way he could. He had a huge and annually increasing family to feed. A smallholder's existence was always a grim one, wherever he toiled.

After he'd kicked off his boots, the Boss, warm with contentment, peeled ten shillings off his wad and slipped it into Babs' pocket. In the presence of her mother, a drudge chopping cabbage at the cold stone sink, Babs gallantly refused the money. The Boss smirked. 'Have it yer way then,' he said, patting her back, and quietly went off to his room and bolted the door.

Under the bed there was a coffin-sized box in which he stowed cash and important papers. It was secured by two heavy locks. Babs went to the sink and, taking a knife from the drawer, helped her mother, while her father got down on his knees before the open box as if in prayer to worship his money.

46

JACK RAN DOWNHILL across the Pit, his schoolbag swinging, the dewy grass soaking his leather boots. He was alive, alone and thrilled to be out in the wonderful morning, far away from his father, from his sisters, from everyone. He stopped to toss stones at his reflection in the pool below the Corporation estate. If ever there was a fat bottle to stand on the wall he would smash it, thrilling at the sound of splintering glass.

The sky was unoccupied, except for a flock of starlings arrowing towards the telegraph wires. Neary's red barn, packed with yellow hay, was visible between the trees. An old hay turner anchored by thistles and garnished with clumps of feverfew stood outside. From his bedroom window Jack watched that rusty old machine alter with the seasons: a snowy chariot in winter, adorned with blossom in spring, camouflaged with dead leaves in autumn.

Leaving the Pit and its sloping fields Jack joined the road where horses and carts delivered bread and milk. On the forecourt of the new petrol station a huge blue and silver petrol tanker was crouched, humming like a great bee, its proboscis filling the new underground vats with petrol. The new service station grew from a hole in the red clay to a majestic glass castle filled with new cars. It was the first of its kind, a last chance to fill up before the mountains.

Jack could see the shiny granite school, an elephantine monolith with immense bronze bells which had once so terrified him he ran from their booming. In the school lane he stooped to collect spiky leaves from under the monkey-puzzle tree.

As he neared school and heard the screaming of children Jack felt his chest tighten. Inside, the smell of polish and poverty overwhelmed him. Drawing in his snot he tried to concentrate on the blackboard. Outside, the world went about its business. Sparrows scrabbled in the eaves or bobbed about the yard. The sweet smell of manure wafted through the school. Jack imagined men in braces toiling in the sun, their horses sweating, the cart tracks disappearing over the hill. He did sums and scribbled stories behind rows of nameless girls and boys. No one seemed interested in him but it didn't matter.

Jack longed to be in the fields with the wild creatures. After school he wobbled home; a bundle of rags, but with a mind that whirred in peculiar ways. He helped his father as much as he was able.

Jack had discovered the paradise of comics. Boko Rooney, had the *Beano* and *Dandy* delivered every week. Like a starving mongrel, Jack haunted Boko's house, waiting patiently, while the spoiled brat turned the sweet smelling pages.

When Boko loftily handed over the precious gift Jack dived on it and was away, his head bobbing through the Rooney's thistles, to find a secluded place. Behind the sties, where the river ran and Neary's cows came to sniff, Jack opened his crisp comic and his eyes sparkled. How his eyes sparkled. Oh, the hunger in him as he ravished pages, eating words, the stream stippling his smiling face.

Lost in world of bears, cats in bow ties and smoking cigars, Jack heard a plaintive sound. The sun was lower, the cows had moved on, leaving their cloven prints. He folded the comic and stowed it under his jumper. The sound was coming from Kitty's stable.

Jack approached cautiously and saw Pam crooning to the old pony, her creamy arms around the bewildered Kitty's neck.

Pam leapt back when Jack appeared. 'Yeh scared me!' she exclaimed, stepping away from the pony. Kitty, experiencing tenderness, bared her teeth angrily at the intruder. Pam had plaited the old pony's mane with geraniums and daisies she'd picked from the bed in front of the house where every year the Boss grew a tangled medley of scent and colour. 'Worra yeh smirkin' at?' Pam asked.

'Nuttin',' Jack said.

Pam tore at her handiwork. Kitty, her eyeballs like gobstoppers, reared, her neat shod feet pawing the air, dying to get a foot on the sly, snotty intruder. Pam cried and fled in her gauzy frock, like a waif from *Alice in Wonderland* running towards the house.

Jack muttered, 'Yeh feckin' ould hoor,' and kicked the stable door. Kitty bared her teeth as much as to say, 'C'mon, you cowardly little shite, let me get my brown teeth into the back of your fecking neck, you stinking little spoilsport.'

Jack heard her wheeling angrily in her concrete stall, trampling the decapitated flowers. He left the yard with its rotting hayrick and its pig and hen shit smell and made for the house. He was glad to find that Pam had left the kitchen and gone to her room. Isolated and wounded, she was in there dabbing her face with the pink powder Mary kept in a small gold case with a small cracked mirror.

When the Boss took a bucket of water to Kitty and saw the mess on the floor, Jack was quick to incriminate his sister.

'Bloody fool,' the Boss said, 'feckin' dotty, that wan.' Over tea he asked Pam what she was up to with the pony, but she remained silent.

'Bloody t'ick, th'oul pony didn't know wedder t'ate the poxy flowers or feckin' wear them.'

Pam hung her head, the buzz of ridicule bringing tears to her eyes.

'Yeh bloody fool, yeh shou'bey doin' yer sums instead a tryin' ta practise flower arrangin' on poor oul' Kitty.' The Boss chortled and the other children joined in, enjoying his humour – each one relieved it was not directed at them.

At last, Mary snapped, 'Fer God's sake, will yeh l'ave the poor child alone. What's wrong wit' hangin' a few flowers round the pony's head? Poor t'ing doesn't get much attention.'

'Don't be talkin' rubbitch,' the Boss snarled, 'I don't want that pony excited. She's gorra long day on the road tomorra.'

'I can't understan' how yeh can abuse the poor child fer doin' somethin' so harmless and . . .' Mary ran out of words.

But the Boss was just warming up. 'That's because yeh're from the country an' they love that sorta t'ing, them gobdaws bein' half mad from inbreedin'.'

For the sake of the children Mary let him have the last word. 'Come on, pet,' she said to Pam, 'ate up.' Pam picked up her fork but she had no appetite. Instead, she glared at her brother like she had once seen Jean Simmons do in a photograph.

As Babs helped her mother clear the table she paused by Pam. 'Sorry, Sis,' she said, 'it seemed funny at the time, that's all.' She touched Pam's hand and her sister's head came up. Pam's eyes were wet as she took a great slice of bread and started eating, clownish mascara tears running down both sides of her nose.

'L'ave her alone,' said the Boss, from his seat in the corner. 'She's a bloody oul' fool like her mother.'

'Daddy!' Babs said sharply. The Boss picked up his *Evening Mail* and silence blessed the remainder of the evening.

47

THE BOSS VISITED Babs in her room. From behind the closed door came the slushing of lemonade, the blessed breaking of a bar of Fry's Chocolate Cream, the holy handing over of two squares. Outside, deprived of luxury, the rabble listened with one ear to Mary's agitated commentary. Hurt and jealous, she pressed her ear to the varnished plywood. Slyly, the children watched for the brass knob to turn, signalling the Boss's exit. He barged through them like a matinee idol, went to the turf rick in the yard and returned with a sod in each hand.

Re-entering their deprived and starless world he carefully placed the turf on the embers, then with a smile he turned to tickle his nearest infant, to the child's huge and unexpected delight. Mary scratched her oily hair as it flopped over her glasses. She was pretending to read. Jesus Christ, she'd get even one day.

When the Boss slammed home the bolts on the kitchen door the room moved in on Mary and the children like the closing jaws of a salivating monster. Collectively, the breath was squeezed from them and they fidgeted, jumpy as fleas under a tenement bulb. Mary flattened the pages of her *Messenger* and cast an occasional bug-eyed glance at her children. The night was going to be long and silent.

Jack went to bed and listened to the sink in the scullery fill the drain by his window. The Boss, hairy and naked to the waist, was purging himself with cold water. He stood, caked in soap, his braces hanging, like a gorilla in a shopping bag. The last droplets could have been tears as they entered the drain. Feeling small and fragile, Jack crawled under the bedclothes and drew up his knees.

Next day, hatted and spooky-looking with his scowl and black jaw, the Boss waited outside the school to pluck his son and his eldest daughter from the stream of children caterwauling through the door.

The bit-part actors could walk. The Boss had the two he wanted, the slave and the pale goddess. Babs mounted the cart while the girls from her class, where she was the star pupil, sniggered bitchily. The Boss, making room, said, 'Sit in the front, yer man can hunker down in the back.' Babs tucked the tails of her gabardine coat around her bottom and put her feet up on the rail in front. Jack clambered behind her and sat on the damp floor. Half a Ritchies mint was handed to both children. The Boss was feeling generous today - all previous convictions quashed.

'I wan'cha ta get a bit a oul' bread from the Landy fella while me an' yer man get tha guts,' the Boss said, shaking the reins.

'OK, Daddy,' Babs said, smiling sweetly up at her father's worn face. He cast his small pale eyes on her, signalling the love he felt. Babs had no reservations about loving her father.

Feeling the wetness from the damp cart seep up through his trousers, Jack sucked his half mint, turning it gently with his tongue. They crawled by the convent, the big black gates, the little shop on the corner, the Shamrock Stores where he had so stupidly thrown away the half crown he'd got from the nuns for picking potatoes, hooked and mugged by the one-armed bandit.

Kitty headed up the hill past The Yellow House, the Church of the Annunciation and Whelan's the barbers, Madigan's pub, the Mascot, before coming to a halt outside the abattoir. The Boss tied the reins to the cart.

'Babs, there's two bob,' he said, 'don't let them hoors wipe yer eyes.' Babs hopped off the cart, her ankle socks white blobs as she crossed the quiet street, her head thrust forward, showing the same energy and purpose as her father.

The Boss and Jack crossed the street to the slaughter house. The doors opened, releasing the smell of dung, blood and death. Kitty, head down, waited by the kerb. A passing child caught her eye and she gave it a wicked look. Inside the blood-splashed abattoir the Boss dug a fork into the entrails of dead animals. Flies, buzzing loudly, swarmed through the open window. Holding his breath, the Boss loaded steel oil drums that would slide easily on to the cart. With strong arms he wrestled the heavy drums, spinning them like tops, their metal edges gouging the dung-covered concrete of the abattoir floor.

As an ancient Jesuit crabbed by, the Boss's mind raced with old hurts cramming into his head. Momentarily and picturesquely, the priest was framed in the sunny glow of the big oaken door. Disguising his hatred of the breed, the Boss lifted his hat. The old priest saluted, stooped to see what the shadow inside was doing, and walked on. 'Feck off,' the Boss swore in a low growl. 'That oul' shite is pimpin' on us ta see if we're stealin' an'tin'. Feck'im!'

A crow landed unsteadily on the pole outside Landy's shop where Babs was queueing. Fresh loaves were carried in on wooden trays, the baker's name stencilled in black on the side. Customers stealing a few minutes from lathe, sink or counter pinched their cigarettes and waited. Children wrestled loaves into the open jaws of their jackets. Babs waited, trousered legs brushing past her. Labourers smelling of porter grabbed their bread with blackened fingers. 'Grand day.' . . . 'Isn't it lovely weather we're havin'.' . . . 'An' how's the missus?' . . . 'Oh! on the pig's back, an' how's herself?'

Peering down at Babs, Mrs Kelly, the shop manager, called out. 'An' how's Babs this mornin'?'

Crimson filled Babs' face. Her loaves occupied most of the counter, a goods train of them hitched together, warm with terracotta roofs. Mrs Kelly wrapped the bread in old *Heralds*. 'Couldn't yeh get yer Dad to help, love?' she said, leaning over, her fat breasts cleavaging. She took the money and patted Babs' head. 'Yer tuppence short, but don't worry.'

'What in the name a God's keepin' yeh?' a voice growled. The Boss was standing in the doorway, dripping soft dung on Landy's floor.

'Sure, the little girl can't carry alldem at wanst,' Mrs Kelly said.

The Boss, elbowing customers aside, grappled with the loaves, pressing green thumbprints into the soft dough. Babs gazed at the Swiss rolls and the doughnuts oozing jam until her arm was yanked by her father. Blind behind the bread, the Boss's wellingtons strode out in front of him.

When the loaves were stacked under the cart seat he leapt aboard and shook the reins. Kitty obediently galloped.

'Oh, Daddy, I jus' 'membered,' Babs said. 'Mrs Kelly said I was tuppence short.'

The Boss laughed. A little victory at last. 'Well, she'll be waitin' a long time fer that I can tell yeh,' he said. Fuelled by this triumph, he gave each of the children another half of a greenish mint. Jack sucked deliciously, the guts beneath him slurping about grotesquely as they galloped home.

The instant Kitty was released from the cart she rolled in the ash and dust of the garden, leaving a hairy impression in the ground. Babs carried the loaves indoors and left them to cool on the windowsill. Children's hands like blind snakes, fastened on to the soft doughy bread and, if a scab of crust came away with them, so much the better. Thundering curses would reverberate round the bungalow when the Boss found out.

After tea the Boss, putting a rough hand on Babs' cheek, swept away her dark locks to feel the soft underside of her chin. 'G'wan now, an' do yer sums,' he said.

When he at last got away from the yard, Jack blew the dust off his collection of birds' eggs. Snug in cotton wool they had taken him a couple of years to accumulate. He removed one tiny egg, white with reddy-brown spots. It was his first success. Generations of wrens had lived under the bridge in balls of leaves and moss. The starling that lived in the cracked willow was next, unwittingly donating one of her clutch. The hedgerows around the village were full of blackbirds, thrushes and finches. The mallard he watched for a week from the back window yielded up one green egg from her nest in the reeds, as did the robin in the pigsty and the pigeon in the holly. To get at the tits who built in the crack in the wall, Jack had scraped out the stones.

Then there was the little black and white dipper that lived beneath the weir. He killed her with a rock and tore her body apart with bare hands, trying to find an egg but she was barren.

A pair of scald crows built their untidy nest at the top of an old elm in Kennedy's field. Jack climbed the swaying tree and descended carefully, an egg in his mouth, rotten twigs cascading all around him. Soon, the box was full of eggs, all blown and labelled.

Only when he examined the dried empty shells this time did he realise he'd robbed the birds of an opportunity to live, to soar, to dip, to drink from fresh streams, to sing for the people who needed their song. He put the box back on the dresser.

Staring out of the small four-paned windows down the incline to the yard, Babs caught a glimpse of her father's head approaching. The Boss pressed his face to the glass, whispering and beckoning. She tried to open the top part but her small thumping fists were unable to break the window's painted seal.

Mary was in the kitchen when Babs appeared from the bedroom. She looked hard at her daughter. It was a look she reserved for those who had seriously *transgressed*, and normally lasted only a short time. What worried Babs was the way the look went on day after day, the wildness of it accusing her.

'I saw him at the winda,' Mary said in a disinterested way. 'Up to his oul' antics he was, like an oul' monkey hoppin' up an' down.'

Babs knew the worst thing to do was to ignore her mother. She had learned that a long time ago. It was better to change the subject. Babs backed down. 'Daddy was on'y showin' me an enormous potato shaped like a baby he had in a bucket,' she said.

'Potato is it?' Mary queried. 'Why didn't he show me then?'

'Ah, sure his top boots was filt'y,' Babs said, selecting a red apple from the bowl on the dresser. Innocent and carefree, she sauntered into the kitchen and listened for her mother to make working noises. Putting on the kettle for tea was a positive sound. Everything was going to be all right.

'Mammy, I wan'ta help yeh,' Babs said.

'Oh, so what's got inta yeh all ovva sudden?' Mary said coldly. 'Is it guilt?' she snarled. Babs ignored her, recognising the jealousy. Her mother was unloved, and each day became less lovable. She was scared and wild-looking, no longer bothered about her appearance. Babs sidled to the sink, took a potato and started peeling. For a while Mary ignored her and they worked side by side in a snivelling silence. When the kettle whistled Mary made tea and poured two mugs, placing one by her daughter. Babs took it and sat down. Mother and daughter sipped, eyeing each other. Then Mary began to talk, quietly at first. Babs encouraged her. Mary laughed at some funny thing she'd thought of. Soon, she and Babs were swapping gossip like friends. Pam joined them, wrapping her vampirish nails round her mug. Bridgid cut herself a thick slice of bread and Marmite. They sat together and talked, draining some of the sadness from their mother.

At the sound of Boss's wellingtons clumping up the concrete path, and his harsh voice yelling and cursing, the girls took off. By the time the door was flung open Mary's hunched silhouette was back at the sink. His nagging started immediately but, fortified by her children's love, she refused to be drawn into a row. The Boss picked up his evening paper, sat by the fire and read while Mary, on stout varicosed legs, lumbered around in the cold gloomy kitchen, making the evening meal for her grateful brood.

48

ONE PARTICULAR MORNING Mary was uncommonly happy. She was humming an old Irish air as she waddled about doing her chores. A precious letter postmarked *Galway* had plopped through the letterbox and she had managed to get her hands on it before the Boss had returned from his daily visit to the paddock where he kept a few sheep. Eileen Sinott, Mary's oldest and truest friend, her only friend, was threatening to visit. Eileen with her Quasimodo looks and vocabulary of a navvy, was a crooked-eyed monster with a complexion that reflected a lifetime of poteen sipping in Ballinasloe. It was impossible for Eileen to be polite to the Boss. She loathed the man anyway but especially for what he'd done to her old friend. Like a great she-ape, Eileen would protect and defend her battered mate, to the end if necessary.

Eileen arrived on a fine Saturday morning on her big sit-up-and-beg bike and flung it on the gravel. The children rushed to welcome their outrageous 'aunt'. 'How are yehz, yeh poor, neglected little divils?' Eileen asked.

Babs turned her head away. She was growing out of Eileen and no longer looked upon her mother's friend as any more than an uneducated and uncouth Galway woman. It was a view shared and fostered by her father who hated all country people and who had put the likes of Eileen near the top of his lengthy hate list.

'An' the girls?' Eileen asked. 'Isn't Babs a lovely child? Is she doin' an oul' line yit?'

Mary looked vacant. 'Whatja mane?' she asked.

'Jaysus, yeh're such a t'ick oul' hoor I don't know what I'm doin' comin' ta see yeh,' Eileen roared and her great blotchy face cracked. 'I mane is she gettin' her oats? Fer the love a God, Mary, has she got a young bucko?' She nodded helpfully but Mary wasn't forthcoming.

Eileen tried again, this time trying shock tactics. 'That wan Babs is lookin' very mature all of a sudden,' she said. 'She'll soon have them lads from the cottages offerin' her their little mickeys.'

'Oh Jasus, don't be sayin' such t'ings,' Mary said.

Eileen rumbled with laughter, and the children were equally shocked and amused. 'Babs'll be gettin' th'oul langer soon enough,' Eileen continued, 'and lucky is the gossoon that gets in there first.'

Mary ground her gums. Eileen always went too far. Babs looked stern and totally disinterested. It was all she expected from such a culchie. Mary chewed her cud in silence. Although she sometimes, in her sad and confused mind, thought the worst of her eldest daughter, she would not countenance an outsider taking such liberties with her child's purity.

The conversation flew harmlessly above the younger children's heads. They were innocently contemplating Eileen's fat brown-paper bag.

Eileen spotted them and roared, 'Hey, yeh starvin' little bastards.' The children pushed forward as she opened an obscenely large bag of sweets. 'Take a handful,' she shouted and laughed, and the children, like famine victims, thrust their hands into the bag. 'Ah, yehz poor little feckers,' Eileen said, tousling heads like a saint. 'Sure, it's a little treat yehz'd be wantin'.'

Like furry-tailed marmots the children galloped to their roosts and filled their mouths to bulging with gorgeous bull's-eyes and nancy balls. Their faces were screwed up and twisted with sheer pleasure, their eyes danced and their hands did tricks. Eileen, the most wonderful 'aunt' in the world, watched, sharing their pleasure.

Then Eileen rushed over to her old friend to hug the life out of her. 'Jasus, Mary, yeh're lookin' awful,' she said, 'that melt is going' to kill yeh soon. Yeh sit right there and let me and Babs make the droppa tay.'

In the kitchen Eileen washed and dried dirty cups and saucers. She set the table with a big cake she'd brought. She lifted Mary's arm as though she was the Queen of England and led her to the best seat. The children unravelled from their perches and joined them.

'Now,' Eileen said, 'tell me all the news, and don't leave an'tin' out.'

Mary slurped her tea noisily, savouring every warm drop. She closed her big gummy mouth on to a slice of fluffy sponge.

The children loved Eileen's obscene anecdotes about her experiences in Galway haylofts. 'Them dirty Dubliners t'ink country mugs have no gas but they're talkin' t'rough their bloody arseholes.' Eileen roared with laughter, while Mary fretted in case the Boss overheard. Eileen cared little for priests and Hell-devils were bogeymen invented by spineless celibates. She teased Mary about the Boss's narrow-minded views and laughed loudly at his ridiculous theory that hard work was the shortest way to Heaven.

'That cunt'd be down on his knees prayin' and at the same time figurin' out how he could steal the priest's drawers,' Eileen said.

'Yeh can't expect them poor kids ta grow up as stewpid as yerself when it comes down ta yeh-know-what,' Eileen said, continuing her one-track conversation.

'Oh, Jasus, Mary an' Holy St Joseph,' Mary said, as she grasped what Eileen meant. 'My daughters are as innocent as I was at their age, God fergive yeh, Eileen, fer suggestin' udderwise. Christ, yer man wouldn' let the sign ovva lad within a mile a' the house,' she added, shaking her head at the improbability of it.

Eileen listened with a contemptuous sneer. 'Sure, th' oul' cunt is jus' plain jealous. Yeh can tell be the eyes on him he'd scuttle an'tin' in knickers.'

Mary laughed and hid her face the way the chronically shy do. Eileen continued to ask the most intimate of questions and Mary was both mortified and relieved. It was the only opportunity she would have to talk to another woman, until Eileen's next unpredictable visit.

Time flew dangerously close to when the Boss was due home. Mary's mind was back in the Galway lanes of her childhood. When the sound of Kitty's hooves thundered on the bridge she jumped up, her distant dream shattered. 'Jasus Christ!' she cried. 'Himself is back! Quick, t'row out the tay, an' clane the crumbs offa the table. Putcher coat on.'

Eileen looked at her friend with pity, and slowly lit a cigarette.

'C'mon,' Mary urged, 'he's back, yeh'd better be goin', y'know what sort a man he is, he hates the t'ought of us eatin' his food.'

Eileen exploded. 'God blast the baldy little bollicks,' she shrieked. 'Sure, didn't I bring the bit a cake we're atin' meself, an' if he won't allow his poor ould drudge of a wife a cuppa tay then it's a bloody bad deal, I can tell yeh.'

Mary peered nervously out of the window, her hands shaking, the cake choking her. 'Look, c'mon Eileen, don't worry about finishin' yours, l'ave it, the kids'll be glad of it.'

'No, I'm not goin' ta be chased off. He can go feck himself,' Eileen retorted. 'I'm not a bit afraid of that mean little shagger and I'm stayin' here whether he bloody likes it or not. I came to see yeh, not him, I wouldn't piss on the little bastard if he was burnin' alive. Gi'me another cuppa tay out a that and relax. I'll handle him when he comes in.' Eileen took a long casual pull on her cigarette.

'What bitch's bastard put that feckin' bike right across me path?'

The door flew open with a bang. When the Boss saw Eileen his face cracked into an obsequious smile. He flapped his hand to her. 'Well, there now, isn't it lovely seein' yeh after all this time,' he said. 'Aren'tcha lookin' the very picture.'

Eileen took the hard, rough paw and shook it without enthusiasm. 'Yis, I'm in great form but it's Mary that's not lookin' that well. Can'tcha lay offa her fer a while. Get the kids ta help a bit more; yehz'll bury the poor ould cow if yehz are not a bit kinder ta her.'

The Boss's grin vanished.

Mary recoiled, angered and terrified by her friend's impertinent remarks. She knew the Boss would come back to the topic with a vengeance the moment Eileen was out of the door.

'Will yeh be wantin' a cup a tay an' a slice a me cake?' Eileen sneered.

'No!' the Boss said, reversing out of the room. 'Some of us is killt workin''. Choking on a string of oaths he returned to the pigs, whose screams were heralding feeding time.

'Feckin' cheek,' he muttered as Jack arrived to help. 'The gall of it, comin' here, an' atin' my bit a grub, then tellin' me how ta run me affairs. Stupid Galway heifer. Never trust them ignorant bastards from the west of Ireland,' the Boss concluded.

Before Eileen put on her coat she produced a parcel for Mary. She knew she would be accused of meanness if she didn't pay admission to see her old friend in her private zoo. It was usually a pair of gloves, or knickers, pressed into Mary's fumbling hands as she held open the door.

'Remember now, Mary, don't let that baldy runt get yeh down. Fight back, keep yer chin up. D'yeh hear me now?' She grabbed Mary to her and slobbered big kisses all over her old friend's face. 'Goodbye now, and say a prayer for me. The bloody devil's as good as got me on his feckin' great horns,' Eileen said cheerfully as she put on her hat and gloves.

Mary sobbed as she lurked in the shadow of the curtains, waving frantically until Eileen disappeared down the hill, wondering how long it would be before her dear foul-mouthed friend returned. 'If only I could go home with her,' Mary murmured, but her reveries splintered as the kitchen door crashed open. It was time to pay for Eileen's indiscretions. There would be the usual cursing, the sound of struggling, slapping and screaming, with Babs trying to intervene. Jack would disappear behind the sties with *Desperate Dan*.

49

WHEN GOLDEN ACRE was built, the developer jabbed his shiny knife into the heart of the dying village. It was an artificial estate of tiny box houses. The occupants were transient, clerks and commercial travellers. Marriages collapsed. People went quietly, after trying in vain to pay their mortgage. Men got sacked, parents worried that their children would be impregnated by the inbred thugs who inhabited Rathfarnham. Furniture vans often lumbered up the new cement roads. *For Sale* signs went up, new villagers came to try their luck.

'Don't be goin' near them starvin' bastards,' the Boss warned his children, 'unless it's ta collect their swill fer th'ol' pigs. They have nuttin' else we want.'

Jack had no reason to mix with the children of Golden Acre. He was poor, ugly and filthy. Occasionally, he would watch a little girl with ringlets and think it would be nice just to speak to her. But the children came and went too. The old village was becoming a sort of clearing station instead of a place where everyone had the measure of everyone else.

Then, a man of real substance moved in. Jack saw the long-necked stranger in a swinging-open trench coat and a reporter's trilby on the back of his head.

It was the kind of calm and mild evening only early summer can bring. The trees around the Pit were sprouting leaves, pink-tinted seagulls streamed west, houses were showing off their whitewash, panes in their windows sparkled as they caught the flowing gold. Jack, his hair blowing, his eyes wide, was watching a football match. Lads too good for him were playing each other. Jack watched them flying and falling, then getting up and running, admiring their bravery and strength. How he wished he was as brave as they were. Perhaps they would consider picking him, if only as a last resort.

The long-necked stranger was taking the shortcut to Golden Acre, the path taken by gleaming city men. He was walking with an easy stride, steps long, arms swinging. He hopped over rabbit holes and anthills, floating past the rolled jumpers and the lemonade bottles just as Mickey Doran slammed a goal past Eamonn Lee. Jack watched, his mouth open, as the stranger took the flying ball high up and with a curl of his toe had it dead at his feet. It was the best bit of trapping Jack had ever seen. The man tapped the ball back to Eamonn, who took no notice, as if all fatherly-looking men should be able to trap like that. Jack edged nearer as the man stopped to pass a few words with the goalie.

'D'yehz play here all the time?' he asked.

'We're on'y havin' a birra bootin',' Lee said, and he turned away to clatter the ball upfield.

The man turned to Jack. 'An' yeh? Are yeh not interested atall in the game?'

How could Jack say he yearned to be good enough. Even to stand like a statue on the field of play would be enough. Jack stammered. His voice was so indistinct that the man had to flop on his hunkers to hear. 'D'yeh play yerself?' Jack mumbled.

'Ha,' the man said, picking up a stone and rolling it around his hand. 'I used ta.'

'Who do yeh play fer?' Jack asked, his confidence growing with the man's smile.

'Well, to be honest, I haven't gotta team at the moment. I'm lookin' for someone who wants me.'

Jack suddenly felt so excited his saliva started to fizz. He was going to ask another question. Something about the man's modest demeanour alerted Jack. Here was a man of substance. Jack's lips moved as he rehearsed his question. He took a breath. 'Who did yeh play fer before?' he asked and waited for the man to say, 'Listen son, yeh're gettin' cheeky. Mind yer own business.' But instead, he said two words that lit Jack's eyes like candles.

'Aston Villa,' the man said, putting out his hand. 'The name's Paddy Daly.'

'Yeh played fer Aston Villa?' Jack said slowly. Of course he had seen their claret and pale blue colours in his comics. They were famous, really famous, and one of them, Paddy Daly, was talking to him.

Suddenly awed by the man's greatness, Jack went quiet. In the presence of such glittering fame Jack lost his ability to speak.

Paddy Daly put his hand on Jack's head and sort of spun the greasy hair with his fingers. 'Well, I must be goin', I'll be seein' yeh.'

Jack strolled in a daze back down the pitch to the halfway line. He'd lost all interest in the game. They were only lads messing around. They weren't that special. Paddy Daly, he was *special.*

As the players pulled on their jumpers and lit butts Jack caught the goalie's arm.

'Wor yeh want, snotty?'

'That man there,' Jack said, 'that's Paddy Daly.'

'So feckin' wot?'

'He played fer the Villa.'

'Well, heh, heh, heh, they're jus' feckin' shite, an' if yer man's been dumped he's shite too. Everton, now, they're class.'

The boys laughed and walked off, leaving Jack behind, but his eyes were still afire. He walked home alone but it didn't matter. He had met *the* Paddy Daly, who had played for Aston Villa.

While Babs regaled her father, whose interest in everything she did drew him from the *Mail*, Jack waited, eager to pour out his story of what had just transpired in the now dusk-laden Pit. At last his chance came. Babs had stepped out with a contented smile and was humming as she emptied the drawers of an old tallboy in her room. The emptying of the drawers was an entertainment, a time-passing hobby. When she had taken out every old brass army button, every broken pencil, every needle, broken compass, and mouldy magazine, she put it all back again until the next time. As she was pulling out the drawers Jack was allowed centre stage.

'Guess who I saw in the Pit t'day,' he said to his father. The Boss's bald head remained buried in the newspaper. Jack spoke again.

'Shu'rup,' the Boss snapped, 'I'm after tryin' t'read this bloody paper for the last hour.'

'An' yeh would have finished it be now if it wasn't for Babs,' Mary snapped. The Boss let that slide.

'Paddy Daly,' Jack injected into the stillness of the room. The effect was the same. Jasus, he was burning with great news that no one wanted to hear.

'I'm listenin',' Babs said returning quietly, polishing an old button with Brasso. Jack went to his sister's side. 'He played fer Aston Villa. Aston Villa in England.'

'Who did?'

'Paddy Daly.'

'Did he now?' Babs said, her black curls vibrating as she rubbed the rapidly glowing button.

'Paddy, me arse,' Bridgid muttered as she struggled with her homework. Jack spun towards her. 'Paddy Daly, he played fer Aston Villa.'

'Will yeh feck off, yeh an' yer Paddy Daly,' Bridgid whispered.

Jack waited, scratched his head, looked at his father, the toddlers on the floor, his mother. All were quiet, not doing much. He gathered his socks off the fender and went to bed. Alone in the darkness he played football with Paddy Daly, rising like a bird to head Paddy's crosses past the stricken Eamonn Lee. The goalie flung himself this way and that but he couldn't stop the goals pouring in past him. Jack soared and scored, and was smiling when he went to sleep.

Straight after school one day, Jack was trundling a barrow of turnips when he heard the front knocker rapped hard. Dropping the barrow he sped to the bungalow. Standing on the doorstep was Paddy Daly. 'Ah, Jack,' the footballer said with a big smile. 'I promised yeh these ages ago.'

Jack held out his hand to receive a pair of tickets for the game on Sunday. He scratched the tip of his nose with a dirty thumb.

'Transport is playin' the Hoops this weekend at Milltown. If I can I'll getcha inta meet the players after, Paddy Coad, Liam Touhy, Maxie McCann, all them fellas.'

'Hey!' Jack jumped at the sound of his father's voice. The Boss snatched the tickets out of his hand. 'Who are yeh, an' worra doin' here? Back t'work yeh,' the Boss snarled and he pushed his son away. 'Now, what's yer problem?'

'You mus' be the lad's father.'

'I am, what ovvit?'

'Well, I play a birra football. I've been playin' wirrim.' Daly was knocked off balance, his tongue in knots.

The Boss thrust the tickets back into the footballer's breast pocket. 'Don't come in here tryin' ta bribe my childer,' he said.

Daly looked at the ground, then back at the Boss. He could grab the dirty little runt by the ears and knee him in the balls for the insult, or he could walk out of that kid's miserable life forever. He waved at the face staring at him through the wire and walked away.

50

THE BOSS GRASPED Bab's Primary Certificate in his uncultured claws and examined it from all angles. 'Yeh done well, bloody well,' he said and, tilting back his trilby, he laughed with vicarious pleasure. 'God bless yeh, Babs,' he said, then his face sagged into an expression of self-searching.

'I never hadda chance meself,' he said sadly, his eyes turning away from the fluttering paper. 'I had ta work night an' day fer a few oul' crusts to keep me from goin' mad wit hunger.' Babs waited as she always did for her father's attention to return to her. 'Yeh can't have enough a these t'ings,' he said at last, waving the certificate like a triumphant flag. 'Don't be mindin' them bits a nonsense that lives in them Corporation cottages. Them'll be stewin' in their own p'ison when yeh're livin' in the lappa luxury wit' yer own house an' everythin'. Now, yer next step is to bate that bloody Pitman's,' the Boss continued happily, adoring the smile on Bab's small face.

'The Pitman's,' he said almost reverently. 'Yeah, that's what yeh want next, the Pitman's.' Then, after a short, proud pause, 'Yeh can't bate th'oul Pitman's.'

Glancing up at the bungalow to see if he was being watched, the Boss allowed the pleasure he felt at his daughter's achievement to propel him to touch her - something he rarely did. With an arm around her like an iron trap capturing a butterfly, he briefly and secretly cuddled Babs, his brilliant favourite. 'Yeh done reelly well,' he said, his eyes sparkling and almost generous. 'I betcha it wiped the eyes a them in them snotty houses, yeh gettin' such lovely marks, an' in the music, too, bejapers yeh'd make a fine little musician if on'y yeh'd let me send yeh on a few oul' piana lessons tiddat ould dame beyant in Ballyboden.'

'It's all right, Daddy,' Babs said, feeling slightly guilty at all the encouragement she was getting, and not wanting her father to waste money on her when the whole family needed it.'I'm satisfied Daddy, honestly.'

'Well,' the Boss said gruffly, as if coming out of a trance,'off yeh go now an' do yer homework first, don't be wastin' yer time, yeh're nearly fourteen, life soon passes yeh by.' He returned to the brutal monotony of the squealing pigs and worked alone, talking to himself. 'If on'y I'd had a chance,' he muttered, and his voice was drowned by the pigs clamouring.

That night by the quiet bedroom window Babs showed Jack her Primary Certificate and explained to him what it meant.'Yeh're intelligent, too,' she said, breaking the biscuit she had with her cocoa to share with him.'Yeh can do as well, can't yeh?'When her little brother shufffled, drew in his snot and looked at the floor, she insisted. 'Yeh can, Jack, yeh can. Yer readin' is very good fer yer age an' I have two more libr'y books in me bag ta show yeh.'

For the past few months Babs had read to Jack, sitting by the side of his bed, his spiky head turned towards the wall, his eyes bright with wondering, as battles raged and men screamed and died.

When Babs showed Jack her shorthand he was enthralled. Little maggots wriggling about on the stark white page meant the same as words. When she wrote him a little note he held it from him and laughed.

'It's hard ta believe,' Babs said, 'isn't it? Wan day yeh can take it up, too.'

'That'd be grand,' Jack said, wanting to be nice.

'Don't be wastin' yer time wit' that fella,' the Boss's yell battered the sweet talk into silence.'Hey, you,' the Boss roared at Jack,'ge'rout dere and gather them wisps a hay that's stickin' into the hedge after the wind.'

'Shorthand, huh,' Bridgid sneered at Jack. 'A lo'ra good that'll do yeh when yeh live in a ditch.'

Jack elbowed her in the ribs as he went by.

'Yer man is on'y jealous,' Mary said,'he doesn't want yeh t'do an'tin' wit' yer life. He's dead jealous. That's his problem.'

Catching sight of himself in the kitchen window Jack wondered why that should be so.

The Boss would leave no stone unturned to find Babs a job once she had conquered the magic sixty words a minute. He would use every influence, genuflect before every tin God in the last of Rathfarnham's big rambling houses. No matter what it took, the Boss would find employment for his lovely daughter.

'To t'ink that child might hav'ta folly all them poor bitches ta England,' the Boss muttered as he tossed a small bundle of straw into each sty. England, with its festering back alleys, diseased prostitutes selling their precious bodies, filthy foreigners with their medieval habits, terrified the Boss in sweaty nightmares. 'No, bejasus,' he croaked with emotion, 'Babs won't go t'England. I'd run 'er t'rough wit' a fork before I'd let 'er go off ta dat feckin' hole.'

When Mary asked in her dumb but reasonable way what jobs were available in Ireland the Boss choked with frustration. The woman was insane. She had never been anywhere in her life. She had come straight from the bogs of Galway to Dublin. That was the extent of her worldliness. How could she know anything?

He felt justified in never discussing Babs' future with his wife again. That woman was determined to destroy poor Babs. She would send Babs to Hell. Well, she wasn't going to get the chance.

Poor Mary had little grasp of what went on in the great, struggling, corrupt world outside the prison her husband had made for her.

The Boss would crawl on his belly to those with class and clout who might find Babs a good clean job in Dublin, from which she could return every night to her loving minder. He would love that, his Babs earning money. She could tell him of her day in the exciting metropolis, the gossip and the politics. He'd never had the chance. He began with the priests. If only they could be manipulated, used in some way. Every evening, after another dissatisfying day, his hands scrubbed, a biro in his lumpy fist, the Boss slowly scribbled painfully illiterate letters that were destined for posh wastepaper baskets.

'Yeh'd kiss their arses for *her*,' Mary grumbled. 'What abou' the rest a the childer?'

'Shut yer gob fer Chrissake, I'm concentratin',' the Boss said as, with lousy bald head lowered, he wrestled with the stubborn words.

After the clergy, he tried the gentry. A few replied on embossed paper, still using old army titles, telling him politely they couldn't help. In best jacket and trousers the Boss wobbled on his bike up gravelled drives to every surviving mansion, trying with all his energy and cunning to find work for his beloved daughter. Babs must stay at home with him. She must not go away.

One evening, he came back hot and puffing, flourishing a letter from Lord Armstone, who owned a thousand acres of Wicklow. Babs, her dark hair long and satiny, the way her mother's had been when she'd first known the Boss, ran to meet her father who held the letter up and watched her leap for it like a little puppy.

'We've struck gold,' he said, smiling, 'we're laughin''. Wait now, will yeh, I'll letcha read it in a minute.' Noisily, he parked his bike in the shed and slammed shut the two big padlocks. He removed his jacket and wiped his brow. 'Curse a God on that same feckin' hill,' he said. 'Make me a cuppa char will yeh,' he shouted to Bridgid.

There was a single shuffle as the children all gathered round. Even Pam came out of her dream, her rouged cheeks, spattered with beauty spots that made her look like a clown suffering from the bubonic plague. She drew up a chair.

'Don't bother ta ask me, will yeh. Yehz all t'ink I'm yer bloody skivvy,' Bridgid was heard muttering sulkily from the depths of the kitchen, but with the excitement created by the letter the Boss was too involved to take offence. 'Don't read it yit,' Bridgid pleaded from the kitchen, but Bab's high, sweet voice was already silencing the room within.

'"As I know you to be a very hard-working man,"' Babs read, and smiled at her father, '"I am pleased to be able to recommend your daughter for an interview at Easthams . . ." Easthams!' Babs cried. 'That's the big book shop near Nelson's Pillar.'

'"I cannot, of course, influence their reaction in any way,"' the letter rambled on, '"but I take this opportunity to wish her the best of luck. Yours, Armstone."'

'Isn't that the tops!' The Boss was beaming. 'Isn't he the fine gentleman ta be offerin' a total stranger such a grand chance? T'anks be ta God fer gentlemen like him in this rotten country,' the Boss concluded.

'It was the likes a Lord Arsehole that encouraged the Black an'Tans,' Mary mumbled from her chair.

'What are yeh tryin' ta do?' the Boss snarled, barging a hole through the ring of onlookers to get at Mary. 'We all know where yeh stand,' he said. 'Yeh'd send the poor child off ta England an' ruin her.'

'Daddy, Daddy,' Babs said, drawing his fire, 't'anks fer gettin' me the letter.'

'That's all right,' the Boss said, 'it's jus' when a poor fella breaks his back gettin' somethin' fer one uv his childher yer woman has ta t'row cold water on it.'

For the first time, the Boss hugged Babs openly. 'Yeh'll be needin' a few oul' t'ings ta wear for th'interview,' he said.

'No, that's all right, Daddy, I won't be needin' an'tin',' Babs said. 'I've got some nice t'ings.'

Mary heard her husband reply, 'Not at all, sure yeh're goin' ag'inst terrible cute young wans from the city. Them'll be done up t'da nines. Yeh wan'ta bate them fair an' square on that game. Look, I've got a few bob from the last lot a pigs. I can spare a bit ta buy yeh a frock or somethin' that'll make yeh look the part of a secaterry.'

Early next day, the pony was harnessed and the Boss was puffing vapour around the dawn yard. When he'd finished his jobs he knocked on Babs' window.

'Y'ol' shite, will yeh shu'rup,' Mary, without her teeth, lisped sourly from her baby-warmed bed. She listened to Kitty's hooves clop down the road and heard her husband whistle as the cart clattered away. Slowly, she raised herself on an elbow, wondering how she could force herself to face another day, when the youngest children clambered on to her like fat little piglets, howling their needs. 'Ah well, here goes,' Mary sighed, and putting her big pale feet on the floor, she got up from the bed.

She had a heap of buttered potatoes and chops on the table by the time the travellers arrived home. It was a peace offering to her husband and wronged daughter. All day, Mary's mood had swung from a hate-filled frenzy of boxing walls and smashing vases to a flurry of cramming gifts of repentance on to the table. She was happy for a while and was in a clean floral frock and her best shoes. Even her fat legs were baited with nylon and suspenders to lure the Boss. 'The on'y way ta win yer man is ta decorate the goods an' fill his belly,' Eileen had told her. 'But why yeh wan'ta bates me.'

The meal was tense with Mary wanting instant approval, her nerves twanging, her guts twisting with hurt. In the cacophany of children's questions, the gaiety and unusual geniality of the Boss, Mary went quiet and drifted into the kitchen to stoke her hurt into a conflagration.

Babs got the job over twenty-five other girls and the Boss wrote a spidery, subservient letter to Lord Armstone, who didn't reply.

51

'BABS! WAIT WILL yeh.' The Boss came to the gate for the third time, his face honeycombed against the chicken wire. 'Now, listen ta me,' he wagged a finger. 'Don'tcha be listenin' ta them gurriers from the slums if the melts try talkin' t'yeh or an'tin'. Ignore them bastards, they're on'y ou'ta rob yeh.'

'But, Daddy,' Babs laughed, 'yeh tole me a hundert times.' She reached out a small black-gloved hand and touched her father's crooked fingers. She looked smaller than her four-eleven. The bike the Boss bought for her seemed impossibly large, with the big basket in the front holding only the small plastic handbag she'd snatched from the last charity parcel from Aunt Dolores in Chicago.

'Don't worry, Daddy, I'll be all right,' Babs insisted, her face creased with emphasis. She pushed the bike over the bridge and with her father watching anxiously she got astride, looked back smiling, and pushed off into the future. She was employed, the first wage earner in the family.

'The little genius,' the Boss softly addressed the pigs' upraised snouts, 'she'll not have her poor hands broke like mine, workin' fer nuttin'.' With a last glance towards the dip in the road that had swallowed his beloved daughter, he turned back to attend to the squealing demands of his pigs.

Babs hadn't seen Mary's clouded face peering out from behind the curtain, her fat belly resting against the cold bedroom wall. 'Will yeh look a'im,' Mary had muttered, her old horn-rimmed glasses turning from Babs to her husband. 'The little shite, "Take care now, won'tcha Babs",' Mary was a poor mimic but the strange voice she'd put on to imitate her husband attracted the toddlers, who laughed.

'Again, Mammy,' young Paul said, looking up at his mother, then back to his little brothers, his dirty fat little hands curled as if to applaud.

'Bad cess ta that little spiv,' Mary said. Her whole being aching for attention, she steered her fat stomach out of the door like the prow of a tramp steamer and into the kitchen to work at the scummy sink. Another sunless day without love. At least now that Babs was away from the house Mary wouldn't have to listen to the sick, sentimental rubbish the Boss reserved for his eldest daughter alone. 'Yeh'd t'ink he on'y had the wan child,' Mary grumbled as, with potato peeler in a red hand, she looked out of the lichened window. 'I'll be watchin' yeh, me bucko,' she growled, her eyes wide.

Mary could listen to the radio for an hour whenever the Boss had yoked Kitty and clattered off somewhere. It was a sweet and blissful hour. She put her fat, wrinkled-stockinged legs up and took the terrible pull off her stomach. But too soon the gate clanged, Kitty's hooves thundered on the bridge, and the gate clanged shut. Mary knew the remainder of the day would be tense and tiring. She hated the way her husband rushed into the house as if expecting to find her in bed with a dozen lovers. Every time a man passed by Mary felt her skirt rise. Men were dirty bastards. She had become obsessed, thinking all men carried sticks to lift her skirt to look at her nice fat belly that sat, big and white and blue like a monster's egg, on top of her stout veiny legs.

'Well?' the Boss said with mock geniality as he stormed into the room. 'An'tin' strange or comical occurred while I was out?'

'What are yeh blatherin' about?' Mary snapped, brushing past him, shoving her fat belly into his smug little face, using her unborn infant as a battering ram to cleave her way past him. Sourly, she said, 'If yeh t'ink there's a fella or two in me bed go an' look for 'em.'

'Huh! That's a good wan,' the Boss said, but he was reassured, his face a laughing mask. He put a paw on his wife's massive bottom.

'Get out a that,' Mary shouted and slapped the hand away.

The Boss made an unseen fist. She shouldn't do that. She mustn't hit him.

He could knock her arseways with a punch if he wanted to. Instead, he said in a cold and controlled, if slightly high-pitched voice, 'Any chance of a cuppa cha?'

'Make it yerself,' Mary said, sweeping past him again as she ferried pots of cabbage, potatoes and carrots to the greasy cooker in the corner.

The Boss sat eating a folded slice of wholemeal bread, his hat still on, his feet on the tiles, his trousers tucked into his socks. He chewed pensively, poured another mug of tea and drifted into an uneasy sleep. He was worried about Babs . . . Jasus, if anything happened to her . . . What if she was kidnapped, taken into some filthy subterranean tenement in the city, raped and tortured? He had often thought of that happening, and knew exactly what he would do.

He would get the little Smith & Wesson he kept in an oily rag in the shed, where not even Babs knew about it. He would take a box of bullets and go into town on his bike. If he found the man who had ruined his daughter that man would wish himself dead because he would be required to die a million times. Having drifted into an uneasy doze, the nightmare of something awful happening to Babs became so real the Boss woke up stinking with sweat, his hands together as if they were bound, his feet tucked up helplessly. In his dream Babs was screaming, and he was in no position to save her. He was made to watch her suffer.

'What's that!' the Boss yelled as the gate snarled open. He left it unoiled to warn him of intruders so he could spring from his bed and be ready for the doorknob to turn.

'It's on'y Jack home from school,' Mary retorted.

'That bloody sleeveen, what duzzy he want, startlin' a poor fella?'

In her softest voice Mary greeted her son. 'Didja have a gran' time darlin'?'

Jack's lips disappeared as he made a funny twisted little expression that meant *stupid bloody question.* 'It was OK,' he said listlessly, collecting the slice of bread and jam his mother offered.

'Go aisy on that jam,' the Boss barked, 'that's the last a the lovely Mixed Fruit.' It was the cheapest jam on the shelf, the Boss got a penny off it at O'Beirnes (Grocery and Provisions since 1875). He was well in there because he cleaned out the shop's rubbish. The paper he burned, but the orange, grapefruit and tomato boxes were smashed into kindling. O'Beirne was a 'darlin' friend'. The Boss saw the neat well-stocked shop as a potential job opportunity for Jack, if only the boy would wash himself and scrub his snotty nose.

Jack looked at his father. It was unusual to see him indoors when it was still daylight.

'Get that inta yeh then go an' see to them pigs,' the Boss growled. Jack felt his way into his boots with his toes without bending down. Slovenly little bastard. The Boss watched with contempt the way his son refused to put the fecking bread down while he pulled on his boots.

As Jack clumped off down to the sties Mary rounded on her husband. 'It's no use yeh sittin' there,' she said, 'yer precious daughter won't be back fer at least t'ree hours, and yeh're in the way.'

The Boss looked at the clock, got to his feet, and peered over his wife's shoulder as she peeled apples. 'Yeh're l'avin' none a that bloody fruit at all,' he said as Mary's knife dug deep into the skin and cut around the apple in one long fat strip. 'Cut it t'inner,' the Boss said and went out.

'An' yeh can feck off,' Mary said with the peeler upraised like a finger.

Bridgid and Pam buzzed in. 'Sorry Mam, we were watchin' the Dowlin's fightin',' Bridgid said.

'Animals, ghastly,' Pam said archly. She showed more leg than was encouraged by the nuns, having rolled up her skirt at the waist to show off her developing calves. In time she would have attractive legs, but at the moment they were pale, goose-bumpy, unattractive, and hardly different from the legs of her brothers. Mary had to scold her for this and also for wearing Babs' brassiere.

'Anyway, yeh've got nuttin',' Bridgid said. Pam looked back at her plain, manly sister with a devastating scorn.

'Wonder how Babs is gettin' on?' Bridgid asked her mother.

'Yeh're not the on'y wan wonderin',' Mary said.

'The old man, too, eh?' Bridgid said. 'Am I right?'

'Yeah,' Mary said, 'he druv me mad sittin' there waitin' and worryin'. Yeh'd swear she'd gone off ta Morocco or somewhere like that.' Mary sat down, the bulk of her chores were, for the moment, done.

'Wonder what this wan's goin' ta be like?' Bridgid said, smoothing her hand over her mother's belly.

'Ach! Who cares?' Mary said, 'just another bloody worry. Yer man doesn't care, couldn't givva shite wan way or th'udder.'

At last, loud voices in the yard heralded Babs' triumphant return.

The girls ran out into the yard to greet her, letting off a barrage of questions. 'What was it like?' . . . 'Was it hard?' . . . 'Were there nice lads there?'

Babs, laughing and assailed on all sides, pushed her big bike before her.

'Leave it there,' the Boss said, grinning widely, 'I'll put it away fer yeh.'

'Will yeh look it him now?' Mary said, looking out of the window, 'he's like a dog wit' two tails.'

'Ah, yeh're grand,' the Boss said and almost kissed his daughter in front of everyone. 'Yeh mus' tell me all about it later. Don't fergit now.'

'I won't Daddy,' said Babs, looking like a little Judy Garland in her big gabardine.

Smiling, she went up to her mother and planted a kiss on the heat-reddened cheek. 'Mammy it was great, but it's gran' ta be home again too.'

'Yeh mus' be famished,' Mary said, 'I'll purron the chip pan.'

'I'd luv a mugga tea,' Babs said, slipping off her coat and making her necklace of phony pearls rattle. She let down her hair and, with clips in her mouth, made it tidy. Finally, she sat down to tell the tale of the journey, and the first few exciting minutes when she walked through the office door. Still down the dusky yard with Jack, her father was working away, and missing it all.

Friday came and with slender fingers Babs splayed the first green pound notes she'd earned like a fan in front of Jack. 'Lookit that!' she exclaimed. 'Money.'

Jack was gazing mistily at the fortune when Bridgid appeared. 'An' yeh can ferget that, oul' son,' she said. 'Yeh won't be gettin' yer filt'y hands on any a dat.'

'Ah, come on,' Babs said, 'yeh're awful cruel, yeh know that?' Unclasping her purse, she fished a sixpenny piece out of the brimming silver. 'Here,' she said, 'take that an' buy yerself sweets at Rice's.'

Jack took the new sixpence as if it were the Holy Sacrament. 'T'anks,' he said, and scuttled off.

Stubbornly, her chin on her chest, Bridgid held out her big dirty hand. Babs smiled and, after rooting among the larger coins, produced another sixpence and held it up in front of her young sister's eyes.

'I should ge'ra shillin',' Bridgid growled. 'Yeh gev him the same an' I'm older.'

To take the shine off her big sister's success Pam entered the room quiet as a zephyr. She was wearing lipstick and a big Rhode Island Red feather in her hair, and swanned about dreamily.

'Fer feck's sake,' Bridgid cried, 'it's Brigitte Bardot lookin' fer her tanner as well.'

'Yeh're wrong as usual,' Pam said loftily. 'I don't want money. It's not something I worry about.'

Bridgid laughed. 'Have yer shite then,' she said.

'Bridgid!' Mary's voice reverberated in the cold. 'Come on, giv'us a hand, yeh can lay the table at least.'

'But I peeled all them bloody potatoes on me own,' Bridgid shouted back. 'Ah, g'wan,' Babs said, 'give Mammy a hand. Sure, I'll be out in a minute when I get changed.'

Soon after Babs had returned to help, the door burst open and the Boss stood for a moment, transfixed by the little wad of notes she had left at his place on the table. Fierceness drained from his face. 'Jasus, aren't yeh the sweet little angel,' he said. 'Begod, that's a whole lot more'n I can earn in a week. Three notes, that's the stuff ta give them.' He shuffled the money almost sensuously. 'Is this all fer me? Don't yeh want a bit t'spend on a pair a k's or an'tin'?' he laughed. For some reason, using the initial letter for *knickers* made him laugh like a prurient schoolboy.

'I'm all right,' Babs said, 'I've kept back fifteen shillin's fer meself, that's enough. I joined the Christmas Club, that'll take care a the presents.'

'Toppin', toppin',' the Boss repeated again as he fingered the lovely green Irish pounds.

'Wor about some grub, yeh out there?' the Boss shouted into the dark kitchen. Mary, not daring to turn on the light, grumbled in the gloom.

Bridgid's voice could be heard cursing her father for his 'maneness'.

'What did that little bitch say?' the Boss demanded.

'Nothin', Daddy,' Babs said.

'I won't have her abusin' me,' the Boss said, charging into the kitchen to give Bridgid a wallop that sent her crashing against the sink. 'Don't be talkin' abou' me like that,' he said, holding her by the collar so she could hardly breathe. 'Don't be cursin' me.' His eyes were glinting blue and icy.

With great dignity Bridgid came to the dinner table and deliberately sat directly opposite her father. The red mark remained on her face throughout the meal to embarrass him every time he looked across the table. Bridgid also knew it would make Babs cool towards her father for the rest of the evening.

The meal, like many before it cooked with such suffering by Mary for her family, was eaten in an uncomfortable silence.

52

JACK BARELY KEPT up with Polly, the new cow, as she trundled hungrily towards the green patch of grass in the Pit. Mary watched from the window. For the first time her son had been given responsibility. A tousled and tatty eight-year-old, Jack clumped along in old boots, a switch in his hand.

'Don't let the darlin' baste excape,' the Boss said, 'or yeh'll be gettin' it in da neck when yeh come home.'

The Pit was ripe for development. Rathfarnham was sinking under a sea of concrete, speculators were busy driving up farm lanes, greasing palms, making promises. 'Them bastards'll never build on that pool a piss,' said the Boss, referring to the lakes that swamped the Pit in winter. Having purchased a cow to oust the Nearys as the family's milk supplier, he was fearful of losing the only scrap of free grazing around.

Jack followed the cow's haunches, nervously shadowing her every move as she rolled along, and jumping with fright when she tossed her head and snorted with the joy of freedom. He sat down when she found a patch of grass untainted by mongrel shit. With a café au lait coloured tongue, Polly tugged at the grass and chewed it with a kind of melancholy, her huge lashes flickering, her tail swishing away the silvery flies that crawled over her rump.It was going to be a long day but Jack had a little book of Irish poems that Mary had given him to kill time.

With the finished book on the rock beside him Jack gazed and wondered, his big eyes sweeping over the surrounding scene. He saw women returning from shopping, old men weaving about on squeaky bikes, dogs running in and out of the wheels of carts drawn by tired horses. He saw boys skulking along the hedgerows on their way to caddy at the Grange Golf Club. He saw the smoke of their Woodbines and heard their curses. When Polly at last lay down to chew her cud

Jack relaxed. If she did suddenly decide to make a mad dash for it on to the unfenced road there was nothing he could do about it.

He saw Kennedy's milk float, followed by Johnston, Mooney and O'Brien's bread van hurtling around Cullen's bend as if they were racing. Unemployed men came on to the flattest part of the Pit and began chasing a football. Shark Donnelly shouted, 'Hey snotty, yeh wan'ta go in goal?'

'No,' Jack called, shaking his head vigorously, disguising his delight at being asked.

'Oh, feck yerself then,' Shark said. Jack hated the Donnellys. They were big and loud and not a bit afraid of the Guards.

As he watched them tear around in their old swinging sports coats, with their trousers tucked into their spiv's socks, Jack wanted to yell, 'Yeh're all shite! Paddy Daly's the best.' They would only crowd and threaten him, and the cow might be driven off. They wouldn't hit him, no, for in spite of their rough talk they were terrified of the Boss. Even though a few like Shark were over six foot they couldn't handle a man made of steel, a man with nuts and bolts for eyes, a man who would clout them with any implement to hand.

No man could best the Boss, a fact that made Jack proud.

Jack watched their game and listened to the uncouth shouts of the men as they slipped and cursed. It was something to do, until they lit up cigarettes and with their coats slung over their shoulders they slouched home. As he watched them go Jack felt desolate. He wished he could belong to a gang.

The cow stood up stiffly, her tail out straight she urinated and defecated, the nitrogen-rich grass pouring from her like green custard. Contentedly, she continued to graze some more.

Like a small Greek shepherd, Jack sat patiently, the hours slowly ticking by, the sun edging nearer the trees. He could hear the faint squealing of the pigs. He was cold but he couldn't go home yet, not while there was still light in the sky and Polly kept munching, her piebald hide darkening with the gradual loss of light. A fox barked, an owl hooted in an oak somewhere. Jack saw the single yellow bulb go on in the bungalow behind the trees. He had to wait until his father whistled.

Jack sat on a rock and, having stirred Polly's soft cowpat, he flicked his green stick and watched the men coming home from the City. Brisk silhouettes, they crossed the Pit, their heads bobbing, clutching important looking briefcases. He saw them climb the hilly track to Golden Acre. Where was Paddy Daly? Surely he couldn't have moved on already?

It was a fine,warm Rathfarnham evening filled with the whistling of blackbirds. The excited shouts and squeal of the habitués of the Pit had all but ceased. Jack failed to notice the frail old man who climbed the path and had paused to watch him. The sun had almost set, a last splintered flashlight burnished the little cow, her udder now swollen. Why didn't the Boss call him home? Jack was too deep in thought to notice the shadow creeping from bush to bush towards him.

Dusk was robbing the field of its hues. The skyline of Golden Acre was etched like a stage, skeletons of half-built houses, telephone poles waiting to carry the new householders' chatter across fields and out of the time-warped village.

Ghosting from one half-finished house to the next, the old man was down the path and beside Jack before he knew it. Ragged and greasy capped, he opened his toothless mouth to talk. It was as raw and foul smelling as a hen's arse. 'Evenin' son.'

Jack jumped up.

'What's yer name?' The man spoke in a strange piping voice.

'Jack Dunne, I live over there.' Sensing something that was not right Jack began to move away.

'All right kid,' the old man said in a strangled castrato. His eyes were half boiled, his chin was stubbly. He reached out with boney hands. 'Com'ere, I'm not goin' ta hurtcha. I know yer da. Nice man. Hard workin''. I'm the night watchman above in Golden Acre. I gev yer dad a few planks. I know yer house. I've been in it. Yer mother made tea fer me.' He pointed a twig-like finger in the direction of the bungalow. 'Nice man yer da, wouldn' tell the cops what he done, y'know, knockin' off them planks an' all. I wouldn' hear a bad word abour'im.'

Jack remained silent. How was he going to get away? He felt trapped and sensed danger but could do nothing about it.

'It's gettin' kind a late fer a lad ta be out. What ar'yeh doin' out here at this time a night. What's up wit'cha? Why don't yeh say somet'in'? Are yeh dumb or what?' The old man's tone was getting sharper.

'I'm mindin' the cow fer me daddy,' Jack whispered. 'I hav'ta be home in a minute.'

The old man shaded his eyes with his hand. 'I don't see no cow,' he said. 'Where is she? Come on, son, don't gi'me that! Yeh're pullin' me pisser.'

Jasus, Jack prayed, why didn't his father shout, whistle, curse, anything. 'Over there,' Jack pointed vaguely at the deepening shadows.

'What's over there?' The old man's voice was shrill. He moved a couple of steps nearer. Jack smelt the tobacco juice on his vest, the fishy pong that came off his unwashed body. Darkness seemed in a hurry to descend. Warnings echoing in his head, Jack tried to move away. With quick steps the man followed him.

Jack had forgotten the cow. He was running now. For God's sake, why didn't his father whistle? The old man's concrete-encrusted boots rushed through the grass.

Jack was fifty yards ahead but was gasping with fear. His legs seemed to be made of lead. His energy evaporated. He was slowing down. The old man seemed to have gained new wind. He dissected Jack's intended path, shepherding the boy towards a broken cowshed. A sliver of moon hung impaled in the trees. 'I want yeh ta help me,' the old man whispered. 'I lost the shank a me pipe in here when I was havin' a shit.' He pushed Jack into the cowshed. A slant of moonlight illuminated half of it like stagelighting. 'I'm distracted wit'out it.' The old man said. He was calm, hardly breathing, while Jack's breath came in ragged gasps.

Jack shivered, dampness was curling up from the river. 'I t'ink it's over here,' the man said, grunting as he pushed the boy before him. The floor was slippery underfoot. Jack's face shone white in the moonlight that was pouring in through the open roof. No sound came from the village. Outside, the cow grazed in the dark, sensibly heading towards the bungalow gate, where she would wait quietly to be admitted.

Jack's bare knee roughly scraped a concrete wall. He smelt shit, old newspapers, stamped out cigarettes. He was in the old man's power, totally and absolutely. 'Yer young eyes is betther'n mine,' the old man said. His hand patrolled Jack's back while the boy searched desperately in the dark, his bare hands touching unseen filth on the cowshed floor.

'Sorry, misther,' Jack said, 'I can't see it, I'll give yeh a hand tomorra. I swear.'

The old man prodded him. 'G'wan, try dere.'

Light from the moon penetrated the thick air, casting shadow on the old man's thin, evil face. Jack continued to rummage ineffectually as the old man closed in on him. 'Hey, whoa there,' he said, 'she's here.'

Jack turned back and blundered into the old man's boney embrace. 'I have ta go,' Jack cried out loud. 'Mey dad'll be waitin' fer me.'

'Nah, yer da's fergotten yeh,' the old man said. 'He's sittin' be the fire now, drinkin' tea. Yeh're on yer own, kid.'

Jack watched helplessly as the thin old arms closed around him with a strength that was stifling and terrifying. 'Come 'ere, me love,' the nightwatchman groaned. With his unshaven face rasping against Jack's soft cheek, he fumbled inside Jack's pants with a rough chapped hand. The old man's grip tightened in smothering, suffocating ecstasy, forcing his dirty nails into the boy's penis.

Jack screamed. He was choking, the old man's crusty greatcoat against his face. The old man convulsed, his grip getting tighter. The pain too horrible to bear, Jack wrestled desperately, but was easily restrained.

With an hysterical scream, Jack looked up and saw God's clean, innocent stars above. At last, he heard his father's whistle. It pierced the dark air, flew like a grappling hook to a man lost in a ravine. It gave Jack strength.

With a cry he broke free and staggered through the dark with its wild brambles and clumps of poisonous nettles that reached out to clutch and sting him. But he didn't feel a thing he was running so madly, tears falling down his face, heading for the light, the bungalow, his father, home.

Jack fled through the blackness, the shouts of the old man echoing behind him. 'Come back, come back,' the wild man screamed. Confused, used to obeying, Jack, to his eternal damnation, stopped, turned back and dumbly watched the silhouette coming towards him, spilling coins into his hand. 'Now, feck off an' be quick about it,' the man said, 'yer da'll be worryin' about yeh. An' if yeh tell 'im an'tin', I'll say it was yeh wanted it. He'll believe me an' feckin' murdher yeh.'

Running, scratching his legs on rusty tin and spiny green things, Jack finally made it home. Then, like a screwdriver through the brain, it came to him: he had sold himself. He was spoiled, ruined, destroyed. He ran to the yard, scattering the rats, gulping in the warm stench of the boiler, its fire flaring in the wind. Vomit lurched up his throat. Clutching his head, he heaved until his stomach emptied. Then he cried again, howling like a run-over dog.

Cold seeped into Jack's bones where he sat, a disconsolate smudge on the bungalow wall. God would hate him for ever. He could never be clean again. Desperately, he pounded the electricity pole that stood outside the gate, smelling its friendly creosote. Through his tears he saw a light shining from the kitchen window. Mary, on tottering legs, would be preparing tea, the smell of food filling the room, the kettle bubbling on the hob, his sisters laying the table. The Boss, in his chair by the fire, would be reading the paper, spectacles on the tip of his nose.

Touching the scented pole, Jack pressed his lips against the wood, and confessed his guilt, then in his agony he remembered the cow. Still choking on his tears, he rushed past the window to the byre. The cow turned a large worried eye on the approaching shadow. Crying out loud Jack threw his arms around the beast's soft neck, feeling her innocent warmth. Deeply he inhaled the milky, secure smell of the animal.

'Hey, what's goin' on out dere?' The window had been thrown open and the Boss's shiny head protruded. 'Dat yeh, yeh bloody sleeveen? Come in an' be quick about it. That lovely cow had to find her way home, yeh useless little bastard.' His father's awful drone penetrated his brain. 'I had ta let that poor baste in meself. She wandered home on her own. Where'd yeh get ta, eh?'

Jack turned to the cow and looped the chains around her head, continuing to embrace the cow's thick neck as she vigorously tackled the few handfuls of graveyard hay the Boss had left for her in a perfumed bundle. As he passed the window he was cuffed around the head, his father holding him steady with one hand as he slapped him with the other.

'That's fer not comin' in when yeh shoulda,' the Boss said. 'Now ge'rinta the house yeh schemin' melt.'

His teeth rattling with a phantom fever, Jack sobbed out loud as he walked the last few yards to the kitchen. Blessing himself, he opened the door. Sheepish and dirty he entered the light of the room. His brothers and sisters all stared at him as if they could see his dirt-black soul and the big sin throbbing in his breast.

Mary looked him up and down, and with fear in her look wiped the gob of grey semen from his trousers. 'What's this?' she exclaimed.

Her tone alerted the Boss. 'What's what?' he demanded.

Showing unusual mental dexterity his mother said, 'The poor lad's afther catchin' a chill mindin' that blasted cow. G'wan darlin',' she urged, 'take yer bread an' milk off ta bed wit'cha.'

'I wouldn't feel a bit sorry fer the waster,' the Boss muttered into his *Evening Mail*. 'I warned him 'bout mixin' with them gurriers from the Corporation houses. They're walkin' with disease, that lot.'

Jack said his prayers more carelessly than usual and crawled under the covers like a wounded dog. Why hadn't Jesus saved him? He lay in the darkness, a thin arm upraised like a small white branch as if to ward off blows. Nothing could be undone. Before he slept he heard footsteps in the hallway, the doorknob turning, stockinged feet on the bare wooden floor. The Boss stood in the dark for a while before turning back to where the rest of the family were clustered, then picked up his paper and resumed his reading.

All through the night, in moments of fierce clarity, Jack woke and endured anew the pain and the shame. He moaned and turned his sweaty face in the moonlight. If only Paddy Daly had come along, he would have saved him. If only he possessed his father's manly strength he would have kicked the old man to death for what he'd done. But he was cursed with his mother's gullibility and cowardice. Jack stared blindly at the ceiling, his hands curling. He would hate himself for ever, and he prayed fervently for forgiveness. Dawn was rekindling the day when weariness finally overcame him and he slept.

When he woke up the hobnailed ghost of the old man was standing by his bed. He felt ravaged again. Jack got out of bed a different person. He would neither forget nor forgive. No one, he promised himself, would ever get the better of him again. Even if he had to kill that person.

When Babs interrogated him over the next few days he couldn't talk about what had happened. And he never did, but left it bottled up inside him like a phial of poison leaking into his system.

53

THAT SAME NIGHT the nightwatchman was attacked and badly beaten. Later, Jack imagined the battered man in his greasy clothes on his back in his hut, his upturned brazier lighting the grass all round, his dark viper's blood trickling on the ground, his whimpering lost in the coughing up of blood. Jack hated him so much he wanted him dead.

At the breakfast table Jack moped, his head in his hands. Bridgid cracked the thick duck egg shells with a knife and spilled the orangey yokes with their rim of rich albumen into hot fat. Outside, the hens were clamouring to be released. 'Ah, c'mon Brud,' she said. 'It's not th'end a the world.'

With unexpected understanding and tenderness she continued, 'Ol' fellas like him are sick. Yeh hav'ta feel sorry fer 'em. On the udder hand yeh mus'n' let a dirthy oul' perve ruin yer life. C'mon, yeh love th'ol' French toast. Here, have a slice, it'll cheer yeh up.' She looked at Jack, her face plastered with a smile. With her bib a size too small, her fat belly, her kind face and unkempt black hair she looked the image of Mary. 'How many slices? Six? I betcha I can ate more'n yeh can.' Jack forced a smile, shiftily took a slice and began to nibble. After polishing off another two he felt better.

Mary appeared, stiffly, as if she had corns on the soles of her feet. Sour-faced, she plonked her heavy frame at the table. 'It's all right fer yehz kids,' she groaned, 'so young, and yehz haven't made a mistake yit. Lookit me. Ruined.'

'Any more for any more?' Bridgid cried.

'No t'anks, darlin', th'ol' stomack's not up to it. Be the way, Jack,' she continued ominously, 'that stain on yer trousers, an' the cuts on yer face an' legs. What have yeh been up ta?'

Jack played with his French toast.

Bridgid shoved some of the toast in front of her mother, 'C'mon,

Mammy,' she said urgently, 'have wan slice, it won't kill yeh.'

'Ah, maybe just a tincy wan then,' Mary said, the direction of her conversation safely diverted as Bridgid handed her mother a massive, love-drenched slice. It was a masterpiece, cooked to perfection, a perfect blend of yellow and russet with dark brown frilly bits on the edges. It smelt delicious. Mary picked it up and began to eat. Bridgid poured her a mug of dark brown tea.

'But Jack–' Mary began again.

'Mammy!' Bridgid gave her mother a very stern look.

'I was just goin'ta say that oul' quare fella won't hurt an innocent child again afther what yer daddy done t'him las' night.'

Jack finished his breakfast and went outdoors.

Calling in a high plaintive voice, and carrying a saucepan of grain, he let the coloured flood of feathers spill out into the yard. The younger fowl were sent squawking as the old birds planted their dirty feet in the middle of the little pool of corn, their lice-infested bottoms hanging, their scraggy wing feathers dipping. The Boss arrived after milking the cow. Jack lowered his head. 'See that oul' wan there?' his father said. 'The hoor hasn't laid fer a munt'.' Unaware of her death sentence, the old hen would enjoy the morning, filling her useless old body with good food, depriving the young layers who would afterwards haunt the hedges looking for secret places to lay their eggs. The Boss watched the hens for a moment, his lips moving. Perhaps he was praying.

The sun, having unveiled early that morning, was already several notches up in the sky. Soon, kids would be clattering down from the terraces of Ballyboden, smoking and throwing stones into the stream like their fathers did. The Boss tacked up the pony and with a shout he was off, urging Kitty into a gallop. Jack watched him go.

Bridgid escorted Jack to school that day, making a point of passing close to the watchman's empty hut. The brazier was still upturned, cold cinders scattered round. And on the way home she made sure Jack walked with some of the lads from the Corporation houses, just to show them he was no pansy.

That evening, all was tranquil in the bungalow. Friday brought an easing of the pain, a couple of days respite from schoolwork. It helped heal wounds and elevate stunted souls. Bridgid was studying a book of palmistry. 'Ah, yeh poor oul' shite,' the Boss had sneered. 'Sure yeh're a bloody fool if yeh t'ink that stuff is good fer an'tin'.'

Feck you, Bridgid thought, shifting her big awkward feet and continuing to stare at the creases on her palms.

Pam lay rump-upwards on her bed, her false eyelashes in place, her beauty spots re-sited, gorging herself on a magazine full of sinful glitter. If only she could be discovered. If only one of those producer fellas would come by. She kicked her legs and hummed, showing her lean calves in the purple dress Mary had cut down from an old ballgown Aunt Dolores had sent.

His work over, Jack went down to the river and gingerly dipped his toes into the cold river water. Broken bottles and rusting scrap lurked in its muddy bed. The Boss used the river to clean bleach bottles which he then sold to a dealer in town. Occasionally, tanners and bobs slipped out of his top pocket when he stooped over. Jack often found the treasure winking in the shallows. He should have given the money back but he kept it.

'Hey!' Dung-caked boots edged nearer. 'I'm afther workin' like a bloody nigger all these years t'put a bit a bread in yer mout's,' the Boss said, 'so tomorra, I'm goin' ta th' Phoenix Park, ta hell wit' the expense.' Jack waited for an invitation. 'I'm takin' Babs,' the Boss said. 'Yer man Liam has a couple a cripples runnin'. We'd have a right bit a skit if one a dem was ta run away wit' the Fifteen Hunderd.'

So, the Boss's recent empathy didn't run to taking Jack to the races. Never mind, Babs liked horses.

Uncle Liam wallowed in Krug champagne while his brother wallowed in pig shit.

'To t'ink I got the little fecker that lovely job when he had nuttin',' the Boss said, not for the first time. 'I could've had that lovely job fer meself. Sir Courteney wanted *me* ta look afther them hunters, not that little shite. I was workin' at twelve for them rotten Augustinians, keepin' that melt fed while the lazy little bastard sat at home wit' his feet up. I blame me stupid bloody mudder, the ould bitch. And that drunken father a mine. But I reelly blame me bloody mudder. She, the feckin' oul' eejit, t'ought the sun shone out a yer man Liam's arse!'

Oh the terrible, wasting, bitterness of the Boss's memory. The deep cuts in him that never healed. Every time the Boss opened the racing pages he seemed to be confronted by his brother's pompous smirk. It made the Boss spit bits of his liver. Liam's success seemed limitless. He lived in a 'bloody great mansion', and fannied around with the racing set, inarticulate football managers from the Gorbals, glitzy gangsters, men high up in the Catholic Church and every other shamshite; while Johnny, poor bugger, had to feed eight kids on sweet feckall. While Liam in his specially built-up shoes bobbed like a hungry terrier among the self-made, the conmen, the Bishops and the English nobles, his poor brother, the very man who'd made him, swapped dreary obscenities with junkyard rats and shovelled shit for peanuts. The fact that Liam felt neurotically inferior to the jumped-up scum who paid his wages and poured his malt whiskeys, never occurred to the Boss who envied and hated his brother with equal, unfathomable bitterness.

Next morning, all was temporarily forgotten as the Boss stood in the hallway splendidly turned out in his best coat, smartest trilby, brown brogues and yellow gloves. As he adusted his tie in the mirror he said to Babs, 'Wouldn' it be grand if we wor to pull off an oul' coup and come back wit' a few bob?'

'That'd be great, Daddy,' Babs said as she put a slide in her hair and adjusted the smart jacket Mary had cut down from a hideous green velvet thing Aunt Delores had sent them.

'Yeah,' the Boss said absent-mindedly as he looked at his cute little face in the mirror. Not bad for an ould shagger, he was thinking as he tightened his belt. 'Come on, Babs,' we'll show them hoors how ta behave.

Baldoyle was an hour away on the bus. What a picture they presented to the casual passerby as they walked to the bus stop. Who could tell what was in the Boss's mind as he swung along with the beautiful young lady at his side? Was he thinking of the days long gone when an equally attractive and dark-haired young woman fresh up from the country had held his hand and twittered into his attentive ear? Mary watched them go and dropped the curtain back ito place. Rubbing her hands together she put the kettle on, cut herself a slice of cake, tuned in the radio and sat down to a pile of darning.

'Fancy the hoor chargin' them prices fer a little thrip like that,' the Boss grumbled as he got off near the racecourse. 'An' the cheeky sod charged full price fer yeh and yeh on'y a slip of a child. The melt!'

The crowd was as colourful and busy as a swarm of tropical bees. They milled around near the parade ring to rub shoulders with farmers with faces like blue arses, boozy entrepreneurs in their vulgar Barbour coats and herringbone suits.

The women were turned out like prize specimens exhibited at a dog show, their tails were brushed, their coats were slky, their cracks were filled, their legs waxed and their bodily odours suppressed. Babs and her father sat under the lime trees looking up form in the list of runners torn from the *Mail.*

'There's P.J. Prendergast,' Babs excitedly elbowed her dad.

'I bet that crafty fecker's got a winner or two here,' the Boss said. 'He always wins the big wans. He could teach yer Uncle Liam a t'ing or two about settin' a horse out for a race.

'There's Phil Canty,' Babs said. 'An' Aubrey Brab'zon. Oh, look here comes Vincent O'Brien with wan a them Arab fellas, a sultan or somethin'. Don't look now, Daddy, bur is that Uncle Liam that's drivin' into the trainers' area in the big Jag.'

'Will yeh look a' the cuttov him, the little shite,' the Boss said, watching his brother from under his eyelids, his pupils white with malevolence. He observed his short little sibling step out of his car, hand the keys to a valet and walk straight towards the President of Ireland, Sean T. O'Ceallaigh, and shake his hand as if they were first cousins. 'The little scutther, an' him wit' th' arse out a his trousers on'y yisterday.'

'Daddy, Uncle Liam's been a trainer fer twenty years at least,' Babs said.

'Shakin' hands wit' the bloody president, wouldja believe. Pair a miniature shites the both a them,' the Boss said.

'There's Jimmy Eddery, an' Scobie Breasley,' Babs said. 'An' who's that little fella talkin' to Uncle Liam?'

'That's Christy Roche th' apprentice,' the Boss said.

'Daddy, that's, that's . . .'

The Boss looked up. 'That's feckin' Din Joe, the big oul' Cork shite. Come there, take the feckin' floor.' And he laughed. 'Jasus, Babs, all the feckin' superstars is out t'day,' the Boss sneered. 'Now here's the rale McCoy, Michael O'Heir. Christ Almighty, he's on'y gone over to talk ta the Liam fella. C'mon Babs, I can't stand much more a this. Wondher what they're talkin' about. If yer man O'Heir wan's ta know about horses he shou'bey talkin' t'me. Yer man knows less than Katie Barry.'

Babs went to the parade ring. With her dark hair flopping over the snow-white rail, she studied the horses as they pranced and sashayed in front of her. She laid her little bet on a fine bay with a diamond blaze, not because of its fine appearance but because of its name, Galway Breeze. 'Fer Mammy,' she said.

'Galway Breeze, me arse,' the Boss said. 'Look at its form, five noughts. Who's up? Paddy Power. Even so that t'ing'll be lucky ta come in before dark,' the Boss said.

Uncle Liam watched the race from the stand, while his brother stood surrounded by denizens of the inner city with their crates of Guinness and pork pie hats.

Galway Breeze won by five lengths. Babs leapt in the air yelling I'm rich, Daddy, I'm rich!'

'Yeah, yeh've won precisely four and sixpence, the Boss said as he tore up is own ticket.

'Uncle Liam has Fame an' Fortune in the next,' Babs said. She had to drag her father over to the parade ring. Liam was hidden among a crop of four-foot-nothing jockeys in their bright silks and revealing pants. Attractive ladies in their finery gathered around the parade ring.

'I'll betcha them bloody jockeys have the pick a that lot after the races,' the Boss said with no attempt to conceal his envy. He walked past the women as if he were judging cattle. 'Yeh can see the hoors are up fer it,' he hissed.

Babs ignored him. She was too busy taking stock of Uncle Liam's horse. Fame and Fortune was a big, good-looking gelding with a fine, active walk. When the jockey mounted and took a double handful, the horse catapulted himself out onto the track and moved sweetly down the course to the mile start.

'That t'ing's got no chance,' the Boss said, but he sneakily put ten bob each way on it.

Under strong driving the horse took the lead a furlong out. The Boss didn't know whether to cheer it home or hope it dropped dead in front the packed grandstand.

But Breasley timed his run to a fraction of an inch to pip the big gelding on the line. The Boss was furious. 'That feckin' Power couldn't ride a bloody bike,' he said.

'Daddy, I got second at seven to one an' won more money,' Babs said. 'Hooray.'

The Boss was counting his winnings into his little purse when Liam surprised him. 'Wor yeh doin' here, Dunne,' he said.

'I'm not backin' yer bloody cripples anyway,' the Boss said.

'Yes yeh are, Daddy', Babs said. 'Yeh had ten shillin's each way on Fame and Fortune.'

'Oh, he did, did he, the bloody liar,' Liam said. 'That's right, Babs, yeh keep an eye on this fella. Yer da's always been an awful conman.'

The Boss clenched his teeth and his fists. Liam bent down. 'Anyway, how's my little pet? He touched Bab's hair. 'Are yeh winnin' all th' money?'

'Yes, I've got lots,' Babs said and she opened her hands and showed her Uncle Liam a little pile of silver and copper. Liam, in rare good humour after his recent English Derby success, opened his wallet and handed Babs a five pound note. 'Buy somet'in' fer yer Mammy. An' I have a nice wan fer yeh in the next, Dan Donnelly, named afther the great bare-knuckle boxer.' Then, noticing someone he knew, Uncle Liam put on his most important stride and marched away.

'Babs, gi'me that money, I'll mind it fer yeh,' the Boss said. Babs handed over the fiver, and the Boss rooted in his purse and gave her a sixpence.

The hours flew by for Mary and all too soon she was disturbed by the sounds of feet pounding on the gravel. Mary didn't have to look; the Boss was back and would be wanting his tea. She turned off the radio and put on the kettle.

The children gathered. They desperately wanted to know the full story of the day at the races. 'From the beginnin,' Bridgid cried as she elbowed Jack out of the way.

Her hands fluttering like birds, her body fully animated, Babs began. 'God, it was super. The buses an' the cars, yeh've never seen an'tin' like it, people everywhere.'

'Never mind the bloody buses,' Bridgid groaned, 'ge'ron wit' the feckin' story.'

'All right,' Babs said, 'I'm gettin' there.'

'Anyway, where was I? Yeah, the women looked wondherful in their fashions.' Pam pressed closer. 'What sort a perfume were they wearin'? An' did they have fur coats on?'

'It's feckin' summer,' Bridgid said exasparated. 'Forget the bloody make-up an' the bloody dresses, let's get to the main action.'

Mary paused from leafing through a pile of old knitting patterns to say, 'Will yeh stop cursin', Bridgid. Yer mout' is gettin' fouler every day. Anyway, Babs, I don't know why them hussies have ta show off their legs. An' as fer wearin' their sunglasses on their hair, what's that about? It's stewpit isn't it? Makes them like big bug-eyed spiders. Showin' off fer men? Psaw!'

Not appreciating their mother's tedious intervention, the children egged Babs on with smiles and nods.

'Oh, I must tell yehz this. When Daddy was rootin' in wan a the wastepaper baskets for a race card, Uncle Liam saw him.'

'He bloody well didn't,' the Boss said. 'Sure, yer man was well gone be then.' The children enjoyed that story. They could just imagine their father with his head down in the wire basket, rooting about in it like a pig. He was always rooting about for something. 'The hoor never said hello, goodbye, kiss me arse or an'tin',' the Boss grumbled without taking his eyes off his paper.

'He did t'me,' Babs insisted. 'An' Mammy,' Babs's voice rose with excitement, 'Uncle Liam gev me a five pound note ta buy somethin' fer *yooou*!'

'Ah, now wasn't that kind a him,' Mary said. 'Liam has always been nice ta me, I'll say that fer 'im. Oh, that's grand Babs, where is it?'

'Daddy's got it.'

'It'll go towards the cost a the day out,' the Boss said firmly.

'Burrit's mine,' Mary said. 'Giv'it t'me.'

'Yes, Daddy, it is Mammy's afther all.'

Once Babs had proclaimed the fiver's ownership, the Boss conceded glumly. He pulled his fat wallet out of his trouser pocket where it sat like a rupture, and grimly handed Babs the note to pass to her mother. The children followed the fiver across the room as if it were a fine green bird until it nestled with Mary who held it up to the light. 'It's the most money I ever had in me life,' she said.

'I'm not a bit surprised,' the Boss grumbled. 'The way yeh t'row money away on sweets fer them bloody kids.'

The children gathered round her, hoping to share their mother's good fortune. 'Some wan hasta give them somet'in' more than curses an' kicks,' Mary said quietly.

To quickly kick a pinless grenade into touch, Babs said brightly, 'Oh yeah, I meant ta tell yehz, although yeh won't like this, Jack. One horse was called Lazy Bones,' Babs giggled, 'an' Daddy said it reminded him of yeh.' The Boss's brow wrinkled at that revelation, and Babs continued, hopping about like an actress performing on a burning stage. 'There was hundred a priests an' Daddy said they wor backin' horses with our money.

'Them priests do no such t'ing,' Mary said, looking hard at the uplifted *Evening Mail*. 'They do a lot fer the poor. Yeh're always cursing them and criticisin' them, an' yeh'll go ta Hell fer it.'

Babs talked freely as if her father was not sitting uncomfortably screwed up a few feet away. 'An' when one of Uncle Liam's horses, the grey, what's it called, Plato, that's it, kem in last, Daddy shouted at the jockey, "Why don'cha get down and milk it?" I was mortified to hear him shoutin' like that in such a crowded place wit' important people there.' Babs bounced a cute grin towards the Boss who caught her eye and allowed a smile to smooth out his frown.

But he had heard enough. 'C'mon Babs,' he said, folding the newspaper and slipping his stockinged feet into his slippers, 'quit that oul' talk and let them chisellers get ta bed.' The Boss prodded the sack under the door, indicating the performance was over.

'If Daddy was nicer ta Uncle Liam we could all go ta his big house fer holidays,' Bridgid said wistfully in the dark.

As he lay in bed thinking, his teeth grinning at him from the glass by his bed, the Boss's face was lit by the glow of light that shone through the window from the roadside lamp. 'When I t'ink of how I helped that cur get started in the lovely racin' game,' he whispered, 'me feckin' blood boils.'

When driving Kitty through the Dublin backstreets with a load of bones, mowing grass with a scythe alone in the Dublin hills, or with his head in a barrel of fetid pigswill, the Boss would repeat the same lament a thousand times.

54

JACK TWIDDLED HIS white toes under the water. As he sat in the midge-ridden silence he saw Jack Perkins outside his tin-roofed shack. He was slicing tobacco from a block and sticking it into a toothless mouth. Cheerfully, the old man called out across the water. 'Bejasus, yeh'll get footrot wit' all the pig-shite yer ould fella dumps into that river. The Jesuits'll have his tripes fer that, I'm telling yeh.'

'*Jack! Yeh dopey melt!* The voice bawled from behind the henhouse where the Boss was hiding. '*Com'ere!*'

Jack fumbled into his wellingtons and joined his father. 'What in the name a Jasus did yeh want talkin' ta that oul' hoor-master?' the Boss hissed. 'That cunt'll corrupt yeh. It's bad enough that bloody fool of a mother a yers encouragin' the fil'ty oul' dirtbag to come up the garden talkin'. I saw her wavin' ta the rotten bastard. I've a bloody good mind to knock his feckin' head off, an' her's too, the stewpit pile.'

Jack felt like puking every time he heard this sort of diatribe against his mother. 'Please don't–,' he heard himself say, but his words were swept away in a flood of vicious invective.

'I've had them watched,' the Boss said, prodding the air with a thick finger. 'I know what I'm talkin' about. I'm not wanna them gobshites from Galway wit' th' arse out a me trousers. Oh, bejasus no! I could buy an' sell them lop-eared melts. Wavin'! An' me sloggin' meself from morn till night. An' what t'anks do I get? The hoor conspires behind me back an' makes little a me an' me breakin' me poor heart to earn a few shillin's ta keep yehz alive . . . the curse a God may light on her fer it . . . yeh don't see me hangin' aroun' the corners wit' them bowsies from the labourers' cottages beyant. Oh no! But I'd be betther t'ought of if I did. . . . Jasus, me blood b'ils ta t'ink of it.' The Boss's eyes flashed with hatred; he could charge across the river and kill old Perkins now. Jack looked away, hoping the abuse would stop, but his father ranted on. The big red sun was slipping down, sectioned like a pomegranate by the trees. The wind blew gently, a lovely evening was coming to an end and still the Boss's voice crashed in his son's ears.

As the last colours of day were lost in darkness and the animals settled in for the night, the Boss walked to the house where the kitchen window blinked its yellow eye. His shoulders were stooped, all vitality apparently drained from his step, but at least he had temporarily exorcised some of the pus from his mind. Jack followed heavily behind.

The weak bulb in the kitchen was quickly flicked off when Mary heard their footsteps, and the silent house closed in, trapping everyone inside.

That night, Jack dreamed Perkins had found the shiny gun in the attic and fired at the Boss, hitting him smack in the middle of the bald pate, sending shards of skull spinning slowly in the sun, a delicate pink plume of gore flying lacily after it across the yard, the Boss lying like Nelson in his shift, a pained look on his face. If Perkins had shot Tans, he might as well shoot Irishmen too. Once a murderer, always a murderer.

'Even Black and Tans are God's creatures,' Mary was saying next morning, as she told the story of a lorry load of Tans tearing down the boreen in Galway looking for IRA men. 'I was sweepin' the floor,' she said. 'I was on'y about ten at the time. The head Tan must a been an officer or somet'in' 'cos he took the brush off me an' said, "Le'me finish that for yeh and yeh run off an' help yer mother make the tea." I butthered the soda bread, so I did. But Jasus I was terrified. Anyway, yeh know what?'

'*What?*'

'He gev me sixpence, that's what.'

Jack was furious. 'Agh, Mammy, yeh're rewriting history now. In her peacenik version, the Tans were all friendly floor sweepers who gave tips and helped injured IRA men to hospital. Double bollocks.

'Yeh'd've been shit scared if one a them Tans as much as looked crooked atcha,' Bridgid said.

Jack loaded his imaginary Tommy gun and acted out shooting his sister in the back. The fat bitch.

55

EDNA, AN OLD maid, an occasional friend and professional nosy parker was due any time. Mary had the house tidy, the Boss was wearing his best shirt and braces. He was looking forward to Edna's visit. She was no Diana Dors but she was good for a bit of skit. The Boss, smelling suspiciously of aftershave, cracked open his paper and began reading. Stiff-backed, he devoured the *Mail* as if it were steak and chips.

'Bejasus, them rotten yella fellas is not gettin' it all their own way, t'ank God,' he said. 'Them bloody Yanks is a match fer any communist hoor. God blast that feckin' Kruschev, that Red melt wants ta kill everyone an' rule the world!'

Mary opened her big slack mouth and said quietly, 'Now stop that cursin', them childer is listenin', and anyway communists is human too.'

The Boss let his wife's idiotic comment go unpunished. He was too busy thinking of Edna, and for the same reason suddenly sprang from his chair like Early Mist tackling Becher's. 'Jasus, the feckin' fire's goin' out.' The Boss rushed into the yard and began frantically splitting logs and swearing.

Mary sat on her broken chair with its straw stuffing oozing out, like a sad old hen sitting on a ceramic egg. Her children were scattered around the room, filling every nook and cranny. She entertained them with the thought that, 'One day, yer Daddy's goin' ta kill one uv us.' The children rubbed their scruffy heads against her just as the Boss kicked the door open and clattered an armful of logs into the basket. The fire must be kept burning tonight. It would make Edna feel nice and relaxed.

There would be no need to boil water tonight. There was usually a big blackened cauldron of boiling water blocking out the fire, with the children, like tiny, robotic slaves, taking turns to ferry lapping saucepans from the rainwater barrel at the corner of the house. As a useful exercise it was akin to whitewashing coal.

'Edna'll be here any minute,' Mary said. The Boss lowered the paper, his pale eyes on his wife. 'Wonder what yer woman wants?' His slippers, incongruously red, were planted on the stone-flagged floor. A forty-watt bulb dangled directly over his head, giving the Boss's large pink ears a pixyish glow.

'Well, if yeh wan'ta know,' Mary sniffed, 'when Edna came las' time it was yeh wanted her back.'

Remembering something delicious, the Boss wiped the acidic look from his face and folded the paper. 'In that case,' he said, 'I betther be puttin' on me new shoes,' he said. Mary made a spluttering sound. 'New shoes? Yeh baldy oul' fecker, yeh'd need more than shoes to make Edna fancy yeh.'

Edna was well preserved but lonely. To the average male she was without sex appeal, except perhaps for a lonely gorilla with personal hygiene problems. But as founder member of the Society of Prick Teasers, she had a real talent for double meanings.

The Boss danced back in wearing not just his best shoes but his latest off-the-peg brown cords. 'How's that?' he asked as he appeared from the blackness of the hallway in a bilious symphony of dung colours and did a mincing catwalk swagger which caught Mary's eye and made her laugh. The children watched their father as if learning some new truth about him.

As soon as Edna's bicycle bell sounded on the bridge, the Boss was out of his chair and opening the door. Overwhelmed by cheap scent, and fired up by the friction of her rubbing nylons, he couldn't wait to touch her up. When he felt her heavily larded cheek, his temperature rose. Edna coquettishly sidestepped with a smile and removed her gloves like a stripper. With her back to the fire and her legs planted apart, she talked and the Boss drooled.

As if stung he ran out the door, returning with a loaf of Landy's bread and a small pot of pure strawberry jam from his personal larder.

'Yer very kind ta me,' Edna simpered, giving the Boss that look.

Mary turned her face away. With her big feet in fur-lined boots she looked as if she had stepped on two dead rabbits.

'Slice a brad Edna,' the Boss asked, his voice rising half an octave.

'I don't mind if I do,' Edna said. And the Boss began slicing, his eyes all the while mauling Edna. In her maroon blouse with the large cream bow, her tempting breasts were securely anchored.

'An' I tell yeh another t'ing,' the Boss said, putting his hand on hers, 'Yeh're lookin' grand. What age are yeh now? Have yeh got the key ta the feckin' door yet?'

'A deed I have. Sure, I'm forty-t'ree this comin' June.'

'Are yeh, bejasus, well yeh don't look it,' the Boss said with a fetching smile.

Mary grimaced.

The Boss shuffled nearer and squeezed her thigh like Terry Wogan. He was powerfully aroused by this scented harlot. If only he could get her out into the yard. Maybe he could pull a stunt. Jesus Christ, he'd be in business. It was bloody frustrating, Mary sitting there, her fishy oul' eyes blank, like a bloody sin eater, wrecking his chances.

The conversation went on with Edna and the Boss swapping *double entendre* until Mary'd had enough. She waited until there was a lull in the duologue from which she was clearly excluded. Then with no attempt at subtlety she said, 'Well, Edna, I t'ink it's time yeh went home.' The Boss who sat like a fox mesmerising a juicy pheasant looked shocked. 'Them roads is very dark now, wit' all them lads from the new houses above in Golden Acre tearin' round on their bloody Hondas, an' them full a stout. Besides, we've all gotta be up early in the mornin'.'

'What areyeh blatherin' about?' the Boss snapped. 'Sure, it's on'y half nine. Let the poor woman have another cuppa cha at least.'

Breathing brimstone, Mary slope-shouldered past Edna's finery and shuffled into her small room. There, she sat on the bed and removed her false teeth as her husband - that virtuous, little electric-light-saving, early-to-bed, miserly bastard - entertained Edna. And the brazen bitch was enjoying it. Like an old bear in a dank cave, Mary thought about the goings-on in the kitchen. 'T'anks be ta God Jack is doin' his homework,' she muttered. 'That dirty oul' swine wouldn't dare thry an'tin' in front a the boy.'

Edna tittered at the Boss's worn jokes. 'Didja know I was a great little horseman in me time?' the Boss asked. Jack's eyes rose from his homework.

'Is that a fact now, Johnny?' Edna asked. 'Sure, yeh're the right size fer a jockey.' The Boss tickled her and they both laughed.

The Boss's smile faded. He must take the initiative before his chance disappeared. 'Have yeh ever seen an oul' racing saddle at all?' he asked.

'No, bur I've a feelin' I might see one soon,' Edna said and she laughed again, tears swamping her eyes as she lowered them. 'How could I, Johnny? An' me a town girl.' She threw her head back and roared, her tremendous breasts looking like six pounders on a battle-ship. Jesus, the sound of the ripe bitch's lovely townie's voice. It was a real turn-on after Mary's boring Galway brogue.

'Come on, I'll show yeh one.' What are yeh goin' ta show me at all,' Edna said with a meaningful wink. Cue more ribald laughter.

'Geroff to bed,' the Boss ordered Jack, who quickly obeyed even though he was thoroughly enjoying the foreplay.

With the field now to himself, the Boss got to work. He whipped the sack away from under the back door, drew the bolts quietly, and with Edna following like a fat lamb, he went into the darkened yard. Now he had her, the soft bitch. To think of what delights lay waiting for him. 'It's in there,' he said. His tongue seemed to be swelling in his mouth.

'Where's the light?' Edna asked a little nervously.

'Ha, ha,' the Boss replied, 'there's no light. Yeh hav'ta feel yer way round.'

Edna laughed smuttily, 'Feel yer way round, ha, that's a good one!' Then, quick as flash, there was a pop of buttons, a slight tearing of silk and the Boss's short leathery fingers were on Edna thick nipples.

'Jasus, Mary an' Holy St Joseph,' Edna squealed, but the Boss succeeded in finding her lips and shoving his blue-veined tongue between her teeth. They kissed for a moment, his stiff penis hard against her fork, his long viper's tongue down her gullet.

'Right, I t'ink that's enough fer now, Johnny,' Edna gasped hopefully, trying to push him away.

But the Boss was burning. 'Ah, come on now,' he said.

But Edna had had more than she wanted. No harm was done. 'Come on now, Johnny, don' be silly.'

Delirious with ecstasy the Boss twanged, pulled and caressed until he'd doused the flames.

In his little bed Jack's ears were cocked. He heard them coming in laughing and flustered. 'Wouldja like a Power's?' offered the Boss, still massively aroused.

'No, no, I'm goin' in a minute,' Edna said. She sat for a moment on the Boss's knee. 'Ah, ah, that was nice,' she said, patting the Boss's hand which was in vain massaging a fat thigh.

After what seemed like a painfully long time Edna rode away, but not before Mary heard a scuffle in the hall. The Boss watched from behind the curtain in the parlour as Edna slid her lovely big arse over the saddle and evaporated palely into the thick darkness. The excitement she had provoked in the Boss was unabated. Friskily he washed and went to the bedroom where Mary lay, silent, mountainous and pregnant.

In rare good humour he swiftly undid the laces of his new leather shoes. Mary sniffed under the covers, smelled Edna's perfume as strongly as if the bitch was in the room. 'A grand little person,' the Boss murmured. Mary was pretending to be asleep. His hands closed on her and pulled her round to him. The Boss grabbed her tender breasts, squeezing them till they hurt. He felt her large soft buttocks and pressed himself vigorously against them. Mary struggled but the powerful arms turned her as easily as a kitten. Mary closed her eyes, her hand in front of her hard against her husband's throat as he drove into her with irresistible power. Frantic with visions of Edna, the Boss pumelled and bucked like an enraged bull. When he'd climaxed he slipped out of bed and put on his old clothes. Mary wept, the tears wetting her face and neck. Around her in cots and cradles her babies slumbered.

The Boss crossed the road in the moonlight. Stars were winking in a vast expanse of inky sky. He walked as quietly as he could through a stark moonscape of half-built houses, holes for septic tanks, and piles of sand and bricks.His feet sunk into the churned up mud. He was heading for the huge portable barn that builders had erected the day before and stocked with building materials. Producing a lever from inside his coat he smashed the lock.

The noise hung in the air. He saw a solitary light and pressed himself against the shed and waited. Probably someone coming back from a night out. When the coast was clear he went inside the shed and selected two large tins of black gloss, boxes of nails, a new clawhammer, a pack of wooden-handled screwdrivers, a tub of putty, and a trowel. He was soon safely back indoor hiding his booty in the roofspace above the scullery.

Next morning, he watched the gardai get out of their Cortina in heavy navy greatcoats, tilt back their peaked hats, and light up their fags. 'Them fellas couldn' ketch gonorrhoea,' the Boss muttered and went back to work. He would have liked to be a cop. Easy money, scare the shit out of everyone. Lots of young'uns inpressed by the shiny buttons.

56

JACK OFTEN WATCHED Billy Riley's pigeons flying - white dots against a blue sky. One day he returned from school to see a snowy hen on the roof. It spent most of the afternoon there. Jack was delighted she wanted to stay. It would be fantastic to have a pigeon loft. Maybe he could make one. There was plenty of wood about the place. Nails and roofing felt too. When the Boss returned, Jack rushed to him bursting with the news.

'Wait!' the Boss snarled. 'Don't disturb the bird till I'm ready.'

The Boss returned with a ladder, and as his father's small feet climbed the wooden rungs Jack asked, 'Are yeh goin' ta get it down fer me?'

The Boss reached out and caught the tame bird. He looked down at his son. Then with a flick he broke the bird's neck and threw it down to him.

'Fling it in in ta the pigs in case Billy hears of it,' the Boss laughed, his bottom reversing.

Jack carried the warm bird to the pigs. He felt nothing.

It was Pam, her eyes accentuated with mascara, who saw Riley urgently cross the Pit to emerge like a bear from the hedge. He snapped open the gate and marched towards the house. Pam curled up on the windowsill and smiled at the big man as he approached the front door.

'Is yer da at home?'

Pam slithered from the window and ran down the garden.

'Must'a found out about the feckin' bird,' the Boss grumbled.

Carrying the billhook he'd been using to chop down nettles, the Boss went through the side gate and took Riley by surprise. 'What d'yeh want Bill?' the Boss asked gruffly.

'Um . . . I was jus' wonderin' wha' . . . happened ta me . . . em . . .'

'Pigeon?' the Boss offered helpfully.

'Yeah . . . it . . . she . . . em . . .'

The Boss waited for the words to be assembled by the slow brain.

'C'mon,' he said sharply. 'I'm a busy man. Spit it out.'

'My pigeon . . . she's dead. Right? An' . . . yeh . . . eh . . . killt it,' Riley finally got out.

'Yeh're not wrong,' the Boss said. 'Last time I saw it, it looked a goner. It's in the pig's belly now.'

'Bu'rit's . . . I mane it was . . . was . . . erm . . . a . . . prize bird,' Riley said. 'It won loads a com . . . com . . . competitions.'

'Well, it won't win any more oul' son,' the Boss said, and he was laughing. 'It's dead all right. What of it? The Boss's smile was replaced by a mean grimace.

'Oh nuttin',' Riley said. 'I don't mind reelly. She was jus' . . . yeh a kind a fav'rit. But don't worry, Misther Dunne. It's all right, I'm not kiddin'.' Riley smiled. 'I'm not gonna bring up a garda or an'tin' like dat, know what I mean?'

'Bloody good job yeh're not,' the Boss said, ''cos I'll sue yeh fer lettin' them rotten birds come over here and ate my bloody chicken's corn.'

Riley smiled as if he had just sealed a bargain.

The Boss waited for him to leave. 'That's not the main reason I kem today,' Riley said, his confidence growing and his words flowing. 'I got a tart, I mean a woman, a girl.' He grinned and wiped his big hands on his dungarees.

'So?'

'Well, it's like diss,' Riley said, scratching himself. 'I wan'ta take her out, see. May Nolan's a lovely, kind person.'

'What's she doin' wit' yeh then?' the Boss asked.

Riley laughed. 'Yeah, good joke,' he said. Once unclogged, his brain positively whirred. He was talking fast, afraid if he didn't get the message over the Boss would heave him into the river. 'Yeh wouldn' know 'er, but she's gorra nice job in Jacob's, packin' biscuits.'

The Boss frowned. Jacobs was where Bridie Mansfield had worked all those lost years ago. 'So what's it got to do wit' me?' the Boss asked sharply. He was getting fed up with this.

'Good prospects, she has, yeh know wor I mean.' Riley grinned.

'Well, plenty a broken biscuits anyway,' the Boss said without a smile. 'Let's finish this conversation anudder time, I'm busy right now,' the Boss said, attempting to shepherd the big man towards the gate.

Riley shrugged and hooked his thumbs in his belt like some extra in Oklahoma.

'So, d'yeh want her to come over an' give me a han' with the pigs, eh?' the Boss asked, relishing the idea of having May in the sheds with a big yard brush in her hands and nothing on but her wellingtons.

'No,' Riley said, hugely amused. 'I don't get no wages till Saturday–'

'That's what yeh get workin' fer them t'ievin' bloody nuns,' the Boss said.

'I wondered if yeh . . . could–'

The Boss was way ahead. 'So yeh wan'ta take this smasher out somewhere? How much would yeh like, Billy?' There was a sneer in those pinprick eyes.

'Oh! Oh . . .' Riley said as if suddenly given a 72-ounce steak and a magnum of de Vogue's '49 Musigny. So his visit was not as crazy as his brother Dan said it would be.

'Mmm, well . . .' Riley began to think about how much he could spend. The Carlton, something with Alan Ladd in, bag of toffees, single of chips and a wedge of rock salmon each afterwards. Yes, a couple of Tullamore Dews at The Yellow House on the way home to a nice long snog and maybe a bit of a feel if he was lucky.

'Ten bob should see me all right. I can't believe how kind yeh are. Them fellas in Cullen's said yeh were a miserable oul' shite. I'm sorry,' Riley blurted, 'I shouldn' a said that.'

'Ah, no,' the Boss said. 'Them boys have their little joke; the fact they're all wankers doesn't matther. Yeh hav'ta take this tart a yers somewhere reelly expensive.' He tilted his trilby. 'Le'me see, how about the Gresham? Yeh, that's the very place for a nice girl like May.'

Riley's foolish slab of a face lit up and his teeth showed in a melony grin.

'Fer that yeh'd need more than ten bob, Billy. Come on, let's t'ink big,' the Boss said, looking serious.

'How much would I need then, Misther Dunne?'

With a shuffle of lips the Boss calculated. 'Yeh'll be wantin' a fiver.'

Riley couldn't believe his ears. A fiver! His week's wages only came to two pounds. 'Misther Dunne, yeh're the best,' he said with feeling and he put out his hand.

The Boss didn't take it. Instead, a smile spread across his face, and the small eyes filled with water. 'Jasus, yeh're the limit, Billy, d'yeh know that?' The Boss's loud laughter floated across the river to where Perkins was lobbing spits into the river and listening. 'Yeh know what?' the Boss mused. Riley waited like a victim of a crime awaiting sentence. 'Fellas like yeh make me laugh.'

'Wha'd'yeh mane?' Riley said dully. His suffering was obvious.

'Well, I'll tell yeh what I mane,' the Boss said, his eyes staring into Riley's empty soul.

'There yeh are, a big lazy, t'ick, gobshite, wit' no responsibility fer an'tin' 'cept what yeh sling inta yer gut. Then yeh decide ta go out ta get some poor mott inta throuble on my hard-earned money! Listen, Billy, fer Jasus's sake, go back over there ta them nuns yeh work fer an' ask them. And keep them bloody pigeons a yers off a me property.'

Riley left the yard, silent and humiliated. He felt his neck glowing with embarrassment as Pam, who had followed the conversation, resumed her place on the sill in the sun. Hugging her knees, she watched the big man retreat through the hedge and cross the Pit, his massive shoulders slumped. 'Poor Misther Riley,' she said quietly, and rushed to tell her mother.

'Poor fella,' Mary said, 'he musta been desprit ta come beggin' off a beggar. Take that make-up off a yer face, Pam, or yeh'll ketchit when yer man comes in.'

'But, Mam,' Pam said, clinging to her mother. 'I like wearin' make-up. It makes me look beautiful.'

'Yeh're t'irteen,' Mary said. 'G'wan, wipe yer face. I don't wan'cha goin' round lookin' like a prostitute.'

Pam smiled at her gorgeous image in the mirror, and washed.

57

JACK HEARD THE sumptuous sound of someone kicking a football. He climbed a tree and saw a tracksuited figure running across the Pit, dummying and dodging, the ball perfectly under control. Without a word Jack ran across the road.

'Hi,' a familiar voice called.

'God!' Jack exclaimed. It was Paddy Daly, and he was on his own, the sweat oozing through his tracksuit top, his blond hair so wet he could have wrung it out.

Daly picked up a towel. 'Jasus, I'm knackered,' he said. 'Haven't trained for weeks. Transport want me on a match-by-match basis. I suppose I'm getting on, even by their standards.'

'Yeh'll be playing at Harold's Cross?' Jack said incredulously. 'Kevin Blount in goal, Olly Conroy on the wing.'

'Yeh know yer football,' Daly said. 'T'anks,' Jack said not letting on he only knew it from reading the *Mail*.

'Gorra get fit,' Daly said. 'Here, giv'us a pass.' He rolled the ball to Jack then stood on the balls of his feet, bouncing like a boxer for the return. Jack toe-ended the ball girly fashion. 'No, widda instep,' Daly said, 'like this.'

Jack watched and copied. Soon he was able to pass the ball into Daly's path as the professional streaked down the field taking it in his stride and lashing it into the distance. Lobbing, square passing, wall passing, it all flowed smooth as oil.

'Hey, yeh're a good footballer, ja know that?' Daly said. 'Yeh've helped me a lot. T'anks, kiddo.' He shook Jack's hand.

'Are yeh lookin' forward to playin' fer Transport?' Jack asked timidly.

'I'm too old for the top English sides, I'll hav'ta settle for it, I s'pose.' Daly picked up the ball and spun it on one long finger. 'I'd like ta've stayed over there,' Daly said sadly. 'It's where the great players are: Matthews, Shackleton, Lawton, Carey, etc. Mindja, I'm not that good,' he said quickly with a self-deprecating grin.

The Boss's whistle cut through the air like a samurai sword but Jack ignored it. He wanted to play all night.

'Yeh'd betther go,' Daly said.

'Yeah,' said Jack, resigning himself. 'Could we do this anudder time?'

'Mebbe. See yeh, son.'

Jack trotted home, where his father was waiting at the gate. 'Who's that bowsie?'

'That's Paddy Daly,' Jack told him. 'He's–'

'Never mind that oul' shite,' the Boss said, manhandling his son. 'I don't care who the hell he is. Ge'rinside an' do yer lessons.'

The sums floated in front of Jack's half shut eyes. At dinner time he saw his father pass some of his lethally greasy meal to Babs who in turned passed it on to Mary who cut it up and gave it to the children. That night, Jack was so tired he was asleep before he'd said his prayers.

The next day as he returned from school, curses screamed from the back yard. Through the chicken wire gate he saw his mother, big-bellied and demonic, her babies squealing and clutching at her apron, chasing the Boss with a broom. The pot had finally boiled over. The worm had turned. Mary's eyes were wild, her hair unkempt as she raised the broom, determined to whack the Boss's bald head. Cornered, he wheeled and brutally twisted the broom from Mary's grasp. They wrestled briefly, until she fell heavily to the ground. Jack saw the sharp chippings digging into her fat, bare legs. She cried like a banshee and tried to get up but fell back like a great big bug, bawling loudly. The children looked down at her in terrified awe.

The Boss rushed past Jack like a fleeing dervish, ripped open the yard gate and disappeared among the pig sties. Jack had never seen his father look frightened before. 'C'mon,' he shouted, 'there's work tubby done.'

Jack threw his schoolbag on the ground and raised his mother from the dirt before joining his father. Shovelling and muttering the Boss delved into a barrel of rotting pigswill.

'Jasus Christ' he said looking up. 'I don't deserve this. That woman is drivin' me mad. She's crazy, yeh know that. The least t'ing I say ta her and she just goes mad. She won't listen ta reason. God help us,' the Boss cried, carving the wrinkles into his ageing face.

Jack shook is head and remained silent. What sort of madhouse had he been unlucky enough to be born into? Did anyone deserve such parents? At that moment he hated them both.

In leaking wellingtons, Jack waded disconsolately through the gluey pigshit, using a broom to push the stinking morass into pools that lapped up against the corrugated walls and ran down the bank into the stream, turning the clear mountain water into a foul soup.

The Jesuits were always quick to castigate the Boss for polluting their precious stream, but would leave the yard with curses ringing in their ears: one day one of the lop-earred, culchie breed would die wriggling, impaled like a rat on the Boss's pitchfork.

The sun flashed on the wet floors and the pigs darted into the mottled shadows. Sweeping around their legs like a lazy waitress in a teashop, Jack moved among them without fear. Pigs are better than humans, he decided.

Soon, the Boss's face loomed over the half doors, lined and serious like Randolph Scott in a close-up at the Classic. 'How ar'yeh doin'?' he bawled. 'Finish off Betsy then wash yer feet in the river.'

Jack sprinkled sawdust where the pigs lay, then went into Betsy's sty. She was a young sow with her first litter. Incredibly clean piglets scurried and nuzzled her teats at the sight of the intruder. Jack chucked the sawdust, made piggy noises, then went down to the river. He glanced up at the house and saw his mother's bulk filling the kitchen window. She had recovered, as usual, thank God.

The girls flew in like tropical birds, the air full of their falsettos as they charged into the steamy kitchen. Mary told them quietly of the latest fight and lifted up her thin cotton dress to show the blue bruises. The girls cooed uneasily and Bridgid felt the marks with a cold hand. 'The rotten melt,' she said.

'Don't be cursin',' Mary snapped. 'He's corrupted yehz all, an' the sad t'ing is yehz don't even know it.'

'Yeh should tell Father Orlston,' Babs said when she came in from work.

'Ah, sure, an' what good would that do?' Mary said. 'It'd on'y giv'us a bad name.'

Protective and guilty, the girls laid the table with an odd assortment of cutlery and chipped crockery. In the centre, on a piece of board, sat a fresh loaf from Landy's bakery, its aroma encouraging little fingers to pick. As they crammed their mouths with warm dough the younger children sang an old song they had learned on their mother's lap. Mary turned her sad eyes on them and joined in haltingly.

'Little Sir Echo how do yeh do, hello,
Why don't cha come over an' play,
Yeh're a nice little fella,
I know by yer v'ice,
But cha always too far away.'

When the Boss came in from the yard, milling children made a path for him like small fry avoiding a killer shark. Sniffing rebellion, he turned on the jovial *bonhomie* he usually reserved for outsiders. Mary, coughing contemptuously, trundled around, pouring emerald peas into a bowl, plopping a yellow knob of margarine on the potatoes.

'Well,' the Boss said, with an attempt at gusto, 'aren't we well off while the rest a the feckin' world's fallin' ta bits. Begob, them oul' Russkies is right vicious snakes. If them hoors get us we've had it.' The Boss tried again and again to force attention onto goings-on half way round the world but he was ignored. Gradually, he was left abandoned on his own selfish little mudbank as an alternative conversation, defiantly started by his beloved Babs, sailed off without him.

Jack left the table first and went out into the yard to do his homework. Pam joined him. 'What yeh doin' Brud?' she asked.

'Writin',' Jack said gruffly as his big fingers propelled a pencil in a bockedy scrawl over the page.

Next, Bridgid appeared noisily and, looking over his shoulder, said, 'Don't know how yeh have the nerve ta hand that in. Hey Pam! Will yeh take a lookit yer man's homework. It's crap, isn't it?'

'Ah, I don't know,' Pam said. 'The poor lad's doin' the best he can.'

'It's still crap,' Bridgid insisted.

Jack wiped his nose on his sleeve and, encircling the page with a protective arm, carried on writing. When Babs quietly closed the kitchen door behind her he smelt the scent she'd been buying ever since she'd begun working at Easthams. It seemed an alien fragrance in a place poisoned by the stench of pigs. She picked up a crumpled page. 'That's good, Jack,' she said, her arm lightly on his. Jack, looked up, accepting her compliment like communion. Bridgid rolled her eyes. Pam went down the dusky yard to talk to Kitty. When she returned she joined the others who were clustered round the window, peering in at their parents. In the unlighted room the Boss and Mary lingered as if sculpted from coal. There was just enough grey light to see the two of them, silent and apart like statues in a park.

When the Boss went to bed, Babs took charge. 'How 'bour a game a Tip and Tig?' she asked. There were vigorous nods of approval. Mary made for the sink.

'No l'ave it, Mammy!' Babs commanded. 'We'll do the washin'-up afther.'

Smiling, Jack discarded jotter and pencil, stretched and joined in. The children ran about the darkening yard, their youthful blood rushing through them. They stayed out until the light faded, and the darkness captured their squeals of pleasure. There was no interference from the cowed Boss who lay on his side in bed, his eyes open, his mind racing. Soon his thoughts turned to the mountain of old Parazone, Cyprus Sherry and Australian Tawny bottles he had assembled in the garden.

58

NEXT DAY, AFTER school and his usual chores, Jack carried armfuls of newly washed bottles up to the cart and stacked them as he was trained to do: greens, blues and browns one end, clear glass the other. 'An' cover'em up,' the Boss yelled. 'We don't want that louser Perkins knowin' what we're doin'.'

The sun had disappeared by the time Jack drew the ragged tarpaulin over the stacked bottles. Going to the city meant a day off school, an exciting journey into the bowels of Dublin. Jack didn't share his father's hatred of the town; he found Dublin noisy and lively, especially in the back streets where the rag-and-bone men lived.

The Boss collected and recycled everything: rags, bones, bottles and jam jars, scrap iron, copper wire. Anything of value was kept in a locked shed: copper piping, old taps, bits of brass, scraps of lead, all stored in separate sacks. As he roamed the housing estates the Boss's sharp eyes were everywhere, in back gardens, skips, rubbish tips. Dustbins left outside lock-up garages were rifled for valuable metals.

Old wheels off mopeds, bedsteads, engine blocks, dead car batteries were collected, piled high like a Turner Prize sculpture and sold. Wine, sherry, beer bottles and cider flagons, all had a value. Those fine, clean, clever 'ladies' who lived in spacious houses with a dog and two children - 'usin' contraceptives, the dirthy bitches' - and husbands in suits, saved kitchen scraps for the Boss.

'No throuble at all, missis. I'll take everyt'in'. Them dustmen is a lazy lotta bast– Jus' keep all that ould stuff fer me, I'll take it offa yer hands. Keep the place tidy fer yeh. Ha, ha.' The Boss's laugh was sad and hollow and as soon as he turned a corner he was effing and blinding the 'snotty hoors' who looked upon him and his kind as some sort of pond life.

In the Boss's world of want and despair nothing was wasted. Unsaleable bottles were broken up and used under the floors of the pigsties. A gashed and bleeding snout stopped the pigs rooting up the floors. The best bottles were reused by the Red Biddy manufacturer who operated cobwebbed bodegas in the unromantic back streets of Dublin. Their sweet brown blend of reconstituted grape juice, deadened with industrial alcohol kept many a lonely tenement dweller's head out of the gas oven.

Skulls of cows, sheep and pigs were stacked high, whitening in the sun and rain, each one neatly drilled with a bullet hole. They were taken to the bone mill in Dublin. A new pile was started which soon attracted rats to the banquet of glazed eyeballs and gristle.

After a sneaky glance at the personal page of an old *Woman's Own*, Jack slipped off to bed. Without bothering to wash or remove his shirt and socks he crawled under an assortment of blankets and coats and fell into a satisfying sleep.

It seemed only minutes before a cold hand on his face woke him up. Dreamily Jack peered out of a small slit between his eyelids. It was a glorious, pink morning, the sky full of childish drawings.

'Ge'rup,' the Boss hissed in the dark, ''cos,' Jack mouthed the words with his father, 'It gets late very early.' He tiptoed to the kitchen to lace up his boots. The Boss had gone out to harness Kitty and would expect his breakfast to be ready when he returned. Jack lit the gas under the frying pan and cracked two big green duck eggs into the bubbling fat. The way the eggs spat and crackled was musical.

Soon the kettle was whistling and a pot of tea brewing on the hob. He plopped two slices of bread into the fat and yawned as he watched them rise like little magic carpets in the hot fat. It all felt magical, with the anticipation of a day in the city, a day away from the nuns and the thick bullies.

Jack laid the table, and when the Boss breezed into the kitchen he placed the breakfast in front of him. 'Ah sure, we're on the bloody pig's back now.' He glanced at the clock. 'Jasus, is that the time. Hurry up an' gettit down yeh.' His cheeks puffed out and a dribble of egg yolk leaked from the corner of his mouth.

Staring at the worn pattern on the oilcloth, Jack ecstatically devoured a slice of fried bread smothered in egg yolk. *Bloody smashin'*, he was thinking.

The Boss ate his food noisily, sucking his tea through the ruined stumps of teeth that had never felt the rasp of pig's bristle. Jack finished his breakfast and leapt to his feet, vigorously rubbing his hands together. He felt like shouting. The Boss swept the crumbs into his hand, rinsed out the things and left them on the drainingboard. 'I'll betcha they're still there when we come home,' he said, 'that bloody woman does shag-all in this place.'

Jack wasn't listening. The pigeons were cooing in Neary's field. Jackdaws chattered and dived in the yard. Rabbits sat near the hedge at the back of the house like brown stones. The road to the heart of Dublin city stretched out, quiet, grey and welcoming in the early morning.

'Make sure yeh pass wather,' the Boss said, 'I don't wan'ta be stoppin' till we're there.' Jack watched the bulging neck topped with the sweaty trilby bob up and down until it disappeared below the level of the window. He picked up his beret and pulled it down over his big ears. A smile brightened his pale and gentle face.

The house was silent. His sisters were lost in the fastness of sleep. Mary was quiet in her room. The babies snoozed like mice in their collection of cots and baskets. The joy of the early morning was tangible, the garden like a painting, everything subdued, the colours quiet. Jack padded past the silent windows.

In the yard Kitty snorted impatiently, the heavily laden cart harnessed to her. The Boss was already in his seat, his strong hands on the reins. Jack leapt up beside him. 'G'wan,' the Boss ordered. With a shake of her head Kitty took the strain and the cart creaked away. Soon the wheels were singing as, head down, Kitty ate the miles with her freshly oiled hooves. Jack shared a sack across his knees with the Boss. His father was strong and powerful, a good man to have beside you when entering the City. 'Here,' the Boss said, annointing his son with a whole Ritchies Mint. No boy had a right to be happier.

A seagull, lost in the morning sky, flapped in delirious circles, squawking. Kitty's hooves beat a rhythm on the deserted road, the Boss flicked his switch to keep her trotting. There was a sharpness in the air which held great promise.

Jack feasted on the passing scene. Kitty drew sparks from the road as she raced past the Church of the Annunciation crouching behind its stockade of pines opposite The Yellow House. On Sunday mornings, men quickly crossed the road here to read the sports pages in their best suits while waiting for the pub to open. And part time Sinn Feiners would walk up and down crying out '*United Irishman*! Ge'rit here.'

The Boss muttered a prayer and crossed himself. Jack copied him. The gates to the church were still locked. First Mass was at seven. The verger Flanavan, clad in black, had not yet arrived to sweep the sun from the steps and welcome the believers. Most were pungent spinsters and lonely old men with food stains on their fronts. On Sundays, the church overflowed. Women and children at the front, farmers and dairymen kneeling at the back, farting.

The Boss glanced at the clock in a window above the pub door. 'Jasus!' he roared. 'Will you ge'rup out a dat!' And Kitty picked up pace. 'I told yeh we should a got a bloody move on earlier,' the Boss snarled.

Tom Kennedy raised his long whip in salute as he turned his milk cart across their path further up the road. The Ben Hur of Rathfarnham stood in the huge milk float and drove his foaming horses mad with lashes. He had killed a couple of good horses by driving them until they dropped dead between the shafts.

'Dat fella's the biggest chancer in the bloody counthry,' the Boss said as Kennedy swished out of hearing. 'He started out wit' one oul' bony heifer above in the Kilmashogue Hills when he was a jus' a chiseller. Now look a' 'im. The connivin' git has a nice little milk round and as fine a herda milkin' cows as yeh'll see round here. But it'd be a right gobshite that'd be buyin' off yer man. Sure it's half wather he's sellin'. I knew his father when I was a lad in Tallaght,' the Boss mused bitterly. 'Another right go-bey-the-wall-an'-tickle-the-bricks. The devil took him in the end. It was the drink that nailed the hoor,' the Boss added with relish.

Jack ignored his father's monologue. Instead his eyes followed the line of the old stone wall that wound round Rathfarnham Castle. Earthquakes from all over the world were recorded there. Jack was proud of that. The whole world, right here in Rathfarnham. Amazing.

Places, crowded and dirty, were quickly entered and left behind. Soon they were in the City. With a spirited snort, Kitty drew up outside a dust-covered emporium in a cramped backstreet. Piles of rubbish spilled out of boxes and bins where hordes of snarling dogs rummaged. A fishy breeze from the docks played with flying litter and slapped it into the resigned faces of tenement dwellers grunting along the narrow, sun-splashed streets, their handcarts laden with junk. A smoky sign attached to a door declared: *Reuben Goss. Zinc, Lead, Copper Bought. Also Good Clean Bottles. Best Prices.* Jack sat in the cart. He felt a little creased from the journey, but exhilarated too.

The Boss bounced from the cart and, shading his eyes, peered through the window. He rapped noisily and stood back, peered, and peered again. Making little clicking noises with his tongue, a sure sign of his growing impartience, he turned to Kitty and wiped the froth from her mouth with his hand. A shabby yellow-faced youth with an unlit butt dangling from his lips emerged. He slapped the Boss heartily on the back.

'Mornin' Johnny,' got more a them oul' bleach bottles fer me? Jasus, yeh'll be p'isenin' all the Red Biddy drinkers in Dublin wit' dem filt'y bottles a yours.'

The Boss turned with narrowed eyes, grabbed the youth and said, 'We'll let yeh have yer little joke, but yeh know me, my bottles are pure and ready fer usin'. May the Little Flower forgive yeh. C'mon oul' son, open th' feckin' door and we'll even carry them inside fer no extra charge.'

He pummelled the boy's concave back, making him cough horribly. The lad returned, after a clanking of bolts, and lifted the first box of bottles. 'Mey father's in bed sick, me mother thinks it's flu, but I've got me doubts, he coughs all night an' his hanky's always red wit' blood.'

The Boss was delighted. Reuben was seriously ill. Maybe he could pull a fast one on the scrawny son, who was now seated in his father's 'smelling seat'. Like a consumptive monkey, he sniffed at each bottle at great speed. The rejects were piled up on one side. An offer of tuppence a dozen was refused with a derisory laugh then accepted. A pound note and a handful of loose change were pressed into the Boss' purse. After a farewell thump that started the boy hacking again, father and son were back on the now empty cart and slowly ebbing into a stream of cars and lorries. Kitty's ears stuck forward.

She could smell the hills beyond Rathfarnham. The Boss whipped her out of the city's maze, heading for the tinted hills.

Kitty tugged the reins out of the Boss' grip as she put her head down and galloped, her brasses flashing in the sun. 'Them oul' Jewboys is the biggest paira rogues in Dublin,' the Boss remarked. 'Did yeh see the way the sneaky whelp sniffed them bottles lookin' fer pethoril or bleach? Me arse. That fella wouldn't know bleach if yeh put it in his tea.'

Jack gazed at the tall buildings rolling around the sky, the tatty shops spinning backwards. As the cart creaked by a small bakers the Boss drew hard on the reins. Kitty shook her head. Jack held the reins while the Boss vanished inside. A honey-coloured cat slept among doughnuts and cream buns. Sugar-coated wasps lay dead, their tiny feet curled in exquisite death in the shop window. An old woman with a beaten face and grey hair piled as high as one of her loaves, dragged two large buns from under the cat's backside. The Boss also bought a sponge cake which was well past its sell-by date. The Boss paid her with coppers slyly palmed, and with his trilby slanted low over his eyes, he raced from the shop like a robber and vaulted into the cart. Kitty was already scuttling along.

When she was at full speed he offered the weeping bag to Jack who extricated a sticky bun and squeezed it till the cream gobbed on his knee. 'That bloody oul' bitch robbed me,' the Boss said. 'A penny each fer them. The curse a God may light on her.' Devouring his in two bites, he wiped his mouth and set his jaw. The Hellfire Club was wedged in a cleft in the distant mountains. Kitty trotted towards them, her ears pricked, her shaggy coat matted. 'We made a few pence out a the trip, God help us,' he said and he passed the mints.

That evening the Boss made his six-monthly visit to see his mother and sister. He poured them a drink from a small bottle.

'It's like cat's piss' the old woman said.

The Boss shoved the cake he'd brought towards her, a grand half-price bargain. 'Come on now yehz miserable bitches, stop that oul' naggin' an' get some a that grand cake inside yehz.' The Boss joked.

The women looked at the cake, their faces twisted with contempt.

'It's got feckin' hairs onnit,' Molly said.

'So have yeh, yeh oul' cunt,' the Boss wanted to shout at her but he stopped himself.

'I hate sweet t'ings,' his mother moaned. 'I hate the sighta sweet t'ings. Why d'yeh insist on bringin' them ta me?'

The Boss wanted to throw the cake in their grim old faces, chuck the watered whiskey on the fire and kick over the furniture. Instead, he tried humour. 'In honour a the Congress,' he said, 'will yehz dhrink that lovely drop a Power's and thry not ta look like slapped arses.'

His mother played her usual cruel game. She brought Liam out of his tabernacle, dusted him off and placed him in front of the Boss. 'Now Liam's a real gentleman. He kem here afther the races th'other day and left a whole big bottle of Jameson's.' She slammed the bottle on the table with a flourish. Exibit A. 'Now that's what I call bein' nice to yer mother.' She rammed her jowly old face, with its runny eyes and warts into the Boss's. 'Liam loves me more than yeh do, yeh . . . He's twice the man yeh're. An' thank God fer it.' She put the bottle back in the cupboard, wheezing and grunting as she knelt down on grey, stockinged legs. The Boss smiled; it was more of a hateful smirk.

The cat came up looking for attention. It smiled flat face, its whiskers sticking out, its tail ram-rod straight. The Boss petted it. 'Lovely oul' animal,' he said, thinking how lovely it would look with its feckin' head chopped off. He would gladly chuck it in the boiler just to spite these twin hoors from Hades. Putting on his hat he edged towards the door, shaking a rickety dresser as he moved. 'Yeh're not off already, ar'yeh? Jasus yeh can't wait ta get away from yer poor oul' mother.'

'God bless us an' save us, is that the time?' the Boss said as he opened the door. He bent down to kiss his mother, allowing the cold and ancient lips to barely touch his.

'Looker'im,' his sister said, watching him depart. 'Yeh'd t'ink the bloody divil had him be the balls.'

'He will in due course wit' the help a God,' said the Boss's mother.

59

'I'M TOO BUSY ta bother about them gobshites from the labourers' cottages an' their feckin' match.' The Boss said. Jack's smile faded. His father was unexpectedly invited by the Dowager, who was still trying to play peacemaker, to take part in the annual kick-about between the older men of the village and their sons.

Although his father hated soccer, Jack knew that if the Boss played, the fear of failure would goad him into heroics. And the men in Cullen's would all be hoping the bull-necked pig breeder would break a leg and succumb to gangrene.

Jack desperately wanted to be on the same side as his father, to show him the tricks he had learned from Paddy Daly. 'But yeh're no feckin' good,' the Boss said. 'Yeh're a liability. If wanna them bastards gev yeh a kick in th'arse, yeh'd collapse an' die on the spot.'

'Paddy Daly said it's all about skill,' Jack said.

'Yeh, an' what'd that chancer know?' the Boss retorted.

'Yeh hittid wit' yer instep.'

'Yeh're a right gullible t'ick,' the Boss said. 'Tellin' me how ta kick a bloody ball, an' me playin' since me arse was the size ivva shirt button.'

Jack knew silence was his best bet. He could never beat his father with words. As he helped in the yard Jack imagined himself in new boots. He was running down the wing, hurdling scything tackles, and crossing sweetly. Colm McKenna, a blond shite from the new houses in Golden Acre, who walked around the Pit with his boots hanging round his neck, rose like a helicopter and lashed the ball into the net. Jack was still smiling to himself when he heard the Boss sneer, 'Yeh'll never ge'ron any team, yeh bandy runt.'

His father scraped a barrel for a last fetid spoonful of rotting pig feed. 'There's too many a' them gurriers from the cottages that dooby hittin' walls wit' them tennis balls all day. They'd mesmerise yeh wit' their trickery.'

Jack stood on tiptoe to see if he could see Paddy Daly . Wouldn't it be great t'have him in the team. It'd be like having Desperate Dan, Jack Flash and Buffalo Bill all rolled into one. But Paddy was a professional. He wouldn't want his leg broken by playing kick and rush with a bunch of thugs and vindictive old spastics.

On Saturday afternoon the Pit was cleared of rocks, fridges, and knotted French letters.

60

'AREN'T YEH GOIN' tidda game, Ma,' Babs asked Mary as she dusted the large picture of John F. Kennedy.

'Jasus, no. Yer father'd say I was lookin' at the men. Anyway, I don't want them Corporation wimmin lookin' at me.'

Babs, Pam and Bridgid would join the other girls to look at boys in shorts. Mary would stay at home. She was looking forward to the bit of peace.

As he sweated over the pigs Jack was dreaming. While the other Dads were at that very moment eating fatty rashers, thick slices of black pudding mushrooms, three eggs and a quantity of chips for breakfast, the Boss was nibbling a nettle and wholemeal sandwich with two big walnuts from Neary's big tree to follow. While other men smoked five Afton Majors the Boss gargled on fresh spring water from Mount Vernon. While the old ragged men of the cottages waited nervously, dreading the occasion, the Boss was on his knee praying to Ely, the God of War.

Jack could see his father, tanned and tough and reeking of Wintergreen, march into the Pit on boots he had shined to a dazzle. He saw the other men look up and he could see they were terrified. He saw them one by one hobble to the bushes, their trousers tucked into socks, their bellies flopping over their belts, to urinate.

Flinging his silver sword aloft like some Neanderthal Prod on July the twelfth, the Boss stamped his feet and wheeled, making sure to show all the oul' wans the considerable lump in his shorts. While old Ned Cummins the coalman was sending lacey spits like leaping green frogs into the gorse from an ulcerated stomach, the Boss was rock still, his eyes ahead and alert, his shield in front of him, emblazoned with the family crest in gold rivets and the motto: *Carpe Diem*. Sieze the Day!

Then, ready and eager to do battle, the Boss jogged on the spot, his oxhide boots pounding dust out of the parched amphitheatre floor.

He creaked his neck from side to side and waited for the beautiful Lady Moore to drop her finely crochetted handkerchief to begin the battle. The Boss strode towards the centre of the field like a colossus. The muscular young men came at him in waves. He easily repelled them, breaking necks like twigs. And still they came at him, their studded fists raised. The Boss, his face stern as a great eagle, resisted until they all lay about him, their blood slaking the Pit's thirsty soil. Foley was the last to go, the sword entering his rectum and coming out of the roof of his head. The Boss spun on hairy legs and stamped his booted feet again. He seemed to be saying, 'Anyone fer anymore?'

Jack paused with broom in hand, shook his head and smiled. In fact, he couldn't stop smiling. On this one day of the year he was so proud of his Dad. He puffed his chest out like a pigeon and whispered to the pigs. 'My Dad is the toughest man in Rathfarnham. He could bate the shite out a the lotta them put toget'er wit' both arms tied behind his back.'

The Pit began to show signs of life. Fat mothers, with children crawling over them sat on the grass while older sons and daughters carried cardboard boxes of food. A knot of men from Cullen's arrived with their hands in their pockets. Geriatrics representing the oldies worked out with fags lit. Some wore double-breasted suits, nylon shirts and hats.

'Get them pigs swept,' the Boss roared just as the cheers went up in the Pit. When he heard the sexy, high-pitched squeals of the Bloomfield Laundry girls, the Boss growled, 'Tarts, hope they get what they kem fer.' When he climbed on the empty cart to look down on the Pit and saw Colin Doyle, the youngsters' captain, greet the girls with his hands inside his shorts blatantly cupping his genetalia, the Boss was disgusted. He saw Father Orlston there. Why wasn't he stopping that melt Doyle showing off like that?

Babs brought a tray of tea into the yard. 'I'm goin' down tidda match,' she said.

'What d'yeh be wantin' ta do that fer?' The Boss asked. 'Yeh'll get inta trouble wit' that scum.' That Doyle melt is upta no good.'

'I don't care,' Babs said, 'I'm goin' anyway.'

'Little bitch' the Boss growled. 'She's been list'nin' ta yer woman up there. I on'y want her safe. That's all.'

With excitement wriggling like a maggot in his guts, Jack joined his father on the cart. Longingly, he watched young men as sleek as race-horses dribble and shoot. What he would give to be that fit, strong and confident.

As the Boss watched, he too wished he were playing like he used to. He would of course be on the young men's side. He had nothing but contempt for his loathsome contemporaries, weak-kneed derelicts, afraid of their own shadows. How he hated weakness, especially in men. Women were different. They were born weak and pathetic.

Jack barrowed and shovelled, fed and watered the animals. Every few minutes he ran up to the cart to climb on board and view the Pit in all its excitement and colour. How he wished he were there, stripped to his vest and flashing down the wings like Maxie McCann of Rovers.

The teams were picked and the game was started by Father Orlston. 'Yeh blind runt,' the Boss screamed at the Dowager, from atop the ponyless cart. 'Yeh couldn't pass diarrhoea.' He swore as much as he pleased, ranted as much as he liked. When Tommy Rooney, the youthful captain dribbled past several ineffectual tackles Jem Rice rushed from goal and swung a right boot. The nimble-footed Rooney did a smart drawback and when Rice fell on his back, Rooney rolled the ball into the net.

'Foul, foul, yeh blind oul' cunt,' the Boss roared but Father Orslton plodded on ignoring the barracking.

Babs, Bridgid and Pam timidly ventured out of the bungalow to watch from a distance. Village girls, more forward and better dressed, brazenly cheered their young men and leapt into the air showing their legs. Babs brought her sisters home. They didn't belong.

After the match the young men drifted away, heading the ball to each other. Their blood warmed, they talked of sex. A few girls hung around, looking for romance. Jack heard the boys catcalling lewdly: 'Jasus, will yeh lookit the diddies on yer woman.' . . . 'Hey, Maisie, decorate yer ankles.' Their voices were muffled by a cold breeze. The girls turned away, and the boys ran after them, shouting obscenities. The sound of their bantering voices continued to drift up to the house until they were swallowed up by the advancing night. But by that time Jack was indoors sitting on the form with his sisters as his mother, wreathed in steam, made supper.

61

JACK WAS WORKING alone. The Boss had left him a pile of cuttings and a crowbar, and given him a planting demonstration before he left. The work had to be completed and the tools put away by the time the Boss returned. His hands nicked, pricked and blood-smeared, Jack worked silently and slowly until each thorny little shrub was standing straight and watered. He was contemplating the neat straight row and expecting a word of praise when he heard a whistle through the tall willow branches.

Across the stream and over the wall he saw a familiar figure holding a full-size football. Paddy Daly had climbed over the wall and was standing on Jack Perkins' patch. Skeletal and approving, Perkins was standing beside him.

'Gor somethin' for yeh,' Daly said. Jack's stupid smile almost cut his face in half. He wiped his nose on his sleeve. 'Well? D'yeh want it or not?' Daly joked. This made Jack's wellingtons accelerate towards the fence, his eyes fixed on the big ball. He wanted to rush out onto the road, throw himself upon his benefactor and hug his knees. He was dumb and dirty, stupid and inarticulate but in his heart he was so grateful. 'Will yeh t'row it over ta me?' He heard the words coming out of his mouth.

Jasus, fancy talking like that to an ex Irish 'B' International. 'Right son, here she comes,' Daly said and he flung the ball the way goalies do, right over the tall trees. Jack followed it, running, as it sailed and turned and spun like a planet to land in the garden. It bounced as Jack gave chase.

'Jasus, it's goin'ta go in the river and over the weir,' Jack cried to himself. 'Oh, my God, please don't let it.' The ball stopped like a big brown ostrich egg and nestled in a hole the pigs had made in the garden.

He picked up the leather-skinned ball and clutched it to his chest.

'It's autographed be all the lads at Transport,' Daly said. Jack glanced at the squiggles. He recognised Kevin Blount, the goalie, always in black, who dazzled with his diving and fancy fingertip saves. And Olly Conroy, the weaving winger Jack read about every week in the *Mail*.

'Happy now?'

'T'anks,' Jack mumbled.

'Well, I'm off now,' Daly said. 'The offer of tickets is there any time you like.' He waved and as he jogged away Jack's hand rose and made a vague wave.

Now he could look at the ball more thoroughly, every stitch on the leather panels symetrical, the tight lacing, the rubber nozzle in the side bent back and tightly sealed. Jack fondled the ball as if it were a live animal. He put it to his nose and inhaled, it smelt of dubbin and oil, of the cobbler's shop.It smelt beautiful.

Jack didn't hear Kitty's hooves on the bridge. It was only when the gate squealed he knew the Boss was back. Jasus! He looked around, quick as he could he shoved the ball under the hayrick.

The Boss leapt from the cart. 'Well?' he snarled, 'have yeh done that bit a work I gev yeh this mornin'?'

'Yes,' Jack said, wanting to hug his father for not seeing the football. Tearing around with joy he took the crowbar, scraped it, smeared it with grease and put it back in its place. Then he ran to help his dad unload the heap of scrap metal, logs, old car batteries, empty bottles, turf and potatoes he had collected that day. Jack worked so willingly and with such rare commitment the Boss must have wondered, but he said nothing and between them they finished the job and were washed and ready for dinner in double-quick time. As he passed the hayrick Jack saw the ball's silhouette but his father didn't look down.

Later that evening, Jack slithered out of the bedroom window, retrieved the ball, took it lovingly indoors and hid it under his bed. Claiming he was tired after all the work he had done in the garden, he soon slipped away.

The Boss's ears picked up the remark. 'Sure, that wasn't work. When I was a boy, work was work . . .'

Jack wanted to be alone with his ball and after a cursory prayer he was in bed with it under the covers, fat and soft, big, round and smooth. It took him ages to get to sleep and when he finally dropped off the ball was in his arms. He dreamed of balls of all shapes and sizes sailing through the air, bouncing about the garden, him running after them. When Jack woke he still had his lovely ball, his own ball, his own FAI approved ball. It was far too precious to kick, with all those signatures on it. The ball would live with him in his bedroom.

62

MARY WAS ALMOST hysterical with happiness. Her sister Dolores was coming home after thirty years in America. The road to Chicago seemed gravelled with gems when Dolores left Galway to escape the leaking thatch, tribal hurling matches, priest-led ignorance and no electricity. She was a soft, pale child but America had soon taken away her innocence and given her an accent. It had also given her wealth, enough to stable two cars as big as bungalows, and to build a house called *Connemara.*

Dolores had married a German who made mountains of gold selling printed string. Who in the sodden boreens of Galway would have thought money could be made from selling twine? Dolores sent letters bulging with dollars and photographs of her cars and her children. They'd always made Mary jealous. But Dolores had remained a Catholic and that was the main thing.

Mary watched the mean Dublin seasons waste themselves against the windowpanes, full of envy for the flown bird. Dolores had holidays in Hawaii and perfume sent from New York. She had even been to Alcatraz. While Mary was followed around by a string of needy children coughing and crapping, her sister sat in a house made from chrome and glass and let a maid look after her blonde babies. But, in spite of her hardness, Dolores' thoughts were often wrenched back to Galway's crumpled fields and rocky bays. She even dreamed she was standing in the boreen of long ago, her hair lank, she and Mary on the same old bike, nothing but stillness all around.

When paying her dues at the shrine of her youth, now a hacienda owned by a Greek millionaire, Dolores headed for Dublin to clap eyes and hands on her sister. Mary prepared for the visit with manic enthusiasm, cajoling and bullying her children with cuddles and threats to help her clean the house, make cakes and beat the threadbare carpets.

Failing to grasp the immense importance of the visit the Boss carped. Visitors frightened him. 'She'll ruin them slips a girls wit' her ideas,' he complained, and his wellingtons disconsolately slip-slopped him back to his pigs. The house hummed to the sounds of polishing and scrubbing. Emulsion paint was dabbed where the damp grown tumours on every wall. Jack sang in the back kitchen as he knelt on a sack and buffed the tiled floor.

Dolores arived in style. On seeing her hired car the Boss skulked back out of sight, as wary as an old cockerel needing to sniff out a new arrival in the chicken run. He was armed with a fork, its tines impaling apples and potato skins. His eyes glittered as he stood like a poverty-stricken sea god behind the chicken wire, his trident raised.

In the hallway, like an actress awaiting her cue, Mary stood mountainously. In a panic she adjusted her home-made maternity dress, worried about her veins, and teased her still-dark hair with sausagey fingers.

Colourful and loud, Aunt Dolores nonchalantly waved notes at the driver and crossed the bridge buried in presents. She pushed at the door to the bungalow's dark interior like a plump Victorian anthropologist investigating a burial mound. Warily, she stepped inside, and burst out, 'Mary, Mary, I'm home!'

Like an overworked horse before a plough, Mary agitated on the spot for a few seconds before trundling on her unfamiliar high heels to hug and slobber wet kisses all over her sister, almost sucking every shred of powder from her face. The two women whinied and squealed.

'Darlin',' Mary whined, 'how ar'yeh afther all these years?'

'Hey, Sis, hang on there, lemme breathe a little,' cried Dolores. 'Hey, I'm jes' wunnerful. You sure write great letters, I know all about yer kids. This one's Babs right?'

The children lined up like famine victims in a Protestant soup queue, waiting to meet the great aunty, whose boxes of clothes had made her famous. They shuffled in line, smiling shyly, their hair watered and slicked.

'Hey, what great kids ya got,' Dolores said, as she pecked each child on the cheek. 'How many ya got sis? Ya sure have been busy. Ain't ya got no TV in Ireland?'

Mary said nothing. The remark was intended to be funny but Mary had heard it all before. The children watched the two women and wondered how they could be sisters.

'I kept my guy occupied.' Dolores said. 'A six-pack of Bud and The Bears on TV, and he left me alone.'

Mary hadn't warned her sister she was pregnant for the ninth time. Dolores, who could only manage four, looked at her sister's belly. Poor thing. But there would be time later for the women's talk.

'Jeez, them hogs,' Dolores said, holding her nose. 'How d'ya stand the smell?'

'What smell?' Mary asked, offence written on her forehead in capital letters.

Dolores took her sister's worn face in her hands. 'I guess I forgot how the country smells, that's all,' she soothed.

The Boss slyly appeared from the bedroom where he had rushed to change. He smelt as if he had poured the entire contents of his secret cache of Old Spice over his head. If he'd intended to make an entrance, it backfired, because when Dolores saw him she whooped, 'Why it must be Johnny!' and she planted a smacking kiss on his bald head as if to emphasise her size and his insignificance. Knocked of his stride the Boss fumbled, gushed, and retreated. Feckin' cheek!

He took stock of Dolores's well upholstered arse and the way it rolled and quivered as she walked slowly to the table and plonked herself down with a sigh. 'Jeez, honey,' she fanned her face, 'I'm just about pooped. Y'know how far it is to Dublin from home? One hundred and thirty miles. And the roads, they are so bad.'

'So yeh still call it *home*?' Mary said. 'Well, so do I.'

'And so ya should,' Dolores said over her chained specs. 'Galway is your home and always will be.'

The Boss said nothing, but just stood like a grievously offended Red Indian Chief whose sacred ground was being pissed on.

Mary drew back the white sheet covering the feast as if she were a detective inspecting a dead body. The children gasped. Bridgid clapped like a seal, but Pam merely cocked her head as if such a feast happened every day. There was a spectacular mountain of cakes, ham, cheese and chicken sandwiches, and green, white and orange jellies. As a huge pot of tea was hustled in, Dolores was already refusing most of the food being offered to her. Mary was upset, but trying not to let on.

Dolores tapped her stomach, 'Sorry Sis, but the doc says I gotta get it off. Ya know what my cholesterol is? Nine. Would ya believe that?'

Clutching her plate to an aproned lap, Mary fired questions about their past but Dolores had lived away too long. Ireland had died for her years ago. She'd come over to lay the ghost, so she could die happy in America, no longer a foreigner. Faraway hills might be green but close-up they were also pretty shitty.

'Pity ya never came over to the States, Mary,' Dolores said, curling a finger round her cup handle. 'You'd a loved it there. The men are so cute.' Mary's eyes darted to her husband. 'I was lucky, I guess, meetin' Heinz. It was, as I recall, at a party for young Catholics. He was real charming.' Dolores genteely licked her fingers, the crimson nails made it look as if she were eating them. The childen ate like famished mice around a tray of poisoned corn. Feverishly, they elbowed each other out of the way as they steadily demolished the food.

The Boss sat on the edge of his chair with the pained look of a man eating a razorblade sandwich. He did not like strangers invading his house. The sooner this loudmouth woman left the better.

Tiring of her sister's obsequiousness, Dolores turned to her brother-in-law. With a victorious smile the Boss slipped easily into his role of entertainer. Seeing it as a lying sham, Mary left him the stage and retreated to the kitchen, firmly rejecting all offers of help from the children. She wanted to suffer. As darkness fell, the flicker of firelight leapt across the ceiling. Mary heard laughter and it made her feel worse - her sister and her husband were obviously bonding nicely. Blast them.

The washing-up done and the kitchen tidied Mary braced herself before re-entering the warm room. She was in time to hear the Boss brazenly inviting himself to Chicago.

'Oh, ya'd just love it there, Johnny,' Dolores said, clutching a large Power's. Another rabbit the Boss had produced from his tawdry hat, and it was working. That bottle had lasted five years till now. By doling it out in miniscule portions it had oiled many a wheel. And Dolores didn't need much persuasion. Why she was American and, hell, the Yanks sure knew how to party. 'You come over, Johnny,' she said. 'Ya'd jes' love it. I mean that. You should a gone when ya were a kid. You'd've done real well there, with your energy and initiative. The

Americans like hard-workin' guys who play hard an' pay their taxes ta Uncle Sam.'

Mary winced. The Boss, his little blue eyes dancing, placed a hand on Dolores's knee. 'Bejasus, yeh're right!' he exclaimed. 'If on'y a poor fella could sell them oul' pigs and raise a few shillin', he could still go an' make a minta money in Sheecago.'

'Why, it's little Mary,' Dolores said as her sister crept near her like a whipped dog. 'Come in, macushla an' sit with Johnny and me. We were just saying how it would a been just fine if you both could a come to stay with us.'

Mary played with a cardigan button. 'Ach, I don't know,' she said and her voice was whispering. 'Sure, we don't go anywhere.'

The Boss's warm mouth came close to Dolores. He was now captivated by the lovely brash woman with the raucous laugh and the fat wallet. Why couldn't he have found a woman like that? Someone with spunk, a woman who could handle herself in any company. A cute business lady who went to the States a Galway pauper and conquered the damned place. The Boss's admiration for Dolores was in danger of spilling over.

Jack, ragged and dishevelled, padded barefoot into the room. His nose was running, his eyes full of cold tears.

Dolores stopped in mid sentence. 'Jack!'she cried. 'Why, here's the manager of the estate, ah guess.'

Confused and embarrassed Jack wanted to flee from the arclight beamed on him by this multi-coloured behemoth.

'Is it manager?' the Boss sneered. 'Sure, the lad's so pat'etic he needs constant attention from yer woman here. She even wipes his bloody arse.' The Boss laughed. Mary's hands were shaking as she filled cups with streams of tea. 'Come on now, Dolores,' she said, 'the dhroppa tay'll be goin' cold.'

'Sure, what would a grand, big woman be wantin' with yer cold oul' tay?' The Boss said.

'Well,' Dolores said, 'who's coming back with me to the Yewnited States?'

'Me!' Bridgid cried, with her hand held up as though she was at school and wanted to go to the lavatory. 'I wan'ta go,' she insisted. 'Can I?'

'Not you, darlin',' Dolores said, 'least, not right now. Later, maybe, when you have your grades.'

Stuff it up yer fat arse then, Bridgid thought.

'What about you, Babs?' Dolores asked.

'No! Babs doesn't wan'ta go, take Bridgid wan,' the Boss said urgently.

'But Babs is the bright one, I unnerstand,' Dolores said. 'She'd do real good in Chicago.'

'Now yeh're talkin',' the Boss said, 'but she's not goin'. She'll do all right here. Babs is a right little brainbox. Lovely little worker too. She'd be betther off here in Dublin. Yeh wouldn' be wantin' ta go all that way ta America, wouldja now, Babs?'

Her face serious, Babs weighed it all up before answering. Dolores's lipstick-stained cup remained stationary at her lips until Babs said, 'I t'ink it might be good for me t'go. But I don't wan'ta leave home yet.'

'Well, how's about that?' Dolores said loudly. 'The kid knows her own mind. I appreciate a considered opinion. Le'me tell you this though. From what I've seen of this country, it ain't going nowhere. In the States you could maximise on everythin' ya got. Whatever talent you have, America'll bring it out. There's opportoonity everywhere. We jes' about have every sorta evenin' school you could possibly want.'

The Boss studied Dolores's fat lips. She was trying to entice his beloved daughter away from him, but he liked her. He bustled out to his secret cupboard and returned with two gold-rimmed glasses brimming with liquor. 'Slàinte,' he said, handing one to Dolores and poking her in the breast. He emptied his in one breath-gagging gulp, his eyes bright with pain. Dolores took a sip of hers and made a face. 'Jeez, Johnny, where'd you get this, the gas station?' She laughed and the Boss laughed too.

'I'll tell yeh now,' the Boss said. 'An oul' lady gi'me that fer doin' a bit a work on her kitchen. Quare stuff, isn't it?' He picked up the bottle, put on his glasses and tried to read the label. 'Tekweela,' he said. 'Jasus, what the feckin' hell is it atall?' He turned the bottle. 'A hundert percent Ag. Ag. Ah, feckit.'

Dolores leaned across and her big breasts creamed upward threatening to spill all over the Boss's face. 'Why, it's Tequila,' she said, 'Mexican brain damage.'

'Is that a fact?' the Boss asked and his hands assumed a life of their own. For two pins he'd have those big juicy tits out and be munching on their fat nipples. 'Jasus, there's now. Te-bloody-queela. A grand droppa oul' juice.'

'Tequila! Johnny,' Dolores shouted, amused at the man's daring unsophistication, she put her smooth white hand on his.

The Boss felt smoke coming out of his ears.

'We call it *brain damage* in the States. Know why?' Dolores asked.

'No, bedad. Why?' the Boss asked and he heard a punchline cantering towards him.

'Ever seen an intelligent Mexican?' Dolores laughed loudly and pushed him with her hand.

'Jasus, I never seen any kinda bloody Mexican,' the Boss said. 'That's a good wan.' He laughed with Dolores until he caught sight of Mary's eyes. They were frozen with hatred.

'Yeh sure know how ta put away that jungle juice,' Dolores said as the Boss downed another glass and refilled it.

'C'mon,' he said, his voice slurring, 'yeh'll take another oul' dhrop yerself,' he asked shakily.

'Phew!' Dolores said. 'It ain't what I'd call soothin'.' While the Boss turned the ugly little glasses in his fingers Dolores got up with a grunt and went to the kitchen to help Mary, who had slid away and was clanking around doing nothing.

'Are yeh sure yeh injoyed yer tea?' Mary asked, feeling full of guilt and very inadequate.

'Sure, sure,' Dolores said tipsily, 'loved it, especially those itty bitty apple cakes. Ya gotta gi'me the recipe.'

'Oh, them's jus' oul' apple baskets,' Mary said with a weak shot of enthusiasm. 'I'll sen' yeh the recipe.'

'Sure,' Dolores said, absent-mindedly. 'Sure ya will.'

'Mammy, there's a big car at the door,' Bridgid said breathlessly.

'It's got ta be my cab,' Dolores said. 'Now listen, you guys take it easy. Like I said, no use killin' yerself, and mind that dear little baby.' She chuckled something under the chin of the infant who was crawling about the floor. 'Yuh got a real nice home here, and a sixty-four carat guy for a husband. God, that man's humour kills me.'

The horn tooted again. 'An' listen here, Babs. You jus' think about comin' to America. I can fix it for ya. I got two big brownstone houses and a cottage up country. I can make it a damn sight easier for ya than it was for me in them early days. My God, it was tough, but we made out. Well, I gotta go now. Hope ta see you all 'gain sometime.'

Dolores grappled with Mary for a while, two outsize waltzers in a slow motion dance of death. Blood sisters kissing for probably the last time. 'Take care now,' Dolores said pushing a fifty-dollar bill into Mary's bib pocket. 'Ya hear me?' The kids crawled, climbed and cried to see off their magic American aunty. She who had sent the parcels that clothed them and the dollars that helped to feed them.

Dolores went over to the Boss where he sat bemused by the drink, and slipped a twenty-dollar bill into his pocket.

'Hey!' he yelled as if coming out of a trance. He jumped up and threw himself at his sister-in-law, clumsily pressing himself against her massive bust. Dolores side-stepped and stooped into the taxi. The Boss waved, holding one of the children for effect.

After she'd gone he poured her unfinished Tequila back into the bottle, locked it away, and sought out Babs. She was sitting on the bed talking with Pam and Bridgid. 'Yehz two make yerselfs scarce,' the Boss ordered, holding on to Babs' arm. When the room was empty he looked into Bab's eyes. 'Yeh don't wan'ta be taken in be that oul'Yank,' he said. 'That woman talks rubbitch. Yeh've got a lovely little job in Easthams. I got down on me han's and knees ta getcha that job. Don't let me down. Them that has ta go ta the States is poor gobdaws from the counthry like yer woman Dolores, from places where they live in filt', steeped in superstition and ignorance. They have nuttin' ta lose be goin' away. Yeh're not in that situation. Yeh have a lot ta lose. D'yeh hear what I'm sayin'?' His voice was normalised by the urgency of his message.

Babs nodded. 'So yeh'll put any t'oughts out a yer head about America. Right?'

Babs tossed her dark head. 'I wasn't goin' Daddy, I was jus' t'inkin' about it, that's all.'

The Boss fondled his daughter's head, feeling the warm skull under her black hair. He would never let her go. That was the end to it. 'Ah well,' he said, relieved there was going to be no difficulty about it, and left the room.

Babs sat on her bed. She would go to America. She had to escape.

63

THE BOSS TOURED his property looking for cracks and fissures in the walls and ceilings. After months of threatening he decided to plaster the kitchen ceiling. As he crouched on the kitchen table a creamy blob of lime fell into his right eye and it was instantly on fire. The Boss knuckled the eye angrily.

'Mothera Jasus, I'm afther destroyin' me poor eye,' he groaned as he slid to the floor, doubled up in agony. Curses richochetted throughout the bungalow as he staggered across to the sink, and made it worse. 'Lovva Jasus, I'm blinded f'life,' the Boss railed as he twisted his head under the tap.

Mary rushed into the kitchen as fast as her stout legs would permit. 'What's the matter wit'cha?' she enquired, placing a gentle hand on her husband's thick neck. Flinging her away he pawed the eye. 'Will yeh get out a me feckin' way,' he roared as he groped for a towel.

When he had wiped his face and gingerly dabbed the eye, Mary asked, 'Diyeh want me ta send wanna the childer fer a doctor?'

'Jus' l'ave me alone, fer Chris'sake,' the Boss groaned, dropping into a chair.

Mary made gestures of hopelessness. 'Bridgid!' she yelled. ' Ge'over to Dr O'Donnell and ask him to come immeedjetly.'

Bridgid, home from school with a phantom belly-ache, leapt into action.

Dr O'Donnell was more concerned with holing a tricky downhill putt at the Grange. Mary fidgeted behind the curtains , her eyes panning the road. The Boss slumped, his laces undone, a curved hand pathetically shielding the hurting eye.

'Dr O'Donnell's out,' Bridgid gasped. 'We'll hav'ta get an ambulance t'get'im t'ospiddle.'

'Feck th'ospiddle,' the Boss snarled. 'What the hell do I want wit' wanna them places? For Jasus' sake woman have a bit a sense. Could you look afther them bloody pigs if I was lyin' in some rotten 'ospiddle?' He squinted up at her like a dog ready to tear the arm off a postman.

Mary went silent, the way she did when her husband treated her as an irrelevance.

'Get Docthor Carrol from Barton, 'The Boss said weakly, a self-pitying kink in his voice. Barton, recently built, was a mile away with neat lawns, double garages, pseudo-Georgian façades and tennis courts. The new residents were clean and educated. They were the new Irish, not at all like the real English gentry the Boss admired so much. They were 'hungry bastards who druv big cars on the never-never.'

The Boss feared rather than respected the new professional classes. They had scrambled through an inadequate educational system by 'fiddlin' the exams and paying back-handers tidda priests'. Some were accountants and estate agents, devious creeps he had no use for. As for the dentists, they were out and out chancers, 'chargin' t'ree prices to rub a bit a ould bakin' powder on a few stumps.' The only drill an Irishman could use was on tarmac, in England. Doctors were in a different league altogether. He hated them totally, and it hurt his pride ever to be in their power.

Bridgid was sent pedalling again, this time to Mrs Crimmin's shop to use her telephone. When the elegant lady doctor arrived, the Boss's disgust was transparent. To think she was going to touch him, made him squirm. Her tone was insufferably brisk. She was an educated woman, not a doormat like Mary.

'Snotty heifer,' the Boss thought. With his good eye he noted the curve of her legs as she stood over him. 'It's on'y a bit a oul' lime in me eye,' he growled, 'jus' putta dhrop a' somethin' innit an let me out a here.'

The doctor spread the eyelid with thumb and forefinger, revealing the ugly veiny eyeball peering from the slit. A malevolent eye. 'Wash it out,' the Boss ordered.

'This is a serious injury,' the doctor said. Do you want to lose the sight of the eye?'

'I'm not goin' ta 'ospiddle,' the Boss barked like a cur that had been booted in the balls. 'I've got too much work . . . And I'm married to a bloody eejit.'

'*I'll* decide whether you do or whether you don't go to hospital,' the doctor told him.

In the kitchen, Mary smiled.

'Wouldja like a cuppa tay,' a soft voice asked. The doctor looked at Mary who had shuffled in on broken slippers, wearing her cleanest bib. Poor woman. She addressed Mary. 'It is quite serious,' she said. 'I'd advise you to get your husband to hospital as soon as possible.'

Mary wiped her hands in her apron. 'Yes, docthor, a course I will.' She was finding immense comfort in the fine lady's immaculate presence. The Boss's good eye stared as if it was a painted marble. He was ready to leap on his bedraggled wife when the doctor left.

'We'll getcha a taxi,' Mary said, taking charge of arrangements after the visitor's car disappeared down the road. The Boss turned his burning eye on her like a laser. 'Speak a bit a bloody sense woman willya,' he roared. 'Them hoors'll charge the eart' fer a bit of a stunt like that. I'll ride me bike there. If I hav'ta go at all,' he added miserably.

He put on his best shoes, but left on the greasy trousers and jacket. With water trickling from the stricken eye and cursing his luck, the Boss extricated his bike from the shed. He felt the tyres, and set off to cycle the five miles to the hospital.

'I hope he's goin' ta be all right,' Mary said as she watched the stocky figure pedal with furious determination down the hill towards the village and into the hostile atmosphere of the city. 'How would we manage wit'out him wit' all youse young childer ta look afther?' Her face was lined with thought.

The house was so peaceful without the dominating presence of the Boss, Mary put the kettle on for a cup of tea. Bridgid joined her, saying it would be awful if her Daddy went blind. Mary agreed, adding, 'Now, don'tcha be talkin' like that.'

Bridgid smiled. 'Ah, sure, he'll be all right, Mammy.'

Mary cuddled her daughter.

The Boss, his eye glowing like a branding iron, waited cursing at the traffic lights in Terenure. He gripped the handlebars tightly, tears dribbling down one cheek. He pushed off urgently, weaving through the traffic, his head bent, pedalling hard. The hospital, a sterile mountain of red brick, appeared. Flinging his bike against a wall, the

Boss stumbled into Reception like a hunted gorilla.

Jack, home from school, took off his hobnailed boots and padded damply into the kitchen, where Pam joined, haughty but concerned. 'Yer Da's had a'naccident. He's ridin' his bike ta the 'ospiddle in Dublin.'

Jack smiled, disbelieving. His father was indestructible, everyone knew that.

''Clare ta God,' Mary said, sawing a slice from one of Landy's big loaves.

Jack took the bread and walked, shaggy-headed, into the sunlit yard. With the Boss in trouble he might come in useful. Breaking a bit of jammy bread he held it above the heads of the seven cats who, mewing hungrily, had slunk out of their hiding places. They stretched, their tails quivering vertically.

Jack sat in the sun and unfolded a precious copy of the *Eagle* which a boy at school had lent him. Soon he was in Dan Dare's spaceship negotiating the galaxy. Silence, tangible and rare, enveloped him. With supreme pleasure he finished the last morsel of bread and sublimely licked his fingers.

Pam joined him. She had changed into her best casual wear. 'Shockin' isn't it?' she said. 'Daddy in hospital. I betcha he doesn't stay there.'

In the Eye Hospital an irritated bottle blonde slapped down her *Woman's Own* and nodded at the half-blind figure who'd just burst through the glass-panelled door. The Boss held his sweat-stained trilby in his hand. His head was naked and shiny.

'It's me eye,' he growled, 'I'm afther gettin' a dose a' lime innit. Dr Carrol sent me. I don't hav'ta pay an'tin' do I?' He blinked crazily at the indolent girl.

'I wouldn't know about that,' she cried in back-street Dublinese. 'Will yeh fill in dis anyway.' With a pencil she prodded a card towards the Boss as if he had leprosy.

'How in the name of Jaysus can I do that an' me with me poor eye nearly hangin' out?' he roared. Before the startled receptionist could reply, he strode past her and hurried down a long white corridor. He was stopped by an Asian doctor in a white coat who directed him to a cubicle. After a cursory examination he was told he was being kept in.

'No, no! Yeh don't understan'. Yeh can't keep me here,' the Boss pleaded. 'I'm a hardworkin' man witta big family, the on'y bread-winner. me wife is hopeless, she couldn't cope . . .'

'Please wait here, Sir,' the young doctor went off leisurely and returned after twenty minutes with an older man with grey hair and gravitas. By this time the Boss was practically eating the plastic curtains.

The consultant examined the eye. 'I'm sorry but you simply have to stay in here for the time being,' he said. 'You could lose the sight in that eye completely if it's not treated properly.'

The Boss cursed his luck, his wife and the medical profession. A nurse led him into a ward full of men wearing eye patches. They gaped, one-eyed, at the new arrival and one man in faded pyjamas tried to start a conversation. The Boss wrung his hat, staring bleakly through the large windows that overlooked an alien world. He longed for his pigs, for Kitty, for his apple trees.

Mary prepared supper. Babs helped her peel potatoes. Mary said the Boss would make much of his injury. 'They're like that,' she said, 'weak when all's said an' done.' The children gathered round, their eyes fixed on their mother.

'He'll go blind as a bat, Bridgid said cheerfully, 'he'll be feedin' the pigs witta white stick.'

'How morbid,' said Pam, who had recently discovered the word. Her face was pale where she had been applying flour, pretending it was Max Factor.

'Oh don't,' Babs said with a shudder. 'He's our Daddy an' he does his best fer us.' Then, as if the realisation slowly dawned that they were free of the monastic rules of silence and obedience, the children became very agitated and noisy. Their yells filled the brown hall, seeped into the bleak bedrooms.

They found the key and ran into the parlour. They examined the big walnut cased clock that hadn't ticked for fifty years, the chipped vases with the pictures of stags at bay, the chromed horseshoe, the wooden box of dominoes made of bone. Then they stopped and looked open-mouthed at the massive, gilt-framed pictures of their father. Enlarged photographs dominated two walls. Their father's image had been retouched for maximum effect. Like the phoney images of egotistical dictators, the Boss's hair was lush and black. The face was small and almost effeminate, the eyes aglow with false sincerity.

'They'll prob'ly give him a squirta somethin' an' he'll be gameball in no time,' Mary said, slicing potatoes into thick chips.

'I hope so,' Babs sighed, 'It sounds awful t'me.' The Boss's only loved child looked vacantly out on to the yard. 'He's a hard worker, Mammy, yeh've got ta give 'im that.'

'I'll give 'im that all right,' Mary said, 'Pity he's such a bully.'

With a clutch of gingersnaps and a mug of tea, Mary sat with a biro and a few sheets of paper to write to Dolores. She felt a little guilty about her sister's last visit. Mary's brain was expanding like a dry sponge in a basin of water. Without the Boss around she could write well. She told Dolores of Babs' promotion. 'She's got her own phone now, if you don't mind. As for Pam, well one day, please God, she'll make a fine little actress. She'd love that. Bridgid has her father's foul mouth, but she's kind enough, God help her. And poor Jack still has trouble keeping his nose clean. I think he gets the catarrh from my side of the family with the big blue eyes and the varicose veins to come. I hope he doesn't get the meaness and the old baldy head from his father. My Uncle Padge was a snotty old devil but he was nice. Poor Jack doesn't get much out of life except abuse.' Mary sniffed. 'Not a bit of thanks does the poor child get. Yer man just works him into the ground. Poor lad.'

Mary dunked another biscuit, her false teeth pinched so she took them out and laid them on the table. Her tender naked gums sucked the liquid biscuit, loving the gingery tang and the warm brown tea. She felt the pain as she stretched her stiff and bound old legs out in front of her, like a mummy tipped from an Egyptian tomb. The letter flitted in and out of the past. She reminded Dolores of things they shared when they were children. They lingered in the mind because they were either embarrassing or comic. 'Blood is thicker than water', she wrote, scribbling away. The house was quiet, the garden still. Jesus looked down from the wall with his arms outspread, his poor heart crowned and burning. But even He seemed to be smiling. Mary smiled back and took another big slurp of lovely tea.

Babs was doing the washing up. The hand pulling at Mary was Bridgid's, whose big round kindly face mooned up grinning and asking for money. 'Knock, Knock. Are yeh there, Mammy, is anywan there?' Bridgid rubbed her nose, Eskimo style on her mother's cheek Mary licked the envelope.

'Wh'isit, Bridgid darlin'. I was jus' droppin' a line t'me sister in Chicago.

'Ten bob,' Bridgid said.

'What?'

'I'm doin' the shoppin'. I t'ought we could trate ourselves t'a bloody feckin' big cake.'

'Why d'yeh always hav'ta use such language?' Mary asked stroking her daughter's greasy hair. 'Landy's have these gorgeous cakes in the winda. I jus' thought the oul' fella bein' away we could buy one.' Bridgid grinned, the taste of the cake already on her tongue.

'Yer father is in hospiddle.' Mary said gravely. 'Here's half a crown. It's all I have.' Bridgid snatched the coin and flew out the door.

As Mary sank her gums into the fluffy, coconut-topped cream gateau Bridgid had bought, she felt she was committing a mortal sin. But feck it. They would soon wipe it out with a few *Hail Marys*. As she looked around the table and saw her daughters, their faces beaming as they clutched thick slices, she knew the sin was worth the price.

Although the Boss's noisy ghost still floated through the house and around the garden, Mary, Babs and Pam talked happily. Bridgid emptied the shopping and put it away. Jack joined them after he'd wandered around the yard doing what he could. A ray of contentment filled the poky kitchen.

Mary was humming an old tune by the sink as she washed the cups. Looking absent-mindedly down the lane, she turned and shouted, 'Jasus, Mary and Holy St Joseph, he's back. Quick! T'row the tea out and put the pot away.' Jack fled, followed by Bridgid and Pam. Only Babs held her ground.

64

THE BOSS GRIMLY pushed his bike into the yard and turned his face to the house. His eye was covered with a black patch, making him look like a deranged pirate. He flung his bike into the shed and stooped to remove his bicycle clips. A stream of words, loud and nasty, poured from him. 'Them hoors has no regard for a hardworkin' man. That skut of a nigger thinkin' he was Jasus Christ in his white coat, was all fer keepin' me in there. I told 'im that if the pigs could shubble their own grub, and the cow milk herself while I sat in bed gorgin' meself, I'd do it. But not otherwise, no bejasus, not with the help I've got here. Me poor eye is ruined bur I can't just sit on me arse while them poor pigs is squealin' wit'tha hunger.'

The Boss stormed into the kitchen. The atmosphere was electric again, the brief contentment gone. Mary tried weakly to console him but he growled before disappearing into the scullery to put on his wellingtons.

'Jack,' Mary called out, 'go help yer Daddy.'

'I was goin'ta,' said Jack with a big grin, his eyes sparkling at the prospect. He wanted to help his stricken Daddy. This was his chance to prove himself. He raced ahead of his mother and was heading out of the door when Babs pulled at his sleeve. Slyly she palmed him a crisp *Lion* comic. 'Meant ta give it ta yeh earlier,' she said. Jack secreted it under a cushion.

The Boss sat on an upturned bucket, pawing at his black patch and cursing his luck. All around him the pigs squealed for attention. Mary arrived to timidly mention that maybe Jack was old enough to drive Kitty. 'He'll be goin' ta the big boys' school soon now, an' I t'ink he could give yeh a hand.'

The Boss laughed ironically. 'Ah, what help could that fella be to me? An' him still pissin' in his britches?' He peered at Mary with his good eye. Like a chastised child she retreated. Jack hung his eyes with hurt before going to sweep out the pigs and dream.

When he'd finished he slouched back to the kitchen to be among women, and to strip every bit of his comic, like a piranha. 'Daddy doesn't want me to drive Kitty,' he said, 'but I know I could.'

'Course yeh can,' Mary said.

'Never mind Daddy, Jack. He's jus' upset an' angry,' Babs said, but Jack had lost interest in his father and turned to his comic. 'G'wan then, 'Babs said, 'I know yeh're dyin' ta read it.' Jack's mind kept straying from the adventures of Captain Condor, the Robot Spaceman, and his favourite, Rory and Mick the Mountie and his dog. He was certain he could help his father, and went back to the yard where his half-blind father was stubbornly working alone.

The Boss ignored him. With his patch leaking pus round the edges, the tight elastic ruffling the bit of hair at the back of his head, the Boss was a sorry picture. Gone was the bullish aggression, the sneering sense of superiority that, at a crack his whip, could make all before him scurry like mice into their holes.

Mary was amused that her husband went weak at the slightest touch of pain while she, her thick legs splayed filled the world with blood and babies without as much as a murmur. Festooned with placenta, infection, migraine, varicose veins that criss-crossed her ankles with blue doodles, she'd always grimly suffered in silence. She tied on her fat sanitary towels while he was out in the yard, to avoid him slaying her with a string of hateful abuse. And, now, here he was making a big deal of a little soreness in the eye. 'Huh! If he'd ever had a baby, he'd know what pain was.'

When a child tumbled and its head cracked against the furniture Mary felt the pain. While the Boss might look up from his paper with the air of a gentleman disturbed in his club by a clumsy waiter dropping a tray of gin and tonics. 'Stop that fecker's keenin' he'd roar, 'or I'll burst him.' Mary had to pick up the infant, cajole it to a smile, the tears in its eyes, the big blue bump on its head, so that the Boss could read his *Evening Mail* in peace. At last the boot was on the other foot.

It took a day or two before the Boss decided that, while Jack was stupid, weak, uncoordinated, and thick like his mother, he could use him to help collect the pigswill from the respectable suburbs of Rathdown Park, Crannagh Road, Bushy Park, Orwell, Rathmines, Dartry and Milltown. But he would not let him drive the pony. That required a modicum of skill and intelligence.

'Yeh can take time off a school till the patch comes off,' the Boss said, tasting defeat and not finding it palatable. 'Bur, there's no way I'll letcha drive Kitty wit'out lessons. She'd turn the bloody cart over or have yer feckin' arm off 's quick as lookit yeh. That pony 'preciates discipline, an' yeh don't even know what the word means. Get her out a the stable an' I'll show yeh.'

Here was Jack's chance to show his father he was not merely a snotrag. He wanted his father to be proud of him the way he was of Babs. His eldest sister was loved and she loved back.

The Boss took Kitty's fringe and led her out of her stable to where he had laid all the harness on the concreted yard. The Boss went through it with him, identifying each strap and buckle while Kitty's eyes shifted from her master to the boy. Every time Jack touched her she shook her head as if to bite him. When the Boss roared, 'Stand, yeh hoor!' the pony knew he meant it. 'Gi'me that,' the Boss snarled at Jack. The pony let him fit the straps over her velvet ears without as much as a snapping of her teeth.

After trying a few more times Jack was dismissed. 'Ferget it,' the Boss roared. 'Yeh're useless. I'll yoke th'animal meself.' Kitty was quickly yoked to the cart. It was an unfamiliar time for her and she knew it. She should have been out grazing. She knew the Boss never took her out in the evening.

The Boss led her over the bridge, climbed into the cart, and handed the reins to Jack who shivered with fear and anticipation.

'Aisy now,' the Boss snapped. The Whitechurch Road stretched emptily ahead. Soon Kitty was travelling at full trot with Jack proudly sitting there, gently holding the reins. It was so easy. Jack was smiling, wondering what the fuss was all about. He had the touch. He shook the reins. Kitty galloped.

The Boss sat one-eyed and grim. Without warning Kitty veered across the road, almost knocking old 'Bockedy' Rooney off his bicycle. Kitty rushed down to the river. 'Jasus, yeh've done fer us now, yeh stupit bastard,' the Boss roared. Fear was clearly visible in his good eye. But Kitty stopped abruptly on the grassy river bank and with her brown teeth she lustily attacked the thick grass by Sheridan's Garage. Grease-smeared mechanics came out to investigate and laugh.

The Boss was fit to be tied. 'Yeh've got no brains at all. Yeh're s'posed to be steerin' the feckin' animal. Yeh gobshite!' he exclaimed. Jack's face filled with blood. To make matters worse, Rooney had got off his bike and was coming back to complain. 'It's the lad,' the Boss said. 'He's a little shitehawk. Me oul' eye is out a action. I'm tryin' ta teach him ta drive, so he can collect the waste from them ladies that keeps it fer me.'

'That's all very well,' said Rooney, who always was a nerdish arsehole, 'bur yeh near'y knocked an innocent man off a his bike.'

'Oh yeah, an' feck yeh, too,' the Boss whispered.

Jack pulled ineffectually at the reins as the pony wolfishly tugged at the grass. The boy was mortified, losing control was bad enough, getting Rooney involved was catastrophic . The Boss hated Rooney. The one thing more satisfying than knocking the cunt off his bike would be to crush the fecker to death. But the Boss had to make a joke of it, smile and ridicule his son, just to mollify a man he despised. Satisfied he had made a proud enemy eat shit, Rooney rode away while the grinning mechanics lit up, contentedly blew out the smoke, and went back to investigating the bowels of a Fiat engine.

'Now look wha'cha done,' the Boss hissed and gave his son a smack round the head. 'Ge'rout there an' lead that pony away from that feckin' river. A pony never eats grass unless yeh want it to. D'yeh hear me!' The Boss's words hit the top of Rooney's trees and bounced back. Jack scrambled from the cart, determined to get it right.

When Kitty jibbed and snapped at him, Jack shouted, 'Ge'ron there, Kitty. C'mon!' The pony walked obediently and placidly back to the road. The loop around Golden Acre and back to the bungalow was completed without further mishap. By the time they crossed the bridge to the bungalow, Jack was in total control with Kitty as compliant as an old ass. If the Boss was pleased he didn't show it. It was as if he wanted his son to remain a snotty failure, and give him another excuse for heaping abuse on Mary.

65

MARY SCRIBBLED A note for the nuns, and dripped solution into her husband's eye before he and Jack set off. They left the yard at 6 a.m. to invade the sleeping suburbs with their flower borders, trimmed lawns and shiny cars parked in the drives. The pig bins were left outside the silent houses. Jack was tense but proud and determined. He shook the reins and Kitty's well oiled hooves pounded the road past Cullen's and through Rathfarnham. The Boss sat Buddha-like on the cart, his knees under an old sugar sack. He wore his indispensable hat but no gloves, they were for homos. His wellingtons, which he did wear all the year round, were washed and shiny. They travelled in silence.

They returned home four hours later. Jack was pleased with himself. He had negotiated buses, trams, bikes, handcarts and even a herd of sheep on the way to market, all without the sniff of a mishap. Mary was so delighted she kissed him. Jack was late to join the children at school but he ate his lunch in the yard feeling tall, good looking and slightly dangerous.

During the period of his father's convalescence Jack got to enjoy sitting on the hard wooden seat of the cart, driving Kitty from house to house and watching his father operate. The Boss worked with the energy of a man under sentence of death. Everything had to be done at frantic speed. Only if a fine midde-class lady popped her head out of a bedroom window to wish him 'Good morning' did he pause, and then only to grovel. Jack watched his father's wet smile as he raised his hat just enough without exposing his crippling baldness. He noticed how the Boss appreciated well-built women in nightdresses who leaned out for a chat. The sight of a creamy cleavage always made his father take a little longer.

The Boss showed his sunnier side to shop managers and assistants who inhabited his patch and who always had much to offer him, boxes of old fruit, split bags of oat flakes, dodgy looking rashers of bacon, dented tins of marrowfat peas and half-crushed bunches of grapes. He would kiss their feet and genuflect if he had to. No one knew what they thought of the busy little man with his doffing hat and sly smile. Little did the Boss care, his pigs and his children would not go hungry. The Boss had no time for those who couldn't be used.

'Never mess wit' them that's poor,' he often told Babs. 'Yeh folly that which has money.'

Jack hugely enjoyed his weeks off school. It lessened the time he had to spend with the nuns. And his newly acquired street cred made him feel important, cocky almost. And it had its humorous side.

One morning, Jack sat atop the cart parked in a wealthy private estate, watching his father's trilby race along the top of a hedge. There was a surprised curse and the hat disappeared. The Boss had slipped on a patch of moss and fallen on his arse, scattering stale kitchen scraps in all directions. He quickly scrambled to his feet, gathered the fetid pigswill with his bare hands, and swallowed the stream of oaths that queued up in his throat. Whistling in agony the Boss climbed into the cart. When they were out of earshot he fingered a damaged white leg and roared. 'Curse a God on it. Will yeh lookit that feckin' dent in me leg.' When Jack told his mother about it she vibrated with pleasure.

Meanwhile back at the bungalow Mary, her latest baby about to pop out of its pod, was grabbing a few minutes to read the *Messenger*. Like a terrier with a bone she virtually chewed it to dust. There were no books in the house. The bungalow was Cambodia, the Boss was Pol Pot. If Jack did not hide his precious comics they were quickly consigned to the fire.

One day, an itinerant bookseller came to the door. The Boss, shovel in hand, greeted the man suspiciously. 'What are yeh sellin'?' he asked.

'Books,' the man said, opening his portmanteau. 'Only books, Sir,' the man repeated with a wild but educated look. Lovingly, he took a book from his case and fondly thumbed the leaves. As Jack watched the pages fan he imagined great stories from the world beyond the bungalow. He could almost smell the new print. He pressed closer to his father, clutching his long-handled broom like a miniature gondolier. Sensing a sale, the man expanded. 'This, Sir, is a novel by

Miss Annie Smithson, a local lady who has written many.[2] A brilliant tale it is too. Her books are great sellers, rivalling the famous English ladies: Miss Catherine Cookson and Miss Agatha Christie.'

'Is that a fact now?' the Boss asked playfully.

'Yes, indeed,' the man said, and he reeled off more titles. 'Ah, Miss Smithson's *Weldons of Tibradden*,' he continued smiling, 'now that is what I'd call an excellent read.'

'I know Tibradden well,' the Boss said, his one good eye a slit. 'God be wit' the days when I use'ta drive th'oul' hay bogey up there for a few cocks a hay.' He looked at the bookseller with pity. A man of learning, a well-spoken man selling books door to door must, by the Boss's definition, be insane. 'D'yeh t'ink them oul' books a yers'd clane out them pigs fer me?'

The bookseller looked perplexed. The Boss laughed. 'If them books a yers is not able ta feed them pigs while I sit wit' me feet up readin' them, sure they're not a bit a use ta me.'

The bookseller put the book back in his case. 'Well, good-day to you, Sir,' he said doffing his hat, and he went back over the bridge.

Jack watched him go; if only *he* could afford to buy a book. His father shouted and he joined him with the squealing pigs.

[2] Annie M.P. Smithson (1873–1948) Romantic novelist and Anti-Treaty supporter.

66

AS JACK SAT beside his father on the cart every day, sharing his sack, his mints and his bitterness a change came over him. As if drawn to a bully for strategic purposes, he found himself feeling sorry for his father, even liking him. Having heard the tale of how his brave father had crawled out of the cave of despair into which a drunken and violent father had thrown him. How he had rebuilt his life after being rejected by the priests, was nothing short of heroic. How he had saved Mary from possibly a life of prostitution on the nasty streets of hard old dirty Dublin. How he bought his land against all odds and single-handedly built his own house on it in spite of the collective wankerisms of that lot in Cullen's. How he cultivated a garden, built sties and filled them with fat pigs. How he made everything from wood and wire. How he filled his coops with fine laying hens. How he invented the world, swam the Atlantic, cured cancer, scored a hat trick at Wembley, beat Jack Johnson, shagged Greta Garbo and Errol Flynn, rode the winner of the Grand National and climbed Everest carrying half a dozen Sherpas on his back.

The scales fell from Jack's disbelieving eyes. He realised his father was not just a genius but seriously underrated. He was up there with Churchill, Gandi, Geoff Duke and Roy Rogers. He was a man with nothing but blows raining on him from every quarter, with a wife who was stupid and over fertile. How could he have stuck it for so long. Jesus, let's hear it for the Boss. The man was a fecking miracle worker. Day after day, Jack absorbed this fascinating if one-sided story. His father's victory over oppression, racism, Catholicism, shortism, baldism and cuntism was nothing short of incredible. Jack was being drawn into his father's deceitful web. His father rolled him up in spittle and put him away to be fed with injections of royal jelly. Jack had sold out. The weak-kneed, lily-livered, snot-festooned, traitor. Up till then Mary had won the propaganda war hands-down. Her children, the neighbours, the priests, even the gardai all voted for her. But now there were calls for a recount. At one time, only Babs understood the Boss, that's why he loved her. God, it was so easy. Once you get to understand someone, why, you grow to love them. Jack was glad he had seen the light.

As Jack examined his father's crazy outbursts, the insults he showered on Mary, it was obvious there had to be a reason for it. An affection grew between father and son. Jack discovered that when his father's mind was free of the cloven-footed demons that haunted him, he was very pleasant company. Jack became vocal about his mother's stupidity, her laziness and her incompetence.

It was all true. Jack was glad he'd changed sides. He knew what it was like to be alone and friendless. At school he, too, was despised by pupils and teachers, just the way his father was with the Galway culchies. As he steered Kitty through the clouds of diesel that enveloped the pony and cart from the big green CIE buses, Jack excepted a mint from his Dad. He smiled and touched his father's cheek. To be mates was just amazing for the boy. Kitty trotted on gamely, unaware of the change that had overtaken her driver.

Jack gazed into shop windows as he waited for his one-eyed friend to return. He imagined his father teasing the shop-girls, especially the young ones with the big tits, it was natural in a red-blooded man. 'Is that all the broken biscuits yeh're givin' me fer me darlin' shillin'. Jasus, aren't yeh the caution.' He could see the girls eyes light up. They loved him. Jack imagined his old Daddy eyeing up the long, nylon-seamed legs as their owner bent down to fill the bag. And why not. The man deserved a bit of sport.

Like a shabby little prince, Jack perched happily on top of the cart with wet pigswill seeping into the seat of his trousers. Although smelly and uncomfortable it was much better than school with its black-caped nuns, squawking girls and vicious ruffians. And he was with his father, his best friend who also hated to be cooped up.

The Boss scorned cosseting of any kind and yet when he had an unfamiliar ache Mary laughed at his fear of terminal diseases. 'Is it cancer yeh've got? Not one a yer family ever died of the disease. An' yeh, moanin' and groanin' an' lookin' sorry fer yerself.'

Oh, she could talk. And she could grizzle. She had a right, but she should do it in private. The Boss hated moaners. With his beret pulled over his big ears, Jack sucked his Ritchies mint. He stole an admiring glance at his father's determined jaw. The Boss was staring ahead, his small keen eye on the road. What, Jack wondered, was racing through that agile brain? His father's inner life was a sealed tomb. Jack wanted to know his father better. But the Boss was far too self-absorbed to talk to his son. Mary blathered on about everything, and was capable of revelations that shocked Jack. The Boss was silent on all matters personal. Jack decided his father was probably thinking about money, of how to take advantage of someone. He liked doing that, and why not? Cheating was fun. Why give a sucker a break? Analysing old hurts was worthwhile too. Jack looked at the pulsing muscles in his father's face and wished he had the nerve to touch it again. During moments of introspection the Boss seemed to slip away to some hidden place and stay there for minutes at a time. No one knew the name of the place. It was a sort of monastery of the mind, a place to contemplate and reflect.

The flicking whip kept Kitty trotting along smartly, her wild mane flying. Man, boy and pony, an obsolete tableau, slowly moving along the motorised streets of Dublin, heading for the hills where only weird people lived.

Jack grew during the period he helped his father. He enjoyed collecting the chaff from mountainous farms with the heathered uplands misty in the distance, the flocks of wild birds, crops full and fast flying; and the streams snaking and gurgling from a thousand mossy vaginas that marked the hills with bright scars. One-eyed and hectic, the Boss charged through his odd jobs, doing anything to turn a 'wing', or a shilling. When at last his pockets were jingling, he would order his young coachman to take him home, and return like an old gunner-eyed hawk to his tormented eyrie.

Jack's thin body and bony arms developed muscle. The Boss now treated him less like a sickly infant, and more like a useful lieutenant. Jack began to enjoy the free-wheeling, fresh-air life of the odd job man. He admired his father's ability to see opportunities and to take them. The Boss was a cunning go-getter who pounced on small opportunities, recognised a bargain when he saw one. Jack was learning the Boss's ways, the unloved ways of a bitter man. He was a pile of moist clay on the Boss's potting wheel and was being moulded in the man's image.

As the Boss's eye responded to treatment, Jack was no longer needed, so he returned to school. The distance between himself and his father widened again. The Boss's accident was woven into his sorrowful, ever swelling legend, another thorn in his martyr's crown: 'I lost an eye fer yehz an' what t'anks do I get? Yehz all hate me. An' me afther puttin' the bit a food in the press an' the stitch on yer backs.'

67

THE BOSS WAS waiting for Babs on the bridge. ''Member this?' He whistled as he untied the string and poured out various bits of metal, screws and a wooden stock, all sopping with oil. 'This'll take a few minutes,' he said, assembling the gun. Babs watched, amused, her hands folded. 'It'll kill at a mile,' the Boss shouted as he peered down the sight of the completed weapon. His good eye gleamed.

'I don't want'a kill an'tin',' Babs said.

'C'mon, take a hold ivvit,' the Boss said. The .22 rifle felt cold and greasy. The Boss loaded the gun and aimed it at a jackdaw in the trees. He smiled as the dead bird spiralled to the ground.

'Daddy, yeh hittit!' Babs said, pointing. 'It's hurt.'

'Naw,' the Boss said, thumbing another slug into the gun and handing it to his daughter, 'it flew off, I seen it. We're on'y afther them bloody rats, that's all.'

Reassured, Babs took the gun back and held it while the Boss, in dungarees and trilby, his backside upturned, went to the remains of the bonfire and gathered tins from it. His ash-stained hands cuddled a heap of scorched tins to his chest as he went to the wall to line them up.

As Jack watched the sty, the Boss pirouetted in his wellingtons. 'C'mon now,' he said. 'Let's see how much yeh remember. Yeh shubby able ta pot the lotta them from there.' He saw Mary clinging to the wire like a quizzical infant. Her look was far off. 'That oul' bitch is gettin' on me nerves,' the Boss said. Stung by the cracking of the gun, Mary shuffled away in her slippers, her greying hair streaming out behind her like smoke. Stopping, she leaned over the wall looking at Neary's field, her eyes blinded with the wintry sun, wondering what she was doing there, in a Dublin back yard, far away from her home and friends in Galway.

'What did I tell yeh?' the Boss said. 'Yeh've got me eye but that feckin' patch is done me.' Babs noticed that he suddenly deflated as he remembered. He grabbed the gun. 'Line 'em up,' he yelled. There was a lilt in his voice as his mood shot up like a child on a swing. He aimed the empty gun at his daughter's eggshell skull, hooked his nail-blackened finger round the trigger, heard it snick harmlessly against the guard.

Babs turned to face him, her teeth white and smiling, her head still intact on her shoulders. 'G'wan, Dad,' she said. 'Yeh hav'a go.'

Leaning on a broom, Jack watched enviously. He wished he could show his father he was not scared of killing things. His father would respect him for that. The Boss loaded and fired, fired and fired again. There were sounds of zinging ricochets, puffs of powdery cement as he missed, missed and missed again. Without his good eye he was useless. 'God damn that bastardin' eye!' the Boss roared slinging the gun on to the cement. 'The cursa God may light on the rotten ceilin'!' He left the gun on the ground and went indoors.

As she gathered up tins and bullet cases Babs heard the bungalow erupt. The window exploded outward, the glass shattered. She heard the dull thud of soft meat being kicked. Crouching, gathering the brass cases, Babs jumped with fright as a shadow, lengthened on the wall.

'How yeh?' It was Jack. In old boots, twine-tied trousers and cap, with a fork on his shoulder, the tines covered with muck. Just as he picked up the gun the Boss charged from the kitchen, the door slamming behind him. Mary's broom was swiping above his ducking head. Looking behind him, the Boss charged forward until the tip of the gun barrel was hard against his chest. Mary, bathed in sweat, lumbered up to the wire. Jack's eyes were steadfast. He smiled. 'Can I borry it sometime?' he asked.

The Boss grabbed the .22's barrel. 'Gi'me that an' go down ta the river an' wash the shite off them boots.'

Jack took the path to the river. Against the wire Mary roared like a cow in a slaughter house, beating at it like it was some sort of useless carpet. Babs moved to her father's side and shovelled a small soft handful of empty shells into his black claw. 'Fer the scrap, Daddy,' she said, forcing his hand open. He turned, a tiny smile breaking on his beleaguered face. 'Put 'em in the sack,' he said quietly. His eye turned to Jack heading for the bungalow, his wellingtons now wet and shiny, leading his limping mother like a hurt soldier into the kitchen. There he settled her on to a chair like a sack of wool, gathering up the ends so she wouldn't slide off the chair. 'I'll make yeh a porra tea,' he said. Rinsing the brown pot in the kitchen, and looking down the yard, he saw Babs and her father in conversation. Babs was waving her arms, obviously cross.

In his narrow bed pushed against the small window with its four panes of glass, Jack woke up thinking. It was a pure night outside, the air was sharp. Snow was expected. He thought about his father's .22. Jack was about to feel and fondle the sweet little rifle. Guns were totally destructive. 'I wonder if I could shoot my father?' Jack mentally doodled as he inhaled the warm smell of his sleeping sisters in the adjacent room. He had seen a fellow shooting pigeons once with a .22 over the Grange Golf Club wall. He saw the aim, squinting along the blue steel barrel. He saw the man tense in that fraction of a millisecond before he pulled the trigger. Jack watched the pigeon instantly become nothing more than a puff of grey feathers. The sound was sharp, so clean. Even the Boss would have died catching that one in the noggin.

Would Mary be pleased? Jack thought nothing would make her happier. But hate, like love was mysterious. If that beautifully impersonal .22 slug had collided with his father's follicly challenged dome, bursting it like a gut full of shit, Mary would probably put the rifle in her own mouth and follow her lover to Hell. People were like that, very strange.

Jack was in the kitchen two minutes later assembling the .22. With the pennies he'd collected from Babs, he had bought and secreted under his bed a box of slugs. It was white outside. Great blossomy flakes were still settling, layer upon layer of feathery stars heaped one on top of another. Snow covered the cement mixer, a pile of drainage pipes, the heap of bones, the boiler, and every dark hole on the building site that encroached and threatened to engulf the Boss's life's work. Soon, his small patch of land, his sties, his chicken house, his bungalow with the drab additions clinging to it, would disappear.

Jack woke very early, drew the curtain, and greeted the virgin whiteness with a pale smile. Hopping out of bed, he dragged on his trousers and socks. He could imagine big flakes gilding everything in the yard. His sisters' snoring rasped from their shared bed. The whiteness clamped on a silence that was as cold as death. Jack found his jacket, slipped into it and zipped it up to the neck. He felt strong. He would show the Boss he wasn't a weakling, or a snotty encumbrance. He was hard and mean - just like his Da. He would be an asset in a battle.

He glanced stealthily at his father's gargoyled face to check that he was asleep. The Boss lay like a battered monk in his cell, his mouth open as if drowning, head and shoulders exposed, striped pyjamas blossoming in the dark. Quietly closing the door, Jack walked through his sisters' bedroom. They lay like unconscious angels. The floor was strewn with soiled cotton-wool balls, knickers and brassieres. Suspender belts hung limply from the bedheads like something Dr Mengele was working on.

Babs had begun to collect Royal Family memorabilia. Their glossy, idle lifestyle added a little glamour to her drab life. Her room was plastered with craftily retouched portraits of the illustrious famly, every nephew, niece and distant Greek hanger-on was given a place on the brown-stained wallpaper. With their long inbred faces and ears like wings, they looked down imperiously from the walls, dressed like Ruritanians going to a fancy-dress party. 'Bloody bunch a Nazi spongers,' the Boss always said. 'When is them English gobshites goin'ta rise up and slit their t'roats?' The Pope waved a gammy hand, his watery old mouth askew and John F. Kennedy, the Patron Saint of Ireland, smiled his ever-youthful smile. Little did he know.

Jack squeezed past, mischievously giving Bridgid's bed a jolt. Her curly head turned. 'Dirthy dog,' she breathed sleepily.

In the icy kitchen Jack clawed on the light that could shock because condensation dripped on it from the water pipe above. Soon the kettle was steaming on the greasy stove, its lid lifting. Jack reached up and took the .22 and the box of slugs from the top of the dresser. The gun felt wonderful in his hands. He leaned over to the windowsill where loaves of fresh bread sat like toy trucks, and pinched a lump from the nearest one. The kettle whistled. The gun lay on the table, glinting in the 40-watt light. He drank his tea slowly, ripped off another hunk of bread and stuffed it into his mouth. Outside the snow was falling silently. Jack put on the Boss's old overcoat and buttoned it to the top, pulled on navy beret and braced himself.

The door, rheumatic from too many winters, gave way to his tug and a small wall of snow tumbled into the kitchen and began to melt on the tiled floor. Jack crumped across the deep-piled yard to Bab's bike which had been transformed into a magical steed with silver lace wheels. He pulled it from the wall and kicked it back to its rusting drabness. With uncooperative fingers he tied the gun to the handlebars, silently pushed the bike around the side of the hushed bungalow, over the bridge and on to the virgin lane. The whiteness was blinding. His breath came mistily, snowy needles pricked his eyes. Behind him, wobbly wheel lines were already being silently erased. His hands were numb, his raw chilblains stung.

Mouth gaping, Jack cycled uphill to the crossroads. A mile or so later he was in a wooded valley. Stiff and alert, he loaded the gun and loped like a Cherokee along the iced hedges. The valley ahead was inviolate. Jack stopped to inhale the freshness of it, to savour the beauty. He was alone; no pigs, no nuns, no Boss, no Mary, no rows. It was magnificent.

When the snow stopped, Jack gazed up at the marbled sky. A breeze soughed through the pines. he jerked back the bolt of the gun and fed in a brass slug. A pigeon clapped and flew off. He stopped himself firing, then settled under a canopy of snow-weighted fronds and waited.

Snow, eddied by the wind, coated the bent trees. Dead leaves like twisted pennies careered down the hill. Jack pulled his lapels up tighter. The temperature seemed to drop. He swiped a sleeve across his running nose. Minutes passed. His joints were seizing. His feet were stinging. A pheasant fluttered to the ground, its shiny plumage like a broken vase against the background of whiteness. Jack, ever so slowly, raised the gun. The bird winked a small clear eye. Jack touched a branch with his elbow. The snow fell. The bird crouched, but didn't fly off. The .22's sharp crack reverberated through the wood. The bird's head disintegrated. The snow absorbed its blood like blotting paper. Shocked, Jack stared at the dead bird. Its feet were encrusted with dirty ice, the scattered feathers were bloodstained. He picked up the carcass, it was soft and warm. As he carried the dead bird back up the valley the sun climbed up his back. It beamed down the valley, lighting up the icicles like upturned candles on dripping branches.

As Jack veered across the bridge he saw that the bird's wound had left a bloody mark on him. The Boss was in the kitchen, disagreeably drinking tea.

'Who the hell tole yeh ta borry that valuable weapon?' he growled. Wha'cha got there?'

'This!' Jack said proudly.

The Boss fingered the damp bird. 'Huh,' he said, sure that poor fella gev hisself up. There's not a bit a mate on him. He was half dead from the hunger. Yeh may as well sling it tidda pigs.'

'Burrit's a pheasant,' Jack said.

'I know it's a bloody pheasant,' the Boss said. 'I seen a damn sight more pheasants than yeh'll ever lay eyes on. I'm tellin' yeh that's a shadda ivva bird. Disazed it is. No one should ate that. Except the pigs. Jack looked at the Boss, the new love and trust he thought he'd established drained away. His father was jealous of him.

Mary crawled from her room, her face a sad concertina. 'I'll clane out the guts, Jack,' she said.

'I tol'im ta sling it tidda pigs,' the Boss said.

Jack dismantled the gun and put it back in the sack. 'I can do it,' he said softly to his mother. 'Yeh go back t'bed.'

The Boss grabbed the bird. 'Gi'me that bloody t'ing,' he said and sloped off to the sheds, leaving Mary standing helpless and her son powerless. Cats uncurled from the rick to reach out their paws, trying to hook the dead bird as it swung past. The Boss shouted and aimed a kick at them.

He opened Barney's half door. The boar kneeled and grunted before his master, eyelashes flapping like a tart's. Then, with his twisted tail bobbing, he smelled the blood and trotted to the door. The Boss swung the bird once then stopped, felt its breast and slammed the pig's door.

As he started to pluck the green neck feathers Babs, on her day off, appeared. The Boss plucked quickly, covering his daughter with a fish-eyed gaze. Blushing from the wind that whipped round the yard and inflamed her cheeks, Babs sat on a bale. The Boss took the half-plucked bird to her, she moved along to make room. He looked at her with devotion, shook his head and smiled, his stubby bloodstained fingers denuding the yellow skin in brisk tufts. 'This is fer us,' he said, 'ever tried pheasant? It's tasty meat. Babs was fit and supple from cycling to work in the city and back. The Boss was so proud of the beauty that had sprung from his loins. She was his finest achievement. He wanted to touch her every time she came near him, the way an art dealer admires a beautiful canvass.

'I'll only eat it if yeh let me cook it for Mammy,' Babs said. She swiped the dark hair from her eyes and smiled innocently at him. The years of drudgery were finally having an effect on her father. He had lost some of his sheen. Time was leaving its claw marks on his neck and forehead. Arms once solid with muscle and sinew now perceptibly wobbled.

Babs felt so sorry for him. She collected the tiny hair-like feathers that floated all over the shed, and put them into a cardboard box for the boiler fire. The Boss kept plucking until the bird was ready. With his penknife he jabbed up the bird's rear and drew out the guts in one slimy, smelly handful.

'Ugh!' Babs said as he playfully pretended to shove them in her face. Babs laughed and the Boss laughed too. In the kitchen Jack drank tea with his mother. 'I'll cook it fer everyone,' Babs said. The Boss washed his hands in the water butt and said nothing.

68

MARY WAS BEARING another little 'gift from God'. After borrowing the names of dead saints, she'd moved on to Americans to honour Dolores, the celebrated aunt, now back in Chicago and sending even bigger cartons of old clothes.

Mary carried her new baby with her usual fortitude. Father Orlston was pleased but was noticeably reluctant to visit Mary in her bleak bungalow. He much preferred the company of scented and educated ladies of substance who practised birth control and lived in neat detached houses in quiet cul de sacs. Neither did Mary have any visits from a doctor or nurse. Her attitude to their absence was, 'Ah sure, an' don't I know more 'bout babies than they do anyway.' And of her latest child she'd joke, 'I'll get that oul' football team yit,' and grinning like Mick McCarthy she'd add, 'if on'y yer man above blesses me.' As her belly swelled, the older girls showed more interest now that they themselves were approaching child-bearing age, and they poked the big stretched belly with their fingers. The younger children took no notice. They were used to their mother's belly swelling up every few months. They were accustomed to babies too and took no particular cognisance when the time came and the Boss took their mother and her bag in the pony and cart to hospital where she had a season ticket to her own bed.

Mary was sent home as soon as possible. Beds were scarce in fecund Dublin and worried looking women were pulling on fags as they queued up outside like dumper trucks waiting to claim a warm bed and a tumbler of Lucozade.

The wind was whipping the froth off the Liffey as pony, cart and occupants headed for south Dublin and home. Mary, with a good colour restored to her cheeks held on to the latest manifestation of her devout Catholicism, as the Boss grimly shook the whip over Kitty's bobbing head. With his trilby pulled low he sucked Ritchies mints and said nothing. Jesus, what could be worth saying?

As soon as they reached Rathfarnham, Mary put the infant in the cot, sandwiched between the two hot water bottles Babs had thoughtfully prepared. Mary looked down at her new baby and sobbed. Most of her brood were blessed with the Boss's wiryness and instinct for survival, but Damian, named after her wayward brother, was weak from the start. She shouldn't have tempted fate by calling him Damian. The Boss's curses were already at work. Mary picked up the pink nestling and held it to her warm body. She tempted the screwed-up face and the curved-down mouth with a thick, scarred nipple, even ejecting a little warm milk on to its lips. Instead of the usual gummy grab of a baby taking its bait like a conger eel would a juicy, fat worm, this infant turned away. With her full breasts leaking life-sustaining milk as her baby lay weakening, Mary cried.

As the days went by, and the weak winter sun fell behind the black bulk of the Bloomfield Laundry's massive chimney, Damian grew weaker. Like a little scrawl that had fallen from a nest, it was barely breathing in Mary's arms as she kissed and whimpered over it like a cow would a doomed calf. 'It's as if the wee mite's decided livin's not wort' it,' she told Babs, who took the newly minted baby and rocked it gently.

'God, isn't he teenchy,' Babs said. 'Can I try him wit'a bottle?'

It didn't work.

69

THE BABY'S STRUGGLE for survival was forgotten briefly when the latest boxes came from Chicago. What had survived the Customs officer's plundering in Dublin finally arrived in Rathfarnham. The children ambushed the postman at the gate. His peaked cap canted, he smiled as if he were the philanthropist. Toddlers gathered like goggle-eyed fish at the window, leaving trails on the windows with their flattened nostrils. The Boss stopped to stare at the approaching uniform, for a moment thinking it was a garda with a summons. The postman, his Guinness-ruined face atop a huge parcel, puffed across the bridge.

Mary, untidy and worried, opened the door like a recluse, just enough to poke her head out. 'L'ave it on the porch, Misther,' she said.

The postman dropped the parcel with an exhalation of Sweet Afton, and gasped 'Jasus, worra yeh got in dare, a bomb or somet'in'? Declare ta God, but yeh're gettin' bigger bloody parcels din anyone else in da village.'

Mary smiled, wishing she'd inserted her teeth. 'T'ank yeh,' she lisped, her hair hanging over her face in sweaty ringlets.

Before the postman had straddled his bike, children were wriggling through the door's widening gap. Soon, they were tugging and tripping over the big parcel, manoeuvring it into the hallway like worker ants. Babs appeared with her wet hair piled up in a twisted towel.

'Hey, c'mon kids,' she said, 'we'll give yeh a hand.' With Bridgid's considerable strength, and Pam's verbal encouragement, they managed to get the lumpy parcel through the door, and the shoal of youngsters descended upon it.

Mary watched Bridgid tear at the knotted string. 'I hope there's a shirt for Jack', she said.

Gaudy American suits and party dresses were dragged out and

competed for. Jack kicked off his wellingtons and joined in. One year, he got a blue-belted smoking jacket which he wore to school after Mary cut it down to size. But his schoolmates laughed and jeered, and Mary allowed him to leave it at home where it turned green in the wardrobe.

The huge parcel fell open like a treasure chest yielding its contents. Shoes fell out, a pair of shiny black plastic ones with fancy pink whorls. Pam grabbed them and tottered about in them, smiling. Two toddlers were planted by Bridgid in a huge pair of Aunt Dolores' pink knickers, one in each leg, and they staggered round like Siamese twins, falling and frightened. Bridgid pulled on a huge felt hat and stalked into the kitchen like Orson Wells. Children were dressing each other up, and rushing back to the ruptured cardboard box for more comical props.

Soon, the hallway was blocked but clothes still oozed from the parcel. Gloves, socks, dozens of pairs, some with holes, loud sweaters. Then, deep in the heart of the parcel, a small glittery bag of cheap, gleaming jewellery was found. Children plunged in like Polynesian pearl divers. Bridgid sent her little brothers and sisters flying as she settled her big hands around the sequinned bag and was chased around the yard by an hysterical posse.

The Boss was removing his wellingtons. Surprised by the hullabaloo, he raced among his children and sent Bridgid flying into the fence with a stinger to the face. 'Fecker!' Bridgid screamed and made to return to the sanctity of the house.

Hobbling in one sock and boot, the Boss grabbed her. A horrible calmness came over him. 'What was that yeh said?'

'Nuttin',' Bridgid said stubbornly.

'Oh, yis yeh did,' the Boss said, and without waiting for Bridgid to slide out of her predicament he battered her with both hands clenched. Bridgid took the blows on her tough cranium, her head bouncing off the chicken wire like a ping-pong ball. When the Boss's fury abated she sank to the ground, still bravely clutching the small glittery bag, and cried quietly, blood pouring from her mouth.

When the Boss saw the floor covered in Aunt Dolores' throw-outs a hatred welled up inside him. The humiliation of it, his children rooting among garbage like wild dogs at a dustbin. 'What in the name of Jasus is the manin' a this?' he roared, kicking a long red ballroom dress with a lacy white frill.

Mary, who had seen Bridgid on the ground and gone to console her, was angry but weak. 'Yeh've gev that poor child a lump on the face,' she almost whispered. 'I've a good mind ta go straight down to Father Orlston and tell him what a pig yeh're ta yer childer.'

'If yeh hadn't encouraged that bloody sister a' yours ta dump her rubbitch on us it wouldn'a happened,' the Boss said, still spoiling for a fight.

'Hah' Mary snorted. 'Yeh know as well as I do if Dolores didn't send them parcels the childer'd go t'school in rags. If it wasn't fer me cuttin', alterin' and stitchin' they would'n hav'a stitch on their backs.'

The Boss moved in for the kill. His brain was throbbing. His fists were bunched, his lips were thin. Then Mary's magic electrician arrived. Babs came into the kitchen and with a few words she fixed her Daddy's wiring and he backed off with a face-saving, 'Get them kids ta get that rubbitch out a here.' The children, sensing that a potential conflagration row had prematurely burnt itself out, gathered round Mary on their knees and helped her fold the material into neat heaps. They carried them into the parlour, the pious little room smelling of mothballs and damp. The stuff was placed in piles by the Singer sewing machine. Eventually, there would be something for everybody. When Mary was better, the outdated dresses would be cut up and made into blouses for the children to wear to Mass on Sundays. With luck there wouldn't be another smoking jacket for Jack.

The excitement soon evaporated. Bridgid sat silent, ruefully rubbing her cheek. Remarkably, she was still in possession of her prize bag. Soon she would give in to the pleading of the younger children and open it to pour the contents on to the table for all to see. But Bridgid needed to suffer a little longer before her natural exuberance could reassert itself and bring a little light back to the sombre bungalow.

Mary's old Singer would eventually whir frantically for days as she snipped, cut and sewed. For fear of antagonising the Boss, she would work without a light until her eyes grew tired and her whole inside ached where so many babies had lain in their crimson cage. Mary could never show off her handiwork, fearing an outburst of abuse from a man who made a virtue out of never giving credit to anyone for anything. The older girls, now pretty as models, would parade in front of their father in their new finery, but the bald head remained stubbornly buried in the *Evening Mail*.

'Daddy,' Bab's soft voice forced him to cast a wary eye in her direction. Her moulded form, with breasts beginning to fill out and nylons on her fine legs, made him fold his paper. A faint smile of a kind seldom seen, invaded his face like a welcome sunrise. 'Bedad, yeh look grand in that oul' t'ing,' he said, his voice taking on a softness the children all noticed, and they stopped what they were doing to glance at the pair. The Boss smiled and Babs looked at him unashamedly, then, with an embarrassed crack of the newspaper, his brow furrowed and the Boss was lost again in events far from the bungalow and his mean existence. Jack watched his father read the paper, like a guard dog might observe a burgler's hand through a broken window. As soon as the *Mail* was folded and stuck behind the radio, Jack was on it. Ignoring the fact that his father had turned off the light, Jack lit his paraffin lamp and opened the paper as tenderly as if it were the Dead Sea Scrolls.

'Yesss! Shamrock Rovers had Shels at home on Sunday. And Jasus! Archie Moore was fighting Yolande Pompey. Hope the Mongoose knocks the shit out a the English bastard,' Jack murmured, sitting in the gloom with a smile on his face. Nice hat trick for Frankie Durr at Epsom. Will Duke do the double at the Isle of Man? Not if Reggie Armstrong has anything to do with it.

'Ge'rinta bed, yeh bloody shagger,' the Boss bellowed for the third time, but Jack finished reading what he wanted before he obeyed.

70

AS THE DAYS passed, little Damian's eyes remained rheumy slits. His little fists were clenched as if he'd swallowed poison. The District Nurse was summoned. She cast a cursory glance over the sickly infant and said, 'If I was you, darlin', I'd get Father Orlston here immedjetly.' The words were a death sentence. Mary cried, her sad old face staring down at her baby, big tears falling from her eyes.

The old priest arrived and in an impatient whoosh of Barethea was down the narrow hallway and kneeling by Damian's cot. 'Wit' the help a God he's goin' ta a betther place,' the old man blathered mechanically.

Mary convulsed into a fit of crying. 'Dear God,' she keened loudly, frightening the children who'd gathered to watch. The priest shook a few drops of holy water on to the baby's head, then like a gasman who'd perfunctorily read the meter, he quickly retreated outside to the fresh air.

The Boss, returning after a morning gathering pigswill, found Mary sitting motionless in the kitchen holding the purple-faced infant. He glanced at the bundle then went to the shed to get his measuring tape. After an hour of hammering and sawing he returned with a tiny white-wood coffin. As Mary bent to place the dead infant into the cold box she staggered, her tears falling like acid rain. With her shoulders pumping, her old shoes bent and buckled under her weight, a hole in her cardigan big enough to pass a tennis ball through, she was the image of hopelessness. Babs, Pam and Bridgid hugged their mother and they all cried in bitter harmony like condemned witches in some obscure tragedy. The Boss stood by, powerless and calm. Crying was what women did best. The other children, their eyes moist and fearful, stood by silently, praying for the drama to end and for life to return to what they regarded as normal.

Outside snow fell.

The Boss, muffled against the wintry winds, drove Kitty over the icy bridge. The little white coffin tucked under the seat was covered with a sack already flecked with snow. The Boss, his face set like a totem, his collar pulled up to his chin, shook the reins. Kitty dug her frost-nailed feet into the snow and tugged willingly, her unruly mane flying. She headed for the graveyard as enthusiastically as if she were drawing a load of freshly mown hay in summer, or a load of quivering guts from the abbatoir. No one knew what was inside the Boss's head as he sat hunched atop the cart, his bare hands holding the reins.

The old pony stood quietly among the concrete urns, the jam jars filled with plastic flowers and the impressive black marble headstones embossed with clichés and the pink faces of long-dead children. The Boss dug the grave himself. Like some bibbed Van Goghian peasant, the snow falling on him, he raised his pickaxe and brought it down on the rock-hard ground with muffled thumps. 'If she hadn't named it afther that rotten hoor master, the child might've lived,' the Boss said to himself.

Despite the freezing temperature, sweat soon gathered under his hat as a small rectangular brown gash apeared in the snow.

The Boss knelt to place the box in the hole, and with his hands he pawed the broken earth on top of it as tenderly as if he were placing a blanket over the dead baby. The hard stuff he then shovelled in drummed on the lid of the coffin like rocks. He tamped down the topsoil with the back of his shovel. Last, like a fur-muffled Celt in a lonely barrow, he clasped his hands together and sent the baby off to eternity on a muttered prayer.

Kitty stood by silently, her coat grey with melting snow. The Boss shook the snow off his trilby. 'C'mon, Kitty,' he said. The pony tugged the cart through the cemetery gates and headed for home.

Mary prayed for the repose of her baby's soul, but she cursed too. 'He wouldn't let me light a fire fer the poor child,' she sobbed, 'I'll never ferget that.'

The Boss fed the pony, who hungrily scoffed her basinful of vegetarian pigswill with her front leg held up protectively. His whistle silenced, the Boss finally approached the house. It was gripped by cold and despair. Mary sat by the fire, holding on to her daughters as if they were lifebelts. Her eyes were raw from crying, and she had a supply rags by her to mop the tears. The Boss crept into the kitchen, turned on the radio and isolated himself with the Home Service.

Jack dreamed of the dead baby glowing in the ground like a yellow lamp, a little mountain of frozen crystals above it. He woke up, startled and cold. Mary suffered for weeks, convinced she was being punished for some forgotten or uncommitted sin of thought, word or deed. She wouldn't let the Boss near her and she chased him off as if he had personally sold her baby for veal.

Father Orlston eventually deigned to visit Mary, and told her Damian's death was God's idea. Only really special children were rewarded with death. And now, the old priest beamed, 'the child's little soul is up there now, flyin' round and havin' a rare oul' time wit' da udder little dead angels.'

'Ah, that's grand,' Mary said and she put all the money she could get hold of into the priest's fat hand for him to say Mass. While the Boss smiled grimly at Mary's gullibility, Jack felt like puking. The old priest clasped his whiskey money and before toddling off said, 'The best way now ta get back inta His good books is ta fall pregnant again.' He lay a fat hand on Mary's shoulder. It was a blessing, just what she wanted to hear. Mary was uplifted. She washed and combed her hair, smiled, and even spoke civilly to the Boss for the first time in weeks. She connived to please the priest and by coaxing the Boss to her bed she was soon blessed with another pregnancy.

71

BLOOMFIELD LAUNDRY'S SOOT-TIPPED chimney rose above the trees. Trout, their black snouts nuzzling flags of old cotton and discarded paint tins, were silver-speckled against the gravelly shallows. Passing schoolboys stood, drawing sleeves under their dripping noses, gawking at the mob-capped workers. Through the dusty windows the girls, with dangling cigarettes, pointed, 'Look a' dem brats starin' in at us. *Hey!* Who diyeh' t'ink yeh're lookin' at?' They opened the windows and let out puffs of steam. 'Lovely little mickeys. Yehz can have me any time.' . . . 'Dirthy cow,' said a workmate elbowing the girl out of the way. Behind them the white-clad, white-faced girls gathered, laughing over the river until the schoolboys ran off. The laundry girls turned to stewing sheets in bubbling vats. Bridgid had recently joined them and would remain there in limbo until she was rescued by marriage.

On fine days the girls would sit outside during the lunch break, eating sandwiches, their painted fingers clasping cigarettes, catcalling to passers-by. Every morning they hurried there, their flat heels clicking on the pavements. Jobs were scarce in Rathfarnham. Green buses from the Dublin mountains disgorged the girls. White-coated, they scuttled towards the big untidy building on the river bank, where it puffed its sourness into the sky, steam hissing from its poulticed pipes.

When Bridgid brought her friends from the laundry back to the bungalow the Boss pretended to read the paper, but surreptitiously his eyes crawled up a young leg, or snatched a glimpse of breast behind a loose blouse. 'Them's nice girls,' he said. Mary sitting on her poisoned nest like an old she-eagle with addled eggs, cursed him inwardly. She hated the unblemished flesh of the laundry girls, often still in anklesocks, as they sat on the form, their thin elbows on the table, talking films and magazines.

Now that she was working, albeit for a pittance, and able to present her father with a pound note every Friday, Bridgid had joined the human race and was an asset the Boss could tolerate but still loved no more than the rest of his swarm. Only Babs was earmarked for queen, a credit to royalty who had long ago accepted her beatification. She was gentle and kind to her greedy little subjects and tried her hardest not to offend the sour old deposed queen, her mother. Tonight, her engagements included a trip to the Classic in Terenure to see *Captain Lightfoot* with Pam, her lady-in-waiting, and Jack, her bodyguard and chauffeur.

It was Bridgid's girls night at the bungalow. The frump with the double chins was holding forth, her fat legs apart, her nails a wanton scarlet. The Boss put more turf on the fire and told Bridgid to make the lassies 'a porra oul' tay. An' there's a few Kimberley biscuits in me press,' he yelled after her. With trouser'd arse to the flames he squinted round the curves of tasty young bosoms.

Such an entertainer; the way he could turn on the old charm like honey oozing from a barrel. He had a gift for putting young females completely at ease. The laundry girls were uninhibited. They were enjoying themselves. The room was warm, the fire jagged and leaping. The Kimberleys were dunked in tea the way the Boss had smilingly demonstrated, then watched their pink tongues. Seeing them all there ranged before him like nymphs, their white teeth, their hair smooth and luxuriant, their neat feet in narrow-toed high heels, made the Boss feel quite bullish. 'Are the lads showin' any intherest?' he asked one girl.

Mary, taking the hint, heaved herself upright with a grunt and quietly shuffled off to her room. On her knees by her bed, Mary's suffering eyes rose like swollen marbles above her glasses. She knew his little game, get them talking about it and the next thing you knew–

The laundry girls swished their young legs and recounted harmless exploits. One even lit a cigarette, nodding at the Boss who, although he hated smokers, managed a watery smile of approval. Jesus Mary and Joseph but wasn't it grand.

The Boss introduced a game but after a few uncouth and breathy jousts the girls returned to talking. An hour or two passed pleasantly, the Boss sitting among them like an old lion in the midst of his pride.

A knock on the door announced Babs's return. She had not yet been given a key of her own because the Boss always wanted her back and safe in bed before he was.

After Bridgid had seen the laundry girls to the gate, they stood under the street lamp in a gossiping huddle. Bridgid's Da was 'such a great oul' skin', not like their own careworn fathers, but 'that oul' mudder a hers, Jasus she had a face on 'er like feckin' Dracula's granny'.

Bridgid went to bed happy. As she slept, white water continued to gush from the laundry into the cold stream, and its big chimneys poured smoke into the night. Behind the steamed-up windows the girls on nightshift moved about like ghosts. Unless something else turned up Bridgid would be there for life, fading away behind the high walls amid the pulsing steam valves and the white-hot water that polluted the stream.

72

THE BOSS'S COLD hand was on Babs's face. She woke with a gasp. 'It's Sunday. Yeh promised last night, remember?'

Babs, raised herself on her elbows, blinked, then covered herself. 'Wha–?'

'The 'rooms.'

'Wha–?'

'The mushers.'

'Wha–?'

'The bloody mushrooms.'

'Oh, them, right, gi'me a minnit, I'm gettin' up.' Babs struggled into her clothing. Jesus, why had she promised?

The Boss drummed his fingers in the kitchen. Jack lay awake, uninvited.

The bikes whirred in harmony as the pair, shrouded in dawn's blue cobwebs, crossed the bridge. The Boss's milking buckets jangled on the handlebars. The Sturmey Archer gears on Babs' new bike were clicking like a time bomb. Father and daughter rode to a valley where houses had yet to be planned and where trees and hedges had so far survived the ravages of the bulldozer. Lying green and timeless, the valley opened up for the two cyclists whose verbal exchanges carried out into it. Birds, solitary and sleepy, traversed the fields, flying low and silently, their wings outspread like the fins on small brown tank busters. The Boss's small feet were one with the pedals. Babs' slim haunches worked furiously. They were soon at their destination, both breathing loudly, faces rouged with effort.

While the Boss milked a couple of Billy Jolly's cows, Babs waltzed through the pale dawn, leaving mazy prints in the dewy grass. The mushrooms she plucked sat like scattered eggs on the bank where Jolly's cows spent the night, chewing and dolloping.

The Boss's behatted head appeared above a dip in the ground, his galvanised buckets filled with warm milk. 'Hav'yeh got the 'rooms?'

Babs juggled, her arms full. As she dipped to gently prise another swollen fungi from under some dung, those she'd already gathered fell to the ground. The Boss disappeared into the wettest part of the field, and returned with a fistful of bulrushes. He tied knots in the thick ends, then with big man's thumbs he pierced the stalks and slid the mushrooms one after another along to the knot. 'Them's called *hanks*,' he said pleasantly. 'Yeh kin carry a dozen a them at a time.' Babs managed two.

Back in the kitchen the Boss removed the stalks, knocked out the maggots and fried the mushrooms. 'Enough ta grace the pan.' The Boss sprinkled salt on the pink gills. In the dim light, Babs cocked an ear to the sizzling pan, sweetly inhaling a whiff of wild mushrooms frying in bacon fat. The Boss watched her for a while and thought of Mary long ago.

The Boss grabbed the handle of the frying pan and shook it. 'Quick, get out them hot plates, 'the oul' fat'll soon set,' he said. With his large hands he cracked two duck eggs and basted the tangerine yolks. Outside, the yard was still sleeping. Babs fought to stay awake. She carried her breakfast to the table, and they sprinkled pepper over the steaming feast. 'Them's cooked well, betther'n yer woman'd do,' the Boss said, his mouth full.

In her bedroom, shafted with light from the window, Mary felt her belly stirring. She had been invaded again. She closed her eyes and at last went back to sleep, oblivious to the sunshine heralding another day.

As Babs washed and dried she watched her father down the yard. Although she loved her parents and would never be ashamed of them, it was time to leave home. She wanted a more comfortable life, a calmer life, one without the dead weight of her father's expectations. She wanted freedom and independence. 'You'd love it here,' Aunt Dolores had written, 'it's a fine country, full of opportunities.' Babs no longer felt shackled to Rathfarnham, her family, the dimly lit bungalow or the stench of pigs that insinuated itself into everything. It was time to leave all that behind.

73

THE BOSS VISITED Mary a couple of times and brought a bit of cake or some fruit which she shared with the other women in her ward. While she was away Babs ran the house on the sort of orderly lines the Boss approved of.

'It's a great pity yeh can't stay in charge,' he said. 'Th'oul place has never been claner lookin'. Yer woman's an untidy oul' pile.' Catching Babs' cutting glance he laughed it off.

Pam waited for the new baby with particular interest and had the room spotless for its return. A little blue brush, a new baby's face flannel and a Donald Duck soap all ready. It would be a new pet for Pam, something to lavish her bottomless love on. Kitty would be forgotten for a while.

More proof of the Boss's virility was not a thing for which he yearned. If only Mary would take something, have an operation, anything. Jack heard his father growling darkly into barrels of pigswill as he barrowed manure to the festering mountain at the bottom of the garden.

Bridgid's attitude to babies was hard. 'Scutther again,' she moaned, 'filt'y nappies hangin' on the line, slappin' yeh in the kisser when yeh go t'work.'

The Boss removed his boots and padded into the kitchen like a grubby Sultan entering his tent. His daughters gave him a good feeling. If only that bloody woman would stay away there would be endless harmony.

'Well, yer woman's back soon,' he said, eating the tasty sandwich Babs had made for him. As he slipped the crustless segments into his mouth he wished time would erase his life so that he could start again with a caring woman who would look after him as a man, not a hated animal. Everyone got on so well when she wasn't around. There was a real feeling of family solidarity, everyone pulling the same way. Even when Jack entered the kitchen, his head stuck in a newspaper he'd found lining a box, the Boss didn't attack him with his customary savagery.

'Hey. Have yehz heard 'bout Billy Riley's new bit a stuff?' Bridgid, munching a mouthful, asked. 'He's got this new bird, a blonde wan. I saw 'im at the corner waitin' for the 47 bus wit' her.'

'A blonde wan?' the Boss repeated. For a second he stopped chewing and jealousy glinted in his one clear sea-blue eye. 'What would a dacent girl want wit' an eejit like yer man Riley?' he asked. 'She mus' be afther somethin' in his trousers.'

Babs looked at Pam and Bridgid. They smiled. The Boss rarely used sexually explicit language. He effed and blinded as if the words were naturally imprinted on his tongue, but he never uttered sexual terms. Maybe it was because Mary wasn't there to pull him up.

'Is she pretty?' Pam asked. She was slightly put out at the thought of Billy Riley taking out some lovely stranger.

'Where would that dope meet a nice woman?' The Boss was still concerned. The Boss's mind filled with dark thoughts. To think that thick gobshite had his foul hands on some frail, beautiful creature.

The Boss whistled as he helped the girls. Jack twirled his fringe into knots. 'Wouldn't it be grand to have a piano. We could all sit around and sing a few oul' songs.'

'That'd be nice,' Babs said.

'I'll see if I can get me hands on wan,' the Boss said enthusiastically.

Jack was not bothered by pianos or by Riley's girl. He was more concerned with reading the *Intermediate Book of Poetry* the teacher had lent him because he showed an interest. His father was right. Life was good without Mary. Her headaches, her old stained underwear on the line, her miserable sagging face as she stared at you; her obsession with chastity, her mindless adherence to the dictates of the priests. The children of single parents had it all. When he consciously realised what he was thinking, Jack felt ashamed.

Mary, her cheeks glowing healthily, arrived home smiling broadly and carrying her precious bundle. The baby was big-boned and had a healthy appetite. The children would soon get used to her feeding it by the fire. Mary felt optimistic. She looked fit and stable. She would suckle it until growing teeth bit into her nipples and her milk was sucked dry. A child always repaid her love.

The Boss returned to his *Evening Mail* and was once more lost to the children. And they all went quiet again.

74

A LITTLE GIRL WITH pigtails was plonking on the piano keys inside the open garage. Looking down from the roof the Boss teased her. 'That's nice,' he said, tilting the trilby back from his eyes. 'Wouldn' yeh give them oul' shaggy-haired fellas a right goin'over wit' yer knack.'

Drawn to the friendly voice the little girl looked up, her head askew, and smiled at him with all the guile of her sex. 'I can play something for you.'

Unable to resist a feminine smile the Boss said, 'That'd be grand.'

The child, rocking on her feet with her hands out as if she were balancing on a high wire, told him, 'I am learning a piece with my teacher, Miss Wolff.'

'An' what's the name a the tune yeh're learnin'?'

'How should I know?' the little girl snapped. 'It's got a horrible long name, *Backerolly* or something.'

'Never heard tell a that wan,' the Boss said, skimming melted tar over a crack in the wood.

'I'm not surprised 'cos you're just a builder,' the girl said. The Boss gave her a murderous look. 'Shall I play it for you?' she asked and without waiting for a reply she began to prod the keys.

At the beauty of the music the Boss turned on his ladder to listen. The little girl's shadow was thrown across the gravel. 'Begod, if I could play like that I'd be made,' the Boss said with the sort of sycophantic smile his own children never saw.

'All you have to do is come with me to Miss Wolff's on Saturday mornings.' The child's brazen suggestion, delivered in a falsetto from a squinting little face, drew her mother to the garden window.

'Penelope, stop bothering the workman and go and play in the back garden.' And the girl obediently skipped away.

'Isn't she the fine little musician,' the Boss syruped from his perch.

'That wan's a little gen'us, so she is.' The soft soap came automatically, especially when it was directed towards a lady of quality.

'Tosh, the wee girl can hardly tell her right hand from her left. We've all got cloth ears in this house.

'So yeh won't be havin' a use fer the ould piana then?' the Boss interjected. And, before the fine lady could reply he launched into one of his favourite monologues about the time he was in great demand at the dances with his old melodeon. 'Sure, I'd love to be able to play again and that ould piano, funny as it looks, would be a grand ould t'ing to amuse us iv a night-time.'

'You can have it with pleasure. Hasn't been tuned for years. We'll be glad to see the back of it.' With a final remark on the weather she closed the conversation and the window. The Boss applied a lick of tar with a happy flourish and contemplated how he was going to get the piano home.

'There's on'y wan t'ing fer it, I'll have ta use poor ould Kitty.' He looked around the garden and spotted a broken swing with sound ropes attached to a rotten wooden seat. With a couple of swift thrusts he severed the rope and with a quick flick of the hands had a long, single piece tied in a reef knot.

With his immense strength the Boss, grunting and cursing, manhandled the heavy upright on to the cart. Kitty observed him irritably from a whitened eye. There was little room for the Boss so he sat on top of the dusty walnut veneer and drove Kitty home, drawing curious looks from passers-by.

The children milled around the bridge as Kitty trotted in with the huge piano behind her. The Boss was happy to have pulled off such a coup. 'Get ta hell out a that,' he yelled as the children massed like mourners, desperate to snatch a glimpse of the dead body.

'I'm afther gettin' a lovely present fer yehz,' the Boss said, adding solemnly, 'I'm always lookin' out some little t'ing ta bring home ta yehz.' The instrument was noisily unloaded and carefully placed in the parlour.

Never unlocked, except on holidays and special occasions, the parlour was furnished with the best family pieces, carpeted with a slab of flower-patterned Wilton. Along with the big photographs of the Boss there were pictures in chrome frames of the girls making their

Confirmation. In pinstriped trousers, bow tie and flowers in his buttonhole, the Boss stared down as a young buck. His smile for the camera was sly but winsome and with a sensual gleam in his small bright eyes, his pose had the carefully arranged casualness of a born performer. For twenty years he'd been standing there holding his hat and cane against a background of heavy furniture and cumbersome plants. His hair had been curly then, before the embarrassment of his premature baldness. To Mary's later taunts, 'Yer bloody bit a hair fell out 'cos yeh spent so much time puttin' the curlers in,' he'd respond, 'Have yer say then, yeh stupid pile.'

There was only one little picture of Mary, creased and yellowing it showed her on her wedding day. It had slipped in its silver-gilt frame and she was half hidden but there was no mistaking the Boss's proud stance and triumphant smile, the muscular chest pushed out, the tough working-man's hand incongruously on the frilly-clothed table. He was shagging the camera. Mary, a virgin in white, was thin and pretty, her face clear, her dark tresses falling over her shoulders. Her naïve gaze contrasted sharply with the conceited pose of her brash young husband.

Except for the occasional pounding it got from Bridgid's uncultured paws, the piano remained silent until a new still anonymous infant grew tall enough to reach the keys. Then the parlour, always so heartlessly cold, would glow as Paul, his big head bobbing like a young chick, his blue eyes dreamy, cajoled sounds of surprising elegance and beauty from the rough old instrument.

75

THE BOSS WAS unsettled, and sat in his chair as if it was stuffed with holly. Babs was late coming home. She had recently joined the Legion of Mary and had gone on there straight from work. The Boss fidgeted, folding and unfolding the paper. He kept referring to that gobshite Riley and a little vein in is neck began leaping. When he heard the door open he was instantly on his feet and slippering down the hallway. Babs came in labouring under her shopping. Bridgid hardly gave her time to unload her parcels, little presents for the baby, small toys for the younger children, a comic and a biro for Jack. Babs always brought joy to the house on pay day and her appearance made the children come to her like small mammals drawn to a bright and startling light. 'We were in the garden, weedin',' Bridgid said. 'We pulled up hunderts but there's still hunderts more.'

Babs touched her tough young sister's cheek. 'Don't worry,' she said, 'I had ta do it too.'

The Boss who'd returned to his chair, prickling, snapped his paper shut. Wasn't she going to explain why she was late? He laid his paper down and looked calmly at his loving daughter.

Babs said nothing.

Jack sat at the table with volume 10 of the 1952 *Everyman's Encyclopaedia*. 'Pamphylia, an ancient country on the south coast of Asia Minor, bounded by Lycia and Cilicia,' he read aloud.

The Boss darted a look in his son's direction. 'If yeh were as smart as yeh t'ink yeh're, then them melts in the Corporation cottages wouldn' be ahead a yeh in class.' The Boss felt threatened by learning. It was a cudgel with which people tended to beat him.

'They're not ahead a me,' Jack defended himself. 'As a matter of a fact I'm first in everyt'in'.' But the Boss wasn't listening. His mind was on that impudent little bitch Babs. Why was she late?

'Jack, somet'in' fer yeh,' Babs said, handing her brother a freshly minted *Hotspur*. 'Yeh're the right little bookworm,' she said, tickling her brother's head.

'I wonder why yeh'd be wastin' yer money on them oul' comic cuts fer yer man?' the Boss said with a stab of jealousy.

'Because Babs is like me that way,' Mary said. The Boss snatched up his paper; there was plenty he could say but he didn't want to upset Babs.

Later, Babs, who now had her own small room, invited Pam and Bridgid in to talk. 'I saw a lad tanight,' she whispered. 'He was *it*.'

The girls' curiosity was manifest even in the gloom. 'What's he like?' - 'How old is he?' - 'What does he work at?'

Babs giggled softly. 'I on'y saw him the wance. He has a lovely manner.'

'He kept it in his trousers then?' Bridgid said, her face ready to break into a grin.

'Fer God's sake, shu'rup!' Babs said, then added in a whisper, 'Don't jump ta conclusions, in case Daddy finds out.'

'What was Mr Wonderful doin' at the Legion anyway?' Pam asked.

'He was collectin' his sister,' Babs whispered. 'He offered me a lift home.'

'Jesus, Mary an' Joseph!' Bridgid cried. 'I'd give an'tin' ta see the ould fella's face if he saw yeh gettin' out of a car with a lad drivin'. Just the two of yehz. Wow! There'd be wigs on the green fer sure.'

'Shhh,' Babs hissed. 'I have ta be up early. See yehz in the mornin'.'

The sisters were agog in the dark. 'Ar'yeh seein' him again?' Bridgid whispered.

'Don't know, maybe,' said Babs, sleepily.

Back in her own bed, Bridgid lay on her back unable to sleep.

76

THE ROONEYS LIVED in a wooden chalet across the road from the bungalow. Gradually, Jack was allowed to talk to them through the chicken wire. Then one evening they asked him to play football with them. But like some Mongolian warlord the Boss, determined to keep tribal enmities alive, vetoed the peacemaking move, and ordered Jack to spend the evening chopping wood and then to give Kitty her hay.

Jack Perkins watched the lone figure chop and sweat, heard the logs splinter and saw sawdust float on the evening breeze. The thump of the football also carried on the wind. Beret in hand, Jack looked up at the stack of wood and felt pleased with himself. He had earned his bowl of bread and milk. Putting the tools away, he slipped through a hole in the hedge and into the stream which had recently flooded and was full of brown trout. He placed a large paint tin with holes punched in it under the bank where the water was deep and covered it with overhanging branches. With a stick he prodded the trout until one rushed headlong into his primitive trap. He broke the trout's neck and wrapped it in dock leaves. He could feel trout bumping against his bare legs. The river was swarming with them.

He never dared boast of his catches for fear of incurring the Boss's wrath, but Mary always had a word of praise for him and eagerly took each little parcel of fish he'd wrapped in dock leaves to keep fresh. If the Boss found dead fish in the food safe they were flung disdainfully back into the river with a curse, to float uselessly among the bobbing bottles and bald tennis balls.

Jack waded in his wet wilderness, amid the hanging briars and the exotic pink roots of nameless trees. Splashing gently in the cold, clear water, he knew where the kingfisher lived and where the wren built her nest on a girder just above the rushing water.

He explored the river downstream where it swirled towards the weir. In the deliciously foamy water that lapped against his thighs and crept up to his backside, gently tickling his testicles, he urinated. He wanted to lie on his back and let the tiny bumping waves embrace him, to put him to sleep for ever. When the rats had stripped him of flesh, the gimlet-eyed eels could live in his body, slithering through the gaps in his white ribs. Then he saw a monstrous black trout. It had been washed down in the floods. With a fast-beating heart Jack guided it into his tin. He reached inside and grabbed the trout and easily broke its neck. He was wrapping it in dandelion leaves when a rustle in the bankside bushes suddenly banished his dreams. Jack spun. Although it was getting dark he could see among the branches his father's good pale eye, half closed with fury.

'That poor pony's cryin' out with tha hunger. Yeh fergot her, in spite a me tellin' yeh. Get the feckin' hell out a that pissy river while I cut a t'ick switch ta bate the bloody arse off a yeh!' the Boss roared. Perkins left his cottage to watch. This was better than Radio Eireann.

Jack could almost feel the ringing pains in his head; his big ugly ears would be getting it in a minute. When the Boss worked himself into such a state of cold hate, he lashed out to relieve the pressure. Wet and frightened, Jack scrambled up the slippery bank and through the nettles that grew beside the river. Venom kissed his exposed skin. 'I caught this,' he cried.

But his father grabbed the trout off him, and smashed him in the face with it before flinging it into the nettles.

The Boss was holding a branch from the pussy-willow, he had already skinned the leaves with a practised run of his hand. He started whipping. Trapped in the hedge and blinded with pain, Jack fell backwards into the water but made sure he had his father by the lapels. Father and son both splashed into the water.

'Go on, son, do the cunt!' Perkins snarled incitement from the opposite bank.

The Boss was first to his feet. Dripping and shiny like a survivor from a crippled oil tanker he put up his mitts. 'C'mon, c'mon, yeh cowardly little bastard!' he roared. 'I'll give yeh fishin' while that pony's starvin'. Come over here or I'm comin' after yeh.'

Jack splashed and scrambled into the garden, blows raining down on him. Shielding his face and head, he ran towards the house as the stick bit into the thin skin and bones of his arms and shoulders. Enraged, the Boss chased him, the water welling up in his boots. Jack escaped indoors.

His temporary insanity abated, the Boss came into the house. The children looked at him. He looked old and wet. He had suffered his first challenge from one of his offspring. At last, his invincibility had been questioned.

After a wash and a meal he pretended nothing had happened. With the paper poking out from under his arm like a drill officer's stick, he swept into the bedroom to collect the green alarm clock and perform his winding ritual. Jack watched him turn the key, heard the small thin spring that measured his father's life tighten. The clock sat on the table, ticking ruthlessly, counting seconds, minutes, days to his father's inevitable death.

Across Neary's field wood pigeons arrowed towards the trees in Fonthill Abbey. A fury of waiting guns sounded and the birds fell in a flurry of blood and feathers. The survivors raced, demented, over the estate, circling like miniature jet fighters. Then, drawn by some primitive need to familiar perches, they dropped like velvet on to the gore-stained branches only for the guns to roar again and slaughter the remainder. Jack saw the flashes of the guns in the dark and the white specks of injured birds, their wings and legs broken, hopping like wounded soldiers away from the carnage.

Next time Gerry Rooney invited him to play football, he was going. Jack reflected on love and the undeniable fact that some lucky people had it ladled over them from morning to night. The Rooneys had pocket money, comics, new football boots.

Down by the moonlit river an otter, his whiskers beaded, blinked like an old man and followed his nose. He knew there was a fat trout somewhere in the nettles and he was going to find it.

77

IT WAS THE middle of the night. Mary woke when she heard the commotion and smelt paraffin. The Boss stood over her, one side of him illumined in yellow. 'Poor Polly's goin',' he said. 'The curse a God on the same bloody cow.' Testily, he blew out the lamp and climbed back into bed. 'Them bloody vets know how ta charge a poor fella.' The quenched wick spiralled paraffin smoke.

The next day a black Mercedes drew up outside the bungalow. A tall figure with a trimmed moustache stepped from the car and carefully locked the door behind him. He ran a superior eye over the unruly youngsters who had crowded round to paw the sleek machine. One or two of the brats stuck out their tongues, but ran away when the vet turned like Vincent Price in the *Phantom of the Rue Morgue*.

The Boss walked out briskly, smiling falsely, his hand outstretched. 'Yeh're most welcome, Sir,' he said. 'But yeh're not the kinda fella I wan'ta see too often, wit' yer high prices an' funny oul' tonics.'

Not another poverty-stricken Irish comedian, the vet was thinking.

The two men shook hands, the vet replying to the Boss's vigorous grip with a floppy handshake. He found the Boss's remarks offensive. 'Where is the animal, I'm a busy man,' the vet said in his English accent.

The Boss led him to Polly's shed. Jack followed the visitor's after-shave. Concluding a brief inspection, the vet turned to Jack. 'Young man,' he said, 'your father is a perfect fool.' Jack smiled. This was a good start. 'He has allowed a useful beast, worth at least thirty pounds, to die because he was too damn mean to call me earlier.'

The Boss grimaced, a hand on his chin. Jack was a little embarrassed at the vet's remark, but only a little. He watched with admiration the immaculate Englishman, with his military rigidity, giving the Boss orders. It was something well worth seeing.

'Get me some hot water, and then get these bloody kids out of here.' He winked at Jack. 'You may stay. We might need a strong man.'

Jack began to feel a certain warmth towards the clean-smelling gentleman. While his younger sisters and brother peered through the chicken wire, Jack had a grandstand view next to the immaculate Brit. The Boss seemed even more like a scarecrow than usual. He barged around annoyingly, dispensing homespun advice but was so ruthlessly put down by the smooth foreigner he began to shrink. Jack felt sorry for his father, rather than ashamed. But it was also a great gas to hear the bully get stuffed.

'Come on, young lad, don't just stand there, do something.'

Yessir, yessir, t'ree bags full sir, Jack thought, as he did a Nureyev-like leap to attention. Following the vet's instructions he located a rope, and fetched a bucket of hot water with a splash of Jeyes Fluid added. He took off his coat and waited with hands on hips for even more crucial involvement. Polly stood there looking as if she had eaten a couple of bales of hay whole. Her belly was swollen, and there was a nasty, snotty thing hanging from her behind. The vet rolled up his white sleeves and immersed his well-manicured hands in the bucket. He then shoved his wet hand as far as it could go up the trembling cow's rear. His moving, tickling, fingers caused poor Polly to shit all over him. A long spurt of green diarrhoea piled up on the vet's rubber apron and polka dotted his nice white shirt. Jack was so shocked at the cow's indiscretion he laughed. But the vet was neither amused nor shocked. He was concentrating so hard, he didn't appear to notice the manure that was all over him. Having securely tied the rope around the unborn calf's legs, he handed the other end to Jack and his father and told them to pull when he gave the signal.

'Ready? Now, gently, heave . . . heave . . . heave. That's it, it's coming . . . gently, now . . . heave! We're almost there.'

Jack sneaked a look and saw a beautiful, white-headed bull calf emerging as if from a hole in a tree. When it was at last delivered, Jack rubbed his skinned hands and the vet turned the cow loose. The Boss sprinkled oats and salt on the calf's wet back. Polly, giving out a small cry, licked the soggy bundle dry. The vet examined the calf and said it was a fine specimen.

'But,' he said, 'the cow, I'm afraid, is not going to make it. It's called saving a penny at the cost of a pound. The Boss grimaced. Jack shared a bowl of clean water with the vet. 'One day, young man, you might have a cow,' he said, 'or perhaps several. If you ever find yourself in a similar position, do the sensible thing, call a vet as soon as possible. It will save you a lot of money. Bye now.'

The afterbirth was put into the boiler for the pigs. Smarting from the vet's numerous put-downs, the Boss tried to swing the blame. 'There yeh're now,' he said miserably, 'I wanted t'call the bloody vet, but no, *she* wouldn't hear of it.' Polly moaned as she urgently licked her calf.

In the bungalow Jack told his sisters how he helped to save the calf. He was a man now. The vet said so. It was official. Jack felt so proud there was a jauntiness about him as he went to bed to contemplate in the darkness the vet's encouraging words. It was a pleasant change from having the hose pipe of shit directed at him all the time.

Next day when Jack ran in from school, the bungalow was deserted. Squinting through the lichen-splodged kitchen window, he saw his mother hunched uneasily in a sunny corner, her glasses thickly reflecting the sun like two florins, her red hands folding and unfolding in a miniature wrestling match. One of her cotton stockings hung halfway down her swollen leg and she wore a pair of battered tennis shoes which followed the uncertain contours of her feet. Her once-black hair was withering.

She raised herself at his footfall. 'Well, hello there, Jack me darlin'. Sure, I didn't see yeh comin' in at all. Yer Daddy told me ta tell yeh ta start clanin' out them oul' pigs before he gets back. I'll put the kettle on the hob, a cuppa tay won't do yeh a bit a harm. She walked stiffly to the kitchen.

Jack fetched his rubber boots and, removing his sweat-damped socks, pulled them on. Opening the creaking gate he was enveloped in the stench of livestock. He glanced in at the cow; she was still alive. He sang and swept. Dung-flies hovered, a rook flew across the garden like a tattered rag. A pigeon cooed in the oak behind the pigsties. The stream whispered over the weir.

A loud groan sent him running to Polly's shed. Peering over the half door he saw the cow lying on the floor, the chain pulled tight around her neck. The blood-soaked organ-stops she had for eyes would stay with Jack for a long time. 'Mammy, Mammy,' he screamed, 'Polly's lyin' down. I t'ink she's dead.'

'Mothera God, don't say that son,' Mary cried as she scuttled to the chicken wire. 'An' we're here alone, oh dear God yer Daddy should be back be now. Where is he? God blast him, he's sure ta blame us fer it.'

When the Boss returned, he listened impatiently to Mary's garbled story, then, his face pinched in alarm, he ran to the cowshed.

'Ah, Jasus. The poor baste. Why the feckin' hell didn't yeh let her loose?' he screamed. 'Yeh might a saved her life. Wasn't she responding to the rotten vet's tonics? Yeh're just like yer woman above, delighted this disaster fell on me. May the curse a God light on yehz bot'.'

The Boss stormed around the yard like a whirlwind. But it was all bluff. He had killed the cow if anyone had, but as usual he was in permanent denial. Before leaving the yard Jack watched in silence the trout leaping for flies in the black pond under the weir, and listened to the corncrake in Neary's field. Anything to delay having to walk by Polly's shed, knowing that there in the dark a massive open-eyed corpse was lying dead on the cold concrete floor.

Overnight the cow stiffened and was winched, stiff-legged, her eyes lifeless, into a truck and taken to the knackers yard. She was not replaced. A diet of Neary's milk and water was a distinct possibility. But the Boss had other ideas.

Silence hovered over the bungalow; any child who made a sound invited disaster. Huddled together, they played quietly, their eyes darting warily at their father who sat hunched in his chair, his feet in slippers, glasses on his nose, the newspaper in his hands. When at last he spoke, everyone listened. 'I miss that lovely cow an' so will yehz. Them feckin' Nearys'll be delighted. Bad luck to the quare bastards. Bur I t'ink yehz all wan'ta see a poor fella down on his knees don't yehz?'

The children were shocked at the suggestion that they wanted to see their father fail. He was such a model. Mary, her face caving inwards with work, worry and neglect, grinned idiotically as if thrilled at his bad luck. The Boss would never forgive her for this blatant display of disloyalty. There had been a time when he could have counted on her allegiance. But not any more.

As dawn edged into the half dark rooms and birds fluttered sleepily from their roosts, Mary's half-closed eyes followed the shadowy figure of her husband as he quickly pulled on his trousers, snapped on his braces and silently left the room carrying his shoes. He tiptoed to Jack's room and shook him. 'It's milkin' time,' he hissed. Jack played dead. The Boss pummelled the inert lump, glancing all the while at the mounds made by his daughters in their bed. Sighing, Jack turned over, muttered gibberish, and made himself more comfortable. With a suppressed grunt the Boss grabbed him by the collar and dragged him from the bed. Jack swayed and scratched his head like Stanley Laurel. 'C'mon' fer Chrissake,' the Boss growled. Only when his son began to put on his socks did the Boss leave the room.

When Jack stumbled to the kitchen there was no friendly bacon and egg smells or the warm and familiar fragrance of nicely toasted white bread, just a mug of tea into which Jack dropped two spoonfuls of sugar when the Boss wasn't looking.

Eyes still glued in sleep, Jack buttoned his jacket and followed his father out into the cold concrete yard and over the bridge. He carried a shiny galvanised bucket. His father carried two. Chunks of black cloud cruised the sky like sharks. Pink flared on the horizon and a flock of wild duck dashed across Rathfarnham.

The two figures continued on their mysterious journey, taking green paths and sunken lanes to avoid detection. They dipped into a green and dark valley by a stream where cows lay like great mushrooms, quietly chewing their cud.

'Milk that little roan there,' the Boss said while he went to a big full breasted animal with horns like a hat rack. Soon the singsong of warm milk rang into the buckets. Other cows stood up, arched their backs, hung out their tails and crapped noisily. Jack was a novice milker but when the little roan felt his cold fingers tickle her she splayed her legs and yielded copiously. Tucking his head into the cow's side as he had seen his father do Jack enjoyed his work. The morning was coming up bright and fine, the hedges were beginning to be dotted with wild peach roses and the air was filled with a mini orchestra of songbirds tuning their instruments.

The Boss raced from cow to cow until he had both buckets filled to the brim with warm sudsy milk. 'Quick! L'ave it. Here comes the

Kirwan bastard!' he shouted.

Jack looked nervously up the hill to see three men running towards them. They were waving blackthorn sticks and cursing. 'Fer Jasus sake, run, yeh feckin' eejit,' the Boss shouted as he disappeared behind a hedge. Shackled by fear, Jack struggled with his half-filled bucket, his heart feathering like a dud Tigermoth engine. He headed for the hedge like a swimmer caught in reeds, the bucket hammering against his leg.

Using the natural cover like an old fox, the Boss slipped away. If cornered he would have given the three men a fearful pasting. 'T'row away the bloody milk but don't lose that darlin' bucket.' Jack stood like a dark ghost, his back to a field gate. The Boss grabbed him by the seat of the britches and threw him over it. Jack curled on the ground in agony like Pat Taffe coming a cropper at Becher's.

Kirwan gave up the chase and stopped to smoke a Woodbine. He had made his point and honour was saved all round.

The Boss looked into the empty buckets. 'Feckit,' he said. 'Worra we goin'ta do fer a dhroppa milk? Pay them bloody Nearys fer their piss, I suppose. As father and son trudged home with nothing but scratches, Loretto Convent was aglow in the bright rising sun.

'Jasus, that was a near wan,' the Boss said. 'Pity yeh're such a stupit bastard.'

78

BY THE LIGHT of her little paraffin lamp, Pam was leaning on an elbow gazing at a picture in a crumpled old *Evening Mail.* It was of a girl in traditional Irish costume. She was dancing, her legs in the air, her hands by her sides, a fixed look on her face. She'd just won an All Ireland title. Pam saw herself in the photo, dancing, smiling, catching the judge's eye. Most of all she saw herself going out dressed in the traditional green costume and glossy dancing pumps with shining silver buckles. It wasn't Hollywood, but it was a start. Her eyes bright, Pam whispered the dancing teacher's name to herself.

In the darkness the three girls sat wrapped together in a blanket on the sagging double bed, swapping the news of another day.

All the girl's exchanges were keenly absorbed by Jack who sat with both ears cocked in the small back bedroom with the flat roof. 'I got th'info 'bout Miss Doran's dancin' classes,' Pam said, and she felt as light as air with the telling. Her small feet were already twitching, her thin white arms fluttering as in her imagination she skipped across the floor, her audience rapt in silent awe.

'Are yeh goin'ta jine?' Babs asked.

Pam, her eyes alight, said, 'Yeah, 'course I am. The Nolan wan is goin' an' I can walk down ta the Bluebird wit' her.'

'Why yeh wan'ta go fer anyway?' Bridgid sniffed her disapproval.

Pam smiled. 'Because, dumbo, I wan'ta learn Irish dancin'.' Again her heart beat faster and she could see a green and brooch-bound figure leaping as high as the ceiling, dancing hornpipes, jigs and reels on a high stage, with people watching.

'It's a nice idea,' Babs said. 'I wouldn'a minded goin' wit'cha meself.'

The girls climbed under the covers and dozed. But there was still something very important Babs desperately wanted to tell her sisters. Like a glowing ember it smouldered in her guts and had become so painful she needed to cough it up. The news she had was thrilling, so sensational she just had to share it. As sleep was about to drag her sisters down, Babs released her depth charge. 'I'm goin' out with a fella,' she said.

'No!' Bridgid roared in surprise. The noise woke the fitfully dozing Boss in the room next door.

Bridgid rose up from the darkness like a corpse. 'Watcha mane, a fella?' she demanded.

'Shhh,' Babs said. 'D'yeh mane a real fella?' Bridgid whispered loudly.

'A course,' Babs whispered softly. There was a small laugh in her voice but it was scared. 'What udder kind is there?'

'Hey, that's hip,' Pam said borrowing one of Aunt Dolores's Americanisms. 'Does Daddy know?'

'Oh yeah,' Bridgid said, 'Babs sent him a telegram abourrit. Don't be stupit, Sis.'

Next door, the Boss was wide awake. When Babs spoke again he heard her awful words as if they were tannoyed directly into his room. 'What's it got ta do wit' him?' his favourite child said. The unfamiliar edge to her voice clubbed him in the dark.

Unaware they were being overheard the girls collectively quivered with excitement. Bridgid and Pam knew their big sister had brought off a fantastic coup and ten to one the little bitch was pulling a sly smile in the darkness. Christ, but she had every right to.

'The oul' Man'll go feckin' bananas,' Bridgid said. 'Yer new fella'll be a corpse if he as much as holds yer hand.'

'Bridgid's right fer wanst,' Pam said as she concentrated on the glorious matter of the first of them having boyfriend. 'Jus' 'cos yeh're Daddy's favourite,' Bridgid said, 'doesn't mane he'll accept yeh doin' a line wit' some strange guy none ivvus knows.'

'*Strange*?' Babs queried. Her raised voice caused the Boss to yell in agony. 'Babs, stop that oul' rubbitch will yeh, an' let a fella get a bit a sleep.'

The girls' hearts beat faster.

'He musta heard everythin',' Bridgid hissed.

'He couldn'a done,' Babs said, but in a reckless, coquettish, womanly way she didn't care if he did. She got up and went to her own room.

Silence settled over the room. In his own small bed, his knees under his chin, Jack dwelt on the prospect of a new man coming into the house. Brilliant, he might be a footballer. Jack saw only benefits.

Soon, snores ripped through the dark. Troubled and threatened, the Boss lay on his side, his good eye open like a stab wound. He felt suddenly small and vulnerable beside his massive wife as she thumbed a rubbery nipple into the gummy jaw of her latest infant. The baby's contented murmurings penetrated the Boss's skull like a power drill. When Mary moved across the bare wooden floor to put her baby down with soothing whispers the Boss's expression hardened in the candlelight. His face had set itself into a frightful grimace. He would not tolerate his daughter's infidelity. Tomorrow, he would squash the burgeoning romance as he would a crawling black beetle with the heel of his boot. 'Pl'ase God, it's not too late,' he muttered. 'What's up with yeh?' Mary hissed. 'Yeh're talkin' in yer sleep now, yeh bloody lunatic?' The Boss stayed awake long after Mary's ragged snoring became a duet with her baby's breathing.

79

'LISTEN,' BABS SAID as she clanged her old bike in the hall. She was excited and breathless. 'D'yeh 'member that fella I told yehz about? Well, yeh'll never guess–'

'G'wan, fer Jasus' sake!' Bridgid howled.

'Sssh!' Babs hissed. 'Well, he's as'ed me out.' Babs did a little dance, her shoes stuttering on the bare boards.

'Wha'cha tell 'im?' Pam asked, throwing off all attempts at being cool.

'I said *yes*, stupit.' Babs gave a wild little laugh.

'Worrabou' yeh-know-who?' Bridgid said, casting her eyes towards the kitchen where the Boss sat in his chair like a god of pain.

'I'm not goin'ta tell 'im,' Babs said, 'at least, not yet. I'm pretendin' I'm goin'ta the Legion in the usual way, burr I'm puttin' th'oul war paint on and a birra silk and satin.' She twirled her handbag, her hand on her left hip like a tart. 'Yes!' she exclaimed.

'If yeh're doin' that,' Pam said with pouting defiance, 'I'm goin'ta the Bluebird, even though Daddy said I couldn't.' Pam was feeling strong in the shadow of her sister. 'On me own, he'd kill me; wit' you, well . . .' Pam said quietly, 'it's diff'rent.'

'We'll see,' Babs said. 'C'mon, let's get dressed.'

'Wor about me?' Bridgid said, her face sour with a feeling of betrayal.

'Well,' Babs said, stuck for words. 'You can come another time can'tcha?'

'When we've broken the ice, sorta,' Pam said. 'Yeh're on'y fifteen.'

'Oh, shit!' Bridgid said, clouting the wall.

'Listen,' Babs said. 'I've tole Mammy about this guy an' she doesn' mind. O.K.?'

'An' I have too,' Pam said, 'an' she said I could go ta the Bluebird any time I want.'

'So yehz have it all stitched up?' Bridgid said. 'But there is one obstacle, an' a feckin' monster one it is. Yehz seem ta be fergettin' about . . .'

This time, the Boss wasn't listening. His head thrown back he was sleeping like a granite cross. His hands flopped down either side of the chair, hands that had punched, fondled and stolen, been torn by wire, and crucified by rusting nails. They had delved, dug, and even prayed. Those hands had etched into them the whole story of the Boss's struggle. Ugly, mighty hands, with a patina of tar, paint, grease and dirt that had faithfully done the work of the aching brain that drove and directed them. Now they hung like a pair of cured hams, stumpy fingers twitching. The Boss slept like a dead man, as if his whirring springs had jammed or broken. The *Evening Mail*, his world outside the pigsties lay like a small tent on his lap. The belly, no longer reinforced concrete but bearing the softness of physical decline, gently heaved.

The Boss was getting old. Mary looked down at him without love or sympathy, and chuckled. 'Serves the old shite right. It's penance fer his sins,' she murmured. This meanness of spirit was recent. The smaller children responded to Mary's pulled faces, their smiles crescenting their cheeks as, barefooted, they held their breath in case they woke the tired old monster.

The Boss woke up testily. 'What's goin' on in there? Why are them girls wastin' that bi'ra light? What are they plannin'? Come out a there you two, an' l'ave Babs ta write her letthers.'

'Divil the letthers she'll be writin' tanight,' Mary said. 'Them two is goin' out.'

'Wha'diyeh mane?' The Boss's injured eye was running milky water. 'Who tole them they could go out?'

'I did,' Mary said as if she couldn't care less about the consequences of her treachery. Knitting calmly, she said, 'Babs has ta go ta the Legion a Mary, yeh know, it's every Chuesda'.'

'An' where's the other empty-headed little bitch goin'?'

'The Bluebird,' Bridgid said tiumphantly as she ran into the room squatted, legs akimbo on the floor and began to disconsolately pick at the corner of a worn mat.

'What!' the Boss roared.

'There's Irish dancin' on,' Mary sniffed. 'It's traditional, it's Irish and it's pathriotic. And,' she played her ace, 'it's supervised be Frances Doran, the Irish National Champion.'

'Yes,' Pam said. 'An' we're goin' whether yeh like it or not.'

The Boss jumped up from his chair and made a bootless kick at Bridgid who screamed in mock agony.

'Now, now, Daddy,' Babs said. 'That's not nice is it?' She began to massage her father's thick neck as Mary looked on in surprised admiration. He turned to his daughter like a bulldog that's had all its teeth magically pulled, his one good eye filled with love. Babs was using her female guile to tame, subdue and disarm her father, negating his fearful energy. It was a trick Mary had never mastered.

'Bluebird, that feckin' tip,' he said almost listlessly. 'Yeh don't want them pups from the Corporation houses messin' wit' yehz.'

Mary stopped knitting, her needles poised in midair. 'They're old enough ta know their own minds be now.'

The Boss flung a harpoon of a look at his wife; or what might once have been a harpoon.

'Now, Daddy,' Babs said and she led him back to his chair. Babs caught Pam's eye and gave her a thumbs-up. The Boss seemed mollified by the idea of Babs going into a fusty chapel to pray with a bunch of young virgins from respectable homes.

Mary smiled inwardly. The handcuffs were coming off. Her husband was retreating. It wasn't so long ago that he'd have been hitting her by now, and the kids dragging themselves off to bed with terror in their eyes.

80

BABS CAREFULLY PREPARED herself for her first foray into the world of sin and excitement. The mirror faithfully reflected her untinted beauty, her hair cascading to her shoulders as she sat in her slip, combing and brushing until the ends crackled. With the narcissism of youth she examined her face minutely for traces of spots and blemishes. There were none. She tried on a pair of cheap earrings and a ring she'd bought in one of the small shops off Grafton Street. Consulting the mirror again she decided against wearing either. The silk scarf went with her complexion and the turned-up collar of her blouse lent her a sophisticated, slightly racy look. Standing up she drew on a new pair of nylon stockings, hooking them on to her suspenders. Looking behind her she arched her long legs and caressed the back of each to straighten the seams.

In the kitchen the Boss sullenly attempted to read the paper but is mind was on his beloved daughter in her room, preparing herself in a way she had never done before. She was out to attract another male, a stranger, a man of unknown pedigree, a mongrel without morals. His control over everything Babs had thought or done since birth was being challenged. 'Why does she need ta go?' he barely restrained himself from crying out. In the Boss's mind the anonymous youth Babs was dolling herself up for was magnified into a sexual deviant, a serial killer intent on destroying his daughter.

The Boss's good eye darted towards the door from the hall when it opened with a soft sigh he saw only a small child meekly turning the brass handle as quietly as it could in order not to upset its father. The Boss's nose twitched, he smelt perfume. It reminded him of willing girls on their backs, of thrusting and sighing. Of the soft, piston-like sounds of coupling. Of messy, fish-smelling climax. He imagined Babs laying down a scent like a sow to attract a boar. The Boss's leathery hands shook the paper like a dog breaking a rat's back.

Mary shuffled around the kitchen like an old tram in a small dark town, stopping to deliver, to lay, to replace, to wash and to brew another pot of strong tea. Then she staggered to throw a few chocolatey sods on the fire. When at last she sat down it was as if the whole house was in mourning. The Boss was pining for Babs' lost innocence. Babs was about to scale the wall and flee, her shackles flying.

When the door opened all eyes swivelled. Bridgid broke into the children's ooh's of amusement that greeted Babs' entrance. 'Bedad yeh look smashin',' she said.

The Boss didn't want to look, but his thick stubborn neck was being forced around and up by a nervous curiosity that made him tremble. His one-eyed glance caught Babs' two blue, lively, hopeful eyes. She stared at him as if seeking absolution. He knew it and turned away.

'Sure, yeh look grand,' Mary said, stopping a drip from her nose with the back of her hand. She fiddled around in her apron pockets until she found a bit of rag to blow into, then threw herself like a broken prop-forward on to her delicate, scented daughter and hugged her. 'Darlin'!,' she cried, 'Don'tcha look a rale little beauty. I don't know why God blessed me wit' such a fine lookin' daughter.' The Boss swallowed a gob of saliva.

'Wor abou' me?' Bridgid joked.

Mary put her arm around her dumpy daughter and said, 'Yehz are all lovely ta me.'

The children formed an affectionate circle and tried to catch some of the glow their big sister dispensed in all directions. They elbowed each other and exchanged smiles. Their Babs, without any of them suspecting it, had crystalised into a lovely lady. Like a queen she patted their heads with a gloved hand and they smiled and reached up to her, their grimy hands holding on to her.

'Gerrof!' Bridgid, her self-appointed bouncer, roared. 'Yehz'll ruin her frock.' The Boss left the kitchen unnoticed. Pam joined the rest of the family like a Hollywood starlet looking for a photographer. She too looked lovely but her entrance got no applause. The two girls kissed their mother and headed down the hallway and out the front door. The door'll be open,' Mary said, 'I'll put the pee bucket in frontiv it.' She was referring to the large paint tin the children urinated in if they were taken short in the night.

From the back of the bungalow, where softly as a nocturnal animal he had secreted himself, the Boss watched, his face barred by sticks. Above, a cloud-smothered moon shone. His head felt empty. His was a peculiar sort of sadness. His prime emotion had always been hate. Without hate he was lost. He hated no one tonight. Not even the unknown boy who would soon take his beloved Babs in his arms. He trusted to God it would be no more than a clumsy embrace, a fumbled kiss. No. Even that was too much.

The Boss grew angry again and he felt more comfortable. When Babs' light coat vanished in the dark the wind blew colder as if the warmth she radiated had gone forever. He watched her go, then returned to the kitchen whistling with an armful of turf to put Mary off the scent. His ploy failed. He had never shown weakness in all the lost and terrible years of their marriage. But he was showing it now.

The girls were bursting with excitement as they stepped out purposefully, delicately picking their way over the puddles lying in the broken road. The village looked unusually exotic in the dark, The Yellow House pulsed with men. Its flapping doors exhaled a concoction of smells: beer urine and cigarette butts. The two girls parted here, Babs to go into the Church of the Annunciation, while Pam headed left followed by her shadow. She was alone, kissed by soiled privet that fuzzed over broken fences.

The Bluebird glowed like a fabulous jewel. It stood on a patch of council wasteland, bordered by an oily stream that in daylight flattened in the sun before disappearing down a culvert. Men would soon come from the pubs and stand outside, their eyes glued to cracks in the wood, looking for a snatch of underwear as the girls joyously kicked their legs into eternity, driven by a fat woman thumping a piano and a battered man on an asthmatic accordion.

Half a mile away in the cold chapel that smelt of sweat and wet-rot, Babs joined the other girls in the Legion of Mary. Their combined purity was tangible. The priest, a tired looking man with weak eyes, uttered banalities about the Blessed Virgin and the importance she laid on chastity. The young girls, their souls fluttering in the old man's liver-spotted hands, cast their eyes upward, inhaling his musty reverence.

Crossing themselves, they followed the priest's prayers with chants of their own, which lent to the crusty old curate a certain majesty. When the service was concluded Babs kissed her rosary reverently. Clutching her prayer book she went to the chapel steps to wait. A splash of holy water glistened on her forehead. She prayed her parents were safe and quiet and that her seams were straight. She should check, but there were no toilets in churches, even after a thousand years. Catholics didn't do bodily functions.

81

PAM DANCED IMMEDIATELY. She was here to dance. Dust flew from woodworm holes in the Bluebird boards as several dozen pairs of feet pounded the floor, clattering, jigging and reeling. She was gasping, drooling with pleasure, her eyes roving along the other girls who lined the walls. A green phalanx of dancers, their brooches shining like yellow buttercups, clapped their hands. Pam hoped they were looking at her. She recognised other first-timers like herself. They looked frightened. But she was dancing. Pam had, at last, what she'd always wanted, an audience, an opportunity to perform. The music opened a warm wound in her, filling her with its mystery. She leapt higher than she had ever done before, her young legs flying, her blood boiling.

Meanwhile, just down the road out of the shadows cast by a spreading yew, Babs' date appeared. He looked fairly mediocre. He would make a cracking shop manager. Sober and dutiful, he could guarantee Babs a church-going poverty, several children and respectability for the rest of her life. The young couple approached each other like sleepwalkers. Neither showed the faintest trace of joy as they touched. It was almost as if they were attracted to each other by some mysterious fragrance. Babs slid into his Ford Prefect, careful as a nun not to show her legs. The engine started, she was driven away.

Outside the Bluebird, men were gathering, their lust inflamed by alcohol. Their mouths full of rotten teeth, they pissed like dogs against the hut, holding their pricks as they squinted at the dancing inside. The girls, now almost hysterical, were sweating, the music screamed, the fat lady knuckled the piano, the man stretched his accordian as if it were made of Plasticine. The girls kicked higher and higher until some had to stop and crawl to their chairs to sit down. Pam danced on. Like a dervish on magic mushrooms she didn't care if there were a hundred men outside with their eyes to the cracks. 'Look, my knickers, see them, see them,' her legs seemed to sing out as they flew until it was almost indecent to look. The men's raw laughter erupted in the night outside as, hands in their pockets, they frantically jiggled and jangled loose change. When the lid of the piano closed, Pam had to walk a gauntlet of men's arms reaching out like sci fi. 'Show us yer knickers again,' one said. Pam stopped and in the light of the open door, slowly drew up her skirt. The man reddened and turned away. Another, his nose bleeding, kissed her on the mouth. Pam walked away, still smiling as if in a dream. Up the dark road she walked, into the light thrown by The Yellow House. Her sweat was cold. Tomorrow she would probably be coughing. She ran to keep warm, flying home before the rain began to splash.

A car sped up Whitechurch Road. Inside it, two faces blurred. The road glistened in the car's lights. Babs was accustomed to travelling by cart. It was good to be in a car on a night like this. Trees lurched, buildings leapt up and down like delirious children. Babs' face, illuminated by the speedometer's creamy light, was as tense as if she were being kidnapped. The boy drove fast, showing off.

'D'yeh wan'ta go fer a drink?' The sudden sound of his voice made Babs start. 'There's the Lamb Doyles.' It triggered an image of isolation and danger. 'Well?' the boy asked. Behind the wheel, he seemed to have matured.

'No,' Babs said. 'It's betther ta go tidda Gem.'

They sat at a formica table and drank lemonade, avoiding the ordeal of conversation. Frankie Laine was rounding up steers on the jukebox.

The Boss emerged from the shadows to watch the road. When he returned indoors he had another sod of turf for the fire. Mary was cutting and stitching, converting one of Aunt Dolores' skirts into a jacket for little Paul.

When the Boss heard the gate squeal, he rushed to the door, sliding the empty piss bucket to one side with a slippered toe.

'Hi!' Pam said as she slipped by him, smelling of sweat and nicotine. She entered the dimly lit room like a very good jumping pony, on her toes, her eyes shining. She did a little dance for her mother.

'Ah, that's lovely,' Mary said, showing her pink gums. 'Yeh learned an awful lot in wan lesson.' Pam danced again, the Boss watched her kicking feet with a look of frantic boredom, his pixie ears twitching.

Pam's excited voice brought sleepy-eyed children from their nests and they staggered around to find an empty chair, only to be told to 'get the hell back ta bed, yehz bloody melts.' They scuttled away like cockroaches, the door closing behind them. Suddenly, there was the unmistakable sound of a car stopping outside. The Boss jumped. Mary, smiling adoringly at Pam's antics, hadn't heard it as she tapped a leaden foot to her daughter's hectic humming and dancing. The Boss slipped away unnoticed and materialised outside in hat, coat and wellingtons. Stealthily, he waded into the stream further down. The car, like a shiny bug, its yellow eyes alight, glinted under the solitary road light. Breathing hard the Boss climbed the bank from the river, his hands reaching in the dark for something to hold on to, thistles, nettles, anything. He climbed the wall and stalked the car from the rear. Stopping within a few yards of it, he hid behind a twisted hawthorn. Inside, two silhouettes were moving in tandem. The windows were opaque with passion.

The Boss's face was pained as if he had swallowed poison. He saw his Babs embrace the man, they were kissing, his hands would be up her skirt, he was going to take her there and then.

Leaping out like an enraged Zulu, the Boss rushed to the car and attacked its rounded roof, hitting it tremendous blows with his clenched fists. He rushed round to the driver's window and peered crazily inside. Babs let out a scream of terror and the boy instinctively crouched, covering his head with his arms. 'Open up, yeh feckin' sleeveen,' the Boss yelled, shaking the door handle.

Timidly, the boy unlocked the car door. The Boss grabbed him and hauled him from the car, punching and smacking him all over. The boy yelled for help but the dark road was empty. Babs looked on, squealing helplessly.

'Get back in that car,' the Boss roared, 'an' don't le'me see yeh roun' her again.' He stuffed the terrified boy into the driving seat. Not waiting to close the door, the car turned and roared away back to the village, its open door flapping.

The Boss turned to Babs who was crying softly, her hand to her mouth like a child. 'What d'yeh mane lettin' a scut like that kiss yeh?'

he yelled, 'an' what d'yeh want stayin' out at this hour a the night? I've a good mind ta–' He raised his hand. 'That's the last time yeh're goin' ta that feckin' Child a Mary,' he said. 'Yeh're my daughter, I'll decide from now on when yeh go out.' Babs ran indoors in tears, her head bent, her body hunched and pumping.

When he'd prodded the sack under the door and shot home the heavy bolts, the Boss sheepishly went to see her. Expecting to find Babs in the kitchen, he saw only Mary. 'What hav'yeh done ta the poor child?' she demanded, 'she's gone ta bed without her cocoa.'

The Boss's thin lips parted. 'Them rotten hoormasters from the village,' he shouted, 'who da they t'ink they yar, takin' Babs in the car wit 'em. I told the fecker to feck off back ta the slum he came out of.'

'How d'yeh know she went against her will?' Mary asked reasonably, 'Have yeh not t'ought she might a been willin?'

The Boss's lips rolled back, he clenched his fists and stood mad-eyed until he was hauled away by a posse of children led by Babs who calmed him.

'She's sidin' wit' the scum,' he said like a whining child. 'I'm on'y tryin' ta protect yeh, that's all.'

'Babs'll hav'ta survive when yeh're dead an' gone.' Mary said before shuffling off to the sanctity of her room.

82

THE BOSS ROSE early next morning, laid the table and cooked an egg for Babs. Nothing was said about the events of the previous night. Both seemed content to let them remain on the charge book. Babs went to Easthams as usual and seemed none the worse for her fright. But it had changed her.

The Boss brooded all day. He talked to himself with fevered twitching and rapid moving of the lips. As he mended the sties, fed the calf and pigs, and cast a handful of grain into the mud for the chickens, his mind throbbed. What Babs did was unforgiveable. He simply could not understand her. Was he not a wonderful father to her? Didn't she have the best of everything? More than any of the other kids? Why did she think a pimply stranger could offer more? It made him rage within, he felt small and not worth much. All day he ploughed through his work, not bothering to go to the house for lunch.

Mary's powers of recovery were phenomenal. Almost permanently bruised, both mentally and physically, she remained amazingly thick-skinned. She ate a chunky sandwich and drank a pot of tea. Then she went to her favourite place on earth, the stone sink by the lichened window with the one cold water tap. Sitting down because of her aching legs, she scraped carrots and parsnips, chopped onions, peeled potatoes and apples, and made a big apple tart. The Boss would never dream of telling her, but he envied his wife. There she was, her mind apparently free of worry, her babies playing on the floor, while he was driven insane with torment. Why did he have to suffer all the time? Why wasn't she more involved with the children's morals? Why did she feel no guilt? It filled his head to bursting. Now, Babs had rejected him. He was friendless. It couldn't be allowed to go unchallenged.

After Babs had returned from work he entered her bedroom without knocking, and sat on her bed. She had been washing and immediately grabbed a towel to cover herself. It hurt her that he was insensitive enough to invade her privacy so brutally. She waited for him to start. He nagged her; said how disappointed he was, what a great father he was . . . how worrying it was for him that his eldest child went out so recklessly with a total bloody stranger. Did she know where he came from? What he worked at? What sort of education did he have? What sort of property did he live in. State-owned or private? These, he thought, were reasonable questions for a caring father to ask.

The Boss spoke with unusual softness, even tenderness. 'Daddy, he's a nice lad,' was all Babs was able to venture, her voice quivering. 'What can yeh possibly have against him?'

'Yeah, but yeh don't know him,' the Boss said. 'Them fellas is all chancers. Slap on a bit a hair oil and they t'ink they're yer man - wha'd'yeh call'im? - Cary Grant. They've no intherest in yer welfare. Don'tcha see they're dis'ased. They can't hold a job down. They live be robbin'. Then they go out at night t'show off ta innocent bits a girls like yerself.'

Sitting half-naked, with the towel barely covering her, Babs was cold and didn't want to argue. She would have preferred her father to go away and close the door behind him. 'Daddy, yeh're wrong,' she sobbed. 'Niall's got a good job in Sweeney's, in the sport's department.' Noticing her father listening for a change she continued in the same soft-spoken way. 'His Mammy's dead but his father's a hard-workin' man, a plumber.'

The Boss reasserted his authority. 'Listen yeh,' he said, and his fists were impotently clenched for there was no chance of him hitting Babs. 'I won't say any more, jes' this . . . if I see yeh bringin' back any more a them bloody ruffians, I'll, I'll . . .'

For the first time in his life his fists were useless. Babs looked at him and his hands dropped to his sides. She went to her father, who was panting like a bull. 'Niall's a nice lad, Daddy. I know his sister. He on'y took me home, he didn't do an'tin'.'

'Now yeh listen ta me,' the Boss said. 'I didn't say he did an'tin'. It's jes' as well for him he didn't. Yeh know how it is these days, there's so many a them fellas out there, waitin' fer a nice innocent lassie like yeh ta disthroy.'

'Daddy,' Babs said. 'If yeh like I won't see him any more.'

The Boss smiled. 'Ah, now wait, I don't wantcha to, but on the udder hand if yeh t'ink . . . well, I'll l'ave it up ta yeh.' He turned on his heel and headed victoriously for the kitchen.

As she dressed Babs looked at herself in the mirror and vowed to be more careful next time.

At the dinner table the Boss made a great play of helping Mary, he even ordered her to sit down while he and Jack did the washing-up. 'Gives yehz a bit of a rest,' he said, laughing falsely, his small, pale eye watering with joy. With dignity Mary carried on working. The Boss had hurt her once too often. She had run dry of forgiveness. As far as Mary was concerned now, he might as well be dead.

That night, Babs had a terrible dream. A wet chill oozed through the house. Mary, young and beautiful, her hair to her waist, a slinky black dress to her toes, was lying face downward on a white bed. The Boss wore an evening suit, his hair curled and scented, white gloves on his hands, black shoes squinting on his small neat feet. He was leaning over Mary, her face was to one side. Babs saw the red lipstick, the powdered cheek. The Boss was whispering, 'Yeh've hurt me.' . . . 'Please,' Mary was murmuring into the pillow. 'I didn't mean to, it's in yer mind. I wouldn't hurt yeh, I love yeh.' Babs saw her father bend down, he was whispering into Mary's ear. She winced at the hotness of his breath. 'But yeh have,' he said, 'yeh've desthroyed me.' He had his hands around her throat. He pressed down on top of her, his blackness sharklike against the white sheets. . . . 'Let me go,' Mary cried. '*Please*!' She was splayed like a carcass in a butcher's window. . . . 'It's the on'y way,' the Boss was saying as Mary's hands curled up to hold him. . . . 'If it's the only way,' she whispered. A tear formed in her eye and dripped down her cheek– '*Don't* ! Please, Daddy,' Babs screamed, but she couldn't get the words out. It was as if her lips were stitched together.

Babs woke up in a sweat. For a moment, she didn't know where she was. She had to go through her parents' room to get to the bathroom. She splashed water in her face and looked in the mirror. She had to get away from here before it destroyed her. She went to her mother who was lying on her side like a stricken liner, her baby snoozing in the crook of her arm. 'Mammy,' Babs said, bending over her mother.

'What d'yeh want darlin?' Mary asked, her long nose stuck in a dent in the pillow, her fat loose-fleshed arm, bearing an ugly bruise, exposed on top of the blanket. The baby woke and pined for milk. 'Typical yella Jack,' Mary muttered, 'wantin' ta suck the last dhroppa juice out a me.'

'Mammy,' Babs began softly again. What could she say that would undo the years of pain? All she could offer were empty phrases, shallow, useless words.

Mary's faded blue eyes opened wide and she sighed. 'Don't worry 'bout me, I made me own bed an' now I hav'ta lie in it.'

83

WITH THE MORNING came hope. Babs went to her mother who was still in bed. 'I was jus' t'inkin',' she said, 'wouldja like me ta bring yeh back a cake or sumptin? A box a chocolates meybe, jus' fer yerself.'

'No, it's all right,' Mary said. 'Funny as it seems, I don't need an'tin'.' In a strange way this was true. Mary lacked so much and yet she felt self-sufficient. Her problems were of her own making, and as such were insoluble. As Eileen had said, if she'd 'stood up ta that little bollix years ago' she wouldn't be in the state she was in now. Mary felt she'd got what she deserved. Her life would start when she died. Heaven would welcome her into its pine-scented clouds where she would be washed and cleansed of the foul stains of Rathfarnham, and put into splendid robes. She could sit around on gold-braided sofas, with a couple of little cherubs fanning her, another doing her nails, another bathing her great bunioned feet in Radox. That's what she told the kids, gathered around her like a human quilt, scratching their heads at the pleasant thought, believing her and smiling. Everything would turn out all right in the end. Life was but a trial to see if you deserved Heaven. The more you suffered now the better your life would be after. This life was only a horrendous intermission. We were all sinners grubbing about in the dirt.

After a quick cup of tea and a Ryvita biscuit, Babs was ready for the journey into town. Mary was out of bed on her knees, an old thread-bare cardigan over her shoulders.

'What's wrong, Mammy?' Babs asked.

'Oh, its' yeh again, is it?' Mary muttered. 'Well I don't wan'ta talk to any a yehz again.'

'Please, Mammy,' Babs said. Tears started in her eyes. She remembered when she was a toddler and Mary loved her.

'Yeh don't need me,' Mary said, 'he loves yeh, that's enough. He despises me and the rest a the childer.'

'That's not true,' Babs said, but she knew it was.

Mary's face was puffy and grey, her cardigan began to slide off her shoulders, she made a half-hearted attempt to arrest its fall. The bed was unmade, the chamber pot on top of a scrap of stained carpet. Babs cried and threw her arms around her mother.

'Mammy, Mammy, what ails yeh?' she asked, burying her face in her mother's flabby neck. Mary's hands remained by her side. Babs held on to her mother, yearning for the big warm hands, with their fingernails gnawed to the quick, to encircle her like they used to. But Mary's heart had been concreted over, like the fields around the bungalow. The sun would never again shine in either place. Babs let her mother undo her embrace, dropped her arms, left the room, and cycled to work crying.

At work that day Babs thought of her mother, her father and the mire into which they had sunk, dragging their children with them. Babs knew there was nothing she could do about it. The only thing she could do was to save herself, to escape, leave them to get on with it. It was a horrible way to think but there was no other option. She racked her brains all day and kept coming up with the same answer. She must get away before she too was sucked into the vortex and lost.

That evening as Babs rode home there was a hardness in her that had never been there before. After putting her bike away she returned to the yard and looked across the river. In the distance, bonfires were burning where birds used to build their nests. Lorries loaded with bricks and rubble from torn down old houses, and huge excavators brought in to rip up the grass and trees, rumbled back across the ravished ground, their destruction accomplished.

From around the yard came the sounds of evening: the muffled bark of a dog chained in a shed, starlings wheezing in the pines which stood dark and straight in Neary's field, the chiming of bells, Billy Jolly's horse and float clattering up the hill, the piping of a robin in the apple tree. Villagers trooped to pub and church, the moon winked like a coin in water, ragged clouds drifted by. So much was going on, so many animals and humans, living out their short lives.

Babs inhaled the air for a while before she felt confident enough to face the bungalow and the tragedy unravelling within. She was glad to see her mother at the sink. It meant everything was going to be all right after all. When her mother went to change from her shoes into wellingtons Babs offered to take the potato and apple peelings down to the pigs for her. Mary sniffled agreement but, even though Babs stared at her mother, the two women did not make eye contact. Soon, the pots were bubbling on the stove, the smell of potatoes, boiling chicken and the whiff of leeks filled the kitchen with their welcome steam. The children dodged about, racing to get to their favourite places on their form. With hands curled on laps they watched, licking their lips, as Mary carried the big pots brimming with food to the table. The children ate voraciously, greasily grinning as they tore bits of tendon and flesh from chicken legs and speared potato and leek. Every morsel gone, they looked up hopefully for seconds, a knob of gristle or a hen's tail or ribcage to gnaw, then for the pie Mary had summoned up the will to make.

The Boss in his slippers, glasses on his nose, the *Evening Mail* folded under his arm, took up his position at the head of the table. There he sat like some feudal crook-nosed chief, lording it over a tribe of pygmics. His sinister arrival made the blessed aroma of food, which had wreathed the table, vanish like a genie, to be replaced by a coarser devil who sternly oversaw the children's silent licking of the custard-slicked bowls. Without having to be told they silently slipped off the form one by one and trooped off to bed like weary little foot soldiers.

Mary ate her food defiantly, her cheeks bulging. Her severe bouts of depression and blinding migraines seemed to add an edge to her appetite. In a fit of pique she snatched the last helping of pie instead of offering it to the Boss.

84

WASHED AND SCENTED the girls talked and Jack listened through the panelling. He enjoyed tapping into their gossip, and their secrets filled his mind with material for dreams. ''Member the blonde Billy Riley was goin' out wit'?' Bridgid said.

'Yeh mean the May Nolan wan. Wor abou'it?' Pam enquired.

'She's on'y goin' out with someone else,' Bridgid said. 'Saw them at Quo Vadis.'

Babs put down her *Woman's Own*. 'No!' she exclaimed. 'Billy won't like that. They say he's very jealous.'

'Yeh're jokin',' Bridgid said. 'He's a fat bastard wit' the brains uvva flea.'

'Billy's all right,' Babs said. 'May's lucky she's got a good lookin' an' hard-workin' man like 'im ta look afther her. He's no Einstein, bur 'e's dacent enough.'

'The udda fella she's goin' wit' behine Billy's back's not a looker, but very smoot'. Nice suits, hair combed back.'

There was silence for a moment, then Bridgid lobbed in another gob of slander. 'Nelly Quinn sez he has a wife an' kids stashed away somewhere.'

'No!' Babs and Pam said in harmony.

'That's disgraceful.' Babs said. 'There'll be ructions if Billy finds out.'

Jack had lost consciousness by time the moon on his sharp pale face made him look as if he'd been drawn in charcoal.

Jack was breaking branches into kindling when a voice interrupted his thoughts.

'Where's yer oul' fella?'

Jack turned and his heart skipped a beat when he saw Billy Riley's big upper body leaning over him. The voice was slurred as if Riley had been at the porter. 'He's out,' Jack said, 'doin' a bit a tarmacking for an oul' wan in Rat'down Park.'

'When's'e jue back?' Riley said, grabbing at the chicken wire for support.

'Don't know,' Jack said, 'yeh'll hav'ta ask me mammy.'

Riley ambled off, rolling as if he were striding the decks of a ship in rough weather. When Jack looked again the drunken labourer was sitting on a log in the yard, leaning against a cock of hay, his head in his hands.

Jack finished the kindling, swept out five sties, and was taking the last barrow of manure to the heap in the garden. Riley was still there, massaging his face all over with his big hands as if he were rubbing in suntan lotion. Jack hated having to take the barrow right under Riley's snout but there was no other route to the mountain of animal shite that almost covered the garden like a leaking abscess. 'Jasus, he's cryin',' Jack whispered to himself and was about to attempt a U-turn when there was an anguished bellow and he saw Riley stagger to his feet.

'Com'ere,' he roared.

Jack dropped the barrow. Riley was holding a huge knife in his hands. When Riley moved unsteadily it flashed in Jack's eyes like a headlamp. 'D'ya see this?' Riley groaned. 'May's gonna get this.' He made an upward stabbing motion with the knife. 'No mott's goin'ta run out on me. Jack. Sit down here.' His words were slurred as he made room on the log. Riley began gouging out pieces of bark like a bull pawing the ground before charging. 'We were savin' ta get married,' he said, and a funny little laugh came out. 'Every cent I earned I gev her an' she was makin' a fool a me all the time.' He stopped hacking at the log and looked at Jack. His big face crumpled. 'Like a fool I was, she jus' . . .' and, with the knife sticking upward from his hands, he cried into the palms. 'She done me, the bitch, done me.' The misery came from deep inside him. Jack was scared, the garden was quiet except for the hens cackling. 'Yeah,' Riley sniffed, 'afther all I done fer her. Know what she done, son? I'll tell yeh, she was spendin' the money I gev her on udder guys.' The horror of such deceit hurt so much the big man howled out loud and Jack prayed for the return of his father. If only the Boss was here, he would soon talk sense into Billy. 'I'm fucked,' Riley said after a pause, 'an' she's fucked too, be every cunt in the village. Sorry, son, I didn't mane ta curse. Women do that ta a man. It's jus–' and he waved his hands uselessly as if there was nothing else to say.

To Jack's relief the big labourer got to his feet, blew his nose with his fingers, flung the phlegm away, then folded the knife and put it in his pocket. He lumbered off, waving without looking back and had been gone only a few minutes when the Boss returned. Kitty clattered up to the gate, frothing, and barged it with her chest. Jack opened it and with the Boss grimly on top of the cart, the old pony, mad with energy, tore around the yard before he could stop her.

The Boss was on the ground undoing Kitty's tack before Jack had the gate closed. 'Was that hoor Riley in here?' the Boss asked.

'Yeah,' Jack said.

The Boss stopped, his eyes filled with suspicion.

'Was he talkin' t'yer woman above?' He nodded towards the house.

'No, no,' Jack said.

Relieved to hear it, the Boss carried on unharnessing the pony. But he quickly returned to the subject. 'What did'e want then? That hoor should a been workin', no wonder them nuns is sick a him. I heard tell his job's goin'.' There was a trace of cheerfulness in the Boss's voice. He pretended he was not the least bit interested in Riley but he was dying to know. After a further minute or two of silence he roared. 'Come on, fer feck's sake, what's wrong wit'cha? Will yeh tell me what Riley's business was here?'

'Nuthin',' Jack said.

But the Boss's fuse was lit and fizzing. 'Tell me everythin' the melt said,' he demanded. Jack told him as much as he could recall. 'An' he had a knife wit'im?' the Boss said. 'What did the big hoor want that for?'

'He said he was goin'ta stick it in May Nolan,' Jack replied calmly.

The Boss laughed. 'Heh, that's a good wan, yer man's nothin' bur a big shite, a bluffer. So, he had a knife, eh?' the Boss said again, as if relishing the prospect of Riley's knife entering May's nice plump belly. 'Some chance. Billy's playin' wit' a dangerous weapon. What a joke. Hope yeh done them pigs.'

'D'yehz t'ink I should tell May?' Babs asked, when Jack informed her of Riley's intentions. 'Afther all, she's a friend.'

'Don't be stupit,' Bridgid said. 'Since she started goin' out wit' fellas she never comes over here.'

Babs nodded. 'Maybe yeh're right. I'll say nuttin'. It'll on'y frighten her.'

The Boss came in on the tail end of the conversation. 'Don't be gettin' involved in an'tin' like that,' he growled. 'If that oul' Nolan wan heard yeh sayin' the fella her daughter was goin' out wit' brought a knife t'kill 'er, yeh'd have all the Nolans, an' that udder feckin' tribe the Rileys, over 'ere stonin' the house. Let 'em ger on wit'it. Yer man Billy hasn't the bottle ta skin a rabbit; there's no way he'd gut yer woman.' The Boss let out a small, peeved laugh.

Babs felt better about it all and went to bed. Bridgid was right, it was just a lover's tiff; Billy was showing off.

The girls talked as usual after going to bed. The conversation finally came to a halt and the girls went to sleep one after the other. Jack, remembering the sun glinting on Billy's blade, stayed awake.

85

THE CONVENT BELL boomed six times, chasing the nuns from their loveless beds. It was the beginning of a new day in Rathfarnham, a day like all the others. But it was an extraordinary day, a strange day, a day that was to wrestle and shove Rathfarnham blinking into the spotlight.

That evening Jack ran to MacAlinden's shop like a tatty moth drawn to a bright light. He could tell something unusual had happened. Worn old women stood around, nodding and grimacing through the glass window. Jasus, it was a field day for the bitter gossipers. 'An' him a well respected man wit' a dacent job,' Jack heard one buckled old mouth say as he opened the shop door.

'She must'a been a fast bit,' another said. The huddled women parted and stared at the intruder, whose entry had ruined their conversation. 'It's yer man's son from down the road,' one woman whispered, elbowing another's heavy coat and rolling her eyes.

As he pressed towards the stack of newspapers lying in front of him, Jack saw the gore drenched headlines. 'Woman Slayed in Frenzied Knife Attack'. The front page of the *Evening Herald* screamed to be picked up.

'Yes?' Suzy MacAlinden said in her bored way. Suzy was magnificent. The beautiful daughter of the store's new owners, she was a girl of some style in Rathfarham. She was gorgeous and she drove a black Studebaker up the Whitechurch Road at well over the speed limit. And no one stopped her. The unemployed lads who played pitch and toss at the corners gawked at the raven-haired beauty and dived into their pockets to give their naked privates a quick fondle, their eyes rolling with manic lust.

His tongue filling his mouth, Jack collected the *Evening Mail* from Suzy and had the nerve to diss the goddess by flicking to the inside pages as he waited for change. She placed his change beside his outstretched hand in case she caught something.

Buffeted by new customers arriving from work, Jack read voraciously. For once he couldn't care a toss what his father would say about creases in his paper. 'Jasus Christ!' Jack hissed, and hurried home before the Boss heard it on the wireless.

'May Nolan's afther been murdered,' he yelled from the hallway, causing the Boss to leap out of his chair.

'Gi'me that feckin' paper, yeh bloody cur,' he yelled. 'Looks like them Northern bastards been wipin' their Protestant arses wit'it.' The Boss put on his Dr Crippen glasses and, with the children giving him a wide berth, he read silently, his lips moving like a moron in prayer.

He put the paper down. 'Mother a Jasus,' he said, 'I betcha that rotten gobshite Riley's afther doin' yer woman in. The dirty hoor murdered her, the gormless shitehawk,' the Boss screamed almost in delirium. 'An' she a lovely girl. Will yeh look at 'er.' The Boss, his mind full of envy and excitement, looked at the soft blonde smiling up from the paper.

'The poor young wan,' Mary said. 'God help her. It was a bad day for her meetin' that fella. I knew when I saw him gettin' so much pleasure out a watchin' that boar ridin' the sow that nuttin' good could com'v'im.'

'Don't be talkin' shite,' the Boss snapped. 'I got five bob fer that!'

May Nolan's slaying united the family. When Babs and Pam returned from work they walked into an unusually contented household. With everyone's mind on May Nolan there was no time for any rows.

'Will yeh look't dis,' the Boss said, pushing the paper towards his eldest daughters. Jack sat smugly at the table, waiting to tell everyone what the old women in the shop were saying.

'But wait,' Babs said, 'there's no mention of Billy Riley here, how d'yehz know it's Billy?'

'Pshaw!' the Boss said. 'Isn't 'e the fecker that was goin' out wit' the poor gullova woman? The one wha' tol' Jack 'ere 'e was goin'ta knife 'er.'

'Yeah,' Babs said. 'But that doesn't mane ta say it was Billy done it, now does it?' Her line of thinking took the excitement out of their speculation. Jack felt quite cheated as he tackled his boring homework. He paused and twisted his fringe. Yes, he would enjoy telling the lads at school that he'd heard Billy say he'd murder May. Even if the gardai didn't know it.

Mary read the account several times and filled in the parts that had been censored, her mind foaming with the murder. 'Poor May - God help her - may she go straight to Heaven. Poor Billy, may God be merciful to him. Sure the poor lad had a bad start in life, and him wit' the pigeons an' all. A quare lot the Rileys.'

'Shush, yehz gang a bastards,' the Boss roared. He was listening to the news, one pixie ear close to the radio.

'God fergive him anyway. If it was him,' Mary said.

'Will yeh shu'rup, yeh bloody garron,' the Boss bellowed.

Riley was in custody. He had given himself up. The Boss was delighted. 'Rotten melt, I tol' yeh he done it. The big hoor.'

News of the murder spread faster than a virus. Wild and garbled, it leapt from pub to pub, shop to shop, cottage to cottage, until everyone had their own customised version. The only thing that was certain was that Billy Riley had murdered May Nolan with a knife.

Babs, full of guilt, cried all morning at work, weeping as she typed, sobbing as she answered the phone. Mary blessed May all day, and the Boss cursed Billy Riley. Jack racked up brownie points by telling the bullies at school he had seen the knife, and even held it he lied.

Delicious speculation aside, real facts were hard to come by. Sergeant Molloy heard it firsthand, but as the Boss wasn't among the sour old copper's confidants, he had to glean information wherever he could. The trial was the only place the story would unfold fully. The village waited, all domestic dramas suspended, at least until the trial was over.

'Hang the hoor now an' save the ratepayers a lot a money,' the Boss said.

When the case came to court the whole village neglected their dinners to read about it. Like some wizened imam, the Boss snatched the *Mail* and read the reports out loud, but with annoying interpolations. '"Billy Riley was a simple man." Not that feckin' simple, he knew where to buy the right sort a knife that'd go right inta yer woman.' The Boss smiled warmly, his lips moving childishly. '"He was labourer with limited intelligence." Yeh can say that again, t'ick as shite. R'member the time the big twat kem over lookin' fer money ta take yer woman out. Jasus, but didn't I see the big hoor off.' The Boss laughed at how he had treated the fearsome killer with disdain.'

'Riley kept pigeons.'

'Yeah, an' he sent the bloody t'ings over 'ere ta be fed.'

'Will yeh shut up yer comments,' Mary snapped, 'an' read us what the paper says.'

'All right yeh bloody fat bitch wait yer turn,' the Boss said.

'She was a slut, deceivin' the poor, hard-workin' man,' Mary said.

The Boss stopped looking at the page and fixed his good eye on his wife. It looked at her, like the eye of a snake about to strike. The children stopped breathing. The Boss cracked the paper and read on.

'"When he discovered how his girl was usin' him, spendin' the money he t'ought she was savin' fer the weddin', somethin' inside him snapped." An' there's no money harder earned than from them bloody nuns,' the Boss interjected. 'Jasus, sounds like she was blowin' the gobshite's tin on udder fellas,' the Boss ejaculated.

'That was my p'int,' Mary said. 'And that poor simple man might hang fer her.'

'Ah, yeh feckin' dope,' the Boss growled. 'Yeh're always stickin' up fer them that's done wrong.' He read on. '"Th' defence lawyer maintains it was manslaughter and will be claimin' diminished responsibility." Manslaughter me arse,' the Boss said. 'I'd pull the bloody lever meself and l'ave the hoor danglin' an' kickin'.

'Yes, an' yeh'd love that job, chokin' some poor misguided fella ta death fer the fun ivvit.'

'That coulda been Babs lyin' there bleedin' ta deat',' the Boss roared and sent Mary's specatacles flying with a smack. Thrown to the floor, Mary crawled across to retrieve her spectacles as the Boss read on. Jack grabbed the baby who was teetering on his chair and looking bemused, like a flyweight who'd just received a dizzying clip from Rinty Monaghan.

'"The accused acquired a huntin' knife,' the prosecution said–"'

'An' I saw it,' Jack interrupted, leaping into a little arc of glory. 'I had it in me hand, the same knife he druv inta May.'

'Will yeh shu'rup,' Bridgid said, 'an' let us hear the rest a the story. Carry on, Da.'

The Boss looked up and an amused smile flirted with his face but declined to stay. '"He drove the Ford Consul to County Kildare and took the deceased to their favourite beauty spot."' The Boss looked up, his face stern behind his glasses, his bald head gleaming in the firelight. '"An' there,"' he said dramatically, '"yer man ran 'er t'rough ontil her blood squirted all over him."'

Babs listened, her mouth open in awe. Poor May, she must have been screaming.

'"Riley then drove to a police station and gave himself up." I d'clare ta Jasus, if any fella deserved the rope it's that bastard,' the Boss said with a huge intake of breath.

'Wor abou' yer woman?' Mary said. 'Two an' t'ree timin' the poor fella she was.'

'Ah, yeh would stick up fer the rotten evil melt, would'n yeh?' the Boss snarled, 'an' him afther slashin' that poor child ta ribbons.' In the tension of the moment it didn't take much to ignite the room and one word borrowed another until the children watched in amazement as their parents wrestled like two rowdies on the sofa, the Boss throwing hooks and straight rights into the pliable fat body of their mother who gouged, scratched, and pinched flesh for all she was worth.

'Stop that!' Babs roared, attempting to tear her father away.

He stopped immediately and, like a chastised child, went back to his chair. He was almost choking with emotion; the excitement caused by reading the murder report was unbearable. Mary resumed her seat momentarily as if nothing had happened. The Boss's muscles remained tense in case the injured party decided to exact retribution. And she did. The bulky giant almost squashed the wiry dwarf under a sudden flabby onslaught. Blows rained on the Boss who, feeling guilty about what he'd just done, was content to just ward off Mary's worst efforts to pummel and slap him. The children, their hair tangly and awry, cheered silently as the underdog gave a good account of her new independence. Her shoes off, Mary picked up the smallest infant and left the room cursing.

In bed the girls talked. 'Anudder reason ta l'ave this bloody place an' go off ta America,' Babs said. 'I wonder when I can go,' she added wistfully, "cos I can't stand much more of this.'

Pam whispered in the dark, 'Daddy's right. That coulda been me. I coulda gone out wit' a murdherer.' She sounded slightly disappointed.

'How couldja?' Bridgid asked. 'He would'n look twice arra t'ing like yeh.'

'Well,' Pam said, 'r'member that time Riley kem up ta see Daddy about lendin' money off a him?'

'Wor abou'it?' Bridgid growled.

'Well, I saw the look in his eyes that day. He liked me.'

'Sshh,' Babs said through her small window. 'Don't be talkin' such nonsense. Go'ta sleep everyone. G'night.'

Under the bedclothes Jack saw hills of gore tumbling like red hot lava towards him. He heard May's awful dying screams as she arched her back in agony as the big Sheffield knife - the one he'd seen and should have told the police about - sliced easily through her soft skin and penetrated deep into her liver and heart, cutting everything up like the stuff he saw in Mickey O'Rourke's shop. Mad Billy Riley, with his fierce temper and the great power of his big arse behind it, was sinking the knife into poor mild, two timin' May. Right up to Billy's wrist it went. Jasus, he must a been mad. In his dream, May's warm, syrupy blood tumbled down on Jack, smothering him as he slept. A solid red liverish mass filled his tiny room, in the distance he heard May's lonely screams as Billy, with lumps of ice for eyes, was killing her. He saw stray dogs lapping her blood.

It was the biggest scandal to hit Rathfarnham since McMahon, the detective, was shot. The Rileys had become famous overnight. This poor family with their corner cottage covered in creepers, the dark inside where dirt and poverty lay side by side were on everyone's slips. What made him do it? Jack questioned himself in the dark. What did it take for one person to kill another?

After the trial the Boss read the sentence and was appalled and seriously disappointed. '"Guilty but insane",' he read. *Insane*, me arse. That dope is as sane as any of us.' The Boss, his trilby pushed back, his braces red as knife slashes on his shoulders, one bare toe sticking out of a worn slipper, shook his head from side to side. 'They should a made the bastard swing. I would a pulled the rope meself.'

'Yes, yeh would, wouldn' yeh?' Mary said.

The muscles in the Boss's face twitched a warning. 'Yes, I feckin' well would a,' he said. 'It's lousy softies like yeh that lets them hoors desthroy lovely girls and get away wit'it.'

Jack thought about it in bed. Did a person have to be mad to kill someone? At times, Mary was mad enough to kill the Boss but she wasn't permanently insane; and she could be gentle too. She only hurt others when her own hurt had been pushed beyond endurance. The Boss could kill her, but he was much nearer to being insane. He killed things without a thought. Jack had seen his father killing hens, dogs, cats, pigs, turkeys, birds, small mammals, geese, and even a fox he caught invading the henhouse.

Jack remembered that very well because a fox is an unusual animal to kill - unless you're English and on a horse - and along with deer and badgers, the fox is one of the biggest wild animals in the British Isles. His father had held the fox with a piece of wire around its muzzle and while Jack was still admiring the beautiful creature, his father battered it to death with a lump of wood. Vivid memories filled Jack's mind: the fox's lovely bushy tail all smeared with hen dirt, the sharp teeth closed together in agony, the intelligent orange eyes wide open but lifeless, like the glass eyes of a teddybear. Why hadn't the Boss let it go? That must have been how poor May looked when Billy killed her. Her blue eyes glassy. It was a horrible thing to do, cut someone up like that, especially someone you loved.

'Billy Riley is neither worse nor betther than any other man,' Mary said calmly when the Boss read out that he'd been sentenced. 'Yehz're all capable a killin' a poor soul.'

Jack reading the bit of paper the Boss had reluctantly given him, was as tense as a wound spring. If his father attacked Mary again he was going to fling himself between them with a carving knife between his teeth. He was going to lift his father's gansey and whip the knife in. But, knowing Jack's luck it would probably bloody hit his wallet and snap in half, then he'd be in the shit. Up to his neck in it.

Billy Riley was sent to Grangegorman for life and Rathfarnham returned to normal. It had been exciting while it lasted. Jack often thought of poor Billy pacing his tiny cell one minute, his arms stretching out through the bars, his bloodstained fingers claiming the soft stars. There were tiny moons in the murderer's eyes. His beloved May in her cold grave, his pigeons fluttering around the chimneys, missing him. It would be a long time before he saw the sun rise over the convent. From now on he would live with mad men, raving and squealing in their striped pyjamas. If Billy wasn't mad to start with, he soon would be.

Billy Riley was special now, a legend. He was up there with Capone, Machine Gun Kelly, Dillinger, Bonnie and Clyde. He used to be nothing, but now he was a killer and people feared him because they'd thought they knew him but he turned out to be unpredictable.

Whenever Jack ran down the school lane he looked but he never saw Billy again. The big fat face resting on the log-like arms. The sly, bovine eyes following him like some murderous Mona Lisa.

86

FROM THE FIRST red cent he'd ever earned, to the last wad of pig-dunged Irish punts, the Boss put money away. It was hard-earned and sometimes dishonestly gained, but no one could deny the man had suffered for his money. So it was a shock to no one, except maybe God, when money replaced priests on the Boss's prayer list.

He made a coffin for it, a great oaken box with a man-sized, earthquake-resistant padlock. The Boss communed with his cash behind the locked bedroom door, fondling it almost sexually. Mary gathered the children into a whispering huddle around the keyhole. The wooden box lay open on oiled hinges. The concentrating figure knelt as if in prayer at Mammon's alter. Little paper bags of silver and copper were standing in rows, punt notes and fivers in elastic-banded bundles. Like a child with his favourite toys the Boss sat back on his heels, reflecting on his good fortune.

Mary, her big toes pushing through her slippers, her greasy worn apron around her fat waist, peeped again, then quietly shepherded the children before her down the narrow, brown-painted hallway and into the safety of the kitchen. 'Bad cess to th'ol' bastard,' she whispered, 'him wit' all that lovely money an' us wit' not a penny to our names. A lotta luck it'll bring him.'

Her warm arms outstretched like a tatty Madonna, Mary sighed. 'What is oul' money anyway? It on'y brings heartbreak to them that has it.' The Boss's money chest was a constant goad to her. In fits of temper she would attack it, as if it were him, beating it with a broom or whatever else was to hand. Crying bitterly after a row she would pick it up like some enraged King Kong and hurl it to the floor, but only when the Boss was out, for anyone who dared to touch the padlocked box was tired of living.

All the Boss's secrets were in that box, personal papers, letters and photos from old flames, cash and multiple bank accounts. He even had a wad of dollars. When Aunt Dolores sent money for the kids' birthdays, the Boss snatched it and slipped the small grey notes into separate bundles, one for twenties, one for tens, one for fives, one for singles.

No one knew how much the Boss was worth. It couldn't have been much but the corner boys and idlers from the labourers' cottages spent many an evening dreaming about the piles of money that must be hidden about the place. One or two of the more stupid ones even wondered if it were possible to relieve the Boss of some of it. Luckily, they never tried, for it would be safer to break into a den of a starving Bengal tigers than to breach the Boss's domain. The Boss never gave money away. For an uneducated man, he struck wickedly one-sided bargains that left the other party bewildered. He didn't believe in giving pocket-money to children. 'Who,' he would ask, 'needs money who doesn't hav'ta buy food? Is it givin' them wasters good darlin' tin t'spend on toffee and fizz bags? Bejasus, I'd rather cut me head off at the neck!'

If it wasn't for soft old Mary, her brood would never have known the pleasure of sucking a bull's-eye or dipping a lollipop into sherbet. No matter how poor she was, it was worth rooting in her large old imitation crocodile-skin handbag; there just might be a copper or two caught up in the lining. It could be her last penny but the dirty-faced urchins with outstretched hands didn't care. They'd snatch the precious coins and make a dash for Rice's. If Kitty galloped round the corner by Cullen's pub the game would be up and bottoms would hurt, tears would make tracks down grimy faces. But it was well worth the risk.

Granny Rice fumbled with her twitching hands in the furthermost corner of the window for a bar of toffee or a 'ha'pennyworth of Nancyballs.' Like an old lizard the palsied hand crept around the window, touching and picking. The children waited patiently, their mouths leaking saliva, then they rushed straight back to captivity to find a secret place to enjoy a wicked and all-too-rare treat.

Mary watched them from a window and shared vicariously their guilt and pleasure. As a girl in Galway there was always time for the good things. No one begrudged a salivating smile or a tickling of the senses. The Boss killed such moments. Was it her fault? Had she strangled the good she'd seen in him all those years ago when his hair was fluffy and smelled of soap, and his strong hand held hers and his lips, so daring and fiery, had her swooning for his love? With a sniffle Mary left the window. The Boss would soon be home and he would be tired, hungry and dangerous.

87

THE SCRUFFY KIDS, like erect little meerkats constantly on the lookout for strangers, were first to spot the massive car pull up outside. They raced into tell Mary, who nearly fainted in panic. Who could it be? A policeman? An official from the Council? A detective? Nurse Smithson? Had Babs been injured? Or killed? There were so many ruffians in the city. Maybe the Boss had died of a heart attack?

'Jasus Christ!' Mary had just peeped through a gap in the net curtains and who should be marching across the bridge in his impressive size ten, steel-tipped, built-up shoes, but that cocky little shite of a brother-in-law, Liam the 'famous' racehorse trainer. What the feck was that poisonous little dwarf doing in Rathfarnham? Gloating no doubt. Liam, a James Cagney lookalike, stepped into the sunlight, caressed the creases out of his made-to-measure suit with his soft neat hands, jerked himself up to his full five foot two, dipped his trilby over one beady eye and gave the gaudily painted bungalow a withering appraisal. Mary was still trying to compose herself when Liam, accompanied by his wife Joan, grasped the knocker and rapped on the door with impressive violence. Even in his built-up shoes he had to reach up to do it. Mary, lurking in the hallway behind the frosted glass, wiped her hands on her apron once more and tugged the door open. Smelling of aftershave and perfume Liam led the way into a hallway choked with dirty children, their faces grinning, their eyes shifting from hand to hand for presents. Liam stared as one grubby child, its torn pants bulging with excrement, waddled shyly away like the scared inmate of a small, ill-kept zoo. Joan handed Mary a large parcel. Mary was insufferably obsequious and almost curtsied as she took it.

'We're afther been ta Phoenix Park,' Liam said, his elocution lessons slipping. 'Had a nice double. Could a been a feckin' treble if that shite Powell'd folly'd me orders. How's Babs?' Liam asked. Like the Boss he loved her.

'Ah, she's great,' Mary said, shaking with nerves. 'Sure, she's at work, she's got a good job at Easthams, yeh know, in–'

'Yeah,' Liam butted into her story. 'Jasus, I heard that a t'ousand times from yer man.' He tried to relight his cigar butt with a gold lighter given to him by Sir Timothy Aymestry when his horse Petrarch won the big race in Deauville. Despite his deprived childhood, Liam was a talented trainer who'd got where he was through buying good horseflesh cheap and training it to perform to its optimum. But he could never tolerate being reminded of the part the Boss had played in his success, and wanted now to ward off the oft-repeated tale of how he'd got Liam 'the darlin' little job' that made him. According to the Boss, Liam was lucky.

'How's that bloody sod ovva brudder of mine tr'atin' yeh?'

'Ah, sure–' Mary started, but Liam wasn't looking for answers.

'Yer man never was any good. Lookit the way he treats his poor mudder. Even when he buys her a baby Power's he hasta wather it down. Take me word ferrit Mary, he's no good.'

'Well, how ar'yehz all?' Mary asked, trying to divert Liam from his favourite hate subject. 'Did yehz enjoy th'races? Did yehz have any winners? I tole yeh, we had two. Yer not listenin' woman.'

'Isn't that School for Scandal a grand horse,' Mary said trying to sound informed.

'Shows yeh what yeh know, missus. He's not wort' a bloody haport' ashit,' Uncle Liam said testily.

He finally lit his thick cigar and the kitchen was soon cloudy with its smoke. 'Havanas, them,' he said to the children, who looked at him as pygmies would a tiny but talkative king. 'Ten bob each, them is. Y'know, I must have the biggest gang a bloody gobshites for jockeys. Coulda won the feckin' Ulster Derby again this year at Down Royal. I told the eejit Cash to hold the baste back until the last furlong. What happened? The feckin' horse runs away wit'im.' Uncle Liam immediately regretted swearing; it was ungentlemanly in front of ladies, so he'd been told. But Mary was only his poor, ignorant, old sister-in-law from the arsehole of Galway. She didn't count. But there was always a chance he would revert to type when talking to one of his aristocratic owners. That would be feckin' disastrous.

'Will yehz have a bit a tea?' Mary asked. Fussing intolerably, she tried to claw off her visitors' coats.

'Oooh, just a pick of something then,' Joan said, 'we are goin' to the Royal Hotel at seven to meet the De Burcas for dinner and we mustn't sp'il, er, I mean *spoil* the oul' appetites. Well, just a pick then, seein' as yeh willin' to go to the trouble an' all.'

'No, we're not,' Liam snarled, 'we've no time for tea here. Sir Courteney's expectin' us.'

Some of the children were touring round Uncle Liam's big car.

'It's open, go inside,' he shouted to them from the open window.

The children examined the cigar lighter, the radio and the vanity mirror. All smiles, they practised waving like Queen Elizabeth. For all his faults the childen loved their Uncle Liam who brought an all too fleeting whiff of success into their stunted lives.

'Ah, come on now, Liam,' Joan said, 'sure it won't do us a bit a harm if we have a taste a tea, seein' as the poor woman is afther makin' it.'

'It's awright for yeh,' Liam said peevishly, 'yeh don't hav'ta explain tidda gentleman why we kept him waiting.' and, mimicking his wife, he added, 'Oh, we stopped on the way ta drink bloody tea with poor relations. It won't cut any ice with Sir Courteney ,' he warned. 'His skivvy'll prob'ly hav'a bloody feast laid on fer us.' His use of the word 'skivvy' was for Mary's benefit. Liam would never let his hated brother forget he'd married a servant, even though his own wife was said to share a similarly modest past. 'Besides, yeh know what them gentry is like when they meet sportin' personalities the likes a meself.'

Mary watched the toing and froing of the conversation with the dull innocence of a child watching a wasp at a window. 'A quick dhrop then,' Joan said as her husband, his neat feet on top of one another waggling nervously as he sat on the Boss's best chair and sulked, his wide-brimmed trilby still on his small head. If he had to take his hat off to the ladies and gentlemen of the turf there was no reason at all to do so for his impoverished, neurotic sister-in-law.

Mary arranged them around the table, covered for the occasion with a piece of oilcloth with fading blue flowers. On it she had laid a lemony, shop-bought cake, a pile of cut bread and egg cups. 'I'll get th'eggs,' she said, shuffling towards the kitchen. Like a child who had captured an unusually beautiful set of butterflies Mary was afraid they might escape if she took her eyes off them.

'Naw, naw,' Uncle Liam said. 'We don't want bloody eggs. Didn't yeh hear Joan say we wor goin' out? Just a bit a oul' cake'll do and we'll be off before the quare fella comes back, t'rowing his bloody weight around.

Mary stopped in her tracks. She turned timidly, her confidence draining. 'Hmm, ar'yehz sure yehz won't have an egg?'

'Sure, I'm sure. Look, sit down an' have a cup a oul' tea wit'us for Jasus' sake and we'll be on our way.'

Mary turned the gas off under the bubbling saucepan. She took her place stiffly at the edge of the table and listened, eyes downcast, as Liam told stories of the famous people he'd met, the hunt balls he'd attended, the bets he'd won. The monotony of his voice was punctuated by slurps as Mary self-consciously drank her tea.

'Well, c'mon, we got ta be makin' a move,' Uncle Liam said. 'Jasus, will yer lookit yer woman,' he sneered, pointing at his wife. 'She's as big as a Mullinger heifer and there she is, rammin' cake as big as yer leg inta her bloody gob.' Joan smiled a long-suffering smile. She hadn't much in common with Mary, but like her she was dominated by a vicious and vain husband.

Uncle Liam walked towards the door. Looking fondly at his image in the hall mirror, he carefully scattered the few hairs he had left over his large expanse of skull, tapped on his trilby and strode towards the car.

Liam proffered a gloved hand to Mary, who wiped her own on her apron before warmly shaking it. 'I s'pose yer man is goin' ta Baldoyle on Wednesda'?' Uncle Liam said. 'We'll be there but we won't have time for him. He's such a bloody embarrassment.'

Joan made a point of giving Mary a big hug, two poor country women sharing a private moment of unspoken acknowledgement.

The car breathed away leaving a dust haze behind it. Mary and the children waved until it was out of sight.

'That bloody brother of mine has a lot to ask God's forgiveness for. Did yeh see the state a yer poor woman, and did yeh get the smell a the place?' Uncle Liam said as he settled back against his plumped-up cushion to concentrate on making the big car surge through Dundrum.

Mary, covering as many of her brood as she could with her massive arms, smilingly told them there would be hard-boiled eggs for supper.

88

'SO,YER MAN was here, was he?' the Boss said, clutching his *Evening Mail* with callused, black-nailed hands, his bad eye leaking on to the page. 'T'ought I smelt his penny cigars. Pity. I'd a liked ta rub his feckin' little nose in it. I'd a told him if it wasn't fer me he'd a been lyin' in bed wit' his bloody head stainin' the wallpaper . . .'

Mary had turned off and was making the tea. Joan's present, a large box of top quality Belgian chocolates lay unwrapped, a magnificent centrepiece on the table. The children sat on their hands licking their lips.

'Cheap rubbitch,' the Boss snarled. 'Picked it up half price in Woolwort's. Them Kerry bitches know a bargain.'

The children drank and ate their modest repast, hardly able to keep their hands from ripping the lovely chocolate box to shreds. At last, each child wild-eyed and clutching a gold-wrapped chocolate as if they were nuggets of real gold, sat outside to adore, unwrap, nip, lick, suck, and eventually, as slowly as they could, eat their wonderful and unexpected treat.

Then it was back to work for Jack and his father. One of the big-bellied sows was about to farrow. Jack wiped the pigs with a wad of straw as they spewed from the grunting sow. The Boss popped his trilby'd head over the half door every few minutes to yell, 'Are they all right?' or, 'That Netsy's a toppin' sow, wisht I had more like 'er.' The Boss's dribbling, self-pitying, sewage that followed fell over Jack like an incessant shower, but he'd long ago grown indifferent to the drumming of it in his ears.

As his father rushed round the yard, his banging and clanging penetrated the maternity-ward contentment of the sty. Netsy lay on her side, her big hairy ears picking up the first sounds of her young as they slithered out of her. Like a factory worker at a conveyor belt, Jack picked the pigs up, cut their cords and wiped them in one sweet and practised movement.

Then, with a gasp of astonishment, he stopped. The animal he held in his hands, slippery and shrouded, was a freak. Its two squealing heads were demanding its mother. Quickly recovering from the shock, Jack put it on straw where, determined to find its way to its mother's belly, it wriggled and squealed loudly, its pink mouths open wide. Jack rushed out to call the Boss.

'Worisit?' the Boss's face, furious at being taken from his work, appeared.

'One's got two heads,' Jack said, attempting to disguise his fear and excitement.

The Boss, who had seen everything as far as animals went, reached over the door and growled, 'Give it here.' At that moment, more pigs began queueing to escape into the dim light of existence, so Jack went to their aid for his father had always taught him to 'get tha live ones out, worry about the dead layther'.

'Here, bring the freak out ta me when she's finished,' the Boss said, thrusting it back at Jack before his bobbing head disappeared. Jack gently placed the two-headed pig in the straw, where it wriggled silently.

When he had fifteen piglets clean and suckling, and the sow grunting softly with pleasure, Jack tried to place the two-headed pig on a spare teat but the weight of its other head caused it to roll off and dangerously under its mother. He milked the sow into his hand and tried to get the piglet to lick it with its pair of tongues, but without success.

Jack dropped the placenta into the boiler and washed his hands in the water butt. Throwing off his filthy boots he rushed to the bungalow, bursting to tell someone. The children gathered round like urchins at a handout.

'Two heads!' They giggled and screwed up their faces. What fun it would be to have two heads. 'Two mout's t'eat sweets,' little Paul said, 'or ta suck lollypops.' Paddy squealed at the thought of it.

'T'ink a all them teeth to clane,' Bridgid spoiled it all by suggesting.

After their meal was over, the Boss read his paper and Mary rode her Singer like an old hag, treadling furiously, her fat knees pumping like a Portuguese labourer stomping grapes, her hands feeding the cotton under the plunging silver needle. When the Boss had put away his paper Babs sat on the worn arm of his soft chair to talk to him. Their conversation was punctuated with little gurgles of delight from her and the occasional boom of laughter from the Boss, who held her transfixed in his adoring gaze. The children stopped what they were doing to listen in open-mouthed silence as their big sister charmed and unarmed the solid mass that sat in his chair most nights like a fizzing unexploded bomb.

Babs, her ear cocked, listened while her father recalled the lost youth he invariably returned to when he talked. She told him of the things she wanted to buy in the way of clothes, shoes and gloves for the winter. The Boss was either a fine actor or genuinely interested, for his expression was rapt, and his bald head nodded animatedly.

Mary, remembering when she was once the object of his single-minded devotion, listened and occasionally smiled at the tenderness she thought had died within him. Jack slipped away to his room, and slept with the two-headed pig on his mind. He had hidden it under some straw and the Boss seemed to have forgotten about it.

Next day, with the Boss long harnessed up and out in the dawn collecting, mending or painting something, Jack had the table to himself. When Pam appeared for breakfast, her face painted white like a Japanese actress, he told her about the two-headed pig.

'Really?' she said, instantly fascinated, as Jack had expected her to be. Pam, with her dizzy head and soft heart, loved everything weak, or crippled, anything on which she could lavish her abundant love. She still expended her gay spirit on Irish dancing, her long slender legs up there for all to see twice weekly at the Bluebird, with its cluster of sad men like barnacles covering every golden crack in the seasoned wood. This twilight but virginal world filled Pam with hope and helped her shake off the despair of her narrow stunted life in a bungalow crammed with squashed dreams.

'Yer jokin',' Pam said, 'a two-headed pig, that's a good one. Can I see it?' They left their decapitated duck eggs and rushed to the pigsty.

Making little sucking noises, Jack was recognised and welcomed by a series of excited grunts from the sow who still lay on her side like a huge glove, her piglets attached. He rooted in the straw and found the deformed piglet. It was quiet, weak from hunger and nearly dead.

'God, it's horrible,' Pam said. 'Ugh!' And she looked away.

'It's not,' Jack said. He held the pig's silvery satin skin against his cheek, the little pig responded to the heat with a subdued squeal.

'It needs feedin',' Jack said.

'I can't feed it,' Pam said. 'I don't wan'ta go near it, it's so, so . . . unnatural.'

'It's got four legs, an'a tail. OK, so it's also got two heads, so what? Everything else is all right.'

'It's . . . it's . . . it's weird,' Pam said, borrowing another of Aunt Dolores's words. She looked without enthusiasm at her brother stroking the piglet's two heads in turn.

'C'mon, I'm gonna be late for school, make up yer mind,' Jack said. 'Will yeh adopt it? 'Cos, if yeh don't it'll be dead be nightfall, an' cooking in the boiler, an' yeh'll hav'it on yer conscience.'

'All right,' Pam said, 'I'll do it.' Having made her mind up, she rushed indoors, leaving Jack talking soothingly to the little pig, whose heart was beating faster as it sensed the prospect of survival. Pam returned with a teated bottle of warm milk. She followed Jack into the sty and sat on a bale of straw. Holding the pig as if it were a baby, she jammed the teat into whichever of its mouths squealed loudest, until the bottle was empty.

'Berrer pu'it near the sow to keep warm,' Jack said, taking the animal back.

'I'll feed it again afther work,' Pam promised, 'it's nice really.' She grabbed her bike from the shed and pedalled into the traffic and to her new job in Hely's.

That evening Pam was hurrying to the shed with another bottle, when the Boss stopped her. 'Where in the name a Jasus are yeh off ta wit' that precious droppa milk?' he roared. 'Not anudder rotten hedgehog is it?'

'No, it's not,' Pam said defensively, 'it's a pig.'

'What pig?' the Boss said, his face hardening. 'The poor little two-headed one,' Pam said, putting on her Marilyn Monroe voice.

The Boss manhandled his daughter as she struggled to get past him. 'Hold yer horses, there and now,' he said, and Pam stopped.

'Jack! Jack!' he yelled. 'Will yeh come'ere, yeh bloody shyster.'

Tumbling out of the house, Jack ran to his father's side. 'Yeh dopey gobdaw, didn't I tell yeh ta ge'rid a that bonniv wit' the two heads? Now yeh've got this bloody simpleton tryin' ta feed the feckin' t'ing.'

'I was goin'ta,' Jack said, trying to think of a good excuse for having disobeyed.

'*Goin'ta*, me shite!' the Boss shouted, and he clipped Jack's ear. 'Bring that pig out here.'

Innocently still believing her brother was fetching the pig for her to feed Pam, smiled and waited, keeping the bottle warm under her jumper.

The Boss grabbed the pig off his son and, instead of handing it to Pam whose hands were stretched out to receive it, he walked briskly to the tool shed and took a two-pound hammer off a shelf. The pig screamed bitterly at being held upside-down by one leg, and Pam's hand shot up in fear to her face.

'You!' The Boss nodded belligerently at Jack, whose face had taken on a stubborn look. 'Hould on ta this fella,' he said, stretching the squealing piglet out on a patch of cement.

Pam screamed. 'Daddy, oh please, Daddy, what are yeh goin'ta do?'

'Ge'rup tidda house, an' mind yer own business,' the Boss roared. 'Com'ere an' ge'ra grip on the feckin' animal.'

'No, I won't!' Jack cried. 'Yeh've got no right ta kill–' Suddenly his face was stung by a powerful slap.

'Piss off, then, yeh feckin' weaklin',' the Boss roared, and his face was set as he raised and brought down the hammer with a slushy thump on one of the piglet's heads, and as the terrified animal, blinded with blood and pain, tried to gnaw at the hand that held it the Boss let out a roar, and split its other head into fragments.

All the while, Pam screamed dementedly in spite of Jack's feeble attempts to comfort her. 'Oh Daddy, Daddy!' She moaned. 'Why did yeh do that?'

'I'll show yeh if yeh don't shu'rup,' the Boss said, holding the dripping carcass. Pam continued to cry, clutching the warm bottle under her jumper, while Jack silently kicked the sty door in frustration.

'Ge'rout a 'ere, yeh feckin' cow, or I'll smash yer feckin' face in,' the Boss roared at Mary when she came out of the house to remonstrate. In the breezy dusk they hurled curses back and forth, their wild oaths sailing over the stream to where Jack Perkins was nodding his head and tutting.

'Yer mad, yer mad!' Mary screamed, and the Boss retaliated by hitting her across the head with the dead pig.

'It's yeh that's mad!' he yelled. 'Yeh're a bloody nutcase.' And they stared at one another, growling, Mary with the two-headed piglet's blood on her face and cardigan, while Pam sobbed, her face streaming with mascara.

Mary stood motionless, her hair wild and grey, her cheek stained red. Her expression could have been that of a dead woman, her blue eyes lifeless, her hands hanging limply. The Boss had won. He had at last knocked the life out of her. Not even Pam's sobbing could hurt her any more. Jack watched his mother and noted how the Boss had finally accomplished something that births, poverty, pain, cold, and hard work had all failed to do. His father had crushed Mary's soul, destroyed her humanity, reduced her to an ageing, podgy statue with no thoughts, no mind, with nothing but a lifeless clockwork obedience.

Mary stood there for some time after the Boss had gone to the smoking boiler, lifted the lid and dropped the dead piglet into the bubbling water with a splash. The battered piglet sank, one weary eye disappearing under the rotten apples and cabbage leaves. Then, slowly, without looking at either of her children, Mary walked back to the house and resumed her endless chores like an automaton. Suddenly, and without warning she seemed to have lost contact with reality. Her children, those smiling, crying, naked little animals she had dropped into the world like a sow, were now only blurred noises to her in the kitchen. They had to manage as best they could until Babs returned from work.

For Mary, the seasons had become dark. She worried about the light; was there enough of it to hang out her washing on the four lines strung from apple tree to fence post to spikes in the crooked concrete-block wall? Dripping washing had worn furrows in dark soil leavened by bits of old wooden pegs which Mary had made herself or bought from the tinkers who, with blazing eyes, came to the doorstep to cajole and threaten her. Mary, from superstitious Galway, always fell for their 'Buy from me missus, an' God'll bless yeh.' The way the tinkers crossed her palm with silver sixpences, their bright eyes on her all the time, frightened Mary, and she never bought less than two dozen pegs.

Often, when she counted the pegs she discovered that a gypsy dozen meant ten. She had trusted the burning-eyed tinkers and feared their fiery blessings, but they were cheating her. 'They shouldn' a taken advantage,' she'd say, going back to sewing new collars on to the Boss's good shirts.

Before her life had worn her down, Mary had been a worker, babies always underfoot, running between her legs, mewling for milk from bitten teats or plastic soothers. There was always work to do, wood to chop, windows to clean, steaming mountains of washing-up, meals to cook. Mary was exhausted in mind and body, but now she seemed to care especially about the seasons. Sun on the roof, frost on the grass, the sheen on the back of a magpie, mushrooms glowing in emerald cow pastures. She became obsessed by them all.

89

BABS CAME IN from work one day and sat by her brother. 'Hey, Jack, how about me takin' yeh tidda Classic on Sat'day? They're showin' the *Creature from the Black Lagoon*, an' a t'ing called the *Monster Maggot from Outer Space*.'

Jack's eyes widened. Was she serious?

Saturday seemed to take a month to come round. Jack washed his feet and combed his hair and put on his best gansey, the Fair Isle one with just the four holes in. He caught his sister's hand as they walked down to Cullen's and caught the number 65 bus at the Bloomfield Laundry.

It was a cold blowy day as they huddled by the stop. Some of Babs friends came up to talk in monosyllables, their voices muffled by scarves and big collars. Jack peered at them from his hiding place under Bab's arm. People looked so plain and lumpy in the cold. His nose ran in two silvery streams, but he couldn't be bothered to take a hand out of his pocket to wipe it.

They queued in a boisterous crocodile that yelled, sucked sweets, ate chips from greasy bags and and smoked butts. The wiseacres were acting big and cursing. Babs winced even though she had heard far worse every day at home.

The cinema was glowing with exit signs everywhere. White-coated teenagers marched around selling nuts and ice-creams. Despite the cold weather there was still a pinching, fecking-about knot waiting to be served. Babs had made sure to buy a mixed quarter pound of sweets at Rice's before they'd got on the bus. Jack had lost a lot of saliva thinking about them, and with his running nose too he looked as if he was dissolving.

The Pearl & Dean banner unfurled and the big noisy adverts for washing machines and the new curry houses were run. The trailers said Errol Flynn was coming soon in some film. Jack sucked his first sweet and snuggled down in his seat because who was behind him but Foley, the Creature from the Corporation Houses. Luckily, the big blond bastard was too busy acting the shite as usual to notice his favourite plaything, the Woolly-capped Snot-nosed Creature from the Pigsty on Mars.

The support film was horrific, with maggots mutating in a California laboratory, flopping out of its windows, getting into sewers and wriggling in toilet bowls. Jack lost so much of his bodily fluids, and even a small portion of solids watching it, he needed to keep eating the sweets. Babs ended up giving him the bag to keep his hands from pestering her.

The *Creature from the Black Lagoon* was good too but the joins in its PVC costume were obvious even to Jack. Still, it was an inspired double bill and Jack's mind was filled with enough stuff to keep his nightmares interesting for months.

At home, the bungalow seemed horribly normal and deathly quiet after the *Black Lagoon*. The Boss sat like a wooden man, his presence gloomy, while Mary talked quietly to her brood which could now fill a good sized classroom.

Once in bed, Bridgid wanted to know everything about the films and Jack chipped in, talking and swearing as poor Babs tried to recall both the plots. The girls finally fell asleep but Jack stayed awake imagining his pillow was a large maggot.

Soon, there were more serious matters to consider. Jack would be off to the Boys National School, segregated from girls, caged with lads from the Council houses, undisciplined boys bent on flexing their muscles. Babs gave Jack a new pencil case filled with brass drawing tools with pointy ends that he didn't know what to do with. Bridgid, standing four square, her hands on her cotton-clad hips, said, 'Now yeh'll haveta stop wipin' yer nose on yer sleeve or them big lads'll do yeh in.' She, too, was preparing to escape childhood. The Boss would soon be expecting his children to start earning a living. Children were not asked if they wanted to be born but, by God, they had to pay for the privilege.

'Jasus, Mary an' Holy St Joseph!' Mary yelled, scattering children as she staggered to her feet. 'It's Eileen. What in the Mothera God is she doin' here?' She just had time to remove her apron and dab her hair before the pugnacious face of her friend, her poor eye crazily ogling the light bulb, the cheeks blue from drink and poor circulation, banged into the hallway.

Eileen gave her sad friend a sergeant major's eyebrow-raised once-over. 'Sure, yeh're not lookin' bad for an oul' cow two years older than meself,' she said. 'Get the feckin' tay on, yeh lazy hoor.' And with that she catapulted herself into Mary's outstretched arms and they both shed tears.

'It's grand ta see yeh're still alive, yeh feckin' oul' bitch,' Eileen said with her hands on Mary's shoulders.

'It's good ta see yeh, too,' Mary stammered, shyly catching at the sides of her dress.

'How's th'ol' pervert?' Eileen rasped, and waited with her mouth open for Mary's noncommittal reply.

'Ah sure, yer always stickin' up fer the fecker instead a cuttin' the tool off a him an' jabbin' it up his feckin' Jackeen's arse,' Eileen said.

Mary cackled loudly and clutched at her friend. 'Ah, yeh shouldn' be sayin' that in front a the kids,' she said, and the children, all smiling, put their fingers to their mouths and hunched their shoulders, sniggering until their chins disappeared.

'Ah don't be talkin' daft,' Eileen said, 'them childer is shrunk be yer man, lookit them, poor little bastards, creepy-crawly wit' fear.'

'Ah, it's not that bad,' Mary said, leaping to her children's defence. 'An' they're not bastards neither, nunna them.'

'Well, I'll tell yeh this much,' Eileen said, wagging a thick finger in Mary's face, 'if baldy as much as lays a hand on them, off yeh go ta call the gardai, niver mind the feckin' oul' priests.'

'Jasus!' Mary said, alarmed. 'Will yeh stop talkin' like that, yeh'll go ta Hell fer it, so yeh will.'

'Hell, me hole,' Eileen said. 'An' where's this drop a tay? Me guts t'inks me windpipe's severed.'

'It's ready, Aunty Eileen,' Bridgid said. She waved the visitor through royally, and with an exaggerated flourish pulled out a chair for her to sit down.

'An' bejasus, yer woman's comin' along,' Eileen said. 'It's not a year ago she was a right little oul' slob wit' nuttin' but insults fer me, now she's tratin' me like a lady.' Eileen kissed Bridgid's cheek. Mary assembled all the plates of food around her friend as if she were in danger of dying of hunger. 'An' how's that snotty little shite, Jack?' Eileen asked, catching the boy with her piercing eye. 'Doesn't he look the image of yeh, wit' his long nose an' black hair. Is he a cowardy custard, too, like yerself?'

Jack gave his mother's friend a hate-filled glance. Any person who used her crazy language didn't deserve respect. He quietly sneaked out and away before Eileen's unpredictable tongue could get even more out of control.

No one noticed the Boss creep into the kitchen, so engaged were they with Eileen's fierce banter. Breathing easily, he watched them through the window. Satisfied no one was talking about him, he entered the room whistling and made straight for Eileen. 'Well, there now,' he said, 'aren't yeh lookin' grand as usual, sure it mus'bey all me food yer afther atin'.'

Eileen winked at Mary and said, 'Is it all the hand jobs that's makin' yeh lose yer last bit a hair, or what?'

The Boss's false *bonhomie* was wiped clean off his face. 'Ah, I'd be leavin' them dirthy t'ings ta the likes a yerself,' he said, 'an' the crowd a mongrels that bred yeh,' he added coldly. After grabbing a sandwich and pouring a mug of tea, he went outside to sit fuming on a log, watching the house with a look of such one-eyed malevolence it almost had the power to burn it down and destroy all inside it.

'God fergive yeh,' Mary said. 'What on eart' made yeh say that t'him? What are yeh tryin' ta do ta me? Get me killt? It's bad enough as it is.'

'Listen,' Eileen said, her wall-eye staring at the ceiling, 'yeh've been a bloody mat fer too long, how can yeh just sit there like a hape a shite an' take it? Well, fuck him, I say, who does he t'ink he is? If I am goin' ta come ta see yeh I don't expect him ta fling insults at me. I'll jus' fling them back wit' a double dose a interest.' Eileen chewed belligerently, watching Mary's hang-dog look. Then she elbowed her friend, caught her glance, and Mary couldn't keep a straight face at the ludicrous eyes of her friend, one out of alignment, the other glinting with wickedness. Soon everyone in the room was tittering, and the children, fused by the power of Eileen's stubborn and dislocated gaze, laughed.

Outside, the Boss chucked his dregs away and cursed. Leaving the mug on the windowsill, he went back to the pigs.

'How's 'bout yeh an' me havin' a bit of an oul' holiday back home in Galway?' Eileen said as she crammed her mouth with another cup cake. 'Jus' imagine it, the two of us t'rowin' off the dust a dirthy Dublin an' raisin' our skirts, doin' an oul' jig fer the lads from the west, an' them holdin' on to their cocks in case they kem in their britches.'

'Jasus, Eileen,' Mary said, shocked. 'That's disgraceful language that is.'

Eileen blinked, her mouth slack. 'Ah, they'll know soon enough, so they will,' she said. 'I betcha that Bridgid one there knows what she's got in her knickers. An' that little sleeveen Jack. Sure, them sneaky ones is always the worst. Jaysus, sure that fella knows it's not fer stirrin' his tea wit' anyway.' Eileen lit a cigarette.

Mary, who was already in shock at her friend's vulgarity, gasped. 'God, yeh're not goin' ta smoke that cigarette, are yeh?'

'Well, what d'yeh t'ink I'm goin' ta do wit' it, stick it up me arse?' Eileen let out a rude cackle. Mary drew breath. 'Don't smoke, please,' she pleaded.

'An' why not?' Eileen asked, her bad eye blood-flecked and wild. 'Listen, if I want a fag I'll feckin' well have a fag, an' fer yer information, no Dublin Jackeen is goin' ta tell me udderwise.' With that, she lit up and blew a rose of smoke in Mary's direction.

Feeling almost giddy, Mary laughed. 'Will yeh have another cup? I'll put the kettle on.'

'I will if yeh stick a drop a the baldy hoor's Power's innit,' Eileen said.

'Oh, my God, I couldn't do that,' Mary said, laughing like a horrified child.

'Well,' Eileen said with comic seriousness, 'if yeh tell me where the mane bastard keeps the quare stuff I'll help meself.'

Mary half nodded towards the big press in the corner where the Boss kept all his little treats, tins of capers, stuffed olives, his bottles of Power's. And she laughed as Eileen got up and began to tear at the press doors. It was the high-pitched cackle of a person about to be hanged. But Eileen had the bottle and she was pouring a fiery helping into both cups.

'Merciful Jasus, if he was ta walk in here now we'd be slaughtered,' Mary said.

'Not while I'm here,' Eileen said and she took a good slug from the whiskey bottle and smacked her lips. 'That's more like it,' she said. 'Slàinte.'

Mary knocked hers back in a couple of gulps and wiped her mouth. 'Jasus, I'll be killed fer that,' she said, feeling indestructible in Eileen's presence. Eileen was such a powerhouse, a bulwark, big-built, with hands on her like bear paws and a temper like a tiger. In a fight to the death only a fool would not put money on her.

'He's often very nice ta me,' Mary slurred guiltily, her hands wrestling on her big lap, a faraway look in her eyes.

'Who is? Yer man Bluebeard?' Eileen said incredulously. 'On'y when he's afther somethin'. If I was yeh I'd keep the ould half dollar under wraps or yeh'll be havin' another little yella bastard to add to yer collection.'

'None of me childer is bastards,' Mary said defiantly.

Eileen tapped the ash of her cigarette on the edge of her chair and snorted.

As the Boss fumed in the garden, sometimes talking to himself, sometimes whistling distractedly, Eileen sat with her old friend until the ashtray was full and the sink crowded with plates and whiskey-scented teacups. Eileen had made Mary human again, made her feel as if she deserved to be alive, made her feel worth something after years of being told she was worthless. By the time Eileen had mounted her bike and ridden off with her big naked knees touching the bars as she tore down the hill, wobbling and waving, Mary was mentally and physically restored. Bemused and fortified with Dutch courage, she was almost hoping the Boss would step out of line. She would gut the bastard. When he came into the kitchen that evening his antennae warned him to tread carefully. Thanks to the holy power of drink the atmosphere remained tranquil, surreal even, with the Boss watching his wife in a strange and, bizarrely, almost fearful way.

90

JACK WAS NOT sorry to be leaving the convent. The nuns lined up in order of seniority for the prize-giving. Miss O'Halloran, thin and spiky as mountain gorse, shook each small hand and grinned falsely, her lipstick a red slash across her chalklike face. Jack shuffled along the line and with tears of embarrassment accepted a secondhand fire brigade vehicle given to the school by the good ladies of the village. He retreated behind Foley's broad back. How Jack envied the hard blond kid his confidence as Foley snatched his gift and roughly shook the hand that had fruitlessly meted out so much pain to him. The school bully winked cheekily at Jack as he elbowed his way back to his seat.

Jack had few good memories of this place but he would always fondly remember the First Communion breakfast at the school, when all the kids were shiny little saints for one morning. The tiny girls in wedding-white veils of purity, the boys, their scrubbed knees naked in short-legged suits that had cost their parents food and the pub an extra few rounds of drinks. Fresh pure faces, pink and smiling, greedily attacked a fine breakfast served by quiet novice nuns who shuffled along in their flat shoes and long veils. Big brown eggs from the convent's Rhode Island hens were eaten with little egg spoons with saintly figures embossed on the handles. Then there was the Corpus Christi procession, incense mingled with the scent of sun-warmed hay. The winding train of altar boys and nuns, the haunting singing of the priests. The breeze rattling the dark green laurel leaves in the convent garden.

Jack had been swept away by the magic, touchingly believing in the perfumed drama. And there were glimpses of the big open-roofed pig pens at the bottom of the convent lane where fat, pampered sows, flat in the straw, wallowed, grunting greetings to their pink-crubeened babies, while Billy Conlon, as midwife, fluttered around plugging them on to a vacant rosy tit. The smell of the farm, dung and urine was strong and would be eternally evocative. Jack would also remember for ever the handsome stand of broad-leafed trees with clusters of daffodils surrounding their trunks in spring, a fitting avenue to the boarding section of the school, an avenue into which he could only wander in his dreams.

He would never forget his classroom, the earnest scribbling on scarred desks, prayers spiralling up to Heaven. Nuns with their cowls askew, bald heads trying to be saintly and at the same time beat education into poor kids whose destiny would be to die in the brick catacombs of England. Lost, scattered and forgotten, while the well-to-do would prosper and remain in touch with their teachers through another grateful generation. The children were taught that there was but one incorruptible God who would watch over them always. Jack knew different.

He gripped his tin toy and nervously found his seat. Foley sitting opposite solemnly made wanking signs. In a few minutes the whole class would leave for ever. The great convent would remain on the horizon of Rathfarnham like Colditz, a granite memorial to State Catholicism. Its massive green bell would boom for a little longer, frightening shy country kids whose horizons were as confined as those of their parents; at least, until the punt-shagging heathens moved in with their cheque books and their bulldozers.

Pale Sister Anthony, her virtue tangible, read a prayer and asked the children to sing. After their thin, flat voices echoed for the last time in the high rafters and across the quadrangle, the squealing multi-coloured mass of children spilled on to the road. The little girls would stay on until their Primary Certificate, but after the summer holidays the boys would have to brace themselves for the Boys' National School in Rathfarnham.

After four years, during which he had suffered so much and learned so little, Jack broke into his crabby trot for the last time. As he sped past the school farmyard with its neat pile of sweet smelling manure, and the sound of animals being treated kindly in the sound brick- and wood-built barns, he saw the ghost of poor Billy Riley, the summers long lost to him. The big farm labourer's ghost shouted, 'Good luck, Jack,' and grinned, his eyes swivelling insanely like some fairground laughing policeman.

Jack looked back to catch one more glimpse of the school, then ran as fast as he could away from it for the last time.

Foley ambushed him at the corner. 'How're yeh, snotty,' the blond sadist sneered. 'So, yeh're leavin', eh? Can't wait t'get cha be the balls at the National.'

'Yeh an' what army, yeh big t'ick shite,' Jack heard himself saying, and ran off like a madman, terrified that Foley's arms would reach out like Rubberman and haul him back for a good kicking.

91

JACK LAY IN bed listening to the sounds of summer. The hens celebrating an egg, the cats scrapping over the flyblown remains of a dead bird, the pigs snorting in the mucky bath they made in the garden. Mary shuffled heavily into the room followed by a procession of pattering children. She drew the scrap of curtain and looked into the yard, letting a huge golden slice of sun into the room. 'I'm goin'ta leave this bloody kip one a these days,' she said miserably. Shit, Jack thought, the reality of the school holidays meant seeing his mother all day, every day. 'I'm tellin' yeh. Yehz'll all come home an' find me gone. So yehz will.' Jack hid under the blankets. 'But I love yehz all too much. I'd die without yehz all around me.' Jasus, summer was going to be long. She sat down on the bed which groaned and sank under her weight.

'Listen son,' she said. 'How wouldja like ta go ta Galway fer a holiday? Eileen can arrange it fer me.'

'Yes, please,' said Jack, fully awake, his eyes shining. Imagine. Getting away from the Boss, the bungalow, Kitty, the aroma of pig shite. Swapping Rathfarnham for the wild west where men slept with their daughters and ate their illegitimate offspring with spuds. The Boss had so colourfully and so often condemned Galway, Jack wanted to go there. 'Wha'bout Daddy?'

'Ach, he'll prob'ly be glad ta see the back a yeh. It'll be one less ta feed. I wisht I could go wit'yeh.' Jack made a face under the covers. 'Bur I can't l'ave the childer wit' that maniac. He'd on'y kill 'em all wit' an axe.'

Jack smiled.

Mary pulled back the covers. She looked at her son and her tone softened. 'Yeh're not doin' an'tin' in there are yeh? Ge'rup darlin' an' I'll fry yeh an oul' egg or two. Jack waited until his mother left the room before he threw some water on his face and got dressed.

Jack was scooping out the contents of a second egg when the Boss rushed into the kitchen, looked at the brace of eggshells but surprisingly made no comment. Instead, he leaned on the table, his good eye fixed on his son.

'Listen,' he growled, 'I'm takin' a few pigs ta da market, I need a han'.'

'Right,' Jack said. Sure, that'd be grand and he jumped from the table and rushed to the toilet. He passed a leisurely motion reading a damp *Evening Mail* that lay like blotting paper under his feet. He pulled the chain then raced to the window to watch his tumbling turd hit the river and flow down to the Jesuits. Nice present for the men in black. He washed his hands with carbolic soap and joined his father in the yard to load the pigs.

The Boss shook the reins. 'Ge'rup there, Kitty. Yer woman tells me yeh wan'ta waste yer time visitin' them ignorant bastards in the arsehole a Galway,' the Boss said. 'Yes, please,' Jack said, looking at his father's jutting chin as he whipped the pony into a steady trot. 'Well, yeh'd be a bloody fool t'go,' the Boss said. 'Butcha'll find out fer yehrself what rotten hoors yer mother comes from.'

Jack said nothing. He was going and that was the size of it.

Jack mused in tune with the pony's trotting. What a summer it was going to be. The great river Shannon he'd only read about in school books. The culchies. What were they really like on their own turf? In Dublin they were either gardai or priests. Control-freakery seemed to be a culchie craving. Mammy was from Galway and she was OK. Yes, he was really looking forward to the adventure. The bus trip alone was the equivalent of a trek across Siberia. Jack looked down at the pigs squashed into the creel in the back of the cart. They were going to their death and seemed bloody cross about it. Jack, his fringe blowing in the breeze, imagined Galway again. It had to be a damn sight better than where the pigs were going. Poor bastards.

The Dublin livestock market was full of violence, noise and dirt. Jack loved the barbaric colour and buzzing excitement of it. Lorries decorated with soggy straw and dripping urine, stood in patient lines waiting to unload their gasping cargoes. Sheep, pigs and cows lay in their own excrement, and peered with resigned eyes through slats as if pleading for the humans to hurry up and deliver their fate. Jack wandered among the hens, turkeys and geese, the trays of brown eggs, the crates of home-made jam, marvelling at the variety, the bargaining, the smell of shit, beer and myriads of different pisses.

He saw brutish men jab their fingers into the eyes of pigs and laugh as they popped out like the yolk of an egg. He watched the blind and terrified animals beaten, goaded, slashed with knives and prodded into pens. It wasn't the bloody animals' fault that they had no souls. Full of obscene humour, the men wiped their dirty hands and their blood-stained penknives on their brown overalls and lit Woodbines.

The Boss waited with histrionic impatience to be unloaded. It was not a day for doing things quickly. Every few minutes he marched up to the office in his big wellingtons to demand attention. An old bewhiskered clerk gave him a tired look and dragged hungrily on a cigarette. 'Yeh'll hav'ta wait like the rest a them,' he said. 'Some a the culchies've been here since seven dis mornin' and they're not complainin'.'

The Boss tapped his wellingtons with a stick and cast his pale eyes around. 'Hey up there!' He'd spotted someone he knew and went over for a chat.

Jack saw veal calves, pale and wobbly, bemused and shivering, being dragged in by bullying porters who screwed their tails up as if they were arresting them. After much nodding and twitching, bids were received and bettered. The calves, as frail as day-old chicks, were hurried away in vans with darkened windows for summary execution. By sundown they'd be on the menu at the top hotels. A huge bull was led in by a weedy man in a dirty suit. It exuded power and muscular beauty, its great wide feet supporting an acre of back. Its eyes rolled and its ringed nose twitched. Jack speculated on what would happen if it decided to go mad. But with brainless disinterest the lugubrious beast was knocked down to a human not half so impressive and towed away like a broken-down truck.

The Boss's six fat pigs went for a good price. The Boss gave Kitty her hay net and a bucket of water. Smiling thinly he said, 'We may as well have the bit a grub.' The bar was full of raucous men. Remembering his last encounter with drink, the Boss looked uneasy. Smoke hung in clouds above the bar. Five barmen briskly lined up pints for thirsty queues of intimidatingly jolly men. The Boss elbowed his way to the counter and ordered two lemonades and several rounds of ham sandwiches. Crooked men pushed forward in soiled gabardines belted with string. They looked at the Boss, obviously wondering whether to nail his arse to the floor for ordering such homosexual fare. Father and son battled to get outside. The Boss upturned a dustbin and they ate heartily off it. With the Boss supplying celebratory mints, Jack drove Kitty back to Rathfarnham without mishap.

Moving slowly, Mary prepared a nourishing dinner out of a pig's cheek the Boss had bought for a few pence in the market. She boiled it with onions and turnips and served it with potatoes in their skins and a half head of green cabbage. Babs came home and gave Jack a freshly printed Eagle. He wanted to kiss her but didn't know how to. He made space for himself on the table, and frantically twisting his fringe he savoured every syllable.

After dinner he grabbed the little cardboard case Babs had procured for him and went to his room to pack. His collection of old comics went in first, followed by a mean selection of holiday clothes. Bermuda shorts from the good old US of A cut down into a very nasty looking shirt, green socks, and a jumper with a golden vintage car emblazoned across the front of it from the same source.

The Boss sat quietly, the firm grip he'd always kept on his family weakening all the time. One by one, they were rebelling. To his immense displeasure, Babs was showing the way with her loose talk about going to America.

The Boss thought about the insurgence within the bungalow's four walls and felt the need to comment on its inexorable progress. 'What does yer man be wantin' a holiday fer, anyway?' he started quietly, before racheting up the tension menacingly. 'There's me workin' me fingers to the bone an' yeh sendin' that lazy sleeveen tidda counthry. What can he learn that's any good there? Isn't the whole place seethin' wit' filt' an' corruption? Them feckin' brothers a yers'll on'y be afther puttin' dirthy t'oughts in his bloody empty head. He'll come back not wantin' to work at all.' The Boss flicked open his paper again but the words swam in front of his one good eye. He felt defeated.

'Whatever yeh say about my family, at least they're all honest an' God-fearin'', Mary said. 'Unlike some I could name.'

The children's eyes widened. Jasus God here it comes, World War Three. But unbelievably, instead of leaping from his chair to attack Mary, like an enraged ferret sinking its fangs into a blackbird's breast, the Boss focussed uneasily on the *Mail*. After a brief reread of the headlines he went meekly to bed. Snores echoed down the hallway. Mary looked at the children and they giggled like idiots. It was a peaceful night.

92

TRAFFIC NOISES AND the stench of exhaust fumes mingled with the queasy belching of cafés as Jack hurried towards Store Street bus station. He carried the small case in a sweating hand. Behind a low wall the Liffey flowed turgidly, its green depths so dull and menacing they forced him to pause and look into the awesome river. He watched an old beer crate tumbling past in the swirling current before hurrying towards the glass bus station which glinted like a birdcage in the sun.

Gripping his ticket Jack sheltered in the remotest corner of the blustery station, observing the other passengers and trying to tune in to their impenetrable brogue. Some carried brown parcels, some wore new shoes. An old lady with watery eyes nodded pleasantly. Jack avoided her liquid gaze.

A mud-spattered country bus pulled in with a flourish and the driver disembarked and punched the conductor playfully in the balls. 'How's she cuttin'?'

A black-haired country lad with burning cheeks guffawed as he stooped in mock pain. 'Arra, like a plough in a field,' he gasped.

Laughing, they walked to a room marked STAFF to drink tea and pick losers at the afternoon race meeting at Phoenix Park. Maybe they'd pick Uncle Liam's horse. Jack tried to make himself smaller. A crowd gathered. Most had rough outdoor faces and ears like kayak paddles. Cheeky Dublin kids, escaping from a nearby slum, came in to beg. 'Mey mudder's sick, God Bless yeh, sir.' The country yokels daren't refuse; Dublin urchins had reinforcements. One kid disappeared into the staff room and reappeared, running, with a boot swinging near his skinny haunches.

The bus crew strode as proudly as fighter pilots across the station forecourt. The driver swung jauntily into the cab, fitted himself into the big seat, pulled a squashed *Irish Press* from his back pocket, and glanced swiftly at the front page. The conductor checked his ticket machine and collected the fares. The driver pressed the starter. A ball of diesel smoke floated along the station floor and into the yawning faces of waiting passengers.

Gears crunched. Jack glimpsed the green-domed Four Courts whirl past like a great big spinning top as the bus nosed into the traffic and headed for Lucan. He leant forward in his seat, his eyes photographing every scene. Clumps of cottages and pubs whizzed madly by. The man next to him wanted to talk, but couldn't kick-start his brain. Instead, he held a weird conversation with himself.

Passengers, full to the gills with Guinness, dozed. Wind clawed against the windows as the bus battled through Kildare. The countryside was flatter, bleaker. Wind-scrubbed folk, as robust as Russians, talked loudly of pigs and hurling.

The driver negotiated the narrow roads and tiny bridges with enviable skill, swinging the big bus neatly round corners, its heavy engine throbbing. Jack wondered about his mother's relatives. Would they take to him, a despised Dublin Jackeen. Or would they eat him?

He remembered the Boss's parting shot: 'Yeh'll come home wit' nutttin', them melts'd lift the eyes out a yer head.' Haycocks flew by, flocks of birds crowded the sky, cows padded indian-file across muddy roads to filthy milking parlours. Jack watched the thin collies work, fawning on their bellies, driving the lumpy oxen. He saw hens pecking, second-hand cars outside lit-up sheds. Dazzled and intrigued, he stayed awake clutching his case all the way to Galway.

Passengers disembarked. One or two, still K.O'd by drink, had to be shaken by the conductor. Even in sleep, their hard hands, tenaciously gripped their brown parcels.

Jack stood in a street like Dodge City, waiting to be claimed. An empty Sweet Afton pack rolled past and a donkey crapped in the dust. It was a Hollywood cardboard town with dung-splashed walls and paint peeling from everything. A forlorn pub had its big window sandblasted with the words Power's Whiskey. A Ford van trundled by, leaving behind the silence. Jack fully expected Audie Murphy to step out into the sun with his black hat over his eyes and walk on his shiny built up boots to where Lee Van Cleef with his sour eyes, was occupying the pub corner, a Colt 45 in both hands. As the two cowboys were squaring up, one said, 'Hello dere, now.'

Jack jumped. A large man with elephantine ears and a smiling red face climbed off an orange cart drawn by an ass which pointed its furry ears towards Jack. 'I'm Shay, yer mudder's brudder. Yeh mus'bey Mary's lad.'

Quick thinking, Jack thought and he shook hands with the man, then joined him on the cart. With something uttered in Irish the donkey broke into a trot. They drove in total silence. The countryside was bleak and neglected with tall, irregular hedges, broken barbed-wire fences and caved-in cottages.

Occasionally, Shay looked as if he was going to speak. He would draw breath, grunt, raise his cap and scratch his head. The donkey's unshod feet tapped on the dirt road as the winding lanes took them over high ground past bent blackthorns.

'How's all in Dublin?' Shay suddenly spluttered, his eyes firmly on the donkey's arse.

'They're all right t'anks,' Jack mustered.

'Grand,' Shay said.

Jack wanted to say, 'Mammy sends her regards but he couldn't.

At the end of a maze of dung-spattered, pot-holed, nettle-fringed lanes lay Gownagh with its church and pub, where men gathered to recycle stunted lives and where life trickled at a Biblical pace. When the sun fell, Gownagh disappeared.

'We're nearly there,' Shay said. Sniffing his oats, the donkey galloped down a brown scar of a lane to a mud-splashed, four-square cottage in a dip. Jack's heartbeat accelerated . 'Dat's our farm aforenint yeh,' Shay said. He pointed to a tangle of trees and bushes. The cottage was squat and bland looking. Jack hoped for a thatched roof and a rope of smoke and an old man in a rocking chair, with moustaches a yard wide and a loaded Winchester by his side.

A knot of sun-tanned people came out, all talking briskly in a foreign tongue. A tall woman with wicked eyes and flared, snuff-tinted nostrils offered a withered hand. 'Well, how are yeh, Dublin boyo?' she asked venomously. 'Has that blasted father a yers murdhered me poor daughther yit? Not much to say fer yerself, have yeh? Unusual fer a rotten Dubliner. C'mon inside. I expect you dhrink tay anyway.'

Surprisingly, under tube lighting, Jack was introduced to a parade of shuffling people who nodded and fled. 'Well, young man,' his granny asked, looking more human without her grey shawl, 'what will yeh ate atall? Bein' from Dublin yeh'll be fussy no doubt. Well, we have no time fer that here. Yeh'll ate what yeh get or starve. I'll get Ita ta make yeh a sandwich.' The old woman turned and snapped, 'If yeh don't like the way we do t'ings here yeh can hop back inta the cart and Shay'll take yeh right back ta the bus stop.' Jack wondered why everyone hated him. 'Tomorra we'll be havin' the Seannachie over here. Do yeh know what a Seannachie is?'

Jack looked vaguely at the tall old woman and drew nervously on his snot.

'Och! Of course yeh wouldn't, yeh bloody Dublin Jackeen.' The old woman laughed at her cruelty. 'He's a storyteller. Yeh don't have them above in Dublin, but then Jackeens are born storytellers anyway? Bullshitters in udder words. Aren't they now?'

Jack tried a smile.

'The Seannachie also kills our pig. That's mainly why he's comin',' Granny said. 'Yeh'll meet him layther.' She rushed about in her long black skirt, with her silver hair tied in a severe bun. With her mustard-coloured skin, whiskery chin and prominent teeth, all she needed was a broom and she'd be away over the rooftops.

Jack was shown to a dark room with a holy water font, a picture of Jesus, and a brass bed. He unpacked his few things and sat on the bed for a while, postponing his return downstairs. The fields outside the window were dotted liberally with cowpats and molehills. Jack watched a pair of scald crows arguing. He felt tranquilised.

A turf fire glowed in the hearth. The men came in from their work and sat around, their eyes avoiding the stranger. After a bowl of soup and a wedge of soda bread Jack snuck back upstairs. Below, he heard the murmurings of the men who gradually seemed to be finding their voices. He sank into the feather mattress. Already, the pressures and tensions of home were evaporating from him like evil spirits. Jack closed his eyes and in the absolute silence, with just a whispering wind blowing over the fields, he slept easily and deeply.

He woke up to familiar sounds and unfamiliar aromas. Cows mooed, dogs barked. Below in the kitchen bread was baking and thick home-cured bacon was frying. The sun was behind the curtains, the room smelt comfortably musty. It was homely but private. Jack stretched. He was feeling warm, and wet. To his intense embarassment he had wet the bed. My God, what a disaster! He had let down all Dubliners and ruined their reputation for sophistication. He was disgusted with himself. There was no way he could disguise his crime, as there was a large yellowing circle in the middle of the bed. He lay there waiting for his punishment.

Granny changed the sheets and gave him a whispered bollocking. 'If yeh do that again yeh can rot in yer piss.' She bared a few old brown teeth when she said it. Seeing his matchstick arms, the old woman said with a first hint of human kindness, 'Don't worry. Yeh'll be all right here. We don't ate our young in Galway in spite of what yer father might say about us. Run off an' get yer breakfast. There's bacon, eggs an' strong tay.'

The men were already in the fields. Jack prowled the house, peeping in doors, and searched in cupboards until his granny reproached him. 'If yeh're lookin' fer a lav' yer wastin' yer time; we don't bother about them sort a t'ings in the counthry.' With a hand as fierce as a talon she clawed Jack to the window. 'D'yeh see them bushes beyant there? There's yer lav. Take a scrappa newspaper from the kitchen.'

Clutching a page of *The Word*, Jack sprinted across the yard into a spinney of pines. Dodging around rows of furry turds, he found a dry spot and squatted. Looking around nervously, he grunted, creased up his face and tried to get it over with as quickly as possible. But he heard squelching footfalls approaching. He hunched down, vulnerable with his trousers around his ankles. A young girl, her dark hair tangled, paused nearby and lifted her cotton shift.

Holding his breath, with his backside feeling the cold, Jack watched until she let her shift fall then ran like a wild thing back into the bushes. He pulled his braces over his shoulders and, before he made his way back to the house, he stopped and examined a damp spot in the grass. Returning to the farmhouse, he drank more varnishy tea from a blackened pot that was always filled and ready for the tramps, farmers, gypsies or priests, who kept the boreen churned with their visiting.

Jack examined smoke-stained pictures, an old fiddle, and a rack of his dead grandfather's clay pipes. The sun was warming the unfenced fields. A tawny owl sleepily swayed on a branch an arm's length from his window. He saw stone circles from every window where leprechauns cavorted at midnight. Centipedes like strips of shredded orange wriggled under every stone, big lumpy frogs lolloped among the bulrushes, and an army blanket of pigeons filled their crops in a poppy-dotted cornfield.

Jack had spent the whole day wandering, helping the men when they allowed him to. He drove the frisky black donkey, charging along the headlands carrying supplies to the men. He felt at home and happy in his mother's county.

93

JACK VISITED THE pig on Death Row and scratched his flakey back. The fine young male grunted affectionately as he lapped up his last feed to an accompaniment of birdsong. He saw the owl swoop low and lazily for a mouse. This was real country with no cars, no planes, no lawnmowers. He came indoors to sit by the fireside and wait for supper. With the ozone and the hard work he had worked up a gigantic appetite.

His grandmother dominated the hearth with her shrill voice, her nostrils rusting like nail-holes in wood. Supper was freshly snared rabbits roasted on a griddle with potatoes baked in the ash. The rabbits were despatched with greasy hands, the bones chucked into the fire to sizzle. Home-made butter melted on the fresh bread. Poured tea caught in the fire's glow was golden. The family ate quietly.

More quiet men arrived to celebrate the pig's imminent death. They sat in a semi-circle, morosely lobbing spits at the fire and listened to them sizzle on the hot stone. One man shyly started a story while admiring the flames. The others muttered appreciatively. Jack stole away to bed.

The visitors, angular and high-cheeked, whispered and moved closer to the flames. As they talked, one man honed to a murderous sharpness the pig-sticker. He was the Seannachie. Between gulps of tea and the corncrake rasping of stone on steel he told a story.

His tacky black fringe in his eyes, Jack watched the men through a gap in the floorboards. The brown-faced Seannachie thumbed the blade. Women intruded only to bring more tea. Granny flapped around like a wounded plover screeching, 'Move yer arses out a me way,' as she piled lichen-coated logs on the fire. Colonies of woodlice ran frantically along the logs before they blistered.

Jack saw someone produce an unlabelled bottle, small glasses filled to the brim. The Seannachie rose out of his chair. 'Snuff out a few a them candles,' he said. Jack inhaled the sweet tobacco which mingled with the waxy smoke from the extinguished candles and the fragrance of turf and burning wood. He crept out on to the landing to more clearly observe the men and listen to their singsong talk.

A serrated glow lit tanned faces. The pig-killer sharpened a stick and the shavings dropped like snowflakes on to the hearth. With eyes wild and moist he teased the superstitious countrymen, playing them like salmon, until he had them flinging frightened glances at the shadows. Jack thrust his face into the candle and firelight. Outside, a banshee wind howled through twisted blackthorn. A mile or so away seawater attempted to scale the crumbling cliffs, forcing watery claws behind granite rocks that glinted in the moonlight. The wind bent the cliff-top grass and flopped, spent, against stout cottage walls. Animals, warm in a fug of breath and dung, huddled close, their eyes open.

The storyteller took a clay pipe from his mouth and sent a lacy plume of spit skittering across the floor where it splashed into a mucous pool. Reaching down, someone threw an ash log on to the fire, causing sparks to soar. Jack shifted impatiently on the stair riser. The men's heads were bowed. The storyteller raised the brim of his hat and a white, untanned ridge above his nose flared up in the light. He raked the bowl of his pipe before ejecting another gelatinous necklace of spittle which landed with a soft plop on the slimy pool. Men with faces half in shadow, followed the storyteller's eyes. 'The sun was murderous an' it shone till evenin'. The whole damn town was pisspirin'.' He began.

The storyteller halted and slowly turned to his entranced audience, savouring the fear in their bulging eyes. 'What I'm goin' to tell yeh now is the God's troot',' he said. 'It's about the time poor Tom Bolger was taken be the divil.'

Jack shivered.

The Seannachie spotted him. Reaching over, he touched Granny's arm and in a hoarse whisper asked, 'That gossoon there, is it safe for him to be afther listenin' to what I am goin' to tell yeh?'

Jack cocked his head and smiled sheepishly.

'Arra, don't mind him. Sure, he'll hear the same stories a hundert times before he's much older.'

The storyteller shook his head, lit his pipe again, shook the flame from the matchstick and threw it on the floor. 'Ah, well then . . .' The men craned towards him like withered plants reaching for the sun. The storyteller spat again and men who had been saving mouthfuls of mucous joined him in sending a shower of it slithering across the floor. A battery of pipes stuffed with chocolatey tobacco sent up sweet-scented smoke to float in low drifts like sheep's wool clouds above their heads.

Granny crept respectfully from the shadows, carefully skirting the men, who pressed their frightened golden faces forward. Their goblin-like ears stuck out, their caps like brown slates slanted downwards, hiding their troubled eyes. Unnoticed, the old woman noiselessly went towards the stairs. 'Come with me, acushla,' she said, but Jack, mesmerised by the storyteller's compelling mastery, didn't budge. 'Pshst,' Granny snorted and, clutching her skirts above her grey stockinged legs, she stooped and climbed the stairs. Jack let her past but remained rooted to the stair.

'There was not a bit a light from Heaven or Hell.' The Seannachie's voice was rising and falling like music. 'Frightened out a his senses, the poor man started runnin'. In the big black trees wit' their great branches, th' owls squawked. Wild creatures in the fields, whistlin', squealin' and cryin' afther him fer the noise of his boots poundin' on the road.'

Jack's bare feet were frozen to the floor.

'Whissht!' the storyteller suddenly said, and his audience jumped. A heart-thumping silence prevailed as they listened to the wild wind outside. 'Wit' his eyes open wide wit' fear, the poor fella ran, his breat' comin' in wild spurts. Over his head the big trees trembled and tossed their big black manes.' The men's mouths hung slackly, their pipes clenched between rows of gappy, yellow teeth. 'The on'y sound was his own two feet drummin' on the hard black road, slippin' an' slidin' on wet l'aves, his poor side painin' him.' The storyteller's voice dipped. ''Tis then he heard chains rattlin' behind him. The poor man cried out in fear.' The storyteller's voice rose to a screech. 'His legs wobbled, his heart was broke, but he still ran wit' the stringth a the divil. The trees were over his head like a suffocatin' blanket. No sshtar could be seen, an' not a house wit' candle or lamp ta give the poor fella hope. The chain rattled nearer, poor Tom, God fergive him, was done fer.'

The men leant forward, every muscle straining. Jack wished he'd gone to bed when his Granny had told him to. The storyteller drew a last skein of phlegm from his lungs, scraped his pipe and filled it. In the silence there was only the thumping of the men's hearts.

'At last, he seen his house, sshnug in Kilmore Hill. He upped an' made a mad dash fer it an' on'y had time to pound the door before fallin' down sshtone dead on the sshtep.'

Jack fled, pattering rapidly up the wooden stairs, his blue eyes fixed with a glassy stare.

The storyteller dropped his head. The light of the dying fire danced uneasily on woodcut faces. The ash from the fire lifted and spiralled impatiently.

Jack, his mind full of spectres, heard the men below, their girlish titters filtering up through the ceiling. Restlessly twisting and turning in the rigid bed, Jack tried to shoo away the ghosts and the devilish horses that cantered through his mind.

As the conversation below declined at last into grunts and coughing, Jack heard the latch on the door snap and a herd of men stumble out into the concrete yard. Accompanied by sporadic obscenities they urinated in unison against the cottage wall. Jack slept at last.

94

NEXT MORNING THE men strolled in the yard their faces, red with iron-rich blood. They beamed expectantly when the Seannachie threw his sharpening stone on the ground. Tilting back his hat, he said quietly, 'OK, Shay, bring 'im out and lay 'im on th'oul table.'

Shay slapped his big hands together, adjusted his cap and rushed into a shed from which almost immediately came the screams of a terrified pig. 'Will yeh give me a feckin' hand, John Joe?' he yelled. Three or four men struggled to get through the pigsty door to try to grab the panicking animal. Hands tugged and pulled at bristly flesh before the beast was manoeuvred, roaring, on to a scrubbed table. The Seannachie wiped his knife on the jacket he wore buttoned to the chin in spite of the leaden heat.

The pig, now strangely quiet, waited, quivering patiently. It grunted when its head was jerked back to expose the veins in its neck. But casting down its blond eyelashes, the pig seemed to resign itself. A chorus line of sparrows on the shed roof quit chirping to watch the execution.

Pearls of dung-scented sweat hung from every face. The women remained indoors. Slippery pink tongues licked dry lips. His hat shading his eyes, the pig-sticker set his face, then swiftly and accurately slipped the blade into the pig's neck. A bloody scream of betrayal spoiled the innocent beauty of the day. The murdered animal's hot, red blood spurted, drops quickly clotted on the table. The men grimly shook their bloodstained faces but held on to the writhing pig until it kicked itself into oblivion. One last spasm and it lay silent, a pile of bloodstained meat with accusing eyes.

The corpse was hauled into a wooden tub and shaved in scalding water. It wriggled and rolled in the scarlet water like a fat man bathing in elderberry wine. Two men scraped it with cut-throat razors. The pale smooth carcass was strung in the barn, hind legs tied to a beam. The steaming entrails were extracted by the Seannachie who now smiled and joked as he worked.

Jack watched every act of the ceremonial brutality. Subtle glances were thrown his way for signs of city-boy distress. There were none. The men washed down the table and utensils, leaving the cadaver to dangle for the night, its scent tormenting dogs, cats and foxes for miles around.

The men unrolled their sleeves and wandered indoors swapping jokes and backslaps. Soon they were welded back into a picture of timelessness, their faces yellowed by the fire glow in spite of the sun shining outside.

The Seannachie was again ensconced in the best seat, his tales growing in outrageousness and ribaldry as mugs of poteen removed his wits. Feeling unwelcome amid the enclosed order of countrymen, Jack lifted the latch and went to the barn where the pig's carcass hung. It was no longer a pig, just a hollowed out ribcage with legs. All its vital organs were packed in salt, its blood saved for puddings. Jack watched the sun weave fantasies out of silhouetted trees until it was time to go to bed, taking with him the sandwiches and the glass of thick milk his Granny had prepared for him. As drink opened up the men the night was filled with rustic male jollity. Jack slept on his side, a cool breeze tossing the curtains.

95

JACK HEARD HIS uncle Shay chasing someone round and round the kitchen table, laughing loudly all the while. He dressed quickly and rushed downstairs. It was the girl he'd seen in the woods. She was about twelve, dark-haired and ruddy with pellucid blue eyes, a torn jumper and bare legs in wellingtons. She stopped running and breathlessly examined the intruder.

'Ah sure, 'tis the little Jackeen yeh've come to stare at,' Uncle Shay said.

With eyes downcast, her hand smoothing the scrubbed pine table, the girl blushed.

'Dis is Marie, from Woodsend farm beyant. 'Shake hands now.'

Jack took Marie's hand. She snatched it away with a cheeky grin but soon both children were talking. Marie showed Jack the tree where boys hung stray donkeys for fun. 'They drive them over the cliff,' she said, holding back a lock of dark hair. 'The poor cr'atures is killt on the rocks below.'

Jack looked down into a deep quarry expecting bones and hide, but there was no sign of the dead donkeys. 'Why do they do it?' he asked.

'Och, I don't know. Yeh Jackeens ask too many questions.' They climbed down into the deep bowl of the quarry and looked for donkey bones.

Jack chased her around red-berried rowan trees. They investigated the woods and the standing stones, and they fingered the ogham on granite scratching posts. Marie climbed trees and skinned her knees. Jack followed her rump out along the longest boughs and they sat there swaying and laughing. They caught pinkeens in the rocky streams and held them wriggling in their leaking hands. They ran breathlessly, climbing gates and stiles. Jack was playing the way a boy should play, with a sweet companion. Marie was a perfect boy but with a girl's gentleness.

When they returned, running in and out of the sun, wetting their feet in dew ponds, their clothes torn by barbed wire and their legs scratched by the yellow furze which covered much of the poor, hilly land, Uncle Shay had made butter. Both children pressed fingers into the yellow butter and licked its greasy, saltiness. Jack said he preferred it to his father's.

'Ah, yer oul' fella couldn't make butther,' Uncle Shay said. 'Yeh need plenty a fresh cr'am. How could he get enough from one oul' cow?'

'C'mon, Jack,' Marie said, leading him away by the hand.

'Och, she's the quare one, afther draggin' the Jackeen off, an' him on'y here a day or two.' Uncle Shay, a middle-aged batchelor with his torn and dirty coat, rough hands and balding head, seemed ancient and foolish as he shouted after the children, 'She's on'y afther yer washin'.' Then, tipping up his grizzled chin, he chewed with brown-stained lips on his wad of tobacco, spattering the area round him with juice.

They went to Mass on Sunday and tied the donkey up outside to graze with a dozen others. Jack felt totally at ease with these culchies. He liked the easygoing nature of the countrymen, their amiable jocularity, their nearness to life's existence, their belief in God. Galway days were gentle. Galway men threw their doors open to friends and neighbours. Culchies were quiet-voiced men compared to the frenetic Dubliners. Galway men were at one with their history. Jack watched with inherited cynicism, a farmer, his eyes bulging with fear, warily circle a burial mound rather than disturb its mystery. The Boss would have opened up the mound and robbed it.

Every precious moment Jack spent in Galway was one to savour. Whole days drifted past without a raised voice. Haymaking was a joyous celebration with neighbours joining in. Jack brought sustenance to the men in flood-fertilised fields. There were baskets of fatty sandwiches, flagons of beer, cakes, cans of tea, and hayricks to sleep against when bellies were full.

With instructions from Marie, Jack made an adequate rope of matted hay. Every day there was sun and laughter. Rathfarnham seemed a million miles away. Did it really exist, Jack wondered, or was it all a bad horror film he'd seen at the Classic?

When tired of haymaking, Jack followed the smaller children down to the riverside. The Shannon flowed deep and mysterious. Fishing boats bobbed on its smooth surface. There was endless peace, sun and laughter. Jack felt renewed.

He went to the shop where all news was gathered, embroidered and passed on. Every need was provided for: duck eggs and candles, tobacco and paraffin, laces and loaves, snares, whiskey and poison. To country children Dublin was a long-distant, smoke-blackened myth peopled by slick devils armed with tridents. And Jack delighted in scaring the wits out of them with his hair-raising lies.

Green and yellow days slipped by all too quickly. Nature's perfume insinuated itself into Jack's hair, his clothes, the pores of his skin. But the idyll was coming to end and a gnawing anxiety about returning to Dublin spoiled his last few days. Lying awake in bed, pictures of his poor mother flashed on to the red screen of his imagination. Jack wished he could stay in Galway forever. Rathfarnham, forgotten like some screaming nightmare, was once more rearing its diseased head.

Granny, her shawl stirring like the feathers of an old crow, watched as Jack was driven away. He looked back tearfully. The old woman waved a thin arm. Faces were grinning at him from under caps.

'God bless yeh,' Uncle Shay mumbled at the bus stop. Marie watched, her head aslant, her smile teasing him. Jack watched her clamber back into the orange cart with Shay. The wheels turned as the black ass dragged it away. Marie turned once but didn't wave.

Jack endured the journey resolutely, glimpsing headlines over shoulders, the back of the driver's head with a cigarette butt stuck behind one ear. Granny, the farmworkers, the pig-sticker, and Marie were being edged from his mind. The bus's engine thumped in and out of his weary head. Dust swirled as the tyres pounded the dry roads.

Dublin appeared with its poky tenements sprouting television aerials. Behind glass and brick, the inhabitants groped in their twilight world. The bus swept down rubbish-strewn lanes that at night would ring with the wild curses of the mugged and the drunk. The Liffey wallowed to the sea. Clogged in the city's traffic, the bus crawled slowly back to the station. The passengers vanished into the anonymity of the city.

Weighted down by salted pork, goose eggs and a mineral bottle of poteen, Jack stood at the number 17 stop, his face coloured by winking signs.

Shabby streets gave way to suburbs. The smoking stack of the Bloomfield Laundry poked up from the nettled banks of the river. Clutching his presents Jack crossed the Pit. As he approached the tall green gate all the lightness had gone out of his stride as he felt himself being sucked back into the dark and joyless void.

96

'HOW'S ALL AT home, then?' Mary asked. 'Did they ask afther me? Do they even know I still exist? That's about all I do do - *exist* - in this bloody dump with that madman fer a husband.'

The Boss arrived indoors with a tremendous crash. Wisps of straw and hayseed clung to the rough fibres of his ancient tweed jacket. His face was snarling, his false teeth white and foaming. 'Put down the gas tap, yeh feckin' bitch,' he roared, flinging the frying pan across the floor where steaming sausages were scattered like turds and split eggs bled, thick and yellow, coating the skirting board.

'What did yeh wan'ta do that for?' Mary asked, her face looking dismayed at her husband's ridiculous action.

'Bollix ta yeh and yer feckin' fry,' the Boss said, 'standin' here, runnin' me down while I'm out there in them freezin' sheds slavin' on me own wit' not a body ta lift a hand ta help me.' Jack tried to be invisible, but the Boss's hand reached out like the grappling-iron fist of a crane and held him fast. 'So yeh're back from that t'ievin' bunch a tinkers? Now getcha feckin' top boots on, yer feckin' sleeveen, an' sweep out them pigs,' he growled, pushing Jack towards the door.

Mary was on her knees with the younger children around her, gathering up steaming sausages and mauling congealing egg from the walls with a dishcloth. As her fat rear shook with the effort and the strings of her apron danced behind her, she began to sob, her big shoulders pumping. A toddler put a hand on her face and said, 'Don't cry, Mammy.'

Jack slung his case on his bed and watched the blood from the pork Granny had given him bleed into the patchwork quilt. He went to the yard and swept out the pig pens indolently, his heart as hard as a rock. His mother would have to cry, and carry on crying, there was nothing he could do to stop her. The Boss stormed about the yard, his temper showing no sign of abating.

The soothing swish of water from the tap told Jack his father was washing the dung off his wellingtons. The last chore was done for the day.

The final hours of another unhappy day were eked out with Mary and her frightened brood sitting quietly with just the occasional self-pitying sniff and the whiplash sound of the Boss turning the pages of his beloved paper. One by one, the children slipped away and were soon snug in their damp bedrooms. Jack watched the Rathfarnham moon lighting up the yard. It would also be bathing the boreen and the farmhouse in Galway, and brightening Marie's quiet bedroom. He imagined her pale face and wished he was lying beside her. Granny would be in bed, her transparent hands manacled by rosary beads.

When he heard the girls undressing next door Jack told his wad of stories about Galway. The smaller children pulled woolly blankets up to their chins and listened in the dark, enthralled as Jack's imagination ran away with him. Whenever his voice dipped to a whisper, Bridgid yelled , 'Speak up, yeh gobdaw, we can't hear yeh.'

Jack finally went to sleep, his mind at peace with wonderful memories.

Summer, once so full of promise, was flying towards winter. Squalling winds were blowing away the long, dry weeks. Leaves cascaded from the trees and floated down the swollen river. The swallows, that had sat like musical notations on the wires cat-cradling the village, were gone.

Jack read the *Dublin Evening Mails* he salvaged from the Boss's pile. He was almost up to date with the goings-on in the capital city when he read the morsel that stopped him fiddling with his fringe. Paddy Daly was leaving Transport for Bray Wanderers for a fee of five hundred pounds. 'Paddy Daly's goin'ta Bray,' he told Bridgid.

'So what?' Bridgid snarled, her crotch visible as she lounged on the sofa reading some paperback she had been given by one of the girls at work.

'Bloody Bray must've money t'burn,' the Boss growled without looking up. 'Five hundert pounds fer an oul' shagger like dat.'

Jack stared at the curtain behind which a small dark window looked out on the bare yard. He would never see Paddy again. He felt the outside come in and cloak him with despair. He cut out the snippet of news and stuck it in an old album with all his other football cuttings.

Next morning, he took his FAI-approved football off the wardrobe. It was deflated and dusty. He polished the fluff off it with his sleeve and gazed at Paddy Daly's signature.

97

JACK PREPARED FOR his first day at the Boys National School, Rathfarnham.

'Well, goodbye an' good luck, said the drake tidda duck,' Mary said as she handed her son a packet of sandwiches. 'It's on'y oul' lettuce,' she said.

Jack marched to the school in new boots, pausing on the way to look into the river at the Bloomfield Laundry. A big black water rat prowled among the rusty pipes that polluted the stream all the year round, poisoning every living thing except the rats. The discharges coloured the water. Submerged rags waved like weird fish, and bottles stuck up from the riverbed like the periscopes of miniature submarines.

Jack's new school was a granite, three-roomed affair with a teacher in each. It had high, spiked, iron railings around it like a zoo. The playground was a square of grey concrete with a silver birch growing up through a hole in the middle. The rooms were dark, the seats hard, and the only educational tools were a blackboard, a few books and a massive leather strap. At the back of the school there was an ammonia scented, brown-stained urinal and a smelly, single-seat WC that had a piece of string as a handle and no toilet paper. The headmaster, the kind and bespectacled Mr Dougal, used the *Irish Times.* The other two teachers wiped their bums with the *Irish Press* and the *Irish Independent.* Jack crept around, clinging to the walls as if he were climbing the Eiger. A new batch of harder bullies were soon sniffing about him to see if he was kickable. He was and they did, but mercifully not too often.

After roll-call, the new boys sat together, their hair sleeked with water. Ungnawed pencils and new jotters sat on their desks. When Mr Moroney entered, all the boys clattered upright, and sat down again when the master waved at them testily as if he were swatting mosquitoes.

One by one, the new boys presented themselves at his desk to have their credentials checked against a list sent by Miss Hogan. Jack waited for Mr Moroney to speak. He had a big face with enormous brown eyes that were overshadowed by vast bushy eyebrows. When their eyes met the teacher pulled a face. 'If yeh keep yer nose clane,' he reached out and picked up Jack's congealed sleeve, yeh'll do all right here.' Jack's face flushed. When a big hairy hand grasped the leather strap and brought it down with a crack Jack jumped. In a low theatrical voice Mr Moroney said, 'Get back to yer seat, yeh little scutther!' Jack quickly regained his seat and when no one was looking he wiped his nose on his sleeve.

All three masters believed in discipline, and many a tough mountain boy squealed like a castrated ass as the course leather strap was whirled by a bulging-eyed master and brought down with a crash on hands that cradled battered craniums. Jack remained an anonymous student, doing just enough to avoid notice and pain. He kept his nose clean and his trousers dry and he learned to handle the school bullies with diplomatic cunning.

The Boss lowered his newspaper and the room drew its breath. 'I'm goin' ta the abattoir fer a load a guts tomorrow. I want a hand,' he growled.

The pony and cart were waiting outside Jack's new school as he hurried out, ashamed of his father's shabbiness and archaic transport. Even the mountain boys parents had vans. Jack scrambled into the cart, wanting to be on his way before Mr Dougal came to the school gate. Kitty was in full trot before the bell finished its brassy tolling.

Jack had to kick the locked, dung-sprayed, slaughterhouse doors before the ragged figure of Frankie Connelan prised them apart cheerfully and waved the cart through. 'Yehz're in luck t'day,' he said with a smile. 'There's lots a fresh guts in them barrels over dere.'

A bouquet of bluebottles buzzed upwards as the Boss dug a fork into the quivering slush of stomachs. Watery dung showered his back as he swung a forkful over his head to splash into the cart. Jack carried cow heads, each with a hole in the middle of its forehead, their dead eyes staring at him as he held the crumpled horns like a motor cyclist.

Sliding about up to his ankles in dung, the Boss stripped hooks of meat. Rushing to the front of the cart he stowed lacy cardigans of suet and chunks of steak and lamb under a dirty sack. Frankie nodded approvingly, holding his fork and grinning. The Boss winked and bought the lad's silence with a sixpenny piece. 'C'mon, the bogeyman'll be after us,' the Boss said.

Jack was wandering through the abbatoir, a stinking bloody cathedral. He examined the deadly implements. Huge, thin-bladed knives used to slash the throats of sheep, a humane killer in its case, rods used to let the blood of an animal pulse through the newly made aperture in its skull. Bloodstained aprons hung like tortured trunks. Jack battled through curtains of flies. He could hear last desperate cries of animals as they were shot, clubbed and knifed. He saw inanimate limbless trunks of cows that only yesterday had swished their tails in Neary's fields, their piebald backs showing through high grass. He saw new calves that had recently been lolling at foot, their tongues seeking mothers' teats, now cut into sanitised steaks.

He saw sheep, fattened like larva on the hills above Rathfarnham, the wind ruffling their wool, their lambs bleating beside them, now hanging naked and dead. Soon, they would be chopped up and decorated with parsley in O'Rourke's shop window. Jack had met the slaughterhouse men. They were cruel and stupid, with lifeless eyes. They wore trousers tied at the knee, and they enjoyed their gruesome work. Jack had seen how they leapt astride the sheep, breaking their backs, forcing them to the ground, their legs splayed, their joints torn from the roots. He saw their heads with terrified eyes staring as sharp knives slashed their unprotected throats. He saw twitching shit-covered corpses like soft rugs on the wet concrete. Every day, creatures were being killed, were dying silently and courageously.

'Will yeh c'mon out a dat!' The Boss's shout made Jack jump. He returned to the cart. Droning clouds of bluebottles followed them, getting into his hair and mouth. The smell of death and spilt blood was sweet and sickly. As Kitty trotted home, the cart trickled dung. The Boss doffed his trilby to passers-by like some mad despot sitting atop his slain enemies.

When Kitty arrived at the bridge the cats were waiting. Gaunt groups of them had got wind of a meal. They scrambled on to the cart, mewed and tore at the sacks. As the Boss flicked them over the sides they dodged the cart wheels as nimbly as ballerinas.

The boiler was packed to the brim, Jack climbed in and jumped up and down like an old-fashioned wine-maker to make room for the last few forkfuls. The fire's billowing clouds rose into the sky and sailed over the convent spire. Soon, bubbling juice hissed down the sides of the black cauldron. The aroma of meat and shit tantalised the hungry pigs. Sometimes they were allowed to eat the guts raw. The stomachs of cows were ripped open, and undigested grass and dung shaken out of them before they were thrown to the screaming swine.

Kitty rolled, her thin legs thrashing the air. She retained a youthful virility, due 'to a few drops a t'urrabred blood in'er veins', according to the Boss.

Snorting, she regained her feet and shook herself. 'She's me on'y friend,' the Boss said, tickling her ribs. The pony turned to bite him. 'We trus' each other, don't we, yeh oul' hoor.' Kitty pushed her head into her master's chest. He gave her a slap on the hindquarters and smiled as she raced around the paddock, her tail in the air, her scraggy mane flowing.

The boiler was allowed to boil all night. Morning would find insects, like shiny brooches, embalmed in the cold fat.

98

JACK FELT DISGUSTED when he touched the slimy cold spot on his shirt. He got down on his knees and prayed extra hard. Something as pleasurable as that had to be a sin.

After school next day he ran as hard as he could to the river. The Boss was away cutting a meadow in Tallaght. Jack crept close to the tall willow hedge then dropped on to a stepping stone in the clear, fresh brook. With a hop he was on the opposite bank and scaling the Boss's broken-glass-topped wall. He darted across the dusty lane, over a stile and hurried through a stand of pines to The Moat, a shabby chalet with crooked balustrades, shuttered windows, sagging gutters, and sparrows nesting in the eaves. There wasn't a soul in sight as Jack, with heart thumping, ran among the scented pines to the house.

The house seemed deserted. He trotted through the untidy garden, mounted the steps and knocked on the front door. A small voice answered. Suddenly afraid, he was ready to turn back but Sheila Rooney, petite and bouncy, lifted the latch, and her face appeared in the gap of the open door.

In her bedroom the curtains fluttered. It was a child's room: a tidy bed with glassy-eyed soft toys on the bedspread. Schoolgirl annuals were neatly stacked by the bedside. Sheila sat on her bed and kicked her white legs. She was smaller, prettier and younger than Bridgid.

She wore a yellow frock with green leaves embroidered across the front, green ankle socks and sandals. Against the white bedspread she looked as fine and delicate as a butterfly. Her blonde curls were tied with a large green ribbon and bobbed like springs when she moved her head.

'C'mon, sit here beside me.' She patted the bed.

Jack sat down awkwardly. Sheila shook her big yellow curls and, with a wide smile, drew him to her. 'Well, what d'yeh want t'do?' she asked sweetly and her blonde curls danced as the button eyes of a thousand dolls adored her. Jack looked desperately round the room for inspiration. 'Wouldja lend me that *Beano* annual there?' he asked.

'Course I will,' Sheila said. 'I've got lots, look. They're all over the place, me mammy buys them for me an' me brothers all the time.'

Jack looked longingly at a pile of American comics as if he were Desperate Dan looking at a fabulous cow pie. The greats were all there: *The Durango Kid*, *Buck Jones*, *Kit Carson*, *Wild Bill Pecos*, *Hopalong Cassidy*, *Tim Holt* and *The Cisco Kid*. Jack wished his parents were educated, stinking rich and believed in birth control like the Prods.

'Take as many as yeh like,' Sheila said, and as she skipped on to the floor her dress flared and Jack saw her knickers. 'Take the lot,' she laughed and began to pile them on to his outstretched hands and arms.

When the last comic was wedged under his chin Jack said through clenched teeth, 'I betther be goin' now.'

'No, yeh don't,' Sheila said, tumbling the pile of comics out of his arms. Jack looked at her bewildered as she began to do bicycle kicks on the bed, then opening and closing her legs like scissors. 'Well?' she said, gyrating furiously.

Jack watched her in awe. 'Ahhh, em,' he tried, gulping like a snake swallowing a tennis ball. His throat felt sandpapered. Overwhelmed, he could only stand by the bed, knuckling his watering eyes. Sheila sat up and kicked off her shoes.

'Come on, yeh bloody eejit,' she cried and pulled the dumb weeping boy on top of her like a grubby coat. Jack lay there, his head on her floral dress. He heard her heart beating and finches piping in the apple trees. Sheila's breathing was soft and even. Jack could smell her breath. 'Ar'yeh goin' ta da an'tin' or not?' she whispered. But he was content to have her softly beneath him. Sheila opened her legs, the tiny silver hairs gleaming in the sun, and pulled him between them. 'Me mammy'll be back soon.'

Jack uncurled a paw and put it on her face.

'Have yeh got a mickey?' she asked, feeling his trousers. 'Oh,' she said with a giggle, 'an' it's a big wan.' Soon she had it out and peeled like a little pink banana. Sheila beamed and was fascinated. 'Hey, that's lovely, now yeh can see mine.' She pulled back a knicker leg and arched her back. Jack looked fearfully, but only saw a little mouse sliced along its back by a sharp knife. 'Yeh can touch it if yeh wan'ta,' Sheila said. Jack watched an involuntary hand stroke the mouse. The sun was filtering through the curtains as the children lay there.

Jack would happily have died on Sheila's bed but she said, 'Yeh hav'ta go, butcha can come back anudder time if yeh want. Wouldja like that?'

Jack did up his buttons, sighed sleepily and said, 'Yeah, I would.'

'In dat case yeh can't take the comics ,' she said. Yeh'll hav'ta come back fer 'em.'

Jack ran through an avenue of apple trees, Sheila's laugh seemed to be making their leaves dance.

As Jack helped his father unload potatoes and bury them in a clamp, his secret made him strong and defiant. What he'd done with Sheila was a sin, but feckit, everything in Ireland was a sin. 'Them that does be doin' rotten t'ings wit' their privates is headin' fer hell,' his mother was always saying. Then with a slavering grin she'd add, 'Bur dere's no danger a dat. Yehz wor all brung up in the light a God an' his sacraments, an' I won't let that oul' father a yers lead yehz away from the Holy Spirit.'

Before sliding between grey sheets, Jack examined himself in the blotchy mirror that reflected his gaunt body from the wardrobe door. 'Not bad,' he concluded, then thinking of Sheila he wanked himself to sleep.

He visited Sheila as often as he could. When she played with him he saw a bright-eyed devil on her shoulder pointing and grinning, its black horns curled on its shiny head. 'Go on, dip yer wick in the oil,' it seemed to be saying as he jumped up and down. 'It's what it's there fer.' The devil was great, a man of the world. Mary's God was a miserable oul' bastard who believed ever'thin' was a sin.

What would happen if the praying, the church-going, the Confessions and the Holy Communions were all a terrible joke? Jack began to think. What if all his mother believed in were lies. What if all the pain she'd suffered was in vain? What a bugger that would be.

Jack jumped when a cold hand rested upon his shoulder. 'Ah darlin',' his mother said, 'isn't it grand ta see yeh down on yer knees.

Believin' in the same t'ings yer mammy does. God bless yeh, son.' She shuffled from the room like a great dark tanker slipping its moorings in the night, leaving Jack abandoned and confused by his bed. Mary stumbled off, knocking into chairs and careering into the table. She was old and tired, heavy with liquid and blubber, every bit of black had faded from her previously squaw-dark hair.

Her cheeks were an unhealthy mauve as she turned to kiss her children a last good-night. They squeezed her hand and hugged her as she did the rounds like an old worn-out Florence Nightingale. So many babies had been quarried from her body, lovely babies, one after the other, spilling out of her, squealing and bloody, threshing about at the end of their cord, all different, all intelligent, all healthy, a succession of haphazardly created miracles.

Jack had tried to pray, but instead of going straight on to auto pilot as he usually did, he began to think for himself. He concluded the whole colourful, incense-smelling, Latin-droning drama was a sham. As he knelt by the bed - his jaw twisted by the heel of his hand, his brain throbbing like a clockwork toy with a jammed wheel, unwinding but going in circles - he thought of Hell. Heaven sounded better.

When his eyes opened next morning Jack could smell the damp sheets flapping on the line. His mother washed them by hand every week. At school when he saw the boys in their muscular masses, kicking and punching each other, he thought being snotty and weak was no barrier to enjoyment after all.

99

ALL DAY AT school Jack thought about Sheila, oblivious to the masters as they rambled, bellowed and slapped. In the kitchen later, palpitating with a delicious new feeling, he finished his homework, and when he heard Kitty gallop over the bridge hauling a load of grass he went out to the yard to help his father pile it up to ripen on the roofs of the pigsties.

As he worked, Jack observed his father's broad back clad in a shabby blue jacket, the stitching undone under the sleeves. Poor man, he had nothing to look forward to. Madly, he dug his fork into the meadow grass to fling it on to the hot corrugated roof. Jack would have liked to slip Sheila into the conversation. His father knew more about sex than the guy who wrote the Kinsey Report. Jack thought about it but decided to keep Sheila to himself.

He couldn't talk to his mother either. To her sex was a vile deed, swiftly accomplished in darkness. A coupling barely endurable. For both his parents, the thought of fondling, touching or loving a body was a mortal sin. Mary had to report any foreplay to Father Orlston, even if all she had done was to help the Boss with his zipper. 'T'ree *Hail Marys* an' a *Glory Be*, and say a prayer fer me too while yer at it,' the priest would say.

Jack deliriously, desperately, wanted to talk to someone, anyone, about his beautiful half hours with Sheila, but Mary would have killed him, and Babs and Pam were too enmeshed in the nuns' sterile snare to allow such ugly thoughts to enter their heads.

Quietly, selfishly, he recycled his moments of pleasure.

On the weekend he went to Confession. While supposedly examining his conscience, he was thinking about Dickie and Louie Carter who raced bikes and who lived in the village. No one ever saw Louie who raced against top men like Jack Brett, John Hartle, Bob

McIntyre and Derek Ennett in the Northwest 200 and the Ulster Grand Prix at Dundrod. But Dickie rode his bike to work and like everybody else actually stopped at the lights to give way to oul' wans in Terenure. Jack watched him from the cart, him in his pudding-basin helmet and Belstaff waterproofs. Who would have thought he was the same man who raced an NSU Sportsmax against Sammy Miller and Bob Brown in the Leinster 200 in Wicklow?

The old priest was crumpled and stern, a rosary binding his lardy fat hands. He pretended to be asleep as Jack flashed the mortal sin past him like Louis Carter taking Ralph Renson at Rathnew. The old priest, inquisitive and alert, was not one to be caught missing a juicy one. All of a sudden he asked Jack to go back and re-examine. Poor old bastard, his sad mouth opening and closing like an old fish, with all those dirty old ones queueing up outside in their smelly rags, their mouths full of gin and decaying molars. The priest nodded, absolving the child. As the old face peered desperately at him from the shadows, Jack waited for his penance. 'T'ree *Hail Marys*.' Jesus, Jack thought. What does a fella hav'ta do round here t'get a decent, bloody penance.

Jack escaped to the side chapel. The usual brilliance that bounced off into his soul after Confession wasn't there. It didn't mean as much any more. There was no fear, no feeling of frying in Hell, no satisfying absolution and no redemption. Something valuable and fundamental was lost. In the past when he'd received communion in a state of absolute Grace he'd delicately touched with his tongue the little white disk that represented the blessed body of Jesus Christ, Our Lord. He couldn't bear to swallow it whole, and was afraid to sink his teeth into it, or to dissolve it with licks in case the blood of Christ filled his mouth and dropped through his teeth as he wheeled away from the altar, bloodied hands joined in front of him, his bloodstained fingertips devoutly touching. Why did his father hate motorbikes, Jack wondered as he made his way back to his pew.

On Sunday he listened to *Life with the Lyons* on the Light Programme, a new sin Babs had introduced. The Boss wouldn't hear of it but when he was reminded that she had paid most for the new radio, he meekly capsized. 'All right, all right,' he said trying to save face, 'bur only if I can tune it in.' The children closed in on the radio like zealots, their eyes sparkling as if it were a big black cobra curled in a basket. They watched the green light come on and clapped their hands together and laughed when the signature tune played. They listened transfixed and smiling broadly. The second the programme was over the Boss said, 'Bloody right load a scutther, if yeh ask me,' and he switched back to some culchie with an impenetrable Kerry accent talking about great Irish fiddlers.

'Why does Daddy hate mothorbikes?' Jack asked his mother when he got her alone.

'He hates everyt'in',' Mary said. She thought for a moment. 'He caught me once havin' a ride on the back of a friend's big Matchless.'

'Jesus Christ, a Matchless! Was it a G45 or a G50?'

'How the hell would I know? All I do know is yer man went apeshit when he saw me wit' me legs spread an' me arms around Cyril Boland, a lovely lad from Galway.'

'Good fer yeh, Mam,' Jack said. 'A Matchless? Jasus, that was some goin'.

'I'm not as sweet and innocent as he t'inks I am,' Mary said.

'Evidently, Mother,' Jack said, very impressed.

100

WHILE KITTY WAS eating her grub, her matted hair sticking up like an angry pensioner's, the Boss undid the wheels of the cart. 'Roll'em down ta the river,' he said. Jack took a big wheel to the bank and let it fall in with a splash. He soon had both wheels lying under the water like great zodiacs, oak spokes radiating from the hub, the clear river water purpling from the axle grease. The midges were biting, and Jack was scratching his head when a vision appeared. It was not Mary Magdalene, thank God, it was Sheila Rooney.

She cheekily straddled the rounded coping on the wall and rode it like it was a concrete horse. 'How're yeh, Jackie,' she said and her smile was milk-toothed and magical. In her sleeveless dress her arms were tanned and beautiful. Jack wiped his nose on his sleeve, and as if guided by St Christopher, he waded across to the opposite bank. Ensnared by Sheila's brilliance he gazed at her, the sun shining on her ringlets. He wanted to touch them. 'Yeh can touch me hair if yeh like,' Sheila said.

Jack was reaching out a dirty hand when–

'*Jack!*' The ugly sound of his name cut through the sweet air like a rusty machete with dried bloodstains. 'Come back here, yeh bloody waster.'

'I t'ink yer Daddy wants yeh,' Sheila said, 'an' I gorra feelin' he's cross.' She slid off the wall and ran off as if she was afraid. 'Bye,' she called breathlessly, her ankle socks flying.

Jack's face was pained as he re-entered the water and splashed back to the opposite side.

'Don' be talkin' ta that skuttova lassie,' the Boss said. 'Her oul' fella'll be blamin' us if an'tin' happens to her. That fecker'd love ta see us bent and broke an' in court.'

Jack slopped back to the pigs, the cold water in his boots shrinking his toes. He swept the pigsties and could see Sheila's face smiling in the pigshit.

After his chores, Jack was drinking tea in the kitchen when his mother approached as if she was rounding up hens. She cleared her throat and closed the door. 'Jack,' she said, 'I've got ta say I'm very cross wit'cha.'

'Why?'

'Well, let's put it this way. I'm goin' to ask yeh a straight question. Yeh understand this is very embarrassin' fer me.' Jack waited. 'Do yeh play wit' yerself in bed? Now don't deny it, yer sheets are in a shockin' state. It's a mortal sin, an' it's also disgustin'.

'Chinko says wankin's not just normal, it's essential,' Jack said.

'Well, it's not,' Mary said. 'Next time yeh go ta Confession, tell Father Orlston, he's the man ta sort yeh out. Udderwise yeh'll go straight ta Hell. It's yer decision,' Mary said as she left the room.

Babs told Pam she was getting bored with her secret meetings with Niall. They still kissed chastely under the soughing trees outside the church. Flailing hands kept him at bay but in the confessional, her head bent, her purity soiled, Babs had to be cleansed by the old priest's mutterings. She still enjoyed her job at Easthams, even though there was no prospect of promotion until someone died. But Babs herself had no intention of being carried out of there in a casket. She was intent on going to Chicago, whether the Boss liked it or not. She strolled to Bewleys at lunchtime and and ate cream buns and drank coffee with her workmates. Dublin was all right in the autumn.

Pam got a job and worked long hours in Devine Groceries in Rathgar. Her feet were always cold and her hands began to look like sausages, but she was a popular shop assistant. Her pretty face and welcoming manner appealed to the demented old men who lived in bachelor rooms with fat-bellied dogs.

Bridgid eagerly awaited Babs and Pam's return from their jobs. Most nights, Babs sat with the other girls in their room, reading magazines and listening to her small radio. When the Boss prodded the sack under the back door and slid the various bolts, their lives seemed even more desolate.

Babs mentioned Niall's bristly chin against her soft face and told them he was too slow-witted for her.

'Sounds like his number's up,' Bridgid said.

When another letter arrived from Aunt Dolores, Babs grabbed it as if it were a lifebelt. 'I can get yeh all jobs real quick,' she wrote. 'I got influence.'

Mary wiped her nose and said, 'I hope yehz won't go. It'd break me heart.' Wistfully, she added, 'But that's an awful selfish t'ing ta say, isn't it?'

'Yes, Mammy,' Bridgid said, her face serious, 'it is.' She smiled though, and took her mother's hand in hers to give it a little squeeze.

That evening when he returned with Jack from the pigs the Boss washed, spluttering into a basin of lukewarm water. Babs, her face optimistic, read her father the letter. As he towelled his face dry he said, 'That oul' wan wants yehz ta be her slaves. As soon as yehz get there she'll have yehz under the t'umb.'

Babs shook her head sadly.

'Mey sister's not in need of slaves,' Mary said. 'And what have the poor childer got ta look forward ta here? Nothin'.'

'Yeh might t'ink that,' the Boss said, drying his powerful arms. 'I hav'ta t'ink a the girl's morals.' Mary's snigger made him look at her with hatred. 'Yeh're nuttin' but a pile a shite,' he said. 'What d'yeh know about life, an' you afther livin' wit' them bloody tinkers in Galway.'

Mary's fat body quaked and her big pink hands opened and closed in frustration. Her voice faltering, she said, 'Well, go if yehz wan'ta, girls. There's no future in this bloody place. I don't want yehz ta go, but yeh've got nuttin' ta look forward ta here. Nuttin',' she repeated, 'nuttin' at all.'

The Boss stood up, his muscles taut. He leaned on the table, knuckled hands cocked and ready to inflict damage. 'If that child falls from grace, I'll blame yeh,' he said. 'Send yer own bloody fambly,' the Boss jeered, 'that bunch a gobshites from Galway. Drop the whole feckin' lot an' stick 'em in steerage. Let 'em leave me in peace.'

'If anything happened to Babs,' Mary said later, when out of earshot, 'Yer man would be capable of murder.' Her mouth was slack and her hair dishevelled as she finished with the coda, 'There's now. There's now.'

101

HER HEAD ACHING, Mary kissed and patted the younger children before opening the kitchen door to put them outside like milk bottles. The yard was warm and free of noise except for the rasping of crows in the trees. Mary watched them flapping in circles above their fledglings who sat open-beaked on the branches. 'Lookit them, they want feedin',' she cried. 'Why don't them blasted birds go away. There's nuttin' here fer 'em.' Half blind with migraine, she blinked at the birds, her brow furrowed.

The Boss waited for Jack to come home from school and took him to mow hay in the Moravian graveyard up past Whitechurch. The sky was clear except for a few puffs of cloud as the Boss swept his scythe through the tall grass. Under the slanted branches of century-old pines, Jack lay face down, intoxicated by the smell of the damp, warm earth. A lattice of grasses cross-hatched his face as he poked his nose into the fungoid coolness. His head was cracking with the heat. His shirt was damp with sweat, his shoulder blades relaxed and pliable. An insect, huge and shellacked, crawled out of its small, dark hole. It crossed the veined mound of Jack's hand. It was a sympathetic hand that would not crush the white juice from its hideous body.

Behind a veil of grasses, the Boss worked his scythe with manic intensity, sweat trickling in rills down his tan body, his trilby-hatted head moving to the rhythm of the scythe. His feet planted apart, the Boss guillotined the tall grass, toppling it quickly to dry in the sun. Every now and then there was a sharp metallic sound as the swinging blade glanced off a headstone, sending sparks and fragments into the air.

'Feckit,' the Boss muttered, 'I'm afther bolloxin' me scythe.' Breathing hard, he stopped for a moment and with a tired eye examined the thin blade. Holding the scythe by its warped handle, he cleaned the blade with an oily rag, then wiped it both sides with a sharpening stone, rhythmically, the hard hand missing decapitation by the same fraction each time. 'Ar'yeh there?' His shout bounced off the cemetery walls. Jack rose from the grass like a corpse. 'Get that pitchin' fork and turn them rows over there.' His father pointed to yesterday's grass, already nearly turned to hay.

Kitty rested on three legs in a fly-buzzing corner. Tethered to an iron cross, her ears and tail flicked and twitched, a pile of dung lay like a nest of serpent's eggs in the grass behind her. Her belly full, the old pony poked her ears forward at the sound of her master.

On the mountains above, turf dried; furze, rigid with heat, was motionless. Jack squinted at the glaring sky. A sound in the pines made him redirect his gaze. A rook fluttered in the topmost branches, its black wings spread, its feathers puffed out, its beak silently mouthing, a small, pink tongue sticking out. Jack flipped over the rows the way he had been taught while his father laboured at the far end of the graveyard, moving from side to side, the scythe swinging, its perfect timing drawing him along. He could hear his father's raised voice as he talked angrily to himself.

When the Boss stopped mowing he felt the ache in his arms and shoulders. All this effort for a few bales of graveyard hay. 'Don't be feedin' that oul' stuff ta the poor cow,' Mary would say. 'Sure, how can it be good fer her an' it comin' from unholy ground.' What would be deemed worthless to a rich man, the Boss worked angrily to harvest, his mutterings lost among the tombstones. After turning a dozen rows Jack was ready to lie on the ground again, to bury his head in the damp earth and watch the tiny creatures hatch, crawl and die.

He was suddenly aware of a shadow cast over him. 'Well,' the Boss said, 'Jasus, I'm banjaxed.'

'Will I get the tea?' Jack asked, referring to the canvas rucksack that lay on a headstone a few yards away.

'Yeah,' the Boss said, 'A mugga tay'd be gameball.' He squatted and watched his son wade thigh deep through the high grass, his hair flopping up and down as he bobbed. When he handed his father the flask and a parcel of sandwiches, Jack smiled. He worked so hard, the poor man. Full of good feelings, Jack squeezed up close to his father, but the Boss was distracted and moved away.

Jack drank the remains of the cold tea, took the crusts to the pony who gobbled them off his palm and pulled a face. 'It's the Colman's mustard that's on the bit a ham,' the Boss said. Was Jack imagining things or was there a softness in his father's tone?

By the time they reached home it was dark. As they entered the yard Mary tore from the room to confront them. 'An' what time d'yehz call this?'she demanded, her voice breaking.

'Time?' the Boss queried. He looked at Jack and laughed. 'Yer woman's got nothin' ta do but look at the clock all day, while the likes a yeh an' me is out in them bloody hills sloggin' our poor guts out. I'll give yeh time, yeh dopey oul' garron if yeh don't get in that house an' make the tay.' He looked at Jack and laughed again, not sure if his son was sharing in what had started out as an attempt at humour.

Deep inside, the Boss was reassured by Mary's worrying. It meant that somewhere hidden in the mounds of flesh and rags there was still a spark, even if it was only fired by jealousy. The Boss was in a good mood as he released Kitty and even smiled as he watched the antics of the old pony race off around the garden, flinging muck over herself with her flailing hooves. It had not been a bad day. The shed was packed with sweet, graveyard hay.

Jack kept to himself and did his homework. School was uninspiring.He hated going; it seemed such a waste of time. In class he continued to dream of Sheila Rooney, motorbikes, of Galway, anything but lessons.

102

BABS READ THE letter from Aunt Dolores again and again. '"I will send fares for you, Pam and Bridgid. I may as well bring out the lot of you while I'm at it."' Pam and Bridgid were holding their hands to their mouths, squealing like mad and jumping up and down.

'Jesus Christ!' Bridgid cried with tears in her eyes. 'We're feckin' goin'. *Yes, yes, feckin' bloody yes!*'

Chicago sounded like the Yellow Brick Road, a night with Rock Hudson, and a week's shopping in Clery's all rolled into one. '*I will send fares for you, Pam and Bridgid. I may as well bring out the lot of you while I'm at it.*' It was an amazing opportunity to change their dreary lives. The girls were so happy they joined hands and did an impromptu Ring-a-Ring-a-Roses around the yard. But Chicago was a long, long way from home. The thought seemed to strike them all simultaneously and they stopped dancing. They were out of breath.

'We'll be flyin' in a big plane,' Bridgid gasped. 'At night, way up wit' the stars. God!' she said as if she had seen a ghost.

Babs broke the ensuing silence. 'C'mon, it's goin'ta be fun,' she said. 'Jus' imagine it. It's go'ta be a lot betther than this dump.'

'Yeah, yeh're right, Sis,' Bridgid said, and Pam came on board too.

'I'm reelly lookin' forward ta it. Whatever its faults, it has ta be betther than this.' She waved a hand at the broken mangle, the old swing dangling from the pussy willow, the old white chair peeling paint where Mary sat in the sun to read *The Messenger*.

The girls all cried. Could they really bear to leave their mother?

In the kitchen after supper Babs opened the envelope and once more read their aunt's letter . The Boss looked up every time he heard the rustle of the letter being taken from its enevelope. His bald head wrinkled, he was as jittery as an insecure lover about to be jilted by the most beautiful, the most perfect girl in the world. How could Babs think of going away and leaving him? She was obviously trying it on. She wanted a car or something to make her stay. The Boss did his mental sums. There was no way he could afford a car for her; a scooter maybe, or one a them mopeds. But they were bloody dangerous. He was always seeing some poor shite being scraped off the Rathmines road.

But hadn't he done everything he could for her? As for that old cod, Dolores, what right did she have to take pity on his children? He had a good mind to write to her and tell her to mind her own feckin' business – the fat sow.

As the days went by the Boss tried every conceivable blackmail in his effort to steer Babs away from leaving. The torrent of bullying and nagging made Babs sick but it also made her more determined to go. It was a decision only she could make, even though her mother, Jack and the posse of toddlers all tried in their own ways to get her to stay. It wasn't just the Boss who was going to lose out if Babs went, it was everyone. There would be no more new comics for Jack, no more money secretly slipped to Mary, no sweets for the younger ones. With an enormous sigh Babs closed her mind to them all and sat down to write a letter to Aunt Delores, accepting the offer on behalf of herself and her sisters. The deal was done. The Boss was deeply angry. Nothing he could say or do would stop her now. It seemed his beloved had set her heart against him. Babs was ready to dump a lifetime of love for a cheap ticket to nowhere. The sourness the Boss felt inside put him off both his *Evening Mail* and his food.

When Babs told Mary she was taking the letter to Rathfarnham village to post it in the morning, Mary sat in an uncomprehending daze, wondering what she had done wrong to deserve it.

'But Mammy, yeh have plenty of other children left,' Pam said, studying her scarlet lips in her compact mirror. 'Lots,' she added, combing her eye lashes until they curved upwards.

'That's not the p'int,' Mary sniffed. 'I love yehz all the same, I don't have favourites like some people I know.' She nodded venomously towards the Boss who was feeling too down to reply. Leaning on the stick she'd started using to support her gammy right hip, she ruminated gummily.

103

'THEY'RE KNOCKIN' DOWN the Priory next week,' Babs said. 'Jack, d'yeh wan'ta see it before it goes?'

'What d'yeh be wantin' ta do that fer?' the Boss asked. 'It's on'y an oul' place the rotten English built. Anyway it's a dangerous pile.'

'Robert Emmet went there,' Jack said.[3]

'Well, so feckin' what!' the Boss said. 'Emmet was a chancer usin' oul' Philpot Curran's influence ta get himself promoted inta society.'

'That's rubbitch,' said Mary, who was limping around as if her foot were nailed to the floor. 'Robert Emmet died fer this counthry.'

The Boss sneered. 'That sort a nonsense won't put grub in yer bellies. Yer man doin' that Devlin wan over in Butterfield Avenue, bloody imposter.'

'Don't talk like that in front a the childer,' Mary said with a sigh.

As Babs and her brother jogged across the bridge, the sun was setting fire to the new houses. 'At least the Pit'll still be here when we come back from America ta see yehz all,' Babs said as they strode along briskly, their legs cleaving the bulrushes that thrived in the Pit's boggy ooze.

'Yeah,' Jack said, remembering the awful night he'd been molested here by the night watchman. Then he remembered Paddy Daly.

'Ta imagine Rathfarnham without the Pit is impossible,' Babs said.

'Yeah,' Jack agreed.

The sun splintered on the Priory's diamond-shaped windows. The house had been vandalised. Stones had smashed the pretty windows,

[3] Robert Emmet (1778–1803) Irish patriot, born in Dublin. Having joined the United Irishmen, he travelled in Europe for the Irish cause, and met Napolean. In 1803 he plotted an unsuccessful insurrection against the English. He was captured and hung in Dublin.

coloured glass showered the dusty carpets. Echoing through the rooms were the secret kisses of Sarah Curran and Robert. His red scarf flying, a leather-bound book in his tweedy pocket, Robert Emmet had waved from below and was gone, his polished boots pounding the frosty lawn, shards of soft ice in his beard. On to the quiet, rustling lane he would have walked, his footfalls rising as he reached Butterfield Avenue and his bed. When the soldiers had come for him, Emmet was gone. Anne Devlin, the servant, was left to face a red-faced major. Soldiers pinned her arms, punched and kicked her, but she wouldn't tell. They twisted her long hair until the scalp bled. Her breasts were battered, her stomach was kicked until she coughed blood on to the carpet. Devlin's parents were jailed, her brother murdered. Emmet was betrayed but Anne kept Emmet's whereabouts secret. It made no difference to Emmet, for he was already in the hands of Lord Norbury who sentenced him to be hung, drawn and quartered. 'I am going to my cold and silent grave, my lamp of light nearly extinguished. I have parted with everything for my country's cause. I am ready to die . . . When my country takes its place among the nations of the world, then, and not till then . . . let my epitaph be written.' Emmet's corpse had dangled outside St Catherine's Church in Thomas Street on 23 September, 1803. Below it fat white worms wriggled in the earth.

'Let's run up to the Forto,' Babs said.

As they trotted side by side she realised there were parts of Rathfarnham she had never visited. This might be her last chance. Not talking, they took the strain up the steep hill and around by Marley. Inside, gaunt old English aristos stumped around on zimmer frames, tripping over choked chamber pots. There was no one left to empty the buckets that caught the showers through crumbling roofs. Gardens, where children back from boarding school had jumped their ponies, were overgrown, the once immaculately white-painted fences collapsed.

Pools where poets used to swim naked were choked with filth. Tennis courts which had echoed to English accents were now untidy meadows; verandahs, where pink gins and Pimms had been consumed from cut glass, leaned crazily. Hills where tweedy men with dogs had filled the sky with buckshot and blood were tangled and neglected, the pheasants long since shot by poachers.

They passed superbly crafted farm buildings and cow byres, waiting silently for the yellow bulldozers and excavators to tumble their ancient masonry, smash the dressed stone and extract the oak beams like rotten molars. There was no room for sentimentality. Money was the new Celtic god. The English had kept the country's beauty intact, now they were history too. In nooks, speculators had yet to find, smoke still doodled from distant cottages. For the time being, the blackstone cottage and the modest farmhouse would survive the cull.

'That was good,' Babs said, still jogging energetically. As they neared the bungalow Jack said, 'Wish't I was goin' wit'cha ta Chicago.'

Babs stopped. 'Yeh can if yeh wan'ta. We'll sall save up an' send fer yeh one day.

'T'anks,' Jack said. One thing was for certain. It would be lonely without Babs.

The Boss's bike wheels whirred on new concrete roads built on anthills and dew ponds a thousand years old. He watched the estate being built, the surveyors measure up, the lorries arriving with joists and bricks. Instead of putting his few pounds in a box under the bed, why oh why hadn't he bought a small field when they were going for nothing? Why was he so short-sighted? Instead, he'd let the hated culchies move in, allowed them to make their fortunes right on his doorstep.

'How do them bastards do it an' not me?' he asked himself as he gazed through the trees he'd planted at the houses going up all around him. When he saw a ruddy-faced builder drive past in a brand new Humber Hawk the Boss spat blood. There he was on his fecking bike, in tatty rags, hamstrung with a mad wife and a horde of noisy, hungry children, while mongrels from the west of Ireland, scented and coiffured, waved ringed hands at him as they sailed by in satined comfort. Had he been a man of vision the Boss could have bought those fields for next to nothing and made a fortune. Babs would not have needed to go to America. As he cycled alone, the thought stabbed him through the heart.

104

MARY WALKED SLOWLY into the kitchen, preceded by a procession of children crying, 'Mammy's up.' Her blinding headache temporarily abated she made breakfast.

Jack dipped a crust into his soft boiled egg and sucked it. 'Misther Moroney's afther askin' Ben Byrne to bring his gun in ta shoot rats that do be runnin' roun' the schoolyard,' he said. 'I'm hopin' he'll let me have a shot out of it.'

Mary bent down to tuck in his shirt. 'Ah, sure, God help yeh, what would the masther be wantin' lads to shoot an'tin' for?' she asked through blue lips.

'An' there's this lovely hawk comes over every day after lunch,' Jack said between slurps of tea. It lands on the tree in the schoolyard,' Jack said excitedly. 'Ben Byrne's goin' ta shoot that as well,' he added.

Mary turned indignant. 'That's a shame,' she said. 'An' yeh can tell that Misther Moroney I said so. 'Fancy allowin' this lad ta kill the lovely wild bird?'

'Misther Moroney as'd him ta bring in the gun,' Jack repeated as he slung his satchel on his back.

'Don't be late back, y'know what yer Daddy'll say, an' by the way . . .'

Jack quickly extricated himself from his mother's story and ran down the road. He wasn't the first in the classroom. Others were already milling about, excited at the prospect of some sport. 'Where's Moroney?' . . . 'Is Byrne in yet?' . . . 'Diyeh t'ink the hawk'll come over today?'

Jack removed his satchel. Foley turned around and said viciously, 'He should shoot yer oul' fella.'

'I betcha wouldn' say that ta me father's face,' Jack whispered.

Byrne walked into the room surrounded by hero-worshippers. He carried a canvas gun case. When he dropped it on the desk with an impressive clunk, Jack joined the ring of onlookers.

'Give us a look, Byrne,' Foley asked.

'Feck off Blondie,' Byrne replied.

'What sort a gun is it?' Jack asked.

'Does it fire real bullets?' a surburban kid from Golden Acre wanted to know.

'Yeah, gobshite, it's a feckin' bazooka,' Byrne said.

'Watch out, here comes Moroney!' Fetherstone yelled.

'Morning, you snotty-nosed bunch a criminals,' the master said.

'Good morning, Sir Bollocks!' a reedy voice replied.

'Who said that?' the master roared and glared around the room. Jack blushed. 'Was it you, Dunne?'

'No, Sir.'

'I didn't think it was, yeh haven't the nerve, have yeh, yeh little creep.'

'No, Sir.'

The boys all laughed in unison.

'Who was it then?' The master looked hard at Foley. 'OK, smart alec, come out here.'

'Who me?' said Foley incredulously. 'I never said nuthin', honest.'

'I never said nuthin',' the master mimicked in a falsetto. 'Will yeh come out here, yeh thick cur. You can't spell bloody cat, or add two an' two, but you try to be clever behind me back. Well, I won't take that sort of nonsense from rubbish like you. Come out!'

The master's face reddened and his eyes behind his spectacles looked wild. Moroney eschewed weapons, preferring to use his own big culchie hands to take boys apart. He was a thickset brute but he was interested in football and that made him Jack's friend. And he regularly beat up Foley.

Moroney waited until Foley was within a few feet then he downed him with a perfect right cross. Foley got up, dusted himself down and forced a smile as he strode back to his seat.

'Nice wan,' Jack mouthed silently.

'I'd rather be breakin' stones in Mountjoy jail than teachin' yeh dopey, ill-bred feckers,' Moroney said. The boys guffawed.

'All right, yeh bloody rabble, it's break time,' Moroney sighed finally.

'An' don't be lollin' about the yard, keep movin'. Get the lard off a yer arses. God knows yeh miserable scum need the exercise.'

The silence of the concrete yard was obliterated by a great roar as the boys almost got stuck in the doors as they tried to escape. A hundred immature voices were laying bets, telling stories, or shrieking with pain or delight. The hullabaloo filled the tiny playground, as the teachers huddled by the school door like consumptive crows.

The noise spilled over to the Canon's immaculate lawn. Greg, the weather-worn gardener, poking about in the speckled sunlight, his pipe smouldering, started at the sudden disturbance. 'Shite on them bloody gurriers,' he muttered.

When the headmaster glanced at his shoes and started to walk towards the classrooms it was the signal for the boys to cease their activities and march back in single file to their desks.

Moroney droned on. The occasional jotter flew across the floor, spreading its pages. There was a series of thumps as each recalcitrant pupil had his ears boxed. A muted squeal came from some kid who was being molested at the back. Footsteps were heard thumping down the road and all eyes shot up to the big picture of the Crucifixion to see if the pedestrian was reflected in its glass. In the Canon's garden the gardener relit his pipe and raked the gravelled paths.

Suddenly, a silent fluttering was caught in the corners of one or two alert, mountain-reared eyes. The message was rushed by elbows and nods around the room. Moroney ceased his mouthing. The upper branches of the silver birch were nicely framed in one side of the window. On the topmost branch a kestrel preened itself. The master looked at Byrne in the front desk and nodded.

A deadly game between the hawk, glittering in the sunlight, and the keen-eyed boy, began. The bottom half of the window was eased up and Byrne rested the rifle on the sill. Squinting along the barrel, he moved slightly to get the bird in his sight. The hawk eyed the deserted schoolyard, waiting for a hungry mouse to come out to sniff at a discarded morsel. Jack, like most of the other boys, was familiar with guns and watched with dry-mouthed fascination at what they saw as an even contest.

The room was eerily quiet as Byrne aimed for the bird's head and depressed the trigger. There was a crack, the bird plopped softly on to the concrete, flopped helplessly for a moment and died. A cheer went up. Mr Dougal peeped, under his hand, through the adjoining window. When the boys saw his thin face with dark patches under the tired eyes, their heads bobbed down and they pretended to read.

Byrne rushed out into the yard, and carried the dripping bird back into the classroom. Everyone agreed, even while seething with jealousy, it was a great shot. The remaining hours of the warm day crawled by; a fistful of bluebottles investigated the bird's magnificent plumage as it lay stiffening among the crisp packets and browning apple cores in the school dustbin.

When it was time to go home, a defiant roar rushed over the school wall to irritate the Canon's gardener. 'Stupid fuckers,' he grunted, quickly attempting to take the venom out of his remark with the back of his hand as he glimpsed the Canon walking through the shubbery, reading his Office.

Ruffians climbed, fought, and teetered on walls before vanishing into doorways. The road was soon quiet again except for the wind singing through the telegraph lines.

Jack rushed the story home but no one was interested. Familiar chores finished, he read the armful of old comics he had swapped with Foley for the new packet of Gold Flakes he had found outside Rice's shop. Jack was pleased with the bargain, as was Foley who lit up immediately, and sold the rest to his gang at a penny each.

'Yeh should a handed them back ta da shop,' Mary had said. 'Some poor workin' man might a dropped them there. Yehz're all gettin' like yer ould fella, an' me afther breakin' me heart tryin' ta bring yehz up in the light a God an' His Blessed Saints.'

Oh yeah, Jack was thinking, so that's why yeh're so successful and lucky.

After tea, the Boss sat in his chair, brooding over the imminent loss of Babs. The vein over his eye was leaping about like it was electrically charged. The tension was real and the touch paper easily lit. Young Paul rushing to the ring board slipped on the worn lino. His awkward body hit the ground with a thump. The Boss leapt to his feet, the cheap spectacles knocked awry on his nose giving him an insane look. He grabbed the rings and roared, 'I'll spread yer feckin' guts all over the feckin' house if yeh don't shut yer shaggin' mout'.'

Little Paul huddled close to his mother and cried. Mary muttered, 'Use less a the filt'y tongue in front a me poor childer.'

The Boss exploded. A bunched fist took Mary on the side of the face, knocking her glasses across the room. As she staggered blindly, he connected with another cruel blow that sent her sprawling across the floor, her walking stick hitting the brass fender and making it ring. Squealing girls threw themselves in front of her. For a few seconds the Boss was mad. His eyes rolled in his head, spittle gathered around the little mouth that had twisted into a water-spout of insane curses. He ranted about Mary's impressive appetite for kinky sex which had deviants for miles around panting at the mere mention of her name. Jack glanced at the helpless and beaten hulk of his mother, a poor old hag after so many births. She looked anything but a sex kitten. But beauty is in the eye of the blind. He almost laughed at the idiocy of his father's fevered tirade.

The girls rubbed reddened eyes as the Boss, quivering with tension and temper, sat down and tried to focus on the news. The evening dragged its feet, there was sighing, sobbing and the blowing of noses. 'Don't put any more good fuel on that bloody fire,' the Boss barked as someone tried to enliven the dying embers. 'Yehz may's well get ready fer yer beds fer its near time and yehz all hav'ta be up fer school tomorra.'

How feckin' borin', Jack was thinking.

The Boss got up, looking sheepish. Carefully, he folded his spectacles and placed them in their worn tin case. 'Jack, get them lamps,' he ordered. Jack fetched the pink-globed paraffin lamps from each bedroom. In the kitchen the wicks were trimmed and the oil topped up. He picked up his lamp and walked cautiously to the dark, damp bedroom, a spray of gold flowing round him. The sniffing girls dragged themselves into their rooms and listened as Mary and the Boss exchanged abuse. Bug-eyed with fear, the younger ones stared into the blackness. At last they closed their eyes.

As the older girls gripped the blankets in terrorised slumber a sobbing shadow appeared by their bedside, frightening them awake. In a billowing nightshift Mary sat on the complaining bed toothlessly muttering, 'Babs can't go ta America an' l'ave me here. He'll kill me.

How in God's name was I deceived by such a man. I must a been as blind as a bat to marry a cruel beast like that, and him wit' not an ounce of compassion in his whole body. God above, why, why did I do it?' Then, like a big, useless old urn that had been filled to the brim with misery, Mary spilled over and her wretched cries of anguish woke the whole house.

'Will yeh stop that bloody snottin' and snivellin',' the Boss yelled from his bed, 'a fella can't get a wink a sleep, an' him up at six in the mornin'.'

Soon, loud snores confirmed that he at least was deep in apparently untroubled sleep.

105

NEXT DAY, JACK arrived at school to find a noisy celebrating classroom. Moroney'd had a serious car crash. 'Ran his bleedin' car right off a the feckin' road,' one boy reported gleefully, and added with a smile, 'I hope the cunt's dead.'

The boys sat at their desks unsupervised, grinning and plotting mischief. 'Look out!' someone screamed as a log flew the length of the room and hit another boy on the head. The recipient of the blow went on a revenge mission and a scuffle broke out.

Jack was fascinated. It was like watching a coachful of his enemies roll down an embankment into a cold, bottomless lake. One boy lit a Players Extra Strength and handed it around under the desks. Boys smoked, coughed and swore. Foley took a deep drag then ground the glowing butt into the naked thigh of the school sop, a garda's son whose oystery little ear was often blatantly caressed by Moroney in full view of the whole class. The sop's shrill screaming briefly quietened the mob. Twin morons from a dysfunctional family smallholding up in the mountains laughed, their thin faces creased wolfishly in perverted mirth. 'If yeh tell yer old fella, yer feckin' dead,' one of them said, bunching his fist at Chinko for emphasis.

Chinko Hayes, the school gobshite, with his buck teeth and round, yellow face, regaled the mob by taking Moroney's mug off its hook, lobbing out his cock and filling the sacred vessel with pee. Showing a mouthful of broken Chinese choppers, Chinko yelled, 'I'm goin'ta dhrink it.' As he raised the mug to his lips, the boys punched, kicked, squeezed each other's privates, and laughed. Jack laughed too. As Chinko posed with the mug to his mouth, Foley, determined to gain bragging rights, hit Chinko's arm, sending a parabola of piss across Moroney's desk and spraying the boys in the front row. Boys cursed, mopped their fronts and made disgusted faces.

A few went to kill Foley but by hopping from desk to desk he was quickly across the room to safety. The racket drew Dougal's grey face with its long grey nose to his window. He stared in like a cat eyeing a cage full of canaries. Arms were quickly folded and boys silently seated. When Dougal withdrew his miserable visage, the class once more erupted like a cartoon film that had been on hold.

Jack was relishing the anarchy but he missed the massive disciplinary presence of Moroney. Foley's alter ego, Jim Fetherstone, a bull-necked boy from an incestuous homestead in a cleft in the Pine Valley, searched the room for a victim, taking in its contents like a tank gunner finding his range. His baleful gaze fell unerringly on Jack. 'Yes, you!' The kid with the startled look who was suddenly trying to look invisible. The whole room looked at Jack, glad it wasn't them.

'Jack Dunne, eh? Well, thy will be Dunne in a feckin' minute,' Fetherstone punned, and the class laughed, a few of them nervously. Jack fiddled with his jotter, then discovered something fascinating about the tip of his pencil. A hand as rough and bony as if it had been soaked in prussic acid pulled Jack eye-poppingly close to the pock-marked, blackhead-riddled face of the mountain maniac. Jack, unsurprisingly, found no pity in the close-set eyes.

Fetherstone's breath stank, and hair sprang from a wart on his chin. Jack swooned in case even the slighted movement might suggest defiance. As Fetherstone glared at him like a potential murderer, Jack wanted to see Moroney leap through the doors splintering the wood and smashing the glass. Failing that he wished he had a tommy-gun which he could press very close to Fetherstone's flies and effect an immediate sex change. Even bullies have pride in their work, and Jack's obsession with pacifism depressed Fetherstone who only wanted to kill someone with guts. Someone who would fight back. Wearily, he belted Jack over the eye. The pain was excruciating but Jack gritted his teeth and sat blinking, a plum-sized lump quickly rising over his left eye. The boys laughed but left Jack alone to endure his humiliating agony in silence.

As Fetherstone swaggered past his desk, Foley smiled in admiration. Fetherstone's mastery was unbreachable. Everyone in the school feared Fetherstone, while Foley specialised exclusively in bullying weaklings.

'Yeh want some too?' Fetherstone challenged Foley.

'No, no, no, I'm all right pal, jus' watchin's great.'

His needs temporarily satisfied, Fetherstone returned to his desk and entertained his hangers-on with stories of battles won, laws broken, and things stolen or smashed.

When at last the bell sounded Jack went to a corner of the playground wearing his plummy bruise with pride. He clutched his lunch in a brown paper bag oozing with the life blood of squashed tomato. Uncorking a small bottle of watered milk he swigged and chewed, observing impressionistic blobs of boys as they raced around the playground, jumping, spitting and wrestling. He inspected the dark spot where the kestrel had hit the concrete, then went to sit near the school gate.

The two teachers, their lunch break over, took up their positions by the roadside where they chatted, watched the traffic and wiped the dust off their cars, a black Morris Minor and a green Hillman Imp. They talked as they worked, agreeing that Moroney was not just a crap driver, but a crap teacher as well. 'Too keen ta use the strhap, an' not brilliant on the brakes either.' The teachers laughed.

Then Dougal said, 'I don't care fer vi'lence meself.'

That makes two of us, Jack thought.

The bell sounded for classes to begin, and the rooms filled up. Room 3 was ready for more entertainment. Jack went indoors keen to show off his plum. It was Foley's turn to entertain. He took a piece of coal from the fire with the tongs and flicked it across the room where it stuck to a torn old map of the world and immediately set fire to Tasmania. Chinko put out the fire with piss.

Finally, the school day was over. Almost the instant the last bell of the day rang, Dougal appeared in Room 3 to say Moroney's accident was not too serious. He smiled when sighs of disappointment went round the room, and told them their teacher would be back tomorrow.

As he walked home Jack saw Foley and and his outlaws stealing apples from the Canon's garden. Jack ran as fast as his legs could carry him. He knew his father would be standing on the dunghill, his fingers in his mouth, whistling.

That night, the family was left in relative peace as the Boss listened to Eamonn Andrews commentating from Donnybrook bus station on

Spider Kelly boxing Ray Famechon. He fired vicious hooks and uppercuts at the ceiling shouting, 'Kill the French bastard, Spider.'

When the Frenchman got the points decision the Boss abused the referee and loudly cast doubt on his parentage. Around the legs of the table toddlers sparred and giggled at the antics of their dad.

106

AS A PARTING gift to Mary, Babs wanted to make her mother a huge blackberry tart. Jack helped his sister collect the fruit that had survived the rain and the bluebottles. The berries were hard and sharp and not so juicy but the unmistakable flavour was delicious. Babs reached above the pink thorns and closed her fingertips round the dark staining fruit. She would be in Chicago next autumn, when the tangled bushes behind the sties were hanging with fruit. She would be in a hard-edged place with traffic, sterile streets, underground stations, cabs cruising like sharks, like in the *Picture Posts* she brought back from Easthams.

'God, isn't it a beautiful day,' Babs said, 'never thought it was this good out.'

Jack picked the low berries, with the white sun blinding him and caressing him softly through his shirt and pullover. A robin was singing on the top branch of Neary's willow, and a band of warblers on a lower bough were opening and closing their beaks and wings as if they were having an almighty row. Jack was aware of everything around him: the clip-clop of the horse hauling the bread van from door to door round the Corporation houses beyond the stream; the sheep that blanketed every inch of Neary's paddock; the convent bell tower standing out in the clear air; the clumps of nettles growing in green profusion from the pig-dung saturated bank. 'Them oul' nettles is the right man wit'a bit a b'ilin' bacon,' the Boss often said. With impervious hands he would pluck them as if they were flowers and take them to the house, only for Mary to scream, 'Get them lousy stingers out a this house. Only the divil could ate them.'

Babs rattled a handful of blackberries into the pot. 'There's not that many,' she said, rubbing her bare leg where she'd been scratched by a stray briar. Jack, felt good picking with his big sister, even though there were not many berries to pick. He knew she was thinking of going away. When she turned and looked at her brother, she smiled as if she knew what he'd been thinking.

'C'mon, Jack,' she said, 'let's go home, it's gettin' cold.' The sun had crept around behind Neary's big red barn and was backlighting the bronze-leafed birch by the old farmhouse. Jack saw a figure touched with gold carrying buckets into the milking shed. It must have been Tommy Lee.

With the pot only half filled with blackberries, the last he and his sister might ever pick together, Jack followed Babs back to the bungalow to make their peace offering, a big tart the whole family including the Boss could share.

'Yeh can't bate a few oul' blackers ta give tarts a bit a flavour,' Babs said as she kneaded the pastry while Jack boiled the fruit with loads of sugar. He licked the red spoon. It had been such a sweet day.

107

THREE SINGLE TICKETS to Chicago came in the next letter from Aunt Dolores. A quarter of Mary's children were being plucked from her without her having a say in the matter. Their going was now certain, and sparked off a wild flurry of sewing and mending. Though occasionally confined to her bed with a catalogue of ailments, some imagined, Mary was in good heart. Father Orlston visited and she confessed to him an unbelievable litany of vile sins. It made her feel a lot better, and the old priest had no hesitation in giving her absolution. He was such a comfort. Forced to take tea with the Boss afterwards, his frayed cuffs touching the saucer, Father Orlston listened helplessly to the Boss's bad luck stories, his heroism in the face of adversity, his lack of help from any quarter. The priest feigned interest as the bitter monologue piled over him like a steamroller, flattening him like a Looney Tune cat.

Politely refusing another cup, 'It's a grand drop a tay, shame ta waste it, but . . .' the priest rose from his chair. With his black wide-brimmed hat in his hand, he clawed at the door to make his escape. Outside, he stood before the bungalow, breathing in the sun-warmed air. The children crowded at the bungalow's window, a collage of scraggy hair and besmirched faces. 'Well now,' the priest said, with a touch of briskness, 'the blessing a God on yehz all. Sure, it's hard times all round these days, but if we put our trust in God . . .'

'All right,' the Boss cut in. 'Yeh'll come again soon, won'tcha?'

The priest nodded and power-walked across the bridge in case the Boss tried to call him back. Father Orlston continued walking until he got to Deveney's off-licence, where he purchased a bottle of Gilbey's "Odds On" Wine Cocktail. A couple of glasses over a banned novel would help him regain his equilibrium.

As he listlessly shovelled swill into the pigsties the Boss growled to no one in particular. 'It's them bastardin' priests that's havin' it all in this bloody counthry, wit' their lovely houses and maids ta look afther 'em.' He dwelt on the maids for a moment before emitting a frustrated snarl, 'I betcha them rotten oul' wans that do be lookin' afther them hoorin' priests do be openin' their dirt'y gams fer t'melts.'

Mary had taken to her bed with a severe bout of nerves. Recently, her outbursts were increasingly irrational, causing Babs to think that the thought of losing her girls was sending their mother mad. Pam sat outside the back door with bits of coloured delft, the chainies with which she was trying to make something to please Mary. In the fuggy warmth of the darkened bedroom, Babs had given their mother a wash and tucked her into bed.

'That bulging belly a yers,' Mary cackled as Babs bent over her mother to feed her some soup from a bowl. 'It's a baby, isn't it?'

Babs was shocked. 'No, a course not. How could it be, Mammy?'

'Yer def'n'y in the family way,' Mary insisted with a wild laugh. 'Sure, that's what happens when a fella touches yeh. It's natchral.'

Babs stopped and looked at her mother, who was looking up at her with a manic grin. 'Please, Mammy, don't be sayin' I'm pregnant, if anywan hears that I'll be ruined.'

'Serves yeh right,' Mary laughed, 'fer goin' on wit' them lads, oh, I know, yeh don't hav'ta tell me an'tin' 'bout men, they have yer knickers off before–'

'Mammy!' Babs surprised even herself by the severity of her protest. 'Now, I've told yeh, don't be sayin' t'ings like that, it's not true, I've never done that wit' any fella, bur if yeh keep on about it, I'll hav'ta stop comin' in ta see yeh.'

'There yeh are,' Mary said triumphantly, 'guilt always comes out. I can tell be the way yer takin' it.'

'Mammy,' Babs said with a desperate sigh and a sob in her throat, 'yeh know I'm a virgin, that's how yeh brought me up.'

'Sure, that's nuttin',' Mary said. 'Wasn't I a virgin wanst too, an' look what happened ta me. Yer man hadta have me certified, wouldn't marry me unless a doctor proved I was pure. Lookit me now. Virgin me arse.'

While the sun shone outside on Pam with her chainies and Jack sat alone in the Pit, minding the cow, Mary and her eldest daughter both cried.

'Is there anything else yeh want, Mother?' Babs sobbed.

'There's plenty I want and none of yehz can give it,' Mary said. 'Han' me that knittin' wool,' she added, grinning, her mouth a soft red hole. 'I hav'ta make hats fer yehz. Dolores tells me it's awful cold in Chicago.'

Babs crept quietly from their mother's room and into the kitchen which seemed lifeless without Mary. Bridgid was sitting at the table, her knees apart, reading.

'Poor Mammy's mind's goin',' Babs said.

Bridgid looked up. 'Whatja mean?'

'She keeps on about sex. The latest is I'm pregnant. Can yeh believe that?'

'That's a laugh all right,' Bridgid said, 'an' how in the name a Jasus does she t'ink yeh got in the club, be sittin' on the lav? Although, the Blessed Virgin had a baby be a carpenter who swore blind he'd never touched her. Ach she's gone haywire. The oul' man's done the poor oul' bitch.'

'Don't talk like that about yer mother,' Babs said.

'Ah, I'm sick a the whole bloody lot a them,' Bridgid said, 'they're as mad as each other. Lucky we're excapin' from it. I'm reelly lookin' forward ta goin' now. This place gets me goat, big time. I must write ta Aunty Dolores in case she changes her mind. 'Cos if I stay here any longer, I'll be the next wan for the straitjacket.'

Bridgid went to the bedroom to compose her letter. As she wrote she heard her mother laughing, scolding and crying. It made her pause and wonder if it was right to be leaving her at all.

The next letter from Aunt Dolores ran to six pages and included a wad of photos of her on holiday. Babs focussed on the word *Connecticut*. It sounded a dreamy place: blue water, boats, candlelit dinners with wine on white verandahs. 'Tell your mother I love her. Love, Aunt Dolores.'

The girls gathered round, practically hyper ventilating. Mary heard their screams of joy.

'Giv'us a look,' Bridgid said. 'Read what she says 'xactly.'

'Oh, my God,' Pam cried with her face in her hands, 'I jus' can't believe we're goin'. Wonder if it's near Hollywood.' She touched her hair and lifted up her breasts.

It was better than a wonderful dream. Babs slipped the letter between the pages of *Jamaica Inn*, and went to work. That evening she washed the children's clothes at the sink. Her sleeves rolled, the dirty water oozing through her fingers. She beat, twisted and scrubbed holed shirts, odd socks, and dirty grey underwear. All the while as she worked she thought of America. Soon she would be there, building a new life. She would find a nice lad, get married, have babies, not twelve like her mother, three or four would do. She was hanging the heavy wet clothes on the line when Jack appeared, clumping up from the yard, his hair spiked up by the wind, his torn clothes making him look like the sort of little Brazilian lads seen searching through rubbish dumps in *Picture Post*.

'Hi, Brud,' Babs said quietly. Poor Jack had nothing to look forward to. 'Yeh'll join us out there, won'tcha?'

'I will,' Jack said. 'An'tin's betther than this,' he spread a dirty hand. 'Can I give yeh a hand?'

'Not wit' them dirthy paws,' Babs laughed. 'No, g'wan inside, have a wash an' a cup a tea.'

'How's Mammy?'

'She's the same, poor t'ing. Yeh can see why, can'tcha. I don't hav'ta spell it out?'

The Boss came through the wire with a ball he'd made of the twine he'd taken off the bales and tied the ends together. It would come in handy one day. When he saw Babs at the washtub, for a moment he was back in his tough youth with a young Mary, who was lithe, handsome, with a smile for her man as he came in from work. How good it was in those days. He looked back towards the garden. 'Well, a fella can on'y do his best,' he said. 'I've always done me best fer yeh, Babs.' She tried to talk to her father but he had never been a listener. 'I done me best,' he said, going to the water butt to wash his face and hands.

He took hold of his daughter like Clark Gable held Vivienne Leigh in *Gone with the Wind*. Babs stiffened. 'So yer off soon,' he said hoarsely.

Babs stammered, and had to sit down to force her father to release her. 'It's somet'in' I need ta do, Daddy,' she said. Her face was set and her eyes avoided his.

'I don't blame yeh at all,' he said. 'That feckin' bitch in there,' he pointed to Mary's silent and curtained bedroom, 'I blame her. She druve yeh ta it.'

'She did not!' Babs cried. 'An' I don't wan'ta keep sayin' it, 'cos it's not true an' you know it!'

'Anyway,' the Boss said, 'I've decided, yeh're not goin'.'

'I bloody well *am*!' Babs said.

In his shoddy clothes the Boss looked like an ancient Russian serf in the presence of a golden princess. His wheedling sounded hollow and pathetic. His voice became reedy and emasculated . 'Why wouldja wan'ta go? He asked very softly. 'I don't understand it. I gotcha that lovely job in Easthams. Yeh don't want some slip ova one ta come in an' take that away from yeh, now, do yeh?'

Babs' face was pale in the poor light. Her father made her feel afraid. He had the ability to suck resistance from people. 'I'm goin', Daddy,' she repeated with a kind of robotic determination.

With a sort of animal whine the Boss threw himself at her like some character ensnared in a web. 'This'll kill yer mother,' he said, 'don'tcha know that? The poor woman is half mad as it is. Yeh wouldn' want that on yer conscience, now wouldja?'

Babs laughed out loud. 'I'm goin' away from here,' she said. 'I have to. Why can'tcha see that? I'll go mad if I don't.' Babs picked up the broom. The Boss touched her lightly again. Babs kept on sweeping, her bib swaying from side to side.

'When yeh finish that oul' sweepin' we'll have a little trate,' he said. Jangling the keys, he opened the special cupboard he kept stocked with surprises.

Jack, who had been listening to their exchanges looked up from his Irish History. 'Why can'tcha let Babs go?' he asked. 'There's nuttin' fer her here.'

The Boss leapt at his eldest son with such ferocity that Jack could not escape. 'Don't come that wit' me, yeh bloody sleeveen,' he said, smacking Jack so hard it sent him and his homework skittering across the floor. Jack collected his things and went back to work as if his father had done no more than give him a fiver and kissed him. He looked up at Babs who smiled in sympathy.

When Babs finished the cleaning the Boss had a large chocolate sponge cut into wedges which the surprised toddlers, who had pressed around him, were passing round the room. Genially he fed the baby scraps of sticky chocolate and watched it giggle.

'Can I take a bit to Mammy?' Babs asked.

'A course yeh can,' the Boss said, smiling, his lips drawn back as far as they would go.

108

THE YARD WAS hushed. Jack listened to the irregular piping of a desolate robin looking for something to keep it alive, and the slow drone of an aeroplane homing in on Collinstown. With winking red lights it was returning from foreign parts by way of a shortcut across their garden.

Very soon his sisters would be on a plane like that but going the other way, over Galway. Jack felt like some small hairy animal in a swamp somewhere, totally unknown to David Attenborough. He scratched the scalp under his woolly hat. An old dog fox barked in Neary's wood, where some of the trees had been blasted by lightning and gave it the look of a battleground.

Babs arrived quietly at his elbow and whispered that a pink sky always brought a sunny morning. 'Will yeh miss us when we go t'America?' she asked. Jack wanted to say, 'I'll certainly miss the tanners an' the comics,' but he only laid his chin on his crossed arms and stared ahead with a sad, hunched look.

'We'll miss this oul' dump in spite a everythin',' Babs said. 'It'll always be home. . . . Some days I jus' don't wan'ta go, udders, well . . . Ah, well, if yer not goin'ta talk I may as well go.' She stood for a moment, looking at her brother's scrawny neck and wild hair, then turned and walked away. Jack stood for a while longer leaning on his arms. There would be no tears for Babs, or anyone else. She wanted to leave. He was only staying behind because he had no choice. As he turned to go indoors Bridgid arrived with Pam.

'T'inkin' are yeh?' Bridgid asked. 'Wonderin' how yeh're goin'ta get along wit'out us, eh?'

'Leave him alone,' Pam said, 'he's prob'ly tinkin' how nice it's gonna be without yeh around ta ballyrag him all the time. Isn't that right, Jack?' She put an arm around her brother's shoulder. For a moment he allowed his sister to hold him. Then, as if he had suddenly awoken to a nasty and embarrassing moment, he shrugged her off and bent to stroke one of the cats that craved food from behind the wire.

'I wouldn' wan'ta go anyway,' he said, poking his fingers through the wire and exciting the poor cat who pretended to be a kitten to please him. 'There's no Isle a Man TT race in America.' Standing on her hind legs the cat gently pawed at Jack's fingers, her small furry fist closed so as not to tear him.

Pam got down on her haunches to play with the cat, whose paws were striking through the wire like a prisoner pleading. 'Yer'll be betther off here,' she said. 'When we're gone, Mammy and Daddy'll prob'ly ge'ron betther.'

But Jack knew that without his three older sisters he would be exposed to the Boss's full panoply of terror. He would have to plan his own escape, in his own time.

Another fat aeroplane crossed over the garden, climbed above the dunghill and flew over Neary's red barn. Planes featured a lot in Jack's dreams. He was waving at his father from a porthole window as the big silver bird slanted over the bungalow. He was off to Acapulco where the film stars went. He could see himself laughing and pointing down. All the other passengers would rush to his side of the plane to see. 'Bye-bye, Dad. Keep shovellin' the shite. One day yeh'll strike gold or oil. *But don't hold yer feckin' breat'*!' he would yell as the plane roared off and left his father a bad-tempered full stop in the garden below.

'I'll send yeh a postcard, Dad, yeh gobshite!'

109

JACK HAD SET off with his father armed with a saw and an axe. His mind on Babs, the Boss was speaking furiously to himself, his voice carrying along the still avenues of trees. He felled, chopped and cut while Jack stacked the wood in the cart. Like actors in a silent movie, those who had crossed the Boss at some point in his life, filtered through his tortured mind, gesturing at him, taunting him. He slashed at them.

Babs would one day take a lover, who would ride her with bulging eyes. He could save her, but he was trapped in Ireland. The Boss swung his axe again. The village men - whom he saw as rivals, thieves, conmen, and, if given half a chance, rapists and paedophile s - got the chop too, their legs sliced off at the knees, leaving them staggering around on stumps howling with pain. The priests were next: ignorant midgets with enormous power and a poisonous influence over all, including his wife and daughters. The Boss lifted the axe above his head and pulverised a whole black-coated swath of them.

In the Boss's troubled head his enemies lurched and laughed at him all the while he worked. Savagely sawing and chopping, not feeling pain when a finger was cut or trapped, the Boss drowned in his own sweat. A hideous world was conspiring to send him to Hell. He couldn't let it. It had taken his wife, corrupted his son, and now it was after his darling Babs. He must get them first. The Boss hacked at the trees, his eyes wild with fury, his mouth dribbling on to his collar. 'Jasus, I'll get the feckers,' he roared, striking a disfiguring chunk of bark from a fine oak.

It was Jack who saw the black-coated Jesuits unravelling, single-file, from the wood opposite, crossing a latticed bridge over a stream and climbing the metalled forest-worker's road to where Kitty was tethered. Locked outside his father's yelling, slashing and brow mopping, Jack made mute gestures, but it was no good. Soon, the priests were milling round him, patting Kitty's head, examining the cart, fingering the harness and making cracks about their own lives in the country, for their ruddy complexions, lop ears and big hands gave away their low breeding.

'Mornin', a lovely day, isn't it?' one said.

The Boss jerked an angry face at the intruders when he heard their country accents. 'Oh, good mornin' Fathers,' he hissed, at the same time raising his hat. He was breathing furiously, his chest heaving. The Jesuits mingled for a while then marched on, dismissing the lunatic woodman from their minds.

The Boss breathed heavily, the axe in his hand, blood flowing from a wound making the handle slippery. He watched the men's rucksacks disappear. 'I wonder how long them hoors is afther been list'nin' to a fella,' he mused, helping his son to load the logs. The wind getting up stung the wound in his hand. The sweat had turned to ice on his back. With a tired sigh, the Boss threw his tools on to the cart and rested for a moment, his powerful shoulders pumping, his black-nailed hands on Kitty's neck. He was a desperate man. Nothing had gone right for him in his long and awful fight for his place on earth.

After a while he harnessed her to the cart and cajoled the old pony into a trot. Squealing, the cart ran along the foot of the hill and into the road. It had barely gone half a mile when it was overtaken by a motorcar that immediately pulled in, forcing Kitty to rear up.

'What in the name a Jasus are yeh doin'?' The Boss stood up, his whip at the ready. A young man got out of the car and with accomplished ease, held Kitty's head. 'Get out a me way or I'll run yeh over, yeh ignorant bastard,' the Boss yelled, raising his whip.

'Now calm down, will you,' the young man said. His accent was cultured, and English. 'I'll come quickly to the point,' he said, stroking Kitty's drenched mane. 'My family have just bought the Orlagh Forest. In future, trespassers will be prosecuted. Don't deny it, please, I've seen you come from there.' He walked around the cart and drew back the tarpaulin. 'My God! You haven't been cutting branches off the young trees, have you?'

'Young trees? Orlagh Forest?' the Boss said. 'Yeh t'ink I was in yer wood? Ha ha.' The lies the Boss had perfected over a lifetime of lying poured out of him. Why, he was only 'doin' a bit a trimmin' fer an ould lady. Orlagh Forest? Pull the udder one, it's got bells on.'

The young man, half the Boss's age, suddenly scowled. 'What is your name? We will prosecute. I want your name. You are not leaving here until I have it.'

Overwhelmed by the man's confidence, the Boss capitulated. 'Ah sure, what harrm would a fella do ta a few oul' trees an' you wit' t'ousands. Yeh wouldn' begrudge a poor fella, a local man too, that's hard workin' and God fearin', a few oul' bits a sticks ta light a fire ta keep his poor childher from cryin' in the cold.' Jack imagined fiddles playing quietly in the background as the Boss, his cruel face angelically transformed into a Victorian postcard of abject misery, as he appealed to the smooth young man's sense of justice. The ease with which his father had surrendered made Jack want to vomit. Why couldn't he jump off the cart and floor the cocky little swine? 'If yeh turrn a blind eye ta this time, it'll be the last yeh'll see a me in yer wood, Sir.'

'OK,' the young man snapped. 'I will let you off this time, but remember,' and meanness was writ large in his superior face and narrowed eyes, 'if I as much as see you within a hundred yards of my gates you are in for it, my man. The gardai will be informed immediately. Do you understand me, now?'

'Yis, a course,' the Boss said, doffing his hat and smiling, his plastic teeth watery.

Jack watched his father and wondered how such a pathetic creature, confronted by the twin bogeymen of class and cash, could change. He saw in his father the coward, the bully who could only exercise his hold over the weak, mute and defenceless. Quietly, he swore that as soon as he could he would follow his sisters to America.

Fuming behind clenched teeth, the Boss drove on and Kitty felt the repeated sting of the whip on her thin old flanks as he punished her severely. The old pony galloped until she was fit to drop. When the bungalow appeared, the Boss swung into the yard, dismounted and dumped the wood.

'That rotten young bastard, that feckin' English skite, God blast him an' all belongin' ta him. They own everyt'in' in this feckin' counthry, distr'yin' a poor fella's chance a livin' a dacent life.' Dashing swill into roaring pigs' faces, the Boss called down on the Englishman and his family, the vilest calamities he could think of. 'We're cornered on all sides, Kitty,' he said to the mare, eyeing the welts on her scruffy hide. He rested his face on the pony's neck, feeling her warm blood against his cheek. The old pony bared her teeth to nip him, then continued to eat scraps from the bath tub. With sore hands, and a brain that throbbed with hatred, pity and a slow-burning desire to get even, the Boss worked in the dark. Jack escaped into the house before his father could drag him into his personal tragedy.

After a long, almost hysterical conversation with himself, the Boss eventually appeared and sat down heavily to rid himself of his wellingtons. Tired and drained, he walked slowly into the kitchen. Too tired to fight, he asked in a whisper where the 'Jack fella' was.

'L'ave him alone,' Mary said, 'he's doin' his homework.'

Too depressed to argue, the Boss simply washed in the sink and, tenderly stroking his cut hand, he sat by the table, silently dispatched his food, then went to the fire to read his paper. The day had almost defeated him, but he would bounce back when his enormous energy had been recharged overnight. Then everyone had better watch out.

Next morning, Jack looked out of the window at the big, bare pussy willow that had been there as long as he had. It had grown and thrived out of nothing. Wouldn't it be nice to be a tree, he thought, simply going through its seasonal cycles without pain or hurt, providing beauty in the spring, showering the drab yard with furry little silver bullets, and shading Mary through the summer as she did a bit of mending in its shade?

110

FROM HIS DUNGHILL lookout the Boss spotted the small black car arrive. He slowly stabbed the fork into the soft manure and determinedly walked towards the house. The black suit and grubby dog collar, which kept the village in awe of the priest, had the opposite effect on the Boss, who bristled like a ferocious dog at the sight of any uniform.

'Hey there! Can I help yeh?'

The priest's hand was on the door knocker, but the shout made him quickly withdraw it. He flashed a well-fed smile and, with shiny black shoes crunching on the gravel, he approached the sombre face behind the wire.

'God bless you,' the priest began.

'Now wait a minute, Father,' the Boss interjected. 'Is there an'tin' the matter, didjah get a call or somethin'?'

The priest purred into his social worker's routine. In a roundabout way he admitted he had been tipped off by a neighbour. 'I'm sure we're just talkin' about a little misunderstanding, that's all,' the priest said, smiling.

'Now just a minute, Father, hold yer horses.' The Boss undid the latch and faced up to the visitor. 'Can yeh tell me in what way I can help yeh?' His voice was like a razor on stone.

'I'm sure it's a minor matther,' the priest said, as the one pale, cruel eye had him covered like the barrel of a sawn-off shotgun. 'Well now,' the priest continued softly. 'I've been hearin' t'ings are not as well as they should be with yerself and the missus. As your priest, it is my duty to come and help you sort out your little problems–' The priest's sermon was cut short by the brutal prodding of his chest by a dirty finger.

'Listen ta me, Father,' the Boss snarled. 'I'm a hard-workin' man wit' plenty a jobs round here not yit done. If yeh want ta t'row off that nice oul' coat a yers, yeh can grab that shubble there an' give me a hand. But *don't'* - each word was accentuated by a stiffer prod of the finger - 'come in here tellin' me me wife is this, that or t'other. That woman up there is gone in the head, connives behine me back, tells stories that hasn't a grain a troot in 'em. Me advice ta yeh, Father,' - the priest blinked under the ferocity of the verbal assault - 'is ta go over there ta them in the Corporation houses, them that does be drinkin' every ha'port they can cadge or rob, and tell them if they don't mind their ways the divil'll put tha lot a them into his oul' black b'iler.' The Boss roared at his own little joke.

Then he put his dung-stained arm around the priest's fat, unfit shoulders and murmured confidentially, 'Look Father, I know yer on'y doin' yer best but that woman lives in luxury up there in that fine little house I built for her single-handed; she wants fer nothin' and has too much time on her hands now the childer is growin'. Mark me words Father, there's nothin' innit but her imagination.'

After shaking the Boss's leathery hand, the priest pigeon-toed back to the car. The whiff of carbon monoxide was still in the air as the Boss wrenched off his wellingtons and exploded into the kitchen. Mary was on her knees scrubbing the tiled floor. She looked up like a mother would at a difficult child and waited for the flood of anger to peter out. 'How can yeh tell them feckin' melts all them lies? Sure, them bastards is on'y laughin' at yeh. They mus'bey t'inkin' yer the right bloody t'ick ta go tellin' them - an' they strangers - all our poor oul' secrets. Them's the ones that'll gloat an' tell the oul' wans from the new houses what sort a fool yeh're.'

'I'll tell 'em what a monster I married if I wan'ta,' Mary screamed. 'Yeh terrorise the poor childer; yeh haven't a friend in the world an' yeh take it out on us.'

Chastised by her tears, the Boss withdrew to the yard. Against a backdrop of squealing pigs he replayed the event over and over in his mind. Now she was in league with the clergy; he would tell his side of the story to Canon O'Donnell in Terenure. The Canon was a man of the world, he knew how to handle women, he was a good priest, on the side of men in these matters.

111

MARY WAS A traitor. The Boss's jealousy tortured him. Whether out with Kitty collecting pig food or doing repairs on someone's gutters, he thought of nothing else but betrayal. He fumed with anger and frustration. 'That hoor is bestin' me behine me back,' he complained loudly as he thumped nails into wood or drove the pony along with angry cries. Startled passers-by shook their heads at the strange sight of a man ranting wildly to himself. When such anger invaded his brain, the Boss could hardly wait to get home and dish his insane ramblings into Mary's face. Mary would shuffle about, hoping the hurricane of filth would eventually blow itself out. Sometimes it did, other times it erupted into screams and blows. 'I know yer afther him,' the Boss would say, ludicrously referring to old Perkins. 'It's no use denyin' it. I know yeh get yer dirthy pleasure in his pissy bed when I'm out a the house.'

If Mary laughed at his ridiculous imaginings they would become even more fanciful. He stood in his greasy rags, a bucketful of swill in either hand, his hat perched on top of his head, his mouth strangling the words as they sprayed over the shabby woman. 'Yeh hoor, yeh bitch, yeh feckin' bitch.' But Mary kept on with her work: ironing, baking, sewing, sending the younger children out of the house for fear that the horrible things he was saying might taint them.

'Yeh filt'y cow, openin' yer feckin' legs ta dat rotten hoormaster across the river . . . I can hear yeh t'inkin' I won't be back, lyin' on his dirthy floor and him ridin' yeh like a bitch and yer rotten mout' openin' and shuttin' wit' sinful pleasure.'

Occasionally, the pathetic rag would come to life and throw the nearest available object at her tormentor. He so desperately wanted to be reassured, that until the object was thrown he remained convinced Mary's lack of response proved what he said was true. He wanted more than anything else to believe otherwise. He wanted to believe, but couldn't.

Brainwashed by his father's relentless references to Mary's slack morals, or fed up with hearing the same old story endlessly poured over him like the contents of a prisoner's piss pot, Jack allowed himself to slither into his father's insane world and he agreed to spy on his mother.

Being an unwilling Judas meant the odd silver sixpence was pressed into his filthy hand after he'd swept out the pigs. 'Now, all yeh hav'ta do is watch yer woman for me, an' if yeh see anyone comin' tidda house, or see her writin' letters when I'm not aroun', don't ferget ta tell me, an' I'll be a good friend ta yeh and make sure yeh have enough cash ta buy them rotten ould comics.' Jack took the money and like Pontius Pilate he washed his hands. His mother was so pathetically innocent of all charges, Jack was sure he would have nothing to report. The Boss came to the pigsty to reiterate his instructions as though Jack was a moron. 'Watch 'er like a hawk,' he said, 'yeh'll find somethin' soon enough.'

Whenever Jack saw his father innocently engaging with his daughter, telling her stories, patting her head, touching her cheek, he thought about telling Mary. He could be a double agent and get paid by both sides.

He stopped sweeping and looked up when he heard his father clear his throat. The silhouetted trilby sat atop the half door, the round face underneath. 'Look son,' his father began softly, 'I know yeh're on my side. If that woman as much as l'aves the door of the house yeh mus' tell me. D'yeh hear me?'

Jack nodded and hated himself for it.

'It's a nice night fer a walk,' the Boss said.

They walked down the quiet lanes, wet leaves blowing in the blustery winds, rain sweeping down from the waving trees, the wet trunks gleaming in the light of an occasional passing car.

Jack saw kids playing in the light of the streetlamps, his streetwise schoolmates who lived in the Corporation houses. They were from families the Boss looked down on. 'Them poor shitehawks is on'y the unwanted bastards a da labourers from the buildin' sites,' he said sanctimoniously as they passed the lamppost under which the boys dawdled and smoked. 'How they let them poor childer out on a night like dis is beyon' me.'

Glancing at the kids as he went by on his horrible walk, Jack wished he too could belong to a dad like theirs who went to Cullen's, backed horses, drank most of their wages and lived in their comfortable little Council houses in a warm rag-ball of fun and security. Jack wanted to play pitch 'n' toss under the lamplight, then knock the bulb out with a stone from a slingshot. He wanted to talk about girls; well, Sheila Rooney anyway. He wanted to discuss his father to see if he was normal. He wanted to come and go as he pleased, to cook his own meals, pinch money from the gas meter. Instead, sick at heart, he followed his father into the darkness, waiting for the questions to start.

Jack felt the pain searing his heart. He wanted to pick up a big rock and crush his father's sick brain. 'No, she never said an'tin' to me atall,' he replied to each question. His father didn't believe him. It was a case of no sins, no sixpences.

'I wouldn' be surprised if that bloody woman done it wit' her brothers in Galway before she met me,' the Boss said, his boots squeaking as he walked. 'Them is right animals, so if they come here, remember ta watch yer woman. If she as much as goes in that bedroom let me know immedjetly. There'll be money in it fer yeh. I do me best fer all yehz kids, yehz know that. An' all the time yer woman is connivin' behine me back. It makes me sick ta da teet'.'

Father and son walked around the Fortification, with the lights of the city strung out like tears along the horizon. Jack shivered with the cold, sick of having to listen to his father's wild ravings. They returned at last to the tree- shrouded bungalow as quietly as cat burglers . The Boss listened, grim-faced, ear cocked at a previously open window. Satisfied that Mary wasn't belittling him he slammed the door, cleared his throat loudly and entered the kitchen smiling at Mary. As if nothing shameful had happened he warmed his hands at the turf fire.

'Bedad, that was a nice little bit a exercise yer man an' me is afther havin',' he said. 'Yeh shou'bey gettin' yerself out a bit more often; sure, yeh're puttin' on weight like an' oul' sow.' He laughed, and the pink of his plastic teeth gleamed in the firelight.

Jack slunk off to tell Babs the true story.

'Ah, sure, they're such a funny pair, don't be mindin' them,' was all Babs could say.

112

JACK DREADED WINTER, the cold dark nights, the uneasy gloom, the firelit faces, crammed together under a single bulb like chickens in an incubator. As the nights drew in, Mary talked quietly to the little faces staring up at her with interest and affection. She told them stories of her childhood Christmases in Galway - happy stories, retouched with hindsight.

And Christmas was looming now like a great gold express train with all its promise of joy and plenty. Talk of a white Christmas was already in the air and a previous one was being described in a book read on the radio.

As Jack watched from the window there was no snow in the grey clouds that were stubbornly halted over Neary's big red hayshed. Instead, rain fell by the bathful. The big holes the pigs made in the ground would soon be full of water reflecting the clouds. The hens hated the rain. They dropped their backs, tucked their beaks into their chests, and ran for the shed. The cats mooched about, shaking themselves.

Another year was coming to an end but this one was bringing great changes. Soon, the weather would harden the mud and the chilblains would return to Jack's fingers and toes. The fire would smoulder all day, and nights would start at four in the afternoon. The small bungalow with its cramped rooms full of growing children, would be like a waiting room in a Siberian bus station.

But the Holy season of goodwill was better than nothing. Jack hoped to save some money for presents but the work he did for his father was paid in promises. As he fed hay to the cow, or swept out his quota of pigs he heard his father at the bottom of the yard screaming in the rain, his mind unhinged. Jack felt sorry, desperately sorry, for the mess his parents were in. A pair of innocents, and encouraged by the priests, they had embarked on raising a huge family on nothing. Trouble was, neither celibate priest nor parent was equipped for the task. Too much was left to an overworked and overrated God.

I must go down to the sea again, to the lonely sea and sky.

Jack was haunted by the Masefield poem Moroney had introduced him to. In his stifling room he heard sudsy waves play with pebbles, a mighty roar as they rose up and curled and crashed. He saw yellow shores, brown men in red scarves hauling nets. He smelt spices, tasted salt on his lips. One day, *he* would travel – to Africa, maybe, or New Guinea, that sounded a feckin' fantastic place. Jack would wear shorts and smoke, drink rum and catch herring. He could smell the bonfire as he spun the fish on a piece of wire, his face tanned, his hair wild.

As Christmas approached, the activity in the bungalow became frenetic. Confessions had to be heard, presents wrapped, the one big dinner of the year planned. There was such profound preoccupation in the kitchen, with all the children speculating about the presents they were going to get from Santy Claus, that Eileen burst in unannounced.

The children rushed to form a ragged reception party, their eyes on Eileen's handbag. Slyly they nudged and grinned, making their dimples show. 'She's gorra big cake in dere,' little Paul said, doing a celebratory dance.

'Ge'rout a me way yehz hungry little feckers,' Eileen said. 'I've got sompthin' fer yehz all, butcha'll hav'ta wait till I give yer oul' wan a bloody big French kiss on the chops. Will yeh com'ere, yeh oul' hoor till I stick me big tongue down yer t'roat,' Eileen said, and the two women went bust to bust like ships docking. Eileen slapped and wrestled Mary against the wall with rugged embraces and dribbling kisses which left Mary's face blotched with lipstick.

Eileen licked the finger she'd jabbed into the pot of warm custard. 'I kem ta wish yehz a Happy Christmas, an' yehz're all lookin' great.'

Mary was smiling. Only Eileen made her feel human.

'Here,' Eileen said, offering a parcel. Mary ripped it open and held up a large pair of knickers. 'Oh, Jasus Christ,' she said. 'Don't let Jack see 'em, they're private.'

'Ah, *private* me hole,' Eileen said. 'Sure, if he hasn't 'ad the drawers off a yer woman Rooney beyont, then he's not his oul' fella's son.'

Jack blushed in his corner, he always tried to avoid Eileen; her talk had a habit of dragging him into its wild vortex.

Eileen grabbed the underwear and held the legs apart. 'Feck me,' she exclaimed, smoke from the cigarette in her mouth blinding her wall eye. 'But sure, there's a guzzet on 'em that'd cut the prick off a yer man if he caught himself innit.'

'God, Eileen,' Mary said. 'Yeh've gone too far. Will yer shu'rup in front a the poor gossoon. Lookit, yeh're embarrassin' 'im.'

Jack reddened and lowered his head.

Babs came in and turned on the radio. Bing Crosby was singing *White Christmas*.

'I love Bing,' Mary said. 'Hasn't he got a lovely v'ice?'

'Ah, bejasus, he has,' Eileen said, and turned to Babs. 'Well now, I hear tell yeh're off ta the Windy City. Well, good luck ta yeh. Yeh've got no life here at all. An' that Bridgid wan betther watch herself with her oul' talk. Them Yanks'll sort her out in no time. Sure, they're all bloody born-again Christians over there. A load a bloody nutters.'

Mary so appreciated the comfort and support she received from Eileen. If only they had set up house together, what a life of comfort and indolence they could have had. They were closer than sisters.

'Where's the bullet-eyed, bandy little fecker?' Eileen asked, buttering herself a couple of slices of bread to make a sandwich. 'I can tell he's out a the place, yehz are all so bloody continted.'

'Shush!' Mary said, smiling, her cheeks appley-red with the heat of the gas.

'Oh, bollocks ta him,' Eileen said, then, stopping and pointing the knife at Mary, she added, 'I on'y wish he'd come in here an' say some a the t'ings ta me he says ta yeh. I'd run the little fecker t'rough wit' this knife, or betther still cut the mickey off a him, that'd make him stop wavin' it at yeh.'

'Oh, Jasus, stop Eileen!' Mary said. 'Yer language is awful in front a the childher.'

'Oh feck 'em,' Eileen said, her wall eye looking out of the window. 'Sure, they hav'ta lerrin sometime about the divil in all his works and pomps.'

Babs was tired after a long day of typing invoices but seeing Eileen in such great form turned the tiredness in her face to radiance.

'Yeh're a fine lookin' wan, wit' yer lipstick an' yer new hairdo,'

Eileen said. 'How are yeh, pet?'

'Fine, Aunt Eileen,' Babs replied. 'Yeh're looking well yerself.'

'Ah deed, be Jasus, I'm not. I'm a fat oul' hoor wit' a gunner eye but what's the use complainin'. Give yer ould wan a hand,' Eileen said.

'What wouldja like me ta do, Mammy?' Babs asked.

'Ah nothin' darlin',' Mary said. 'Don't be mindin' Eileen an' she doin' nuttin' but fillin' her oul' belly wit' sanwedges.'

'Feck yeh!' Eileen said. 'I'll stuff me oul' gob innytime I wan'ta.' She came over to Mary and put her hand on her shoulder. 'Are yeh nairly finished darlin' ?' she asked. 'Come on, have a bit a oul' grub before the runt arrives wit' his pizenous rantin'.'

'All right then,' Mary said, 'pour me an oul' mug a tay.'

The women talked and Eileen reported on the news from Gownagh. 'It's a lovely oul' place,' Eileen said between gulps of tea. 'I'd go back ta live there tomorra if I got half a chance. Wouldn't yeh Mary, love?'

Mary looked up from her tea and reflected for a moment. 'On'y if I could have all me childer wit' me.'

Eileen grunted and brought her mug to the sink to rinse it at the tap. 'Anyway, I've got a Confession ta ketch meself, me poor ould soul is scuth'ry wit' sins of every conceivable description.'

'Jasus, that reminds me,' Mary said, 'I promised ta light a few candles fer the girls' goin' away.'

'Don't worry yer ould head 'bout dat,' Eileen said, drawing the ends of her belt together. 'I can do dat much fer yeh, it's the l'aste I can do, yeh poor ould shite.' She fell into Mary's arms and the two women hugged each other.

Eileen was no sooner out of the front door than the Boss rushed in through the back. Mary barely had time to say, 'Quick, turn the wireless off.'

'Mammy! Don't be so scared,' Babs said. 'It's our wireless, we bought it.'

The Boss clattered into the kitchen. The cheap decorations shook in the breeze from the open door. 'What was the wireless doin' on?' he demanded, spoiling for trouble.

'It's supposed ta be on,' Babs said. 'It's a wireless, that's what yeh do wit' wirelesses, yeh turn them on.'

'That Galway hoor's got nuttin' betther ta do than come up here an' make mischief,' the Boss said. 'Let her go back tidda gobshite she's married ta an' l'ave us in peace.'

'Daddy!' Babs said sharply.

The Boss left it there and went to stack up the fire for the rest of the evening.

The girls sat on their bed in their new, pink, lace-trimmed nighties. Pam was painting her toenails, adoring her long slender leg as she tilted her chin over the bent knee. She'd had her long tresses cut off to be more like Barbara Rush, her favourite film star. Bridgid was at the sewing machine, shortening a skirt she'd snatched from the latest American parcel.

'Well, brud,' Babs said, 'what's the story tonight?'

Clutching a battered old book of literary pieces by various dead Irish writers, Jack was preparing to read by the light of his small paraffin lamp. He wanted to say 'Shite', but he didn't swear in front of his sisters.

'This is the last Chrissamiss here,' Babs said, grabbing at Jack and frightening him with her fear.

'Jaze, yeah,' Bridgid said quietly, 'I fergot it was comin' up so soon. I like the oul' Chrissamiss though, when all's said an' done.'

'Is it reelly so soon?' Pam asked, dreamily stretching. The tiny tips of her nipples showed as her breasts were flattened beneath her slip. 'God, it's come on so quick, I wisht now it was a long way off.'

'An' afther the New Year we'll be away, out a here fer good an' all.' Babs said.

'Don't say that,' said Pam, touching her hair affectionately as she admired it in the mirror. 'Poor Mammy'll be disthroyed.'

Babs shook her head slowly from side to side and there was a vacant look in her eyes, as if she were imagining Mary breaking down as they said goodbye.

'I don't t'ink she'll be able ta handle it,' Jack said.

'Don't talk about it,' Babs answered. 'It's Chrissamiss time. Let's see that t'rough first.'

'What'll Daddy say when yeh go, Babs?' Jack asked.

'Who gives a shite,' Bridgid muttered. 'He doesn't care fer us, why should we worry 'bout him. Anyway,' she added with a sneer, 'yeh're here, yeh can hold his hand if yeh wan'ta.'

'Com'ere,' Babs said. Jack went to the side of her bed and she offered him a chocolate from a box full of silver and gold paper gleaming in the lamp's glow. 'Take a couple an' let me read yeh the latest letther from Aunt Dolores.'

Holding two pages of long-looping writing on crackling paper to the lamp, Babs read instructions on what to bring, what clothes to buy, how much cash she would need. Jack listened in silence. 'That's what freedom looks like,' Babs said, holding up the three plane tickets. Pam and Bridgid stopped what they were doing and came to her side. 'Anywan wan'ta hold wan?' Babs asked.

'Yes pleeese,' Bridgid said, leaping up and down like a fat labrador.

'Can I hold wan,' Jack asked.

'Sure,' Babs said handing him hers. 'Don't yeh wish yeh were comin' wit'us Jack?' Pam asked, dabbing her face with cotton wool, then throwing the soiled ball on to the floor with others where they lay like a nest of mushrooms.

'I've been t'inkin' about it,' Jack said. 'Yeah, I'd love ta.'

'It's brilliant!' Pam said. 'I reelly am lookin' forward t'it. Sorry ta rub it in brud. Ohh . . .' She stretched her swan's neck. 'Them clothes shops, fashions, them beautiful Hollywood stars.'

'Will yeh reelly get ta meet 'em?' Jack asked, and the light picked out the hunger in his eyes.

'A course,' Pam said. 'Beverly Hills is on'y down the road. Anyway in America, yeh can fly everywhere. Everywhere's near. Yeh jus' hop on a plane, say, "A single ta Hollywood please," and before yeh know it, yer there.'

'"A single ta Hollywood",' Jack whispered. 'Fantastic'.

'Don't get too excited,' Bridgid said. '*Yeh're* not comin'.'

'I don't wan'ta, now,' Jack lied. 'I' might go ta England instead. They have Everton there and motorbikes, an' I'm goin'ta buy wan.'

'Yeah, an' kill yer feckin' self,' Bridgid said.

'Don't use that vulgar language,' Babs said sharply, 'it sounds awful comin' out of a girl.'

'It would if she was a girl,' Jack retorted and ducked.

113

CHRISTMAS EVE HAD an exhilarating expectancy about it. Jack whistled as he dressed. Laughter poured from the girls' room. The younger children jumped up and down on squeaking beds. Brigid's manly guffaw soared above the more feminine sounds of the thinner girls. Jack strode in polished boots through their room, amused at the comic attempts to harness breasts into hand-me-down brassieres.

He went to the kitchen to eat the good cooked breakfast Mary had made. None of the Boss's abstemious diet for him. Jack liked his food with lashings of grease. Two big, orange-yolked, duck eggs, two slices of thick fatty bacon, two cartwheels of black pudding, a sausage as big as a gas cylinder, two slices of grease-oozing fried bread that should have carried a health warning, and a pile of mushrooms. And big pot of Lyons brown tannicky tea.

Jack still had to go to Confession and that annoyed him. He would have to fit it in later when there were fewer dirty sinners about and when the cleansed ones were packed into Cullen's and The Yellow House.

Hens stopped scratching and rushed to the gate as Kitty's iron shoes clattered up the hill and over the bridge. Christmas Eve or not the Boss was still working. 'Get that pony unharnessed,' he yelled. Jack led Kitty into the yard and released her from the cart. She shook herself before trotting peevishly, ears flattened in temper, to a mixture of crusts, squashed fruit and raw cabbage. Then she tore at her hay net.

After a light lunch of eight slices of French toast made from duck eggs, Jack was ready to take on the priests. He mounted Babs' bike and pedalled to the Annunciation. He dipped his fingertips into the holy water font, made the sign of the cross and pushed his beret into his trouser pocket. Before genuflecting he pulled his socks above his knees, then knelt on the gritty wooden floor. Tim Ryan, the postman, was before him in the queue. Tim winked conspiratorially, his weathered face shining. Jack nodded and searched his soul.

The examination took a minute. Jack lined up sins in order of their seriousness, with the one about Sheila Rooney's private parts sandwiched between 'using the Lord's name in vain' and 'disobedience'. He wondered whether he should mention Sheila at all. What if the priest was normal and had a notebook on his lap. 'Yeh wouldn't be afther givin' me yer woman's phone number now, wouldja, Jack?'

Jack knew if he kept any sins back he could kiss goodbye to the main performance, receiving Holy Communion at the marble alter rails with the priest in his best gear and Foley as one the alter boys.

When his time came to shuffle penitentially into the little portaloo of a confessional, and he saw the priest's eyes shining in the dark like a panda in the zoological gardens, Jack rattled off the venials and breezed over the big mortaler that was disfiguring his soul. The dozing priest suddenly woke up and demanded, in a voice loud enough to be heard on the Whitechurch Road, 'What! Did yeh mean yeh did a dirthy t'ing wit' yer own sister?'

Jack stuttered, 'No it wasn't me sister dis time, Father, it was Sheila Rooney.'

Father Orlston was just teasing. 'Don't do it again,' he hissed. 'Say ten *Hail Marys* and t'ree *Glory be ta the Fathers* in honour a Jesus's birt'day. God bless yeh, son. Won'tcha pray fer me?' the old priest said.

'I will, Father,' Jack repliced, and left the confessional quickly in case the priest should change his mind.

Ten. That's more like it. Jack thought as he left the church cleansed as if he had been through a carwash.Free of sin, his soul spotless, he rushed down the church steps three at a time and grabbed the bike. Now he could begin to enjoy himself.

As he cycled home he passed Sheila Rooney, who radiated purity and innocence. Shutting dangerous, lascivious and soul-destroying thoughts from his mind, Jack waved to her. Sheila pedalled away, her sweet knees rising as she demurely held her floating dress down with a small hand. At the exact point of their passing, she had smiled and rolled her big blue eyes. 'God forgive me,' Jack prayed, and he almost fell off his bike looking back.

His body bent into a racing crouch, he tore into Cullen's Bend. He was Reg Armstrong on a screaming works Gilera. As he tore over the bridge, coming to a gravel-spraying stop, the Boss was yelling as usual. Jasus Christ, doesn't he ever take a break? Jack thought. Immediately, he apologised for using the Lord's name in vain. He had a feckin' stain on his soul already and it was only ten minutes since it had been descaled. Feckit.

'Come an' gi'me a hand, fer the sake a Jasus,' the Boss roared.

Full of the joy of forgiveness, Jack joined him.

In the bungalow, Mary worked unaided at the stone sink until the cold and damp had turned her hands and bare arms blue. From the back bedrooms the girls shrilled happily. As wage-earners their pretty hands didn't like cold water. Bridgid was wearing her see-through nightie.

'Modesty gets the men, not showin' ever'tin',' Mary commented disapprovingly.

'Is dat from experience?' Bridgid asked.

'Ah, go ta the divil,' Mary said, blushing. 'Sure, what experience have I got, on'y yer man is all, and I'll regret that till the day I die. I'd be betther t'ought of if I had let some a them lovely Galway lads have a peep.'

'Jesus!' Bridgid laughed. 'Good on yeh, Mam.'

Mary looked embarrassed at her fall from grace. 'I'm goin'ta brew a pot a tay,' she said quickly. 'I'll put the cosy on it ta keep it hot fer yehz.' Bending down to pick up a pillow, she groaned. 'Ah, me oul' hip, bad cess ta it, I must a strained it.' And she returned to the kitchen.

The girls dressed and gathered around the fire. 'T'row a few oul' sods on. I'll be comin' in a minit,' Mary's voice wailed from the cold kitchen as the girls chatted and arranged their wrapped presents in piles.

Mary worked solidly, her legs felt heavy, the bandages showed pinkish at the edges. Her hands plopped in and out of the water. The gloomy silhouette, stooped and old, plodded on, afraid to turn on the dim 40-watt bulb for fear of incurring the Boss's wrath.

A hymn sung by the boys at Christchurch Cathedral was playing on the radio. It trickled through a tide of tension and excitement. The wind whistled through the hallway, then finding its way obstructed it turned and exited through a crack in the keyhole. Outside, the stream flowed darkly under the bridge, and the hens roosted sleepily above their piled droppings. The pigs were lying quietly in their sties as if they knew a special day was coming. In occasional windows trees had sprouted blossoms of mistily glowing coloured lights. At her house, Sheila Rooney was sitting on the sofa by a warm fire, her knees tucked under her. Jack hoped she was thinking of him, because he was thinking of her.

Cullen's was bursting at the seams with red-faced men intent on committing alcoholic suicide. The smoke was thick and the language coarse as men at last had an excuse to ignore they wives and get plastered. The Dowager sat in a corner with his mates, smoking and chatting as usual.

Jack was working alongside the Boss who was running about the yard, his harsh voice puking out a torrent of words. Mary was peeling a bucketful of potatoes, occasionally blowing on her red meaty hands and wishing she had the nerve to turn on the light.

Babs danced into the cold, dark kitchen. Her beauty was touching. She was followed by Bridgid and Pam. 'Sorry, Mam,' she said. 'An'tin' we can do fer yeh?'

'Ah sure, no. I'm near'y finished, just th'ol' cabbage and we're away. Sit be the fire but please turn off that wireless now, yer Dad hates carols. Besides, yer wastin' electricity.'

'Mammy, I toldja a hundert times, it's our radio. We paid fer it out of our wages,' Bridgid said belligerently.

'Now be a dear an' turn it off,' Mary's voice had softened, and she added, 'yeh'll on'y make him mad, an' we don't want that fer Chrissamiss. Now, do we?'

'Oh, fer God's sake, all right,' Bridgid snarled. 'Yeh sicken me, yeh're so scared a dat man.'

'Shhhh,' Babs said. 'Don't talk to Mammy like that.'

Surrounded by her whole family for their last Christmas Eve together, Mary was telling them more stories of her childhood Christmases in Galway. Even Babs had become a child again, her dark eyes sparkling with tears as she knelt on the floor with her arms on her mother's lap. The children flinched at the squelch of muddy boots, and the sound of voices questioning and answering. Mary looked into the coloured flames, 'Sure, I've had a rewardin' life, though yehz might not t'ink it. I've got beautiful childer dat I'd sacrifice me own life fer if any of yehz needed me.'

The dirty faces smiled and, leaning forward, they rubbed her with their unkempt heads.

Jack had saved his pennies in an old tobacco tin in one of the pigsties. Mary had taken in sewing to help with the presents. Jack had counted his cash, made a list of presents, their value decreasing as the festive holiday approached. He'd trotted up to MacAlinden's illuminated window to read the price cards half hidden under fake snow. He was obsessed with a Dinky dustcart, and a lead farm with chickens, fat pink pigs, cows with horns, a donkey, and a hay-baler with little yellow bales. Hands in pockets, he gazed at the tinselly display until the light was turned off. The coldness of the glass and the chill of the night made him shiver as he headed back home.

Christmas, the annual commemoration of the birth of Jesus, was the celebration of the year. To the children it meant small parcels tied with bows, coloured paper, opening boxes, untying knots, gifts laid out on the table or windowsill to be fondled, pressed and the contents guessed at. The food was better than usual too; a big ham, a glossy-breasted turkey, a huge cake, and a dark, round, fruit-packed pudding. When the light of God shone, even the hardest soul melted in its benign brilliance. It was a day when people smelled of soap, not neglect; when salt-rubbed teeth smiled. Jack spent every penny. He had inherited Mary's foolish generosity. So what? It was a time of giving, of spending, not keeping it in a box under the bed.

The children wrapped presents. They tore around, wildly crying out for the one little wheel of Sellotape and the small silver scissors. They wrapped and cut and made a mess. A threepenny bar of soap, a tube of Rowntrees Fruit Gums. They stacked their presents by the little tree the Boss had snaffled for a shilling at the last minute in Terenure. The little children were almost crying with excitement when they finally went to bed.

The Boss remained unmoved. If a hopeful little face had hovered near, it had quickly shrunk away from his baleful stare.

Jack lay awake, eavesdropping on his sister's conversation. He knew the three older girls had bought him presents. Since they were going away to America they had better be bloody fantastic. The Boss read his *Evening Mail.* The children smiled at each other in the shadows of their rooms, and opened their mouths in song. Baby Paddy, dumb in infancy, sat in his cot, his curly head throwing a pale shadow on the wall.

Way after closing time, Cullen's disgorged its disorientated clientele. Men stood in rows indulging in synchronised vomiting or pissing on cars, bikes and each other. Jack heard them staggering by, some trying to sing but unable to get their dulled brains to remember a word of any song. They all carried brown parcels of Guinness to have another after they'd raped or beaten up their wives. Children's voices were still burbling on in the dark about 'Santy Claus'.

Tomorrow was going to be the happiest day of the year. The Boss, as if touched by the magic of the occasion, had decided to accompany them to seven o'clock Mass. Jack, his soul gleaming with purity, slept like a stone, his mind untroubled by dreams.

Finally, the countryside slept in its frosty bed, the peace only occasionally broken by the drunken howls of a lone inebriate blundering though the sleeping village.

114

AT SIX A.M., lights were shining in every house in the village. Jack dressed in his absolute best, sliding on the bare wooden floor with his new black boots, proud of their heavy nails and smell of polish. Clean socks caressed his chilblained toes and a crisp shirt hugged his back.

The bungalow was bright with the old creased decorations. A few strategically placed balloons added a splash of fresher colour and gaiety. Sprigs of red-berried holly were stuck behind every picture. A yard of red candle was lit and placed in the front parlour window where it burned, thrilling passers-by with its little leaping flame. On this one special day the fire would be allowed to burn recklessly, and the lights be left on in more than one room at a time.

The girls dressed noisily. As curlers were removed, cascades of naturally straight hair tumbled like melting chocolate on to slim shoulders. The room reeked of lavender as the one stick of deodorant was passed around. They slipped small feet into mock-leather high-heeled shoes,and ran hands up the backs of legs to straighten crooked seams as a mob of bright-eyed little faces looked on in admiration. When they'd finished their own dressing, the girls helped Mary prepare the younger children, who like little pit ponies would not stand still for a moment, their necks twisting to avoid pinching buttons and scraping combs. With white laminated prayer books in gloved hands, they then queued up in the hallway where the brown paint proved a sombre backdrop to the flashiness of their clothes.

Christmas or not, the animals needed feeding and the Boss had been out earlier, sliding around in the darkness with Jack, their ears and hands numb with the cold. The Boss never lost the feeling of relief each morning when he inspected his premises and found the pigs were as he'd left them the night before. Rustlers didn't take Christmas off. His animals contented, and the water under the broken ice in the barrel already freezing, the Boss led his son back to the warm bungalow that was already vibrating with noise and aglow with light.

The Boss washed meticulously, brushed his hair and his teeth and put on his white nylon shirt, blue Terylene tie and his expensive, and rarely worn suit and a pair of crocodile-skin shoes, the only item he ever wore from the gift parcels from Aunt Dolores. With his pigskin gloves and his heavy tweed overcoat, he was ready to lead his sweet-smelling army to church like any good, righteous man. Mary would remain at home to prepare the father and mother of all breakfasts. She would have loved to accompany her beautiful children to Mass on this day of days but the thought of all those prying eyes made her feel giddy.

The jolly chattering group pattered over the bridge, waited for the Boss to unlock the gate, then swept colourfully beneath the street light. They marched down the middle of the road, the Boss striking out ahead of them, lifting his feet as if he were a Derry bandmaster in the Bogside. Babs was on his right, Pam on his left. The toddlers shuffled along in front of Bridgid and Jack. Villagers cycled by, full of temporary goodwill. The Boss lifted his hand and his hat to everyone he met. He was like an old entertainer doing a farewell concert.

'Happy Christmas, Misther Dunne,' called Boko Rooney, Sheila's brother.

'Good morning,' the Boss snapped as if he were a sergeant addressing a private.

Old ladies, all lace and big hats, oozed out of the posh houses and smiled at the Boss and his entourage, their lips breathing steam in the cold air.

'Happy Chrissamiss ladies,' the Boss said loudly. 'Aren't we the grand wans ta stick it.'

'Stick it where?' Bridgid cracked. Jack, bringing up the rear, laughed.

Lady Moore cruised by hunched in the back of her black Austin Princess. She was being driven by Geraghty to Rathfarnham Parish Church of Ireland where a former organist was collaborating with Percy French on *Mountains of Mourne*, and where Yeats' daughter Anne was once in the Guides.

When the Boss saw the familiar car, he raised his hat and bowed. The old lady's wrinkled face lit up for a few seconds. Nice man that Dunne, wonderful children. Conjured them out of muck and bones. How did he manage it single-handed?

The sound of the combined footwear on the frosty tarmac echoed against the detached houses, where large Christmas trees blazed in misted windows and fat company cars sat smugly in drives. Children planned for happiness, awoke to a mountain of presents in centrally heated bedrooms. Sweet-smelling husbands lay in downy beds pretending to sleep while wives glided about in silk dressing-gowns, serving tea in china cups with hands that never knew drudgery.

The Church of the Annunciation was lit like Tolka Park for a midweek football match. Droves of sinners and their shadows filtered through the gold-tipped gates and blessed themselves with holy water that a boy replenished from a watering can. They flopped to their knees on soft cushions and beat their breasts fervently.

The Boss brazenly led his family up to the ranked backs of kneeling Christians, then swerved past them like Paddy Daly selling a dummy to Shay Gibbons. The Boss marched up to the glare cast by a wall of candles that flickered and waved like daffodils in a breeze. The fractured light from huge candelabras shone on bald heads and faces of every shape. The Boss inched forward. If God was about to appear in person to shake his hand, He had better be on time. The children followed meekly, stepping over boots, their little faces tense. Babs led the girls in a mannequin parade, attracting sideways looks from kneeling farmers.

At home, Mary had painfully dragged herself out of bed, dressed with difficulty then hobbled with her stick to the kitchen to begin cooking breakfast.

As he waited in line to receive the body of Christ into his empty stomach Jack, with hands clasped in front of him, was dreaming of eggs, black pudding, pork sausages, and a great stack of glistening fried bread.

When the Communion was to be taken the Boss was in the box seat. He knelt down as if poleaxed, his face serene. The children fell alongside in a mini Mexican Wave, and with clasped hands showing white knuckles they closed their eyes tight and put out their tongues.

Foley, looking the epitome of virginal innocence, followed the Latin-muttering priest in patent leather shoes and a frilly top, slipping wafers into mouths furnished with the sort of rusty molars that threatened a poisonous bite. He grinned as he held the silver salver under Jack's chin, his eyes saying, 'I'd slice yer feckin' head off wit' dis if I got the chance,' as the protagonists eyeballed one another.

Jack's response would have been, 'Yeah, yeh and what feckin' army?'

The children followed the Boss to their seats, his lips moving piously as he muttered salutations, begging the Lord for forgiveness. A picture of repentance he stumbled to his seat, eyes downcast, hands clasped. His naked dome shining, he bent over as if paralysed by the agony of his guilt. He fooled nobody, least of all those in the congregation whom he had crossed, and that was most of them.

Mary, warming to and warmed by her task, was filling the oven. She shot nervous, red-faced glances at the clock, wanting everything perfect for this Last Breakfast. Her hungry children would just now be leaving the church, trying to avoid the rudely ridden bikes of the old men grimly cycling back to their hovels in Tibradden, Killakee and Woodtown, eager to flee the clutches of God and get stuck into one hell of a breakfast.

His God sorted out, the Boss was overflowing with *bonhomie* as he led the procession back to the open country and the bungalow on the edge of the village. The roads were dense with pedestrians. Lights bobbed on bikes, smiles were flashed at the girls, hands waved. Goodness was everywhere.

Even from the bridge the children were sniffing world-class aromas. They burst in through the door, catching their mother crouching at the gas cooker. The girls screamed, 'Happy Christmas, Mammy!' and rushed forward to bind her with their arms, and kiss her all over.

Gently prising herself from her beautiful children, Mary said, 'Yehz poor t'ings mus' be freezin'. Go in there and putcher yerselves round the fire. Yer brekkers'll be ready fer yehz in two shakes ivva lamb's tail.'

Like an actor after a convincing performance, the Boss went straight to the bedroom to change. Returning in his working clothes he rushed into the kitchen and began turning down gas jets and opening windows. Mary felt the happiness flowing out into the cold yard along with the greasy whiff of melted lard. But with Bab's help she filled plates and handed the first one to her husband who had already taken his seat at the table. Quickly, he got to grips with a pile of food that could have killed a lesser man. Clearly, his usual diet was on hold. His jaws leapt up and down as if they were on well-oiled hinges. His eyes closed with the effort as he poked sausages and fried bread into his small mouth that seemed elastic in its capacity. The children banged their cutlery and scratched their heads in irritation. Soon, all of them had a plate in front of them.

Manners were dispensed with as everyone greedily ate their fill until a last slice of toast was snatched and dispatched. Teapots were drained and replenished and even crumbs were picked from the oilcloth.

While the girls cleared the table the younger children disappeared to their hiding places, and returned with armfuls of presents. They all had something for the Boss, who lined up a row of shaving sticks like little soldiers. 'Yehz should a saved yer few pence,' he said. Little did he care about the months of conniving and penny-pinching that went into the purchase of every humble gift.

Mary shyly handed him a parcel containing a shirt and tie. He handed out nothing. The girls heaped presents on Mary, and Jack gave her two headscarves. She tried one on and was instantly transformed into the lady on the Irish pound note down on her luck.

The children sat on the floor drowning in colourful waves of paper and blowing tinny bugles like distress signals. Babs appeared with two beautifully wrapped presents, one for the Boss and one for Mary. When she handed her father his gift he pulled her on top of him and the resultant kiss stopped the children in their tracks.

'Yeh don't reelly wan'ta go ta America, do yeh?' the Boss asked as if Babs was still under his spell.

'I do,' Babs said, firmly pushing him away. 'It's best fer everybody. I'll get a reelly good job an' I'll send money so yeh an' Mammy can come over ta see me. How's that?'

The Boss shook his head like a terrier shaking a rat. 'No, no,' he said, his voice rising. 'That won't happen an' yeh know it. Yeh won't get work there. Yeh'll be livin' under that oul' Dolores wan wit' no freedom ta do an'tin'. Why don'tcha jus' stay in Easthams. Yeh love th'oul job an' yeh can come back ta yer own bed every night. Yeh'll realise what yer missin' when it's too late. What d'yeh say? Gi'me them oul' tickets an' I'll t'row them on the fire.'

The sound of sobbing made the children hang their lower lips in sympathy.

'Now look wha'cha done,' Mary said. 'Yeh've gone an' upset the poor child, an' on Christmas Day.' Mary put her arms around her eldest daughter and gave her a handkerchief to blow her nose. The Boss looked perplexed. What could he do to persuade Babs to slip back into his shackles and stay?

Mary threw her love around like rice that day and watched it settle lightly on the shoulders of her children. The Boss had condemned his family to dumbness so they communicated with conspiratorial smiles.

The girls went to their room to try their new perfumes, powders and paints. Giggling, they daubed their faces with rouge and dabbed Evening by the Seine, L'Amour, and Vixen behind their ears. Babs plastered her mouth with wine-red lipstick and pursed her lips wantonly. The Boss looked at her in disgust.

He sat jumpily in his chair, killing the enjoyment with his presence. Surrounded by tinselled bric-a-brac, and with no *Evening Mail* to hide in, he groaned. 'Bloody good money t'rown away on a lot a cheap rubbitch.' For him, Christmas was a criminal waste of time. He sat stern and sombre, his face in his hands, praying for normality to return.

As afternoon fell, and the light slipped from the day, frost hardened the muck in the yard. Jack helped his father with the pigs and had to hear yet again the Boss raving to himself about Babs going off and leaving a job he would have 'given his right hand fer'.

In the Boss's mind his girls were bound, gagged and silently screaming inside a runaway express train labelled, *To the Unknown*. He came up to Jack where he was feeding Kitty in the freezing gloom. 'Listen, son,' he said, 'Babs an' yeh is great oul' friends. If she goes off ta bloody Chicago yeh're goin' ta miss her more than me. Could yeh not put in a word fer me, I mean, fer us?'

'Her heart is set on it,' Jack said quietly.

A tranquil interval followed, during which the girls stayed in their rooms and the toddlers played on the floor. Jack spread out his farm and parked his dustcart on a tiny square of lino he'd fenced off with little white painted lead railings. He mooed and barked and grunted, driving his cows home for milking with the help of his little lead collie dog, and feeding his silent lead pigs with imaginary swill that he'd collected in his dustcart. He then drove his horse and cart towards little Paul and said in a gruff farmer's voice, 'Here's the load a hay yeh ordered.' The other children were assembling jigsaw puzzles and shrieking with joy when the parts fitted.

Like a prisoner in his cell, the Boss pretended to doze, but his flickering eyelashes indicated his mind was working overtime.

When Mary put down her *Ireland's Own* and went to her room to change into a blue print dress her sister had sent from America, it meant Christmas dinner was not far off. The girls rushed to help. The Boss had loosened the purse strings for this last great occasion. The little kitchen was like a busy restaurant with the clatter of utensils, sounds of chopping, scraping, hissing and a lively if slightly strained jollity as the girls, knowing it was for the last time, practised being brave.

They watched boiling pots, made gravy and basted the big turkey, a clever last-minute purchase of the Boss's. The big smoked ham that had hung curing behind the scullery door for six weeks was now lying like the open thigh of a hip replacement patient, its pink flesh giving off a fabulous perfume. Mary had boiled the potatoes, scored them with a fork, and roasted them until they were crinkly, flowery and as light as air. A few home-grown parsnips roasted with them added flavour. It was a trick she'd learned from the old lady who had employed her in the big lonely house in Rathgar all those years ago.

Sprouts the size of green golf balls bobbed in scalding water, and fat pork sausages sizzled and split alongside the bird. There were long orange carrots, and thick brown gravy in a blue-flowered Victorian gravy boat Mary had bought in a jumble sale years before she had become afraid of going out. For afters there were wobbly jellies, and custard-swamped wedges of the Christmas pudding Mary had made weeks earlier.

Bridgid organised an army of small helpers to lay the table. The Boss couldn't help turning down a gas jet he saw flaring wastefully.

'L'ave it alone!' Mary screamed, bringing her big spoon down with a thwack that made him retreat instantly.

'It's all right, Daddy, we girls can take care of dinner,' Babs said, feeling sorry for him. He looked at her through his cheap spectacles and smiled.

Jack washed and dried every dusty tumbler and plastic beaker he could find and placed one at every setting. The billowing, saliva-tempting waves of aroma coming out of the kitchen had tongues lolling. It was as if Mary was trying to kill her girls with kindness to keep them at home, buried in the garden were she could take fresh flowers to their graves every day.

The table legs practically buckled under the weight of such unaccustomed largesse. The children gathered round the table, waiting for the signal to dart into their favourite places.

Like an ageing despot, the Boss sidled up to the table and placed half a pint of Guinness at Mary's setting before taking his rightful position at the head, with Babs on one side and Pam on the other.

'Make room for Mammy,' Bridgid called out, using her bottom to shift a pile of children along the big oak form as if they were rocks in front of a bulldozer.

Mary took off her apron and sat down, her eyes owlish behind the round glases. 'I hope ever'tin's OK,' she whispered. 'I'm no cook but there it is, I done me best.'

'Let's hear it fer Mammy,' said Bridgid rousingly, and banged her big hands together. The older children clapped too but not the toddlers who like hungry squirrels were sniffing the feast and opening and closing their little paws.

Mary picked up her Woolworth's cracker and reached over the children's heads to Babs who smilingly pulled it with her. 'Yeh have the hat, Mammy,' she said. Her mother slipped the purple paper over her head and looked like a wilting bishop. She lifted her spectacles to read the joke. The Boss sat on the edge of his chair, his feet shuffling in bric-a-brac. In his hand he held a folded slice of wholemeal bread and his bad eye was watering.

The meal was an enormous triumph for Mary but the Boss made no comment. After the magnificent pudding, the cake was cut and small crumbling handfuls were passed round. As a special treat, coffee for the grown-ups was made with Irel essence.

Tired and overexcited, some of the younger children were fretful - it was all over for another year. His hands burning with chilblains, Jack sat as far as he could from the fire. Mary had applied brown ointment with a funny smell, and bound Jack's hands up as if he were Randy Turpin. But the heat was driving him wild with itching and scratching.

The girls joined the toddlers in a game of rings. The fire was dying and no extra fuel was forthcoming.

'How mane can yeh get?' Mary sniffed.

'Yeh may as well stuff the grate wit' pound notes and set fire ta 'em,' the Boss replied.

In his room Jack lay on his bed, overwhelmed by the sadness of the passing day. Next Christmas seemed a hundred years away and the girls would be celebrating it in Chicago. Never again would the whole family sit around the same table.

115

ON BOXING DAY it rained. The Boss sprang from his bed, snatched his teeth out of the glass and rammed them into his mouth. Mary snored after a restless night, but woke as the Boss left the room. She had blown all her energy on that final Christmas dinner. How she would love to be able to snuggle deeply into her duck-down mattress and sleep forever. But her children had to be fed.

The girls lay in and their murmuring talk could be heard in the kitchen. They were laughing too much for Mary's liking. As she prepared breakfast she was revisited by the horror of her three eldest girls leaving.

Most of the day she spent washing by hand every item of their underwear. Never again would she be able to show her love the only way she knew how, by washing, cleaning, cooking and sewing for them.

The Boss showed the agony of his impending loss in other ways. He bought Babs a jam sponge cake wrapped in cellophane. Babs took the cake into the kitchen, sliced it and handed it round.

All evening there was an intensity in the bedroom as the girls tried on new dresses and hats they'd bought for the journey with Aunt Dolores' dollars. If her children had to go to America, Mary wanted them to go proudly, but in the depths of her being she wanted them to stay.

As the days went by the Boss at last accepted he was going to lose Babs. It hurt him deeply when she came home from work for the last time. Giving up a good job when there were so few around was madness. How he had cajoled, bribed and got down on his knees to get her that job, and now Babs was throwing it away – a job a queue of girls would be after. In the pigsties the Boss loudly weighed up the pros and cons of his daughters' departure. 'They'll be betther off than I was at their age,' he admitted to the indifferent pigs. 'If they use their heads, maybe they'll save a few bob an' come back.'

He went to see Father Orlston and asked him to say Mass for Babs and her sisters. The old priest said it was the least he could do, providing he got paid in advance. 'Can yeh lob in a few more oul' *Hail Mary's* fer luck then?' the Boss asked. The old priest gave him a funny look.

The pigs nuzzled their filthy troughs and by twitching their ears showed they were sharing the Boss's pain. 'At least they're not goin' ta bloody England,' the Boss told them. The pigs grunted agreeably. 'Yeh're right, Boss,' they seemed to be saying, 'the same England's shite if yeh're Irish.'

Mary crossed herself. God was good and everything would be all right. Father Orlston had promised to say another Mass for the girls for nothing. Mary would find the money to pay for it.

She continued to work her old Singer treadle until it was red hot, making or reworking things for her daughters. She was frightened that she might never see her girls again and she wept quietly as she worked. Why could she do or say nothing that would induce them to stay? She pedalled and wept some more. God was all-seeing, everything was for the best. That night she knelt at the bedside, clutched her scapular and her beads to her heart and prayed for all she was worth.

116

MARY'S HEAD THUMPED with migraine. Today, her three beloved daughters were going away. Running her rosary beads through her thick red fingers, her lips working, she wept quietly. As the winter sun struggled to gild the convent spire, the girls slept warmly. Pam woke first and saw a blue sky. She smiled and called her sisters.

Mary got out of bed groggily. It was the last morning of the last day. She would make a last feast - nothing spared. The butter went on in thick layers. The biggest duck eggs spat in the black pan, tea flowed as thick as tar.

The girls appeared, laughing and confident. Mary piled on the steaming food and watched her daughters gorge themselves from a platter in the centre of the table. When the table was cleared Mary went to her room to lie down. The Boss tried to wrench off the covers but Mary held fast. 'Will yeh ge'rup, them girls is l'avin'. He thought of Babs and left the room, cursing.

'The hoor won't ge'rup,' he said. 'Yeh're goin' away an' she can't even ge'rup ta say goo'bye. I've a bloody good mind ta . . . she's the laziest oul' cow around.'

'Daddy!' Babs cried. 'Mammy's ill, but she cooked a wonderful breakfast fer us. It's up ta yeh ta look afther her now. Make her feel well again, Daddy. Promise yeh'll look afther her, Daddy?' Babs pleaded, tears filling her eyes.

'All right, I will,' said the Boss quietly, wanting to reach out and take Babs in his arms. 'She'll be all right. Stop that cryin' now. She's a hardy oul' devil. Don't worry yer head about her.' And the Boss went down the yard to tend to his stock.

Jack helped move the girls' suitcases out the front door and left them in a pool of wintry sunlight. The taxi would be here soon to take them on the long journey to Shannon airport. With time on their hands the sisters were getting nervous. They finished the washing-up and left the kitchen tidy. Mary had come out of her room but was looking very shaky. Any vestige of courage was fast disappearing. Babs talked to her, with Pam and Bridgid holding her pink, work-scarred hands. She was crying quietly, her big eyes pools of tears. The girls were beginning to whimper, watched by Jack and the toddlers.

The Boss came up from the yard in his familiar greasy jacket, wellingtons and trilby. 'Where's that feckin' taxi?' he growled, looking down the road towards Cullen's, which judging by the bikes piled outside was busy. If Jack Perkins thought the Boss hadn't seen his old head through the willow branches, he was mistaken. Nosy oul' bastard. To spite the old voyeur the Boss took Babs in his arms to hug her, smell her, feel his own warm blood in her veins.

With her shampooed black hair in his nostrils, he kissed a female person for the first time in many a year. Babs nervously hugged him back, enjoying the feel of his strong, protective body under his coat of many stains, and the hands of iron that clasped and comforted her. The smaller children watched, their faces canted upwards, their hands in their pockets, and smiled at each other. Babs gently pushed her father away.

'Make sure that oul' A'nt Delores wan looks afther yeh,' the Boss said. 'An' don'bey goin' out at night, that Sheecago is full a criminals.

Babs joined Brigid who was getting increasingly restless. 'God,' she said, 'The waitin's awful. Let's get out a here.'

Pacing the bare boards of the bedroom floor, Pam was looking around for the last time. The place had a patina of memories, some good, most painful or embarrassing. She would always remember the smell of pigs, and of babies. She looked out and watched her father through the window. His fear and anxiety were horribly visible. She saw him rub his hands together and suddenly head towards the bungalow.

He rushed into Babs' room and after clattering about for a moment or two returned with the hurley stick he had bought her all those years ago when Babs was a weak little girl he'd been determined to transform into a great sporting heroine. He'd wanted Babs to be the finest camogie player in Ireland. The Boss would have seen to that.

He stood on the bungalow step, the hurley in his hands. 'Yeh 'member this Babs?' he said, rubbing the dust off the stick with his jacket sleeve.

'Janey, look, it's the–' Babs stopped, her eyes open wide. 'Where'd yeh get that, Daddy?' She shook her head at being reminded of some failure, some unachieved ambition of her father's. 'Ah, Daddy,' she said after a moment's thought, 'yeh keep it fer a souvenir.

'He'll on'y sell it,' Bridgid said, and her joke brought some release of the tension.

Pam, looking quite superior, arrived as if she were walking on to a film set. She peered out of thickly mascaraed eyes. 'Daddy,' she said, 'that's in the past. Babs is not interested in that sort a t'ing now. She's goin' ta Chicago.'

'Maybe so,' the Boss said, 'but I remember a time when she was very taken be this oul' stick.'

As if pitying her father, Babs took the hurley in her hand. 'How does it go, Daddy?' she asked.

'The taxi's comin',' Jack shouted, and Babs thrust the stick back into her father's hand as the black Ford pulled up. The Boss, tightly clutching the hurley, yelled a welcome to the driver.

'If yeh gi'me them cases I'll fill up the boot,' the driver said, knowing from experience how keen parents were for this energy-sapping drama to be concluded swiftly. The Boss followed the driver across the bridge and set Bab's large case by the fat rear wheel of the big Buick. He stepped back began swatting the air with the hurley stick as if he were limbering up for an All Ireland final.

The girls had momentarily forgotten Mary and were surprised when the door opened and, leaning on her stick, Mary picked her way towards them. She hadn't bothered to run a comb through her hair. Her mind seemed distant. The girls steadied her as the tears crawled down her face. All three pairs of arms linked in one fantastic cradle of support for the poor old creature who had borne them.

The Boss, in his wellingtons and trilby, stood square and powerful on the drive. 'Here Babs,' he said, 'show me how yeh'd hit the goal at Croke Park.' Babs took off her gloves, held the hurley and made an uncoordinated swing. The Boss laughed, the taxi driver smiled. Mary stood more erect as if suddenly worried about something.

The Boss took the hurley again and flexed his muscles. 'Now, stand back there,' he roared, and flicking the invisible ball into the winter sky he lashed out with a tremendous blow. As if drawn by some ghastly fate, Babs stepped into the curving arc of her father's swing. There was a shocking sound of wood on bone as the hurley crashed into her face, crushing it. Babs reeled back pumping blood. Her left eye was hanging out. She staggered, and as if in modesty put a hand to where her eye had been to cover the raw hole. Her scream was almost silent, like the muffled mewling of a cat caught in a gin trap. Her knees buckled and she went down on the gravel, her back arched in agony.

The Boss stood for a moment, the bloodstained hurley stick in his hand, then his face creased into a disfigured mask of pain and terror. He fell to his knees beside his beloved and tried to cradle her. He bellowed like a bull falling. The sound went across the river, and left only silence. Jack stared down at his stricken sister, at the blood pooling around her head. None of the family seemed able to move, to help Babs. Her new white silk blouse was absorbing the red torrent pumping from her smashed face. Mary seemed to be smiling, tousled and crazy looking, her head down like a chastised child in her broken shoes, her apron stained and crumpled, its big bow tied loosely at the back, the heavy cardigan unravelling at the cuffs.

The Boss moaned. 'Oh, fer the love a Jasus!' But no one moved to help him. It was as if he had drawn all their pity from them. His cry held all the unshed tears from his life of sorrow. He covered his daughter with his big working man's hand, like a magician trying to conjure loveliness from broken gristle, teeth, torn skin and caved-in bone. 'Jasus.' He sounded very old and tired. Tears, salty and pure, poured from his eyes. 'Mother a God,' he cried in vain. The taxi driver put his hands in his pockets. The cases were still on the kerb. In his hour of need the Boss called upon all the ghosts of his religion to heal his daughter, wipe away the moment, restore her to the pale, kind-hearted beauty he had loved so single-mindedly. She was the one thing of beauty in a wretched life. Mary stood in shocked silence, the cold winter air playing with her straggly grey hair.

The Boss's moaning rose above the high hedge he'd planted to keep the village out. As he crouched like a wounded beast over his fallen daughter, his children stood there like strangers. He had rendered them mute and now they watched him calling on God to help him. Mary looked upon her stricken tormentor without feeling. The taxi driver longed for a cigarette, but daren't invade the moment. The pigs were silently sniffing blood, hearing with pointed ears the distressed cries of their master.

Jack stood with a stern look on his face, as if he were watching a film at the Classic. He heard the sound of shifting gravel under his father's shoes as he swung, the swish of the hurley, Babs' laughter as she stared upward, showing her white throat. He saw the angle of the cheekbone that took the full impact of the blow that sent Bab's small, porridgy brain into collision with the inside of her skull, mercifully removing her senses. He saw the taxi driver move. He saw Mary, her expression tranquil, appearing to ready herself to take the pain from her daughter by absorbing it, by cushioning it like cotton wool, instincts in tune with her first-born.

Jack saw his father's face when the blow was struck, the thin-lipped smile reserved only for Babs, which remained for a few seconds as Babs reeled around bleeding, before she subsided to her knees. He saw the terrified grimace, the working of face muscles. He saw his father's expression shift from joy to surprise, to horror, to tearful agony. He saw him fall to the ground his hands out. He saw Mary move back as if she had taken the blow. He saw Pam and Bridgid clutch one another. He saw his little brothers and sisters, their faces blank.

The men from the labourers' cottages heard the Boss's scream. Like a shabby Greek chorus they headed for the pub and gathered outside. Lantern-jawed they stared at their black, spidery-laced, boots. They leaned against the window as if for support. The Dowager looked towards the bungalow, his little black eyes taking in the tragic clump on the roadside. 'Poor bastard,' he muttered. With his walking stick in his hand he knuckled a tear. Across the river, Perkins shifted his boots and slowly retreated.

'Ge'ra doctor!' Bridgid shrieked. 'Phone fer a nambulance. Do somethin'. Don' jus' feckin' stand there yeh stewpit bastard.'

The Boss crouched over his daughter like a street gambler playing crap, who'd flung the dice and reached down to gather in his winnings. But he'd lost everything. His was a wretched existence, a life of dreariness, of work and dirt, of anxiety and pain, and ultimately of failure. He'd found one unflawed gem among the rubbish of his existence. One small human, one little black-haired, pale-faced girl he would trust with his life. The bitter taste in his mouth was made no sweeter by the fact he himself had done the terrible deed.

The Boss sat on the rockery, crumpled and old. He cried as never before. It was a strange cry, more like the birds and animals he had killed; the kek-kek-ek of a pheasant, broken-winged, creeping in the sun among the rusty bracken on the Dublin hills, or the howl of a pig with its face crushed, or the slow moan of a cow spread-eagled and shot in the abattoir.

As if reluctant to invade the Boss's private hell, the taxi driver took a hand. His trilby turned up, he waddled purposefully towards the stricken pair like Fatty Arbuckle in a black-and-white at the Classic. 'C'mon, Johnny,' he said, 'let's get the poor kid ta hospiddle.'

Like a repentant sinner the Boss was gently dragged to his feet. His hands were heavy at his sides, his face a glazed mask of tears. There was a long slit in his jacket. Jack cried softly. He was crying for Babs, he was crying for his mother and father, but most of all he was crying for himself.